CONTAMINATED

THE SEPARATION TRILOGY
BOOK TWO

FELISHA ANTONETTE

CONTAMINATED: The Separation Trilogy Book 2

Copyright © 2020 by Felisha Antonette

www.felishaantonette.com

Cover Design by Feliant Publishing

Edits by Novel and Kind

Paperback ISBN: 978-0-9913811-7-3

Hardback ISBN: 979-8-2453691-4-3

For information contact:

Felisha Antonette

reach@felishaantonette.com

For updates and new release notifications sign up for Felisha Antonette's Newsletter at FelishaAntonette.com

CONTENTS

For those who have faith...
-FA

CHAPTER ONE

MARC LEAPS back from a ferocious Sean, snapping at his ankle. He's climbing and jerking to his knees, snarling as he prepares for his final attack on his brother. The two male Vojin approach them. Their color-infused silhouettes of latex-like flesh cross the mud as though the ground were clouds instead of slosh. Standing nearly seven feet, one lifts its hand to the sky, and the air stills, particles frozen midair. The other extends its hand to Sean.

Marc shoves the alien back as he stumbles away, managing to lug Sean's transforming corpse and avoid his attacks.

The Vojin rips Marc from the ground, four fingers clutched around Marc's neck as his feet dangle above the dirt. Sean hits the ground, head smacking a rock.

Marc struggles in the Vojin's grasp, nails uselessly clawing at the flesh of his captor.

I gain a foot off the ground, and Luke yanks me back. "They are hurting him," I snap under my breath, ripping my arm from his grip.

"Stand down, Ky," he warns. "They'll help, but you know they don't take well to unnecessary retaliation."

Unnecessary retaliation? We're asking for something simple. Life!

The other Vojin, an exact replica of its counterpart, takes Sean's head in his hand. Sean's growling and snapping at the extraterrestrial being until a hush falls over the land. What feels like vibrations in the air start soft and grows heavier as Sean heals.

Where he was bitten, the torn muscle recoils as the skin stretches over the wound and seals. Blood is still smeared all over him, and his unconscious body is still in the Vojin's grasp, but he's healed. He's okay.

The chirping of the crickets and heavy wind whipping through the tall hills return as the air stills.

Sean is dropped. He crumples and flops over onto his side.

Marc is tossed into the side of the hill, and the Vojin deteriorate into a fog of particles and sink into the circling pits before blowing away into the sky. We're swallowed by the darkness of the desert, with only streaks of moonlight slicing through paths of the hills.

I'm at Marc's side as he's climbing to his feet. "Marc?"

He shoves me away, fists ramming into my chest. I stumble backward, almost tripping over bulging rocks. Taken aback by his roughness, I stall before trying again.

Upright and balanced, Marc holds me back with his fist jabbed firmly to the center of my chest.

"Marc, please? Hear me out," I plead, though I struggle to sound strong.

He shoves me back again. I fall to the ground but quickly gather myself.

"Hey," Luke shouts. "I know you're angry, but stop pushing my sister."

Marc meets my eyes as I rise. His purple eyes shine fiercely through his smudged goggles. I know the look he's giving me very well, with his brows knit and eyes narrowing in on his new enemy, the urge to kill pounding in his chest as he considers the repercussions of doing just that. "Stay the hell away from me, Kylie," he threatens, tone drowned in his husky rasp, now heavier than usual. Marc turns to his idle brother and helps him from the ground. With Sean stumbling at his side, he leads him back the way we came, never looking back.

I didn't want him to save me over his twin. I didn't ask for this. But Luke and I have done everything we can to help fix it. I realize being a mixed Creation—a Vojin—is the worst kind of betrayal, but I can explain. It's not what he thinks.

"Just hear me out, Marc," I call behind them.

With his back to me, he shakes his head, and when I step to go after him, Luke holds me back. "Let him go, Ky."

I halt, tearing my gaze from Marc's retreating frame. My fingertips have gone numb, legs are slightly shaking in my desire to pursue him, and a heavy feeling is growing in my chest. I don't want to let him go. "That is so much easier said than done, Luke," I groan.

Luke pulls off his goggles. Pursing his lips, there's a hint of sympathy in his eyes as he looks at me. "I know, Ky. But you're the enemy now. Though I trust him to say nothing, he is not going to look at you the same."

I flick my gaze to the stars, tears on the verge of spilling over. "But I *am* the same," I whine quietly. This burn crawls up from my chest to my throat. "I'm the same girl I was yesterday."

"Not to him. Not anymore." Luke pats my back. "It'll pass soon. Just keep your head in the game." I pivot, and Luke quickly grabs me, whispering, "Wait."

Whipping around the hills to where we stand, mystic blue and green particles circle us three times before finding a spot to rise and form the figure of a Vojin female. All the Vojin look identical, only their frame separates the males from the females. They possess no identifiers, like bushy eyebrows or wide noses. Standing shorter than the first two, she points to Luke and with an echoing tone says, "You have served your purpose for Kylie's protection. It is time you stand back and allow her to develop as a human."

"It is time you kiss my ass," Luke barks. "She's my sister. I'm not going to watch her get hurt for your amusement. We're done playing."

In a kind tone she says, "You protect each other, which is wise. These bodies that host you are in need of protection from the threats of this planet. However, for your destiny, should you be selected to reside on this planet in the future, it's necessary for Kylie to possess the full experience of what it is like to be human: love, hate, passion, disgust, betrayal..." She goes on, listing out emotions humans have the pleasure of embracing from birth to old age.

I cut her off, jabbing a pointed finger against my chest. "I have those down."

"You're knowledgeable of these feelings, but you are required to experience them firsthand, Kylie."

I squint my eyes. "We don't need you to come here, telling us how to do our job."

Nodding, she says, "Just remember who's in control. You as the implant? Or the host?"

I snatch my helmet and gun from the ground before turning my back on her. "I know who's in charge," I mumble under my breath, not exactly sure if I still want it to be me the host or me the implanter.

CHAPTER TWO

1 MONTH LATER

With the Normals settling into Separation, they've finally given us access to the additional training halls. We seriously need the space, each of us having nearly twenty members in our units, both Creations and Normals. The virtual reality hall that's being opened near the Creations' recreation hall will allow the Normals to train in an almost real environment. This is safest for them, as refraining from putting them in life-threatening situations is imperative.

Babying the Normals also leaves them weak. Though we're all here for the same reason, they get special treatment because they're fragile. However, there are Normals here who could bench press me if they wanted to. So they can be pushed. General Jord just doesn't want me to yell at them, I guess, though he's constantly yelling at me to whip them into shape.

"Month three of Separation and no war. I'm so bored," Fein complains. She contorts a weird face that makes one eye cross and her brows waggle. "All we do, day in and day out, is train. I'm so tired of looking at sweaty Normals, I want to puke."

I chuckle. "I can relate." I've been trying to remain the same, walk around like nothing has changed inside of me even though it feels like there's a permanent knife lodged in my heart. "Let's hurry and make it to the target practice hall before Jord has a cow."

Coming from our short, noonday sweep, where we make sure the grounds surrounding the base are clear of any Zombies, Fein and I jog to the target hall and join our teams sat on the floor.

"Today," the general's voice echoes off the walls in the large hall. "Those of you who are *still* unfamiliar will go through *basic* training. Weaponry and target practice. Many of you have been working on this task for over three weeks. It is not hard to assemble and disassemble a gun. For crying out loud!" He gestures with an angry sweep of his hand across his front. "We are not asking you to defuse a goddamn bomb."

I can visibly see the frustration looming over his head as he cracks his neck and takes in a deep breath through his nose.

Deflated, he peacefully continues. "Leaders, make sure your groups understand their weapons *this* week. It is the final week we will waste time on this minor task. After completing weaponry, you will run laps and complete the obstacle course. This will be timed. If you're not finished by lunch, when you return, just move on to group members fighting a round with your leaders. Respond."

"We understand," the room replies in unison.

We section off in fours, taking the corners of the hall for target practice where our groups can stay out of each other's way.

At a table stacked with guns, grenades, and bombs, I explain each item and the bullets from full metal jackets to hollow points. "This one is an M4 carbine." I leave it in view for those in the back. "It's an assault rifle. It can be used where lightweight and quick action is required. It also has a grenade launcher. This rifle helps in battle with what we'll be going up against. These," I raise two handguns, "are a Beretta M9 and a Colt M1911. They are both semi-automatic weapons, but the M1911 has seven-round mags with a muzzle velocity of 825 feet per second. The M9 has a fifteen-round mag with a velocity of 1200 feet per second and a range of over 150 feet. This should help you determine the distance required for maximum results." I disassemble and reassemble the rifle and handguns. After I assemble each gun, I fire them at a target twelve feet in front of the table. "Now, your turn, and *do not* leave from behind this table. I don't want any of you getting shot because of stupidity."

The Creations have it on the first try, along with those I've trained with back home and in the races. Only a few Normals need to do it twice.

"Okay. Great improvement! Here is the grenade that we will use to kill the dead that walk the earth," I say, picking one up. "They are very effective in slowing down and eliminating your enemy, and because of that, we will not have a visual aid until ordered to by the general or in action." I nod, and they follow. "Okay, everyone go again with each gun and fire after reassembly. Respond."

"We understand," they say in a dry tone.

I step out of their way.

"This is what you all do, shout orders and manage?" Danny laughs, stepping to my side. Separation was the golden ticket for Danny. Ever since the day we met eight years ago, it's all he's talked about. But I guess living on the streets would have anyone looking forward to a permanent roof over their heads, even if the cost was going to war.

"No, we kill people when the time calls for it and *things* now. Tasks and orders are handed down from General Jord and Seits. Higher ranked Creations are required to help with duties like Citizen Management or Order Maintenance in one of the factions, and we're shipped out where we're needed. Other times, yeah, we're shouting orders and managing those in Separation." I match his laugh with a chuckle of my own, though I'm in no mood for jokes. But as Jord mentioned prior to their arrival, we're to be relatable, and as Luke has drilled into my head, I'm never to allow *personal shit* to affect business.

"Seems simple enough."

"It's not that bad."

"What do you think I have to do to get in that position?" Danny is after the male leader position General Jord announced when the Normals arrived. I have been discreetly training him to prepare for it.

"Be better than everyone else." I watch the next person finish and pat Danny on the back. "Your turn. Try a few headshots." He goes to the table, grabbing a M9.

Luke enters the training room. He looks over everyone as he comes over to me. "Wassup?" It is his routine check. He's required to do this since acquiring the new captain position.

I haven't been able to look him in the eyes since I begged him for that favor. "The obvious."

"Okay." He's just as distant. He bumps my arm with his elbow and leaves to check on the other leaders.

Our conversations have been short. He wants to argue about the turn of events. I don't. I can't discuss my moment of weakness or putting Luke's life in danger as I requested his help to save my *crush's* brother. I put both of us on the line for a boy who will not even look at me, talk to me, or want to be caught in the same hall as me. Shaking my head, I throw my hand in my face and suppress a groan.

"I'm sorry, Ky. Did I mess it up?" Rebecca asks.

Oh. "No. No." I smile to pacify her worried eyes. "You did well, Becca. Keep up the good work." *I can't live like this.* This personal stuff is affecting every part of my life, and I need to get a handle on it.

After each member of my team completes the second assembly, I make them take part in target practice. If they hit the same target twice, they can stop. If not, they'll continue until lunch calls.

———

Everyone in the mess hall quiets as Jord steps to the center of the room between a couple of tables. This feels out of place because he'd usually take the stage. "There are leader Creations who are heading out to China and Austria. The Trade has been working on building an alliance with them for the past couple of years. Fifty-six of you will be leaving from this base. We are not going for war. We are going to inform, and we will request they stand beside us in the battle against the walking dead. We will also ensure that these countries are not flooded with the undead. As a peace offering, we will help them if they are. The group of you that were selected will be leaving at sixteen hundred hours."

When Cory came to explain himself after being caught sneaking from Jord's office, I vaguely recall him mentioning something about Creations being shipped off.

"*Great.*" Collins slams her tray down across from me. "Something else I wasn't chosen for."

"I wasn't chosen either, Collins," I tell her before drinking from my milk carton.

"None of us were," Fein speaks up, turning in her seat to face us. "Mostly the older Creations are going, those who have traveled there before. Don't feel jealous, Collins."

"I want to be chosen for *something*," she says through her teeth and takes a bite of her sandwich. Floyd and Cecilia also take a seat at our table. Everyone eats and talks amongst each other. I nod and keep my words short. I haven't much to say.

Sean is sitting between Fein and me. Though I see him every day, healed and the same upbeat Sean I've always known him to be, there are times I still see him covered in blood, missing half his face, and snarling like a Zombie. I dart my gaze in his direction from the corner of my eyes. Not only did his brother put my life over his, but he also believes we're traitors. But mainly it's because of the former that sends a sour feeling rolling through my stomach whenever I'm near him. *Shame: a painful feeling of humiliation or distress caused by the consciousness of wrong or foolish behavior.*

I push the feeling down and wipe my hand over my pant legs. "Hi." Doing this is so awkward I can't even think about how intense it is to be near him.

"Hi," he replies and wraps up a talk with Collins. He gets up as they conclude and walks over to where Marc is sitting at a different table with others.

I stare, and not once does Marc look my direction. He chats, nods, or shakes his head with his new friends. He doesn't speak to me, and I rarely see him. We live in the same house, but he goes out of his way to avoid me. He makes me feel like that hole in the wall we all avoid looking at because we know we can't fix it.

If I go to him, he won't embarrass me in front of the entire mess hall.

I stand, gaze locked on him. His eyes immediately rise, meeting mine the instant my spine straightens, as though he'd been watching me the entire time. His lazy gaze morphs into a glower. The muscles in his face relax, but the glimmer of hate and disgust in his glare is like a knife to my gut. He discreetly shakes his head, rejecting my approach before I even attempt to execute it.

I mouth, "Please?"

"No," he mouths back and looks away from me to Gia. Gia laughs, shoving her bouncy brown curls over her shoulder. She got all the phenomenal Creation genes, feminine curves, a smile that makes the boys stare while in her presence, and a personality that's as courageous as she is genuinely kind. I've never been kind *just because*; my smile is crooked because of my repaired jaw, and if a guy is staring at me, it's because he's afraid of me.

I squeeze my eyes shut to keep from rolling them. How can Marc not understand that I did what I did for him? That I sacrificed *everything* Luke and I have built for him?

I pivot on my heels and march for the doors.

"Where are you going?" Cory asks, smile peeking out from behind his scarf pulled over his mouth. He opens the door for me as I'm heading out.

"I'm going back early to get some target practice in." I need to let off some steam, firing off a few shots.

He follows me out, strutting at my side with his shoulders drawn back and his head held high. "Everything okay? You haven't been yourself the last few weeks."

"I'm fine, Cory." I survey his sudden diversion from going into the mess hall to striding at my side. "You're coming with me?"

"No, I have to be with Haut's group after lunch."

"Kylie?" Luke barks.

I grimace from the disapproving tone in his voice. "Talk to you later," I say to Cory before turning to Luke. "Yes, Luke?" I answer, frustration lacing my singsong tone.

"You keep pushing it."

"I didn't come up to him. He came up to me," I defend, pointing at Cory's back as he's entering the mess hall. "You're always pointing the finger at me, Luke. Get off my case!"

"Stop whining, Ky! You need to watch your back with him."

"Luke," Marc calls from behind us, cutting Luke off. I twist on my heels. Luke faces him. His eyes squint against the sun.

Neither of them speaks before Luke nudges my shoulder. "I'll talk to you later." He jogs toward the rec hall of the Normals, leaving us alone.

Marc steps in front of me, arms folded across his swollen chest. "What?" he asks, rasp thick in his throat. He wears no facial covering, which would help shield me from his subtle, though exigent attractiveness. His head tilts back a bit, and his shadowed eyes cut me open.

"Can we move from the middle of the road?" I ask nervously. "So we are not heard if someone walks by." We get an hour for lunch, and there are thirty minutes left. Someone is bound to be passing soon.

He marches toward the training hall. I follow behind him, keeping a good enough distance for his comfort. I don't want to make him uncomfortable by crowding his space.

I grab his arm when we make it to the side of the building.

Before I can speak, he yanks it away. "Don't touch me, Kylie," he warns quietly.

"Marc, I'm the same. Stay," I insist and bite my tongue to prevent myself from saying what I truly feel.

"I don't care. You know what you are, and I'm not okay with that."

I don't know what to say to make him get it, to make him get *me*. "I can't talk to you here." I drag my palms over my already smoothed down ponytail, sighing heavily.

He shrugs once. "I don't want to talk to you at all."

His rejection cuts me deeper than before, and the jitters in my stomach kick-start, making me nauseous. I breathe away the discomfort that will not dwindle. "Can I come talk to you tonight? Later? So I can explain."

"Ky, there is nothing to talk about. Thanks for helping my brother, but we have nothing, we are nothing, and never will we be anything. I don't fuck with traitors," he says quieter. "Stay the hell away from me, Kylie." He bumps my shoulder on his passing. "And don't come to my room," he adds over his shoulder. "Stop looking for me. Fuck off."

I break my gaze away from his departure.

Frustration warming my neck, I lean against the wall and slam my fist against the brick. I hurt myself more than I hurt the wall, but the pain makes the nausea go away.

Gah. What a punch in the gut. He doesn't have to be that callous. I'm not a sensitive person. I've been through enough to gain a hard exterior, but it doesn't appear to be thick enough to block that out. To block *him* out...

There's a howl, growing near instead of echoing off into the distance. Around the corner of the building that's holding me up from crumpling to my knees, heat waves hover over the dirtied red land.

A coyote races toward me. The image rolls in heatwaves until it comes into clear view. It stops at the edge of the building and stares.

"I don't have time to visit with you right now," I tell it. "Shoo."

Its head lowers, and a soft snarl erupts from its muzzle.

I ram my fist against the wall again and kick the dirt. Approaching it, I ask, "What?"

It gags and barfs up three balls, each dark with blue and green glistening dust-like particles within them.

"Yuck. You want me to touch those?"

It yaps once.

I rip off my scarf and snatch up the slobbery marbles in the cloth. Taking a quick glance at my watch, I see there are ten minutes left before the end of lunch. "Happy now?" I ask the animal, and it takes off. The answer is enough for me.

I hurry to our house, to the sink in the bathroom to wash the marbles, and then to my room to stash them and grab a new scarf. Dropping the balls into a pair of socks, I stuff that sock in another before shuffling them around, nearly confusing myself as to which pair holds the alien goods.

CHAPTER THREE

"Only those of you who are Creations will I attempt to kill... and Danny. The others, you all are safe from being knocked out or having something broken," I announce to my team as we stand in the middle of the empty field. "Anyone have any questions or would like to back out now because they think they can't take it?" Nobody responds. "I'm taking your silence as a no."

"Correct," Adam cuts in with a round of applause. "Because if we were to object and tell you we want to back out, you, precious leader, would make us fight you anyway." Adam's a Normal who learned quickly, but his timing is just as bad as Sean's when it comes to his jokes.

"Adam, sometimes it's better to let me interpret your silence the way I'd like to interpret it. When I need an explanation, I'll ask you for it." He rolls his eyes and shuffles to the back of the group. "Okay, now that Adam has lightened my mood, who is going to be the first I pummel? I can call out or take volunteers."

My favorite evil twin is the first to raise her hand. Jesail. The Creation with the greatest improvement since arrival. She and her sister have stopped wearing their hair in pigtails and now wear one French braid down the middle. They tuck the tail of the braid beneath their vest, and this keeps it from being snagged or snatched in battle. Cracking her neck, Jesail steps before me. She doesn't hold back. Blow for blow, she shows everyone what it takes to climb the ladder. She throws a punch, which I dodge before realizing it is a diversion so she can swipe her leg under mine and knock me off my feet.

"Damn, that was a good move," someone says from the crowd, and I must agree. I bless her with a quick nod and smile. But that's the only move she has up her sleeve. Instead of taking her out, though, I teach other techniques and maneuvers she can use to knock me out or keep me down.

I've dubbed her as my protégé, and I'll help to make her better in any way I can. Because of her change in attitude, I don't knock her out when I can, but I let her know I have her, extending my hand to help her from the ground. "You are getting better," I tell her, pulling her to her feet.

She pumps her fist. "That's good."

"We'll continue to work on it, and if you want and can keep your attitude in check, we'll build you up to become a female leader." She nods and limps back to the group. Her sister takes her spot.

I fight five before taking a break.

I'm good, but not good enough to fight more than twenty of them with no adrenaline and no drive. I'm bruised, and my muscles ache. I'd usually be rapt, able to get them quicker than I did or fight more of them. But with Marc upset with me—*still* upset with me—it's distracting. If he would let me explain, I could change this. But he's too stubborn. He *has* to know I wouldn't turn on my country. That I wouldn't turn on him.

But then again, I don't even know that for sure. Would I turn on my country? Would I turn on the Vojin? After hiding that they are responsible for the murder of our parents, I should be instantly willing to, but I don't know. Maybe it's me who I must turn on, my thoughts finally mixing with the implant. *Ugh*. I press my fist to my forehead and breathe deep.

I leave the training room, searching for Luke, and find him coming out of Jord's office.

"Hey," he greets.

"Can you take care of these deep bruises?"

Luke folds his arms in front of his vest, straightening his spine as he looks down at me through thick lashes. His eyes narrow into a piercing glare as he replies, "Are you going to talk to me?"

For what? So he can tell me over and over again how bad of an idea saving Sean was? Or how I need to learn how to overthrow these stupid feelings of affection, like he did with the girl he killed because he believed he loved her?

"What do you want from me, Luke?" I roll my eyes. "Are you going to tell me to let it go, leave it alone, blah, blah, blah? Or express your disapproval in me asking you to make them help?"

"I might."

I open and close my fists, tearing my gaze away from him for a split second. It makes my blood boil that he keeps holding this over my head. "I don't want to discuss that, Luke. I messed up, should have let his brother die and us kill him. Does that make you happy?"

"I would say that, Ky." He grabs my hand, aligning our palms. "Tell me where you hurt."

"I get it." I gesture to my busted lip and my right shoulder. But I'm not like him, I can't turn a blind eye like he did. Or pretends to do.

"What did he say to you earlier?" Luke asks once he finishes.

"He doesn't want to have anything to do with me."

Luke heads off to the training center, and I follow behind him. "You think he's wrong for feeling that way?"

"He is," I exclaim peacefully. "I'm not what he thinks I am."

"*Yes*, you are, Ky. You are *exactly* what he thinks you are." He lifts his gaze to the sky. "Not to make you feel better or give you hope or anything. But Marc likes you. He's just angry right now. He'll get over it. Don't crowd him, leave him alone until he comes to you."

"I'm caught up in my feelings?" I ask, feeling my attraction increasing into an affection for Marc. I need to talk to him. I need to explain who am—*what* I am. And the decisions I made that night were to save his brother because he picked me, and I didn't want to see him suffer through losing his twin.

"You are," Luke responds. "And you look bad. I told you to stand down, Kylie," he scolds. "I told you not to take it this far. But no, you wanted to sleep in his room and kiss him and save his damn brother. And he's as dumb as you are after what he did."

"Can you not be a jerk about this?"

"Whatever, Ky, I need to follow up with the Creations departing this evening." Turning around, he heads in the opposite direction. He discards me, as though I'm not worth his attention. I should kick him in the back, but I wouldn't want to attack him without him expecting it.

I open the door to the training room, remembering I forgot to tell him about the marbles. I can bring it up tonight. Right now may not have been the best time anyway.

"You weak today, Ky?" Gabe asks when I return.

"You all have a lot of fight. I'm never weak." I stretch my arms over my head. "So who's next?"

CHAPTER FOUR

AFTER DINNER, I go to my room, curious to find out more about the marbles. There are no locks on the doors to alert me if someone opens it. I stick my helmet at the edge of the door so I'll hear it tumble over should someone enter.

Shaking the marbles from the sock, I nervously drop one on the floor. It shatters on impact, splattering its glistening contents onto the hard wood and forming a small circular puddle on the floor. I hover over it, examining the swirling shades of blues and greens daring me to dive into the pit.

There's a knock on my door. I panic. Racing to the light switch, I turn it off, hoping to hide the pit, but the pool has a faint illumination. There's a distant whistle, likely from the atom-sized dust particles scraping against each other as the pit swirls in invitation to be teleported to the Vojin's desired destination.

"Who is it?" I ask with my hand on the knob.

"It's me," Luke says.

Phew. I wipe the back of my hand across my forehead. Cracking open the door, I yank him inside the room as I throw my index finger to my lips and look to the floor.

Luke shoves the door closed behind him. "What the...? How

did this happen?" His whisper is laced with equal parts annoyance and astonishment.

"A coyote threw up three of these marble look-alikes." I show him the remaining two. "I dropped one when taking them out. I think they're calling us."

Luke's face contorts, frustration causing his hushed voice to rise in pitch. "There's no way we can go there while we are here. Not with this stuff lingering around like this waiting for us to come back."

"I think that's why they gave us three."

He rubs behind his ear before pressing the side of his fist to his forehead. "You go. I'll have to stay around if I'm called. Leave me one in case you don't come back."

"I don't want to go!" I lower my voice to a whisper. "I don't care about what they want."

He shrugs. "Well, what then?"

"Tell them to come here," I suggest. "Through this orb so we can get rid of it."

Shaking his head, he says, "That's risky." Rubbing his neck, he adds, "If someone sees them shining through the window or happen to bust into the room..."

"Luke, the Vojin," I whisper the name, "should know where they are coming to since this is where those lying aliens are requesting us to come from. If not, whatever they want will have to wait."

Luke slowly approaches the churning pit, looking it over as though he were peeking over a cliff. Squatting in front of it, he clears his throat and blows green and blue particles past his lips. It flows like smoke from his mouth into the pond. With a quick *huff*, he rushes the last of it out. A call to our extended kind.

He stands, backing away, and goes over to check the already closed curtain.

"Now, we wait," I say, walking backward. "And hope no one needs us." I lean my back against the door.

Two pink lines of particles fluidly flow from the pit. Feet being the first to form, their feminine silhouettes slowly solidify as they take up a spot on the floor before the pit.

"Looks like we won't have to wait that long," Luke says in a surly tone, coming back over to me.

Two pink Vojin females stand before us, dark almond-shaped eyes looking us over. "Hi, Lukahn and Kylie," they whisper in unison.

"You greet us so casually. Is this even important? Here is not a good place for us to speak," Luke tells them. But it should be obvious, them calling a meeting on the Separation base is the world's dumbest idea. They must be desperate.

"It is important. We would not have risked our lives coming here if it weren't." The female on the left steps a foot forward while her acquaintance rests in the background. Though her face lacks facial features to help me judge her disposition, her worried tone and the stressful way she hugs herself tells me she's greatly concerned about whatever is so important. Their display of human emotions is only a manipulative technique to better relate to *hosts* who have been around such gestures for all our lives here on Earth.

I mentally scoff at the thought.

"I am Noranti," the one who stepped forward says and points behind her. "This is Siona. Luke, Kylie." She gestures toward us. "Things have taken a turn for the worse back home."

Back home? That place was never our home. "In what way?" I'm unable to remember what their home looked like the one and only time we visited as children. We've always been treated like outsiders, not trusted or looked upon as their own. And I now know it's because we never were. We're just red and black checker pieces on their checkerboard.

"As you may be aware, domination over this planet was the original plan. After seeing how the humans live, poisoning this universe with hate, pollution, and selfishness, having the planet cleaned of them would be satisfactory. We saved this land after the invaders destroyed the majority of it, and they've made it worse instead of making it better." Noranti bows her head and rubs her arms up and down. "Treason..." she utters the word in a remorseful tone. "That's what changed." Looking back at us, she continues, "Our leaders have been overthrown by the Volones rebels, and we have been instructed to destroy this planet, from the core to the atmosphere. Earth is only the first stop."

My gaze flicks back and forth from the door, hoping no one walks in on us. I also can't help eyeing the Vojin behind the other, waiting patiently with her hands at her sides and dark, large, almond-shaped eyes widely looking upon Luke and me. She remains quiet while Noranti does all the talking.

"Over the last few years, many other planets have been taken over by the Vojin," Noranti says with an edge of fear lacing her tone. She raises her hands, palms up, four fingers splayed out; two center fingers fused together, and what would be the thumb as long as the other three. "When the talk of domination came, many misinterpreted the actual plan." She walks to us, followed closely by the other. "We were to dominate Earth to enforce a change, to make them a better people and have them live happily among each other. Not to overthrow them."

"Or turn them all into the walking dead?" I add.

They nod, but only Noranti says, "This is beyond us, and we have become as bad as what we were set out to change." Her hands lower. "Our leader has been locked away, and many of us have allied and will go against the Volones, but it will not be before the destruction they plan to initiate against this planet."

With a lazy drawl, Luke says, "So this is why you're here. You want us to step in to help you."

The Vojin's thin lips press together. She nods, and the nod turns into a headshake as though she's uncertain of the correct gesture to relay her response. "Right now, we are here to inform. Your parents were a part of our alliance, and when they, alone, tried to take back our home from those who are destroying it, they came here for them. We cannot do this alone. When it is time, you will know. You will gather your fellow Creations and welcome us here using the transports. If we can stand alongside the Creations and whoever else is willing to fight against them, we can save this planet, ours, and others that may be affected in the future."

"Neither humans nor Creations will ever side with the Vojin." Luke tightly crosses his arms in front of his puffed-out chest. "You can count your losses now. Let us worry about Earth."

"Actually," she raises her first finger. "Whereas the mixed Creations were originally placed here to convince other Creations and Normals into siding with us for domination, instead we are asking that you now convince them to stand with us. All it takes is a simple change in words. With the human qualities you have attained and the relationships you've built here on this planet, this should be easy." The Vojin do not wait for us to respond. Turning back into flowing particles, the two sink into the dissolving pit.

I sigh, throwing my head back.

Luke does the same. "What do you think?" he asks.

"I don't know," I say, voice strained from the stretch of my neck as I peer at the ceiling. I pull my head forward and meet his eyes. "They can't expect us to do that, just the two of us."

"They won't. They'll probably want us to connect with the others."

"No one who is mixed will be willing to...admit that," I say uncomfortably.

"Except you," he drawls mockingly.

"Luke," I drone, pursing my lips. "Don't be an asshole at a time like this."

Luke heads for the door. "You heard what they said about our Mom and Dad? They were resistance. *That's* why they killed them. We're their legacy, Ky. Our decision is already made. The real matter is whether we will eliminate them." He taps his throat. "Because let's be honest, who are we, really?" He leaves, closing the door behind him.

I pack the marbles back in a pair of socks and stuff the socks into the drawer. I pause, hand clutching the knob of the drawer. Luke had opened the door to our parents' room that day we'd rushed home from our first big win. They'd missed it, and they never missed supporting us. Crowded by four Waulers, Luke and I were surprised by two hiding behind the door. Before our eyes, they beat our parents to death before knocking us out. We woke up days later in the hospital, Trade member Councilman Luckett advising that guardianship over Luke and I was being transferred to our aunt. But now I know that Waulers did not murder our parents, but instead implants, *Vojin* are responsible. How dare the Vojin ask us for our help? We *are* our parents' legacy, and we *should* avenge them.

I grab my clothes for a shower.

I open my door and see Marc passing. He doesn't look in my direction. He sees me though. He keeps his shoulders back, spine straight, chest pushed out, arms swaying at his sides, and head held high, facing forward. Not once glancing my way to acknowledge my presence. I wait until he hits the stairs before I enter the hall.

Seeing him makes my breath stutter. A heaviness weighs on my chest, and from my heart, cement pumps through my veins. Marc and I weren't together. Togetherness or companionship are not gifts Creations are granted. I've never wanted this, but I may have wanted *something* with him. What that something may be... I don't know. Not yet. But I hope I'll get the opportunity to figure it out.

On my way to the shower stalls, I pass Fein, Floyd, and Sean sitting in the den laughing and talking loudly. Some dispute they're having about sourdough bread versus whole wheat bread.

Collins is in one of the stalls singing a familiar song I never learned the name of. I've missed out on many luxuries most have reveled in, never concerning myself with music or the little things, though I wish I had. I don't interrupt her.

Her singing stops once I cut on the shower. "Who is that?" Her high-pitched voice rings over the water patter.

"Ky," I say, hating that she's asked. I'm not in a chatting mood.

"Hey Ky. How do you feel about some of the others leaving?"

"It doesn't bother me." She thinks she should be picked for everything. "We weren't supposed to be picked for that. We are supposed to stay here and train our teams for Separation."

"You all went to Chicago," she says matter-of-factly, waggling her finger over the stall's wall.

"We were only gone for a day. Not weeks, like they are going to be gone for now."

She goes back to her song, louder than she was originally.

Collins can be an acceptable person in passing. Not a friend. She is manipulative and conniving. And she's heads over heels for my brother. No girl in their right mind should be that crazy over Luke. He doesn't care about her, and yet, if he offered her a doggy treat, she'd bark and do tricks. I wonder what her feelings are for him. Does anyone else here *love*? I wonder if I'm the only person who actually cares about someone here other than their twin. We are not supposed to. Luke did. But I've never heard another Creation say it. It could be because we aren't supposed to; those are feelings we keep concealed. Taking away our human emotions, which they should have stripped from us, instead of conditioning us to believe what we should and should not feel.

These *feelings* are an inconvenience.

I wash my hair, and I'm out before Collins. She takes long showers. Her water has got to be cold.

A folded note lying on my bed catches my eye as I close my bedroom door. I rush to my bed, snatching up the wrinkled, cream-colored paper.

I glance over it.

The words are in cursive, hard to read. The bottom is signed with a fancy *T*. A *T* I know well enough to be the Trade. I sit, trying to decipher the minuscule handwriting. I make out the words parents, death, Vojin, and Creations. The word *Implanted* stands out in all caps. I can make that out clearly—the clearest word in the short paragraph. This isn't even a full sheet of paper, but a scrap likely torn from an eight by eleven.

Luke is also legible.

I study it longer, trying to put together the puzzle. I wasn't born for cracking jigsaw puzzles.

...Implanted your parents were put with the Vojin. They were created to...as Creations, they bred to continue their mission to destroy the Vojin. Successful in discovering the Vojin's plan for destruction... their death after you two were old enough. Luke...untold plan for reconstruction...

T.

I don't understand. I know how my parents died. The Vojin told me they killed them. But I didn't know they were *implanted* into the Vojin. I thought they were Vojin who were implanted into Creations or Breeders, humans. How many roles *did* my parents play? They were implanted by the Vojin to breed for Separation. But this paper that I assume is from the Trade is saying my parents were also implanted *into* the Vojin. Which means the Trade must know about Luke's and my association with the Vojin.

The Trade holds the most power on this planet. They know

about everything that goes on in and outside the world, from delegating tasks among the factions, keeping order in the development of Creations, maintaining a level of communication between the countries that's enough to mitigate but not enough to invoke peace, and they monitor life force outside Earth.

It would make perfect sense if they had a hand in this. They have all the resources. But why? What was the Trade trying to figure out, and why were our parents important to this plan? Did the Trade know the Vojin would use them as implants and send them to Earth to infiltrate Separation?

I don't know if I'll find the answers to these questions, but the Vojin knew, and that has to be why they murdered them. I guess the greater question would be, if the Vojin couldn't trust my parents, why are they trusting Luke and me?

I knock on Luke's door, hoping for his help.

A girl snickers, and he shushes her. "Luke, I need to talk to you right now. She can see you later."

"Ky, wait."

"No, Luke. Now."

The door opens, and Luke steps out. "Wassup, Ky?"

I show him the letter. "Look."

He glances at it. "I can't read this." He grumps at me and snatches the paper from my hand. "What is this saying?"

I point to the words as I quietly read the ones I was able to make out. "What do you think that means? Can you try to make out these other words?" I point to scribbled lines that are supposed to be letters.

"Implanted?" he whispers, crossing the floor from his room to mine just across the hall.

I follow behind him. "I get that part. I know what that means. But I don't understand what it's trying to tell me." I close my door after we're in. "Why is your name on it?"

He sits on my bed. "Luke..." he reads, trying to make out the words. "What is this, a fancy C?" he asks disgruntled. "No, a B. Dammit!" He stomps. "Who wrote this, and why don't they know how to spell?"

"Calm down, Luke. You're too loud."

"This is frustrating. I don't know what it says. Luke knows… maybe. Luke blows… Luke follows…Ky," he shrugs. "I don't know. Our parents were implants from the Trade. You think the Trade wrote this? It's signed with a T."

"That's what I was thinking."

He stands. "It's not enough for us to go by. The words are smudged, we can barely read what it says, and the paper is old and crinkled. Who knows how old it is?"

"What's more important is where it came from. Who would leave this on my bed, and how do they know about it?"

"That is a damn good question, Kylie." He heads toward my door. "But we aren't going to find out the answers to these questions now. We'll try to figure it out later. Keep an ear and an eye out. Make sure we aren't being watched. No more talk about this until we figure it out. No talk about anything, with *anyone*. You hear me?" He looks at me head on with his brows high.

His insinuation is far too clear. "Yeah." I plop down on my bed. He leaves, and I lie across the mattress, holding the letter over me as I reread its cipher.

Luke will go back to that girl, and I'll wait until he comes and gets me so we can sleep. He should stop letting those girls in his room. They are going to catch him, and then we'll have to sit through a lecture about relations among Creations and how they are not permitted. And if we do revel in such actions, there will be consequences. Luke says our government won't care about his actions. But even if they knew you wouldn't choose someone over your twin, that doesn't mean the other person wouldn't choose you over theirs.

I fold the crumpled paper over, following the indented lines.

Someone here knows about us. Especially after reading this letter. We need to find out who.

Sean yells with Fein laughing loudly from downstairs. "What are they doing?" I head out of my room and catch Marc's door close.

Don't do it, Ky. Go downstairs like you planned.

I look left and right before I cross the hall on my tiptoes so I'm heard by no one. Placing my ear to the cold wood, I listen and hear no voices. I take in a breath of confidence and take a small step back so I can look at the doorknob. Grabbing it, I turn it and push the door open before I can change my mind. Stepping in, I shut the door behind me and quickly, but quietly, face him.

He's lying on his back, his head facing the ceiling.

I walk to the side of his bed.

His head slowly turns to me with his left arm resting on his forehead. Even slower, he opens his eyes.

"I can't," I mumble, as I slowly squat down to be eye level with him.

He closes his eyes and returns to his original position. "You don't listen."

"I'm sorry," I say, lifting my hand to touch his shoulder then deciding against it. I rest it on my knee instead. "Can I explain further now?"

He shakes his head. "I already know, Ky. I don't need you to explain anything."

"I can't leave you alone," I admit before he continues with his rejection. "Please stop telling me that."

"Leave me alone, Kylie," he orders, turning and sitting up. I move back, standing. "Don't you understand that?" he fires off. "Whatever it is you think you want or need to explain to me, I don't want to hear that shit!" He's loud enough that if someone were at the door, they could hear him, but hopefully not all the way downstairs. "You need to get oughta here."

"Marc, I–"

"No," he cuts me off. "You are nothing to me." He jabs a finger toward the door, rage darkening his eyes. "Get out."

A rough breath thrusts from my lungs, charging from my throat. I cough from the feeling of the wind being knocked out of me. A fire blazes my throat, and beyond my control a tear falls.

He looks away from me, turning his head toward the far wall and his chest of drawers.

He's hurt me, and I don't like the way it makes me feel. The hurt is replaced with anger. I ball my fists, and a string of hostile words build in my throat.

I try to catch my breath, and I'm reminded of the sound of my cry when I watched my parents get killed. It softly echoes off the walls of Marc's room.

Before it can happen again, I grab ahold of myself and walk to him.

Looking up at him, I whisper, "I only did it to save Sean. If it weren't for me, he would be dead."

Marc straightens his spine, and his frame somewhat towers over mine, but only by a few inches. He takes a step forward, forcing me back. My feet scrape against the rough wood floor. Heavy breaths heave past his nostrils, thrashing against my crossed arms. "No. If it weren't for *you*, you would be dead," he states devilishly, inches away from my face. It sounds more like a threat, that maybe if he didn't have feelings for me, he'd take me out. His gaze shifts from my eyes downward then back before he pushes me. "Or maybe you wouldn't be because *they* would save you."

I scoff. "You are angry with me because you saved me?"

He stares at me, shadowed eyes peering through me as though I were a window instead of solid flesh. He's tearing me apart with his silent glare. "You need to leave."

"Talk to me," I demand. "Tell me why you're really angry."

"You are one of them, Kylie. You aren't supposed to be here. And because you are, there is only one explanation, and it's not a good one."

"I am a Creation. I am *not* one of them." He shakes his head and pushes me to the door. I shove his hands away from me. "Just hear me out, Marcain, and stop pushing me." I continue when he backs away. "I have no allegiance to them. This is all based on a plan that started with my parents. The Vojin thought we could help in it to better this planet." He gives me a disgusted look, and I correct, "Better *our* planet. They killed my parents and lied to us for years, and now things are worse, and they have a different plan that we are not trying to be a part of. We want to destroy them and their plan instead."

"Why should I believe you?" he asks, purple gaze shifting around his room, continuously avoiding me.

"I wouldn't lie to you. I am no different from who I was before. You cut me, I'll bleed like you, and a twin will heal me as yours would. You look into my eyes and see them infused how yours are. I am like you, and my thoughts are no different than they were before."

Marc runs his hands through his dark hair and leaves them resting at the back of his neck. "Even with that said, Ky, you still need to leave. And leave me alone."

"I...can't!" I say slowly. "I don't know why, but I can't. It was easier when you weren't upset with me. Even then, I thought I could forget about you. But I can't." I grab his arm. His jaw works, bulking from the tension in the muscle. "There is...affection for you that won't let me."

His eyes shift to mine. "Don't say that, Kylie." His voice goes down an octave.

"Just stop...trying to force me away. I couldn't tell you, and I wouldn't, and you wouldn't have asked because we won't uncover and discover the bests of each other. But I can't just let you go and see you every day. You know you can't either."

"Don't try to uncover me, Kylie."

"*I'm* uncovered," I yell, shoving my hands through my hair.

"I'm in too deep with you," he says as I walk closer to him. "You're not good for me, and I need to stop this. *You* need to stop this."

"That's a lot easier said than done," I utter, then hesitantly place my lips to his, feeling the empty sentiment fill when he returns the gesture. I hug him as we kiss, but he doesn't return it. "Please."

He kisses me again as his hands slowly push over my back. His arms tightly wrap around me, and he breaks our kiss, moving his head beside mine, beard scratching my cheek. "I want to tell you I hate you…and I want you to leave me alone."

"But you know who and what you are…and your wants don't matter," I quote. His hair blankets my face. It smells like desert air and the light scent of the conditioner they give us.

"*Your* wants matter," he states, leaning away but keeping me in his arms.

"And I want to be with you." I tug him by his neck to me and kiss him with the affection growing in my chest. My body goes numb as all the oxygen leaves it and quickly refills.

His body moves with the kiss, pushing me back until my back hits the wall. He grabs one of my legs, lifting it to his side before doing the same with the other. I wrap around him as his body wedges me against the wall.

I take short, shallow breaths. His room becomes hotter, and the jitters in my stomach kick in, telling me to stop and go at the same time. Pushing over his shoulder, I reach up his brawny neck to his long hair and seize it, letting it fall between my fingers. I yank him closer.

All without interrupting this kiss where our lips join and our tongues meet, he lifts me a little, lips moving lustfully against mine. I'm captivated, sensing he missed me as he tries to pull as much feeling from this kiss as I'm trying to give.

It sobers to a simple peck before he breaks away. "Ky," he groans. His voice sounds like it's forcing itself from his throat. "Stop."

"Okay," I say catching my breath. "Let me down."

"Right." He wraps his hands around my legs tighter, turning us, and carrying me to his bed. He lies over me.

I lightly touch his face, watching his eyes wash me over, from my hair to my neck and back to my eyes. I bite my lip to fight my smile, but it breaks through as I say, "I like how your actions contradict your words."

"I don't mean for them to," he says, dipping beside me and lathering my neck with inspirational kisses. "You just got out the shower?"

"Yes. Why?"

"Nothing, you smell like that soap." He leans back. "I haven't done anything to you so you can't leave me alone."

But you have, Marc. By comforting me, showing me you care, kissing me, showing your feelings too, and saving me over your twin. I owe you my heart. "You have done enough."

His purple eyes bore into mine. "You are not good for me, Kylie. You *have* to leave me alone."

"You want to let me go?"

He looks off to his left, and his head falls forward as he says, "I can if you stay away from me. But when you come around me or address me first, I can't." He glances back at me, then back away. "I need to, but when you're close and weak, I won't."

"I am not weak."

"You are when it comes to me and your parents."

I sink deep into his mattress, feeling the truth of that statement bombard me. Only my parents and him can cause that burn in my throat that brings tears to my eyes. They can make me feel like I'm a non-entity without them. Like I need them to survive and battle the world and its invaders.

His door opens, and Sean charges in, laughing. "Hey Marc!" He's loud and cheerful before seeing us as we move from the bed. He turns, closing the door.

"I should go," I say, looking myself over.

"You should go." He takes my hand and comes closer. "Stay away, Ky."

"Make me." I lean forward and kiss him.

"Mmm…" he groans against my mouth. "I can't." He leaves me for the door. Handle in hand, he says, "But I'm working on it. Make it easier for me."

I grumble. "Marc, stop with this! Even after this," I point between us. "You still want that?"

"You don't get it, Ky. I *cannot* go…any further with you." His voice rises, and I flinch away. "I would put you…" he begins in too low of a whisper. "…before him." He points toward the door. "And I can't live like that. You are important and need to be avoided."

Unfortunately, I understand, but he should have thought about this before he liked me first. Before he agreed to kiss me and kiss me again and hug me. Before he took away my nightmares–allowing me to rest peacefully without Luke—and held me while I cried without crowding me with questions, and… and…a lot of other things.

There are a *lot* of other things I can't figure out either. "You made me this way. You did do something to me, and it started with you pinning me to the floor and not taking me out when you could have. You initiated the point of interest."

"No, you did. With your hidden glances and passionate stares as you watched me. You asked *me* to kiss *you*. Remember?" He leans into the corner next to the door.

I do remember, and what a kiss. He gave me everything without giving me anything in that moment. And now, he's trying to take it away, replace those memories with either hurt or anger as I regret ever experiencing them with him. He changed a lot for me in that moment, and I won't let him steal this from me. "I'll go. Make sure you don't make me stay or kiss me again," I say, now at the door.

There's a sigh as he drawls, "I'm going to make you stay."

"But you don't want me to."

"No."

"And you hate me."

"Yes," he answers matter-of-factly.

"But you like me..."

"Sometimes."

CHAPTER FIVE

WE ROSE EARLY THIS MORNING. The rain brought cooler days, and though we know it's temporary, we soak it up. Still, rushing to meetings before the morning bell dongs makes me regret being a Creation after the long, quarrelsome night I had.

General Jord had Luke and Marc wake the leading Creations and ordered us to meet immediately. He stands before us, leaning over on his knees, clutching a communication device in his hands. "They are building labs on the other side of the hole. The Guidance wants to start dissection of the undead. They think it's more than an infection," he says to the small group of us. It's about time he comes out and explains that the Vojin put forth the threat. Secrets should not be kept from us, the Creations who are fighting against these things. We have the right to know exactly what we are up against, and it shouldn't be by happenstance.

Jord allowed Cory to sit in on this meeting, but in the back of the room. Maybe only as a courtesy. Jord continues, "After the construction is completed, they are going to bring in two bridges they will build to cross over the hole." Those are going to be two very long bridges. That hole was the length of a football field and crowded with Zombies. Posts will need to be built into the hole, among the Zombies. Or maybe they will use a stabilizing structure to handle the stretch. "There will be frequent sweeps by us to make sure the undead do not crowd or hollow in the labs while construction is under way. Because construction will only be permitted in the daytime, they require us to go out and make sure nothing is there in order to keep it secured for the workers. After these labs are completed, there may be a couple of you stationed there permanently."

Jord pauses. We wait for him to finish while he looks over the communicator, sliding his index finger upward on the screen. Over the past month, Cory has been able to sit in on discussions and be included on territory sweeps. He and I haven't talked, so I'm not sure what's going on yet, but I assume he's working to prove himself, and Jord may be susceptible to these actions.

As though he could sense my thoughts were centered on him during the pause in our leader's instructions, Cory takes the available seat next to me.

"They do not have a date yet," Jord continues, "for when the new facilities will be completed. Once they are, we will start sweeps over there. It will be after the bridges are installed." He nods, and we nod in agreement. "Attend to your day as usual. Luke and Marc, meet me in my office in one hour."

We relax once he's out of the room. Cory stands in front of me, smile as wide as his shoulders. "Hey," he greets, extending his hand.

I take it, allowing him to help me from the floor of the auditorium hall. Narrowing my eyes, I question, "What's got you in such a good mood?"

"C'mon." He turns, grabs my hand, and pulls me from the hall. "I can't get my spot back, but I'm no longer an outcast," he reveals once we're outside and out of earshot.

"*Or,*" I sing, unconvinced, "that's what they made you think so they can see what you're up to because we're leaving for war soon."

"They are pushing off the war. Remember the Creations went out to the other countries?"

"Yeah," I nod, knitting my brows, confounded he knows about this before me. We've never pushed off a war deployment for any reason. We should be relieving the other Creations who've been fighting the past ten years.

"Well, they have Zombies tearing through their land as well. Everyone wants the same thing right now. To save humanity."

So the Vojin are to blame. Seems their plan for the Zombies to be a distraction and start the demoralizing of humanity is working out the way they desired. I chuckle, realizing, "We're stopping killing each other so we can kill them first."

Cory snorts and shrugs once. "And then back to the same old same old."

I laugh, shaking my head. Another day in the life, *although* this slight change may shake up our country, our world. "You think it will ever be over?"

"What? War?"

"Yes." Will we ever be peaceful like the aliens planned?

He snorts. "Yeah, after it's destroyed and reconstructed."

My steps falter, though I avoid tripping. I crane my neck to look at Cory. "What?" I snap unintentionally, shocked by the similarities of his statement and the Vojin's plan. I swallow hard and force a smile.

His wide-eyed gaze meets mine, bewildered, aware of his mistake, but he laughs it off saying, "I don't know, probably not. I need to go." Without another word or glance my way, he runs toward the fields behind me.

Only a Vojin would say that. Those are *their* words. A Creation would never say 'destroy to reconstruct.' There is only destruction. We do not try to reestablish what we have destroyed.

There would be nothing to reconstruct. Whatever it was, was abolished for a reason. Why would we waste funds and time putting it back together?

"Reconstruct?" A voice comes from behind me, causing me to jump as I turn back around. Jord's exiting a nearby training hall.

My mouth goes dry. Unsure of how much he's heard and how damn good his ears are as we were over ten feet away and speaking low enough our voices would whisper. I hurry to answer, "The same thing I was wondering, sir." I force my brows to draw inward and my upper lip to curl in disgust. I have played my role well my entire life, and I'm accustomed to lying and covering things up.

"That's odd for a Creation to use that word. *Reconstruction.*" Jord strolls toward me, hands clasped behind his back, shoulders square, and eyes piercing through me with his brows knit tight to their middle. "What do you make of that, Captain?" His casual tone leaks suspicion. His brows relax, and his once accusing scowl flips interrogatively with narrowed eyes, a strict tilt back to his head and lips in a tight line as he glares down at me.

I straighten my spine, bring my feet together, and repeat more sternly. "The same thing I was wondering, sir. It sounded odd to me too, sir," I respond as a Creation would, without opinion, though I am withholding a more typical response. *His words render suspicion, and he should be put to death. A Creation has proven he cannot be trusted, and an untrustworthy Creation is a malfunctioned design. Subject is failure and requires termination.* I reserve this response because I believe Jord may know about Cory's secrets, and I'm the one being tested.

"What else did he mention?" Jord asks.

Looking straight ahead, I answer, "He hopes to be working his way back up, sir."

Jord nods. I spot it in my periphery. "He might be," he says slowly, looking off in the direction Cory ran. "Keep your distance, Captain."

"I understand, sir."

He marches off behind me. I sigh with relief, dragging my hand across my forehead.

"Why are you standing in the middle of the road?" Fein asks at my side.

Where did she come from? "Nothing, I'm walking."

"Well, where are you headed?"

Somewhere everyone can stop sneaking up on me. "Um, to the training hall. You?"

Fein tucks her fingers in her front pockets and shrugs. "I'm tired of looking at my group, and I want to relax for the rest of the day. Thinking about treating it like a day off. They're pretty bruised up anyway."

Nodding, I say, "Good idea. Let's give them the day off from training and have them watch the guides and Trade instructions."

Fein chuckles. "Those boring videos," she drones. "I guess."

We can't let the Normals just sit around. They must be learning something, but I agree they need some recovery time. If the Generals or, worse, Luke, were to walk into the training room and see the trainees lying around, we would hear it for sure.

By the time the morning bell dongs, Fein and I have gathered our groups, and we pile into the projector lecture hall with the comfortable auditorium seats and air conditioning. We ask the cooks to serve breakfast and lunch in the hall, and we spend the entire day playing the Trade's instruction videos from *Introduction to Separation for Normals* to *How to Cope with Loss in Battle*. I even play *The Path Beyond Separated War*, where it goes over how they can submit a division request to be shipped to another faction to be Breeders, Farmers, or even Construction Workers.

None of which have I ever been interested in, but their one- to two-hour run time per video fills up the day.

The ending bell dongs as the sky turns to dusk. Fein and I dismiss the groups and head into the cool evening breeze.

"Let's go to the mess hall and get dinner before it crowds and then head back home and watch a movie," Fein offers. I'd think she'd be tired of staring at the projector light today. I'd prefer to lie in my bed and dissect that mysterious letter to try to figure out the illegible words, but I agree because I'm working on being more sociable.

I turn on my heels, heading with her toward the mess hall. "We would have to make it home before Sean."

Fein bursts out laughing. "That's so true. He will get back, kick off his musty boots, prop up his smelly feet on the center table, and hog the den and the movie player."

Sean is cool with me, but I can tell he doesn't trust me, though he doesn't let it show. He also never brings up that night or discusses Marc and me anymore.

"Ky!" Fire calls, running over to us. "Hi, Fein."

"Hey," we greet. "You're done for the day?" I ask.

"Yes, Marc made us stay behind for an extended training because we didn't finish our trail in the time he wanted. He is extremely hard on us."

"Yep, that sounds like hardcore Marcain," Fein states, chuckling.

"You think they would mind if I came with you all? I don't fit in with the others."

Fein and I share a glance, knowing they would, and we shouldn't friend the Normals. It's one of the first rules as a leader, but I was associated with Fire before Separation. I shrug, and Fein nods.

"I'll sneak you in. Don't draw attention to yourself. We aren't staying there long," I say.

"Just long enough to eat, then we're headed home," Fein finishes.

Fein, Fire, and I enter the mess hall and head toward the food. We shuffle down the counter, grabbing our dinner with Fire between us. There aren't many people here yet, so we should be able to sit before the others notice her.

"Thanks," Fire says again after we sit.

I nod and dig into my lasagna. The food in Separation is far better than the food back home. Danny was right to look forward to this. They give us a variety of options throughout the week, and it's always cooked to perfection.

Luke comes up next to me, sticking his fork in my lasagna before his butt fully hits the bench. I roll my eyes, ignoring him and the full plate of food on his tray. My lasagna tastes just like his! But Luke, who wishes to be in control of everything, always has to eat my food and drink my beverages. He wouldn't be Luke if he didn't.

"Hey." Luke reaches around me to tap Fire. "What are you doing here?"

"I'm an outsider with the others. I wanted to sit with friends." Fire shrugs and shrinks into her frame.

Sean sits on my other side, forcing Fire and the others beside her to scoot over. I don't know why Sean always has to sit by me, but he does at every opportunity. If we are in the mess hall, the rec hall, the auditorium, anywhere he finds a seat beside me, he will take it. "I would not take you as an outsider, Fire," Sean says. His voice is a replica of Marc's raspy tone. The sound of it would usually make my heart jump for Marc, but it twists my stomach coming from Sean.

"Sean?" Fire inquires, smiling.

Sean smiles at me. A wink causes his purple iris to flash, and he turns back to Fire. "No."

"Yes, you are." Fire cracks a flirtatious smile.

"Then why ask?" Sean adjusts to whisper in my ear. "I think she likes your boyfriend."

I nudge him with my elbow. "Stop."

As if on cue, Marc strides over, Collins tight at his side. They sit a little too close for my comfort. She smiles, quietly saying something to him and turning into his shoulder as she chuckles.

"Her too," Sean adds, whispering again as he bows a nod toward them.

I stop chewing the lasagna I've just shoved into my mouth and swallow hard, irritated he's pointed them out. "Thanks." I glare at Sean from the corner of my eye. "I was trying to ignore that." Poorly, but trying. Appetite gone.

Sean laughs.

"Ignore what?" Luke and Marc ask.

I look at Marc, biting the inside corner of my bottom lip to keep from telling the truth. "Nothing," I say with a quick shift of my gaze to Collins and back to him. He averts his gaze and scoots away from Collins. Marc gets on my nerves with the back and forth we so often have. Though Collins appears to be so infatuated with him, giggling and whispering to him, Marc saves those intimate interactions for me.

I turn to Luke, after catching Collins reclaim her closeness to Marc. "You want some?" I ask, picking up my canned soda to cover up my grimace.

"No, I got one." He taps his soda can with his fork. Over the sound, Collins's cackling and moans tempt my attention. She won't get it.

I close my eyes and pinch the bridge of my nose. "Um," I divert my attention back to Luke, "You sure? Because you'll say no and still take it." Honestly, I want the distraction to take my focus away from Collins's obnoxious snickers.

Luke turns down the corners of his mouth and shrugs. "Yeah."

Unconcerned with Collins' sudden change from him to Marc. "You like your food?" he asks.

"It's fine. You apparently like it too." I wipe my mouth before whispering in his ear, "Why is Collins on *him* when she wants *you?*"

He turns my head and says in my ear, "I was finished with her, so I guess she moved on to the next one."

I nod, turning back to the others. Fire is casually flirting with Marc, asking him a million and one questions. Fein is sitting on the other side of her, flicking her peas at Sean. A couple of them scatter onto my tray. The front of her is damp and cola drips from her chin, likely Sean sprayed his soda at some point while I was distracted. Floyd's sitting on the other side of Fire, also flinging food at her.

Luke talks to Marshal and Marc, and Marc tries to hold up the conversation while ignoring Collins and Fire.

I finish my food while the kids play. Someone behind me squeezes my shoulders, and I am so over people sneaking up on me.

Striking a glance over my shoulder, I find Cory looking down at me. He invites me to talk with a welcoming, crooked smirk. I shake off his hands and stand. "What?" Cory swipes his thumb over the corner of my mouth. "Don't do that." I swat his hand away, feeling awkward that he did that in front of everyone.

When it comes to Cory, Marc forgets what role he actually plays in my life and will take up the torch of a big brother, forgetting I already have one of those. He'll run and tell Luke when I won't listen to him telling me to stop. Then there are times when he gets jealous and wants to play the boyfriend. *Don't do that with him, Ky,* he'll say passively, a look of resentment sticking in his violet eyes.

"There was food on your face, and it was distracting. I need to tell you something. Walk with me."

Then there's Luke...The big brother who thinks he's my father.

Luke stands beside me, an inch taller than Cory, shoulders also wider than his. He crosses his arms and looks Cory over. "Why do you insist on talking to me in front of him, knowing he's going to have a cow?" I sigh heavily, knowing one of the three of them is about to start a fight.

"You shouldn't be talking in front *or* behind me," Luke states.

I thought we were talking low, but once Luke says this, the room quiets, and everyone turns their attention on us. "Cool out, Luke," I tell him kindly.

Luke looks from Cory to me. "No, *you* cool out." Since Luke overheard Cory's confession of working with the Trade to sneak the names of the implants from our general, and Cory lost his position, Luke has zero tolerance and no respect for him. We're supposed to be loyal to each other. If our generals were under investigation, as a Creation, Cory should've brought the concerns to Jord before sneaking around his office. Or at the very least, he shouldn't have gotten himself caught.

I look away from Luke to Cory. "I'll, um, talk to you later," I say, scratching the outer side of my left eyebrow. My cheeks burn.

"Ky, everything okay?" Fire asks. She's the only one of our close group who is not used to the disputes between Luke, me, and Cory like everyone else.

I roll my eyes. "This is normal. It'll be over in a sec," I whisper over the table.

"Why is she in here?" Cory blurts as I'm turning back around. He points to Fire, raising his voice. "Why are you allowing her to be in here, Luke? It's *your* responsibility to keep one party separated from the other!" He shakes his head and marches off, shoving the mess hall's doors open on his exit. They slam against the walls and swing on their hinges.

"See what you do, Ky," Luke accuses, following after Cory, likely to prevent Cory from telling on him.

I roll my eyes and throw my hands on my head. "I didn't *do* anything," I say childishly, hurrying outside after them. Dusk deepens the red color of the dirt road and brick homes. I see Cory charging for the General's office, kicking up dust with every step. Luke's a few feet behind him. "Cory," I call once the doors to the mess hall are closed behind me. "Where are you going?"

"To have a talk with the general."

Luke laughs as he slows his pace until I make it to his side. "He's going to tell on me."

I match his laugh. "Cory, you cannot be that childish. I'm the one who told Fire she can come. Tell on me, not him. I thought you wanted to talk anyway, why waste the time. The talk with Sir Jord will take too long. Let's talk now." Cory stops, and I mutter to Luke, "Got it."

He laughs again. "No. Let him *tell on me*. We can all go sit in the general's office and tell him everything, including that conversation you had late night with Ky."

Cory whips around, charging across the dirt. "You told him," he accuses, jabbing a point in my face.

I smack his hand away, and before I can defend myself, Luke says, "Ky didn't tell me anything." He shoves Cory away from us. "I can read snake in your eyes. I know the sneaky shit you do to get back on top. You're low."

"What does he do?" I ask Luke, tugging at his shoulder.

"Nothing," Cory cuts in, giving Luke a warning glare.

Luke laughs loudly, holding his middle. "You think I'm afraid of you. Regardless of you being good or bad, Ky will never side with you over me. It doesn't matter if she knows or not."

"What did you do, Cory?"

"Nothing, Ky. I've always been on Luke's bad side because you like me. He's threatened by me. Thinks I'll become your first pick."

I hold in my laugh, though I snort. Pick Cory over Luke. That will never happen. I wouldn't even pick Cory over Marc, let alone Luke. "The three of us know that will never happen, and you cannot try to sway me from the side of my brother. Are you insane?" I ask but don't wait for an answer. I tug Luke's arm as I turn us around to head back to the mess hall. We ignore Cory's rebuttal as he stomps off, but I don't hesitate to ask Luke, "You'll tell me about what you were talking about later?"

He laughs, arm dropping on my shoulder. "I know nothing. It just makes sense. He has to be doing something under the table. I don't know for sure though."

Chuckling, I nudge his side with my elbow. "That's deceitful."

He shrugs. "Must be true by his reaction."

"He definitely gave himself away," I say, realizing that what Luke is saying is true.

Luke laughs louder as we head back into the mess hall. "The best was that bit about you picking him over me, *your twin*."

I snort. "Like that'll ever happen." I shove his arm from my shoulder, and we shuffle back to our table where we left our food trays.

Fein stands at my approach. "You ready to go?" she asks.

"Yeah." I scoot my tray to Luke as he sits. "Throw that away for me."

He nods.

"Thanks." Passing Luke to meet Fein, a cold feeling strikes me in the chest, sending a freezing scorch blazing my veins. Collins's lips connect with Marc's. Seconds crawl by before I'm in position to lurch across the table and shove her away from him.

Marc calmly breaks away from her, and Sean says, "Exactly, Fein. Let's go." He coolly wraps his arm around my shoulder and shuffles me from the room against my will. Fein follows close behind.

I'm fuming, skin boiling red.

The nippy breeze cools my flesh but does nothing for the rage within me. "What the hell was that?" I shout. I maneuver out of Sean's grasp and turn back for the mess hall. Sean and Fein catch me by my arms and push me toward our house.

"It's cool, Ky. He didn't want her to. Don't be jealous," Sean tells me, hands wrapped tightly around my shoulders, *still* pushing me.

"Am I acting so unruly that I needed to be shoved from the mess hall and escorted to the house?" I snap.

"The fingers you shoot with are twitching and you turned red with anger in an instant, Ky. Sean grabbed you when you took a step toward them."

I wasn't even able to take a step forward. "Why would she do that?" I burst. "Did he let her?"

"Don't sweat it, Ky," Fein begins. "I'm sure he didn't want her to, like Sean said. I thought you and Marc were over anyway."

Sean nudges our front door open, and Fein and I walk in before he does. "Right. I mean, we are. We weren't something to be over. I just didn't need to see that." We amble to the den and toss our vests onto the table.

"Ky and Marc are not over," Sean states halfheartedly, plopping down on the sofa. "He's into her, and she is equally into him. That's why they look at each other like that. Googly eyes, as though they were destined to be Dyads instead of Creations."

I sit on the table in front of Sean, and Fein sits beside him. Crinkling my nose, I scoff, "I'm not at all beautiful enough for being a Dyad, and Marc's too rough for being aired on some billboard and ogled at by onlookers." I wouldn't want that anyway. The broadcasters in charge of the America's entertainment and developing culture match the most captivating individuals, whom they can portray as loving, intimate couples in efforts to encourage the Normals to mate and have families. They use them as an example to imitate, and I believe they're indirectly conditioning Normals to want companionship so that they will be inclined to increase the population. The more people in the America, the greater the economy.

Fein fake gags. "Those well-shaven god and goddess fakes!" She kicks her heel against the table and dust works from the sole of her boots. "They give Normals hope they'll one day look like them and have camaraderie. Ha!" She barks a laugh. "I think they're created in a tube too." Disgust turns up her upper lip. "No one can relate to their beauty."

Sean leaves the couch to shuffle through the movies. "The Trade models those fake couples on purpose. It's for hope and to give those lonely Normals dreams. Just like they make war look fun and sway volunteers with building strong relationships with Creations and Normals before one magical day returning to their normal family." Sean closes his eyes, viciously swipes across the screen, and smashes down his index finger. The projector flickers on, and a movie plays. "While you two may not be Dyad material, that doesn't change the way you two look at each other and walk around, acting like no one knows, or we don't see it." He slumps back down on the sofa.

Fein adjusts to sitting on her left leg tucked beneath her. A contemplative glance steals her eyes as her gaze slices over me and travels to Sean. "I *have* noticed that." When her gaze carries back over to me, I've already looked away from her.

"It's not what you think," I tell her. "It's because she was just all over my brother, and now she's trying to make out with Marc in front of Luke." I groan and shrug not to draw emphasis to my anger, and while I may have Fein convinced, Sean isn't.

"You're right. Collins sure does get around," Fein sings, standing. "I'm going to shower before we get too relaxed."

"Yeah. Me too," I say as the front door whips open and closes, followed by rushing footsteps that plod across the hardwood floor.

"Kylie," Marc calls loudly. The rasp in his voice makes the call echo through the low furnished home.

Nope. No. No way. We're not having this conversation.

I pass Marc to head for the stairs, and he grabs my arm. Without looking at him, I pull my arm through his hand, then grab it, pulling him to come with me. We make it to my room, and I push my door closed. "You kissed her. I'm not mad anymore, and you aren't mine to be jealous over. You can do that to whoever you want."

Splaying his arms out at his sides, he defends, "She was just using me to get back at Luke. I didn't know she was going to take it there."

"It's fine." I snatch up my in-house lounge wear and avoid his eyes. "I'm tired, we're about to lie around the den. Go back to *who* you were doing."

"Kylie," he says in an impatient tone. "Cut that shit."

I lean my shoulder against the door. The scene replays in my mind every time I look at him. "Did you slap her? Push her away like you did me?"

"She is not a traitor. There was no need for me to push her away like I did you."

He grabs my arms to keep me from pushing him. "I am *not* a traitor," I snarl.

"Don't be jealous." He takes my hands in his and raises them over my head, pinning them against the door as he steps closer. Placing a kiss to my cheek, he says, "I only want your lips kissing me." His beard is rougher than his kiss.

I try to move my arms, but he keeps me pinned. "Why do you insist on holding me down?"

"Because I don't want you to touch me."

"I won't touch you. Let me go. I'm getting in the shower."

"You're going to stay down there with them or come up here with me when you finish?"

I bite my cheeks to fight my smile. When I have the grin under control, I say, "Stay with them. We're nothing, remember. You hate me, and I'm working on leaving you alone." I'm happy I have him back, but we're still in this place where we go back and forth. One day, we're forcing distance. Another day, I'm sleeping in his room, cuddled next to him on his bed. I don't think it's supposed to be this way.

"You can't."

"I can't," I admit defeat. "But they'll know I'm up here with you." We try to keep everyone out of it, but as Sean said, our efforts are pointless.

"Okay," he says, releasing me and taking multiple steps back.

I rub my wrists. "Why are you so strong?"

He smiles. "To make you weak." He approaches and nudges me from the door. It opens and closes after he leaves.

One-minute Marc is all *Kylie kiss me, Kylie lie with me, Kylie don't like Cory because I like you*. Kylie, Kylie, Kylie. Then the next minute, he's asking to be left alone and accusing me of being a traitor. He's a walking contradiction that gives me a headache I like to have, an irritation I love to feel, and annoyance I can't avoid. I hate it, and I admit going back and forth with him drives me crazy, but when he does give in…it's worth it.

CHAPTER SIX

FEIN BEATS me out of the showers. She, Sean, and I crowd on the sofa in the den, watching a movie about a giant reptile. Fein falls asleep shortly after the movie starts.

I nudge her leg with my knee, and she is out cold. "Wasn't this her idea?"

"Yeah, it was. I'm probably right behind her." Sean slouches and lays his head back. His voice drawls as he asks, "You and my brother are back at it?"

Though Sean is cordial and oddly nice, he's not that big a fan of mine. He may secretly hate me because of what happened and preferred it when his brother still resented me. "I don't know. No..." I answer.

Sean doesn't tear his gaze from the lizard squashing a motor vehicle as he says, "He can't turn on you. Regardless of the *circumstances*." He won't say it in front of Fein, but what he's saying is even under *these* circumstances of me being connected to the Vojin, Marc won't turn on me. And while I don't even know why Marc is even the least bit interested in me, I push that side of him to give in to me, to want me like I want him. Maybe this is because I'm selfish, and I want the things I've heard others talk about. Maybe it's the parts of me clashing, the Vojin, the Creation, and the trickling humanity still coursing through my veins.

"I'm sorry." I feel the urge to say.

"For what?"

"I try to leave him alone. It's just really hard."

"It's not that hard," he condescends.

"It is when you feel the way I do about him."

He leans over on his knees and cranes his neck to look back at me. The grave expression he wears causes a heavy shadow to fall over his always light eyes, the seemingly permanent rise of his cheekbones to fall, and his brows to pull taut, which I've never seen them do. His gaze flicks over to Fein then back to me and whispers, "You're saying you have prohibited feelings for my brother? Like an affection for him?"

"I'm not *saying* anything."

He shakes his head, turning back around. "Would you pick him?"

I lean back on the couch. I don't know the answer to that question. I could say no and say I'll pick Luke one hundred percent. I just don't know just how truthful that is anymore. But it's what I was born to say. "I'll pick Luke."

He nods slowly. "How can you confirm that feeling? *Attraction*, yes, *that* is acceptable. We don't love."

"I'm not confirming that feeling, I can't. It's nothing more than anything anyone else has going on around here. What I said was, it's hard to pretend like I don't have this attraction, that I can't have it one day and leave it be the next." Confirming restricted feelings would be a mistake, and what's saying Fein's definitely asleep?

"What I've heard from the Normals is if you have those feelings for someone, you don't have to think about it."

I couldn't write this off as just attraction. It's deeper than that.

It's empty and full. It's heavy and weightless. I float, and I sink around him. I breathe as I suffocate with him. And the same without him. It's an odd feeling that I can't explain, and one I've never experienced. But I can't say yes, that's what this is. "I think, though there are restricted feelings and emotions, I don't think it's because we *can't* feel them. I believe we have open access to these feelings, that our brains can manifest them, and our bodies can and will react to them. But they've been working us for so long, training us, and making us believe there's only one path. And while there is...what if there was an opportunity for Creations to be Creations and something more?" I follow up the questions with a half-hearted chuckle, hoping to give off a sense that I'm joking.

Sean shrugs once. "Who knows?" He goes silent and shoves his hands through his hair, stretching his back as he does so. "Look, Ky. I know I haven't said this yet, and it's not because I'm resentful or ungrateful. I've just been caught up in my thoughts about this whole thing. But..." He bumps the side of my thigh with his fists. "Thanks for what you did for me. I know what you risked."

"Don't thank me." Luke was right in saying we shouldn't have saved him and killed him instead, and we are putting a lot of trust in the two of them, hoping they don't rat us out. It may be appropriate for me to thank *him*. "Thank *you*." I give him a shy smile. "For what you're continuing to do for us."

"We're even. What you did was greater than what we are doing."

I appreciate that.

Luke comes in and leans against the door panel. "What's that?" He points to the screen. "Whatever it is, it looks boring, and Fein sleeping proves it."

I yawn. "I'm right behind her." I leave them for Marc's room.

"Not with me, Ky?" Luke asks.

"Nope," I answer, running up the stairs. I knock on Marc's door and wait for him to answer. I wait for a while.

Eventually, Marc tugs the door open and leans against the door frame, blocking the entry. "When did you start knocking and waiting for an answer?"

"You can close the door, and I'll try that again."

He works me over with a lazy gaze. "You aren't working very hard on leaving me alone."

"I'll try harder tomorrow."

He pushes the door open further, and I duck under his arm, entering his dark room. He doesn't get a sliver of moonlight in here. "You aren't sleeping in here, Kylie," he says after closing the door, eliminating the slice of light that split his bedroom in two.

I stretch and sit on his bed. "But I'm so tired and already here." I pat my mouth to forgo my fake yawn.

He moves from the door. "You make it easy and hard to be upset with you."

"Then don't be upset with me and let me be mad at you for kissing Collins."

Standing in front of me, he takes a haughty stance, frame broadening as he crosses his arms. "I thought I could do whatever I wanted with whoever I wanted."

"You can, but I want to be your only whoever."

"We are nothing more than hugs and kisses, Ky."

That is a lie. "We are so much more than a hug or a kiss. You, me, and everyone else knows it. We just can't go anywhere with it."

He lies down behind me and reels me to him, saying, "You can stay in here until Luke goes to sleep, and you will sleep with him."

I lie across him. "Can we talk?"

"Yes."

"Does Sean hate me?"

He shrugs. "Maybe, but he hasn't said anything. Why do you ask?"

"If I had known about Luke's girlfriend before he killed her, I think I would have hated her."

"Why did he kill her?"

I play with a loose string at the hem of his shirt. "I don't want to say."

Marc combs his fingers through my hair, massaging my head with every stroke. "Say," he encourages.

I can't. I don't want to give him any ideas and tomorrow end up dead. "Because," is all I'll say.

"He probably started caring more about her than you." He pauses, then sighs before saying, "I thought about killing you, when we were standing on the side of the training room that one day. It would have been easy, just beyond the cameras' view…"

I jolt up. "You wanted to kill me?"

"I didn't kill you, I thought about it. It is clear I didn't *want* to, or you would be dead."

I look away from his eyes to a scar on his chin, where his beard doesn't grow. Though I feel small, in a firm tone, I ask, "Was it because you were mad at me for what you saw, or to remove me as a distraction?"

He presses his lips together and shrugs. "To remove you as a distraction."

My stomach turns uneasily. I'd feel better if he said he wants to kill me because he thinks I'm a traitor, because he thinks I've led him on, and I can't be trusted. But to kill me because he might care about me more than he cares about his brother, that makes this worse. It also makes me hate Separation and Creations, and I finally understand what he once said… *To be born as an only child and not of Separation so I can have my own wants.*

I clear my throat. "I'm going. I'll see you tomorrow."

He pulls me to him, hugs me tight, and then kisses my cheek before saying, "Okay. Goodnight."

I leave his room and head into Luke's, where I lay on his bed. He comes in shortly behind me. "I thought you weren't sleeping in here?"

"Marc made me uncomfortable."

He sits on the bed, expression reflecting concern. "How?"

"He wants to kill me but won't."

He gets up, worry washing away with a blink. "I can relate. But you're right, he won't kill you." He hangs his vest and stuffs his other clothes in a drawer.

I pull the blanket up to my neck and close my eyes. "I know."

Luke lies down on his stomach, and I press my head to his shoulder. "Why when I lie with Marc, it doesn't matter how I lie, he can take away my nightmares. But when I sleep next to you, I have to be like this for you to take them away?"

His shoulder shrugs. "Beats me, Ky. We've tried everything to help you out, and I don't know why he's the only answer."

Me neither...

I wait a while before I ask, "How did you know you loved that girl?"

Luke clears his throat. "Because."

"A little bit more," I probe.

"I can't explain." He brushes me off like I'm irritating him, but says, "She seemed to make me feel...euphoric. My heart swelled when I was around her. The world was peaceful. It felt good to live. What I was didn't matter. What I stood for wasn't so important. The fact that my body was property of the America wasn't an issue. It's a weird feeling, one that feels wrong, so wrong it hurts...but on the other hand, she settled the discomfort and replaced it with the one thing we'd never have as Creations, humans, Vojin, a rebellious host...*peace*. I didn't need anything else in the world. As long as I had her..." he breathes deep, grumbling. "I don't know, Ky."

"But you can confirm it. You can confirm that feeling, *love*. You can say that's what it was."

"She loved me first, and my feelings somehow copied hers, accommodated hers. We mirrored each other. It had to be."

"How do you feel now?" He takes so long to respond that I have to say again, "Luke?"

"I. I feel...broken," he says slowly, and then clears his throat. "Empty."

I shift uneasily. "Do you, um, regret?"

"No. You are more important than she was. I don't want to talk about this anymore. Go to sleep."

I relax onto the mattress and withhold my sigh. We *never* mention our rebellion, the one thing about us that separates us from other Creations, or even Normals, who are Vojin hosts.

We're subject to death by the hands of the government should they discover we're associated with the Vojin. But should the Vojin find out we've reestablished control over our bodies, that we're no longer hosts and under their control, they'll use us to set an example where we'd prefer death instead of their torture.

It won't matter that the Vojin entities are still part of our DNA, altering our molecular structure. The fact that we've had our implant slain is all that will matter. Our mother took care of it not long before she was murdered. This is what makes us so different, and why we're in the most dangerous situation should someone gain suspicions of us. An ounce of our blood could give us away, but thankfully, they haven't needed that. I think the Vojin and maybe whoever put that note on my bed may be on to us. Someone around here knows our secrets.

"Ky?" Luke brings me back to wakefulness.

"Hmm?"

"Don't pick Marc over me," he states, wrapping my head in his arm.

"Are you worried I will?"

"Do you love him?"

I clear my throat. "I can't say for sure. I can't confirm a feeling I am unfamiliar with."

"Then yes, I'm worried you will."

I couldn't pick Marc over Luke. If Luke goes, I'll be in even bigger jeopardy of getting hurt or killed when we do fight in the wars or against the Vojin. "I couldn't pick him over you. I've been convinced for so long that we weren't supposed to have these types of feelings. Specifically, *us*, beyond the Vojin im–"

"Don't talk about that, Ky," he says, though he just mentioned the worst of it all minutes ago.

"Fine."

The silence soon fills with Luke's snores, and I doze off with death heavy on my mind.

CHAPTER SEVEN

I GET up before Luke and before the loud horns sound. For Marc and Sean and Luke and me, I'll try harder to make this *not* work. Remembering the tone of Sean's voice and the look on his face last night, I accept he's not happy about Marc and me. I can't blame him. What twin would want to be in competition with a girl or boy who has feelings for their sibling? I wouldn't. Had I known about Luke's girlfriend, and known he was more accepting of her than me, I would have tried to kill her myself. It's likely something Luke has been contemplating about Marc, though he won't admit it. That type of affection lives with you even after one of the people dies. Is death even the best answer?

Love: an intense feeling of deep affection.

Love is dangerous. It makes you do things you wouldn't normally do, feel ways you aren't familiar with, and turn on people who would save your life.

Luke is strong. He had a battle with love and won. He conquered love.

Or did he...?

He was hurting last night. I heard it in his voice. Maybe he lost the war to love because he's broken.

There must not be a winner in love and war. If you give in to love, you forfeit, you lose. If you defeat love, by offing the person you fell in love with...you still lose.

I don't lose. I'm not a failure.

Leaving Luke's room, I try to reprogram myself. Marc and I need to end, and I need to revert my attention to the threat, Separation, the bettering of my team, the Vojin, my mixed identity, finding out the others who are mixed, and that letter. I need to find out how my parents played a part in this and are somehow continuing to play a part. I need to be the Kylie I was before I met Marc. Strong, assertive, unable to be weakened or to shed a tear. I must be undistracted by the softness in his eyes when he only looks at me, the smile that wrinkles his cheeks, and the way his touch lightens when he caresses me. He can't deter me from my mission.

And there's one more thing I want to make sure I change. The Vojin, who betrayed us by killing our parents and setting forth a plan to end this planet, will never bring me to my knees again.

I tug on my suit and sit on my bed, waiting for the horn to sound. I need my own distraction to distract me from Marc. If I kill him, he would no longer be an issue.

The horn is loud, jarring me from my thoughts.

There's a knock on the door.

As I open it, I hear Luke ask, "When did you leave?"

I step into the hall with him and pull the door closed behind me. "Just a little bit ago. I couldn't sleep."

"There is going to be a sweep tonight. Six of us will go." We head downstairs and out the front door. "You and me, Marc and Sean, and Collins and Cecilia."

I kick my boot against the dirt, causing gravel to scatter across the road. "Can't we go without him?"

Luke's ice-blue eyes pin on me. "Thought you'd be happy."

"No Luke, I'm not happy about that. Are you coming with me to breakfast or do you have something to do?"

"I'm coming to breakfast. But I'll be out for the day with the general and Colonel Harold."

I stretch my arms over my head. "Who is Harold?"

"Remember the man who went with us to the hole? That's him."

We make it to the mess hall, and I hold the door open for Luke to enter behind me. "Oh! I've wondered what his name was. Where are you all going?"

"Back to the underground labs that they took us to before. They are going to dissect some Zombies and see how they are infused or infected. These are Zombies that just showed up, not that were changed. It's like they fell from the sky. Then they want to test another vaccination on willing Creations to make sure our Creations here can't be changed if they are bitten."

"You'll be back before dinner?" We nod to a few Normals who wave as we walk to the food counter.

"Yes," Luke says. He looks me over. "You seem unhappy today."

I stretch before grabbing a plate. "I'm thinking. Trying to figure out how I can remove this distraction without killing it. Or falling further. And then there are the other things you and I have to figure out."

"Don't worry about him. Stay back. I'll get them to trade us out of the sweep tonight so you won't have to be around him." Luke always comes through when I need him. Even when I've upset him, he looks out for me. Nobody else is going to do that.

"Thanks." I finish packing my plate, and we sit at a table with Fein and Floyd. "Hey everyone."

"Hi," they chime.

"Hey, no groups today. What do you want to do?" Fein asks me.

We don't have that many options. We can train for fun in the simulators, lie around the houses, sit around the rec hall, socializing, or sleep. It's so hot outside. If I were back home, today would be a day that I'd go to the diner and drink a white shake with a basket of chicken fries.

Being here gets boring sometimes. They require order at all times, so we are constantly being watched unless we are in our homes. This is the longest we've ever been in Separation. They usually train us for a maximum of three months, then we're off to manage or control. For war, I've heard they train for five months to prep the Normals. Now that there are some Normals forced to be here, I suppose they need extensive training. But I'm getting bored with the same old routine. Wake up, shower, train, lunch, train, dinner, shower, sleep, and repeat.

The Guidance has got to need us to do *something* in the America. Get me out of Desert Hills so I can see something else other than red dirt hills and heat waves.

"I don't know," I tell Fein. "Probably go talk to Danny and Seas. It's too hot to be outside with these suits on." The heat has kicked out the cool breeze, just when we were getting used to it.

"She's right." Collins sits next to Luke. "It's too hot to be outside. We should go to the theater auditorium. Watch a movie on the big projector or something. Maybe start up the simulator and have our own war."

"Outstanding idea," Floyd chimes in. "And the air is on, so we'll remain cool."

"What are we planning?" Sean asks from beside me.

"Go to the hall, watch something, then set up the simulator to have our own war," I tell him.

He nods, and Marc sits on the other side of the table between Floyd and Collins's sister Cecilia.

Argh. I can't sit here with him. I'll stare, then he'll stare. He'll narrow his eyes as he bores through mine, silently requesting I stop staring. Then I'll give him a tight smirk that tells him he's equally staring, and when *he* looks away, I will. He'll look away then back quickly to see if I'm still staring, and all the time...I am. Then I'll look away and realize how unlawful our actions are and beat myself up about it until I see him later.

"Hey Fein," I say, standing. "Come with me to the group's rec hall. I'm going to get Fire, Danny, Jesail, and Amber." I look around the table. "If that's okay with everyone?"

"Yes," most reply. "I'll get a couple from my group too," Fein agrees.

"Hey, Ky, get Sally and Marlin for me?" Cecilia asks.

"Okay, anybody else?" I ask the group.

"No."

Luke grabs my attention saying, "I'm heading out. See you all when I get back."

I give him a nod, and Fein and I leave the mess hall into the scorch. We nod to the General sitting on his stoop as we pass his office. He returns the gesture and goes back to his tablet.

Fein snatches her black scarf from her vest pocket and dabs it across her forehead. "These suits are only to help boil us, you know that, right?"

Chuckling, I say, "Well, we still have a mile to walk to their mess hall, so we will definitely be well-done by the time we make it."

Fein grumbles, and I chuckle at her frowning face. They've parked five Humvees on this side of the base today, which are usually on the far end, near the entrance. They may plan a further sweep or trip to the city. Or, as I watch eight privates run over with towels and buckets, they just may be getting washed.

"Sometimes, it pays to be better than the sludge," Fein says, gripping the collar of her vest. She strolls with her shoulders back, gloating.

"Queen of the world over there, Fein." I laugh at her cocky sway.

She chortles, straightening. "I'm not serious. I wouldn't mind washing a couple of windows."

I've always known of Fein. She was an all-star statistician who fought with her mind by calculating every avenue of a win before landing the first punch. I've really grown fond of her since we've been here. I shove her shoulder. "You're pretty cool, Fein."

She punches my arm. "Thanks, Ky. Back at you."

Drenched with sweat, we enter the private's mess hall, shouting, "Aye! Hey! We need everyone's attention."

I stand on the table. "I need Jesail, Amber, Danny, Sally, Fire, and Marlin."

Fein stands next to me, adding, "And Rick and Amy. Let's go, you all are with us today."

We jump down from the table as they come without question.

"What are we doing?" Fire asks.

"We are going to use you all as target practice so we can let our anger off from the heat," Fein mutters seriously, wiping her face.

I laugh but don't correct her. The terror on Fire's face is priceless.

CHAPTER EIGHT

EVERYONE'S CROWDED around the film selection table, scrolling through the movie list. Collins stands next to Marc as they decide what movie to watch. She grins, grabbing his arm as they all joke about title fonts and cover images. She lightly slaps his arm as she chuckles and annoys the hell out of me. He's flirting back, *not* pushing her away as she is entirely too close to him.

Though their actions make the nerves squirm in my stomach, I ignore it and find Danny.

"Thanks for letting me join you, Ky," Danny says when he spots me approaching. "I never see Luke anymore. He had other things to attend to today?" he asks.

I sit beside him in the auditorium seats. "Yeah, his new title keeps him pretty busy."

Danny gestures around the room, asking, "What's this?"

"It's an off day and too hot to do anything outside. Sitting around the house alone is boring, so we invited a selected few to hang out with us for the day."

Air blasts from the vent feet above our heads. I sigh and lean my head back, cooling off quickly. The auditorium is wide and open because the simulator is in here. The chairs fold into the floor by the switch of a button and the simulator gives us more direct, in-person training, bringing to life the war or whatever scenario is input into its database.

It can place us in any environment, may it be water, desert, city, fields. It looks very real, especially when we are in a forest or the woods. We can almost touch the leaves and feel them brush against us as we run. A headband is required, which pricks into our temples and causes the real-life effect for its direct connection to the brain. A slim, compressing pair of gloves allows us access to weapons or we can use the laser weapons, which are equally efficient. The vest that straps around our upper bodies zaps us whenever we're hit. The experience is immersing for the Normals and is the preferred training option because we can't actually shoot them.

"They act like it matters which drive they put in." Sean takes the seat beside me. "Just pick a damn movie and press play," he yells at them.

Floyd is with them, shifting through the drives.

"Sean, you remember Danny, right?"

Sean looks over at Danny on my other side. "Yeah, from the diner."

"Wassup?" Danny greets.

"Trying to figure out..." he raises his voice, "...why the hell we aren't watching the movie yet?"

"You are impatient," I say with a laugh.

"Ky," Cory calls from a few rows back. He waves his hand for me to come to him.

I stand from my seat, shuffle past Sean, and climb the few stairs to the row of seats Cory's sitting in. "What's up?" I ask, taking the seat to his left. "Just get straight to the point, Cory. What's really going on?"

"I didn't do anything Luke may have told you I did. Luke and I don't like each other."

"That goes without saying, Cory." I roll my eyes. "Do you have anything useful you'd like to share?"

Cory frowns. "Sheesh, Ky. Can you cut me some slack? My sister even looks at me sideways, and she knows me better than anyone."

I half shrug. "Maybe she knows you're a traitor too."

He stares me down as if he's seeing through my brain. "I work as a Creation, not for anyone else. I've never been a traitor. I serve my country and the Guidance, and I was placed in Separation to do a job. All of my intentions here are pure." He whispers in my ear, "I told you, I only got the names to weed out the implants, not to become a traitor."

"Was your name on that list?" There is definitely something up with Cory. Him stating 'destroy and reconstruct' proves that. He draws back slowly, locking eyes with me. "Well," I push, "was it?"

He moves closer so we are face-to-face. "I'll tell if you close this distance."

I press my palm to his face and shove him away. "I'm not doing that." He pushes my hand away. "I'm only asking a question, not forcing you to answer."

He smirks and drags his gaze away from me. "It might be, but then again, it might not be."

I look away from him when the lights shut off, and the projector turns on, creating a screen on the stage as the movie plays.

The chairs of this auditorium are circled around the large centered stage. No matter which side you sit on, you can see what's playing. The screen the projector creates is large, going up more than thirty feet and spreading out more than seventy-five. It is enormous and feels like I'm in the middle of the movie with how real and close everything appears.

I slouch, getting comfortable in the chair.

Cory is mixed, I know it. And he's going to tell me, just not here. Cory tells me everything. I just need to find the right time to ask.

"What are you doing?"

I look up at Marc. Dark, wavy hair hangs loose around his head and the scruff of his beard emphasizes the twitching muscle in his jaw. His broad frame towers over me. I sit up to lessen the effect and look away from him to the previews. "Today is tomorrow," I say, shrugging.

"You don't say." He taps my shoulder, drawing my attention back to him. "Come here."

I say to Cory, "I'll talk to you later." I see what Marc means about not being able to avoid me when I approach him. I feel the same way. I was fine, but I can't *not* go with him. He has some type of pull on me.

As I stand Cory grumbles, "Your *nothing* is really something, Ky."

"Like the answer you gave to that question I asked. You left me just as high and dry, Cory."

He smacks his lips at my back, and I ignore his derogatory huff. Marc and I walk to the far end of a row, away from the others.

"Why are you making this difficult?" Marc asks.

"I'm doing what I am supposed to be doing, Marc. And I was doing a great job before you bothered me."

"Bothered you, huh?" he objects calmly.

"Yes. Why don't you go sit with Collins and do that thing you were just doing with her?" He jolts up and all but charges past me. Before he gets too far, I grab his arm. "Okay, wait." His nostrils flare as he sighs and sits back down. "I didn't mean that. It's just that...It's really hard to know what we know. A part of me wants so badly for us to leave here and have each other because...I...I...

Because I just do. And that same part of me wants you to be okay with running away. But the more reasonable part of me knows that will never happen. I'd never leave my brother. You'd never leave yours." I pause, but not long enough to give him time to respond. "But this is us. This is what we get, as unconventional and annoying as it is for the both of us. And I'm working on leaving you alone like you want me to and like I need to, *for* us."

"There isn't an us, Ky. There can't be an *us*."

Argh! "Your stubbornness is annoying, Marc."

He slouches on his chair and stares at the movie that's gone quiet as a title card graces the screen. I tap his hand for an answer, and he nods. "It's complicated," he utters.

That is a good title for what we have. *Complicated*. "Good to know you are as confused about this as I am."

"I am not confused. I know what this is, I know what I want, I know what I am, and I know how I feel. But I know I can't have what I want. So I push you off and try to force you to leave me alone to make it easier to leave you alone. But I'm terribly jealous, and I don't want anyone else to have you either. I'm not confused at all," he says with a shrug.

I turn in my seat to face him. "What do you want to do?"

He flicks another glance at the movie. I wait for his answer and tap him again when he doesn't speak. "You can go sit with Cory, and I'll go sit with Sean."

I sit back in the chair, angered by his suggestion and his contradiction. "No, Marc. I'm not doing that. But seeing you would push me off on Cory, like I were an unwanted pet animal, I get it. You make sure you hold up your side too because you most definitely are confused." I stand and shove his legs out of my way as I pass.

"Wait." He grabs my waist.

I shove him off me. "No way."

I look for Fire and Fein in the auditorium and make my way to them and sit down.

Fire gets up and goes to sit next to Marc, and at this point, I really don't care. At least, this is what I tell myself.

I turn my attention back to the movie. It's one I've not seen yet where an alien species battles the human race, and I'm able to call the ending before it's over. The humans win, they always win. Maybe, one day, there will be a place for something a little more than human to take down the aliens and stand up for something like this country.

The movie goes off, and we prepare for our fake war. We put on our headbands, gloves, and vests. The needle from the headband sticks into my temple, and I'm immediately transported to the forest, hidden behind a tree.

Gunshots are blazing, birds sing, and rough waves crash against a nearby beach.

I lean against a tree, staring at my gun. I could be more into this simulated war, but I'm just not. My leg jolts in pain, and I realize I've been shot.

I'm not up for playing with them. Not with Collins all over Marc's back and trying to jump on him. Her laugh echoes through the air, attracting my attention to them near a bush about twelve feet from me. I hate her, and if he smiles at her, Collins will be eliminated from Separation. She jumps on his back again after he's shaken her off twice.

Blaming my actions on jealousy, I aim my gun at her and pull the trigger, sending a bullet into the middle of her forehead. Her head whips back, and she loses her balance, falling backward off Marc.

I remove my headband, and I'm snapped back in the hall. I replace the gear on the charging shelf and leave, stepping out into the scorching heat. The desert is vacant, everyone afraid of getting sucked dry by the blazing sun. Heat waves dance across the ground on my walk back to our house. I hope Luke isn't out in this weather.

I could really go for a nap, but I have a dilemma. By now, I should definitely be able to sleep on my own. I should be able to lie on my own bed and accept a nightmare like anyone else and not jump up from it trying to murder whatever brought me discomfort.

I had my first nightmare experience years before my parents died. It was something silly that would bother a child, and I can't remember it today, but my mother came in my room at the time, calmly. I must have been crying loudly, or I might have screamed. She said to me, "Peace, Kylie. It wasn't real, and you have to learn to separate the real from the unreal. Think of when you have a good dream. You don't wake up thinking *that* was real. Relay those thoughts and feelings to the bad ones."

I understood that, and I didn't have a nightmare after that until the day they died, and then after the incident with my uncle. My mother probably didn't consider I'd dream about things that were real, as if I were reliving them. If she did, she may have taught me a better way to abolish this fear.

Our home is silent when I enter. Though I know no one is here, I still say, "Kylie," and it echoes through the house. We established a rule that each of us who live here will say something, may it be our name, hello, or something that tells each other we are entering and are not a Zombie. Everyone's pretty good at following it, except my rebellious brother.

I run upstairs to grab a change of clothes from my room and go to the stalls for a shower. It helps cool me off, and the change of clothes helps me to get comfortable.

It's not often I get the entire house to myself, and I take the opportunity to dance through the house as I drop my clothes off in my room and boogie into the den to find some music to listen to. It's the best cure for my drowsiness that'll soon loom over me if I don't keep moving.

I press "shuffle Pop" on the screen, and through the speaker blasts an upbeat rhythm. I jump over the coffee table and onto the couch, bouncing on the cushions and pumping my fists in the air.

The front door opens.

I leap from the couch and rush to the music, trading it for a movie. Whoever enters doesn't announce themselves, but it's not Luke. Their footsteps thunder as they plod across the floor, this person's heels drag.

Cory pokes his head around the corner. In a sing-song voice he asks, "Were you dancing?"

I walk around the table to sit in the corner of the sofa. "No."

He gives me a wry smile, teasing, "I bet you were," as he takes off his vest and tosses it on the table. "Do you remember that time we snuck off in the middle of the night to the gymnasium at the education center back home?"

"No," I say, carrying it out. "I remember you trying to sneak out and falling off your roof. We never made it because you broke your ankle and Hanley had a cow."

Cory throws his head back, bellowing a hearty laugh. "Ah-ha. That is what happened. I guess I just dreamed it went differently."

I stifle my laugh and look away from him. "Always dreaming, Cory. It's time you lived in the real life with the rest of us."

"You mind if I sit with you?"

"You're already sitting." I shrug. "But you can stay if you answer my question from earlier." He is going to tell me. If I have to beat it out of him, he's going to admit to his name being on that list. That's the only reason a Creation would double-team with the Trade. And if he reveals this, he may slip up and tell me *he* left that note on my bed, and then I'll know the Trade is up to something mischievous. I could be wrong about all of this. But there are things that aren't adding up.

"How long has this movie been on?"

"Just now."

He grabs my hand. "I trust you, Ky."

"Good," I say, staring at the screen.

"You trust me?"

"No."

"Why not?"

"Because you are hiding something."

Letting go of my hand, he pushes behind me, grabs my waist, and pulls me to his side. "I'm not the only one hiding something," he whispers.

I scoff. "What do you mean?"

"What do you think?" His gaze drops from my eyes downward.

I turn away from him, sensing him trying to kiss me. "You can either tell me or scoot over."

His index finger pushes my jawline, turning my head to face him. "It's the reason I wanted to be the one to get that list, and one of those reasons may have been to remove my name from it before giving it to the Trade."

Yes! I knew it!

I try to turn my head, but he doesn't let me. "Okay," I say and try to turn again. He doesn't allow me to, but he stares me down. "What?"

Distress clouds his features, making his green eyes soften. "I told you, and you had no reaction."

I drop my gaze, looking away from his boyish face that reminds me of our years of laughter and time spent just talking for hours. "I already had my assumptions. Can I move my head now?"

He cracks a smile, flashing two rows of perfect white teeth.

"No. I haven't been this close to you in a long time." The breath of his words wafts against my chin and neck. He's too close.

"There is a reason for that."

"C'mon, Ky," he whispers before his lips touch mine.

I can't say why I have not moved away yet. Stupidly, maybe I want the snake to kiss me. Maybe to take my mind off everything. But it makes me think about it all even more. I break away from him and tug his hand from my chin.

Cory exhales. "With Marc out of the way, maybe we can regrow."

"Marc is not the reason I stopped talking to you. You were. You were pushy and overbearing."

Grumbling, he drags his hand over his buzz cut. "What if I told you I wasn't the only *alleged* renegade? That I am not the only one hiding my identity in our division. The things I know can change your mind about a lot of people here."

I raise my brows. "Are you going to tell me?"

"I could. But we could talk about something else." He grabs my hand now resting in my lap.

"Like what?"

"I would tell you if you shut up." And he kisses me without me moving back as I return his kiss. He leans back, pulling me over him.

Cory's kiss is different; a mixture of pecks and a couple that linger. They aren't warm and affectionate like Marc's, and no feelings of my own lie behind the action. It's a pointless notion, and it feels wrong to even grant him the pleasure.

His hand creeps over my hip and grabs my butt. I shove him away from me, moving back, instantly drawn uncomfortable. "Don't touch me like that," I blurt out. An icky feeling creeps over my flesh, making me want to vomit.

Cory throws his hands up. "I'm sorry."

The front door whips open, and I quickly sit back on the

other side of the sofa, covering my mouth. My breaths are a little rapid as I try to make my disgust pass.

Cory sits up, leaning against the back of the sofa. He throws a foot up on the table.

Luke walks in with Marc, Sean, and Fein. They stare at us for a second, and I feel even more uneasy.

Cory looks in my direction, and I pull my eyes from the screen to see he's looking at me. "Maybe you should go," I mumble in my hand.

"Yeah. I should." He grabs his vest as he gets up and approaches the small group. He bumps Luke and Marc's shoulders as he passes.

I take in the sight of Luke's loathing expression and look away from him to the floor. The heat slowly leaves my cheeks, and I drop my hands to my lap. "Luke."

"Ky." He matches my resentful tone.

"You know, Ky,"

"Don't start, Luke." It was a thoughtless mistake, and I'm going to beat myself up far worse than he can.

He turns away from me and leaves the room.

I get up, following him.

Marc grabs my waist as I walk past him. "I wasn't serious, Ky, with what I said earlier."

"Marc, enough, okay. Leave me alone," I say, turning away from him to continue after Luke.

He pulls me back. "Why are your lips so red, Kylie?"

"Excuse me," I turn, and he turns with me. "You don't have to follow me," I snap.

He snorts. "I need to talk to you."

When we make it to the top of the stairs, I whip around and have to keep myself from shouting. "About what, huh? You keep ignoring how frustrating this all is! It's an obligation for us to keep each other at a distance. So do that." I pivot but turn back to add, "Before you kill me, and you wind up getting killed."

Marc gently grabs me by my waist, stopping me from turning away from him. "Is that why you have been acting funny all day? Because of what I said last night?"

"No. Just…" I grind my teeth and sigh, calming myself enough to say, "just go away. And I promise I'll do the same." In the shadows of the stairwell, his plum eyes shine softly as he glares at me. They stab me through my chest with his silence, threatening me to take back my words.

Seconds pass, and longer than I like, we stand staring at each other. Then he hangs his head forward, nods, and walks away from me.

I grab his arm. I'm not going to take my words back, but him having nothing to say and walking away from me isn't acceptable. His arm slips through my hand as he continues away from me. When his hand reaches mine, it slips away too.

I move my arms behind my back to prevent myself from reaching for him again, and I hold the railing of the stairs to keep me from going after him. When Marc is out of sight, I turn my attention back to my brother and go down the hall to his room.

"Luke," I call at his door.

He whips the door open and turns away when our eyes meet.

"Luke, I'm sorry."

"About what, Ky?"

"I don't know, but you're angry."

"Not angry, just disappointed. I asked to swap out Marc and Sean for tonight's sweep. We will go with Jord and Seits and Marshal and Danielle. Tomorrow is supposed to be hotter than today, and we will have training inside. It will be limited. We don't want people dying from heat exhaustion. You really need to get it together, Kylie," he scolds. He avoids looking at me. The smoke is practically charging from his ears though he keeps his voice even.

"You're not my dad. You don't have to talk to me like that."

"I'm the closest thing to a dad we both have." He slams a drawer closed. "I'm trying to help you. I'm trying to get you to understand. If you want, I could kill both of them to make it easier for you." He finally looks at me, after the anger has washed from his eyes.

I'm disappointed in myself. I sit on his bed. "I don't want you to kill them, and besides, I would want to kill Marc myself. No one else could eliminate that distraction but me."

Luke sits beside me. "What are you going to do? You can't keep going on like this."

"I've been trying to get information from Cory since we saw him leaving Jord's office. He finally told me his name was on that list." Luke's eyes grow wide and quickly sober before he shifts his gaze to the floor. "And he knows who the others are. I don't know–"

Someone knocks on the door, cutting me off.

He gets up answering it. It's a girl I've frequently crossed paths with, but never gave her a second thought.

I scoot from the bed. "I'll go, Luke. Come get me when you go eat."

The girl steps away from the room's opening and gives me a small smile on my passing. "Hi, Captain Kylie."

I glance at her from the corner of my eye. With a single hitch of my left brow and a slight smirk, I acknowledge her with my silent greeting and continue to my room.

I open my door and nudge it closed with the heel of my foot. It's nice and cool in here. I sigh, flopping down onto my bed on my stomach. My muscles relax, and I quickly grow tired.

But sleep is never good alone.

I scream at the Vojin as they beat my parents and at my uncle as he pins me down, forcing me to watch. With no fair warning, I cry, consumed by my weaknesses, by my memories, by my sadness and hate. Everyone is torturing me, and I'm not strong enough to break free alone. I can't save my parents or myself.

"Ky," my name calls out from the light in the ceiling that I shift my gaze to when my father's neck is snapped. The heavy arms pinning me down become consoling, and the bright light fades to a comforting, warm purple.

I relax and hold the shoulder of the arm that holds me. "Thank you," I tell Marc. I don't have to open my eyes to know it's him. I'm familiar with the hold of his body, the touch of his hands, the smoothness of his skin, the scruff of his beard scraping my forehead, and how the soap that we all use smells different on him.

He kisses my head once and says, "You're welcome," as he holds me, rubbing my back.

I fall back asleep in his arms until there's a knock on my door. I act like I don't hear it.

I hear the door open, and Luke walks in.

"I didn't know if it was you or not," Marc says.

"What happened?"

Marc's shoulders move. "She was screaming and doing that jerking thing she does when she sleeps alone. I'm helping her calm down so she can get some rest."

"She probably appreciates that."

"I don't know," Marc says in a mellow tone.

Fabric scrapes against plaster, likely Luke sliding down a wall. "You can't have this. It's getting too serious for her."

"We don't need to have this conversation."

"Why don't you just," Luke pauses, likely thinking of the right word to use, "stop?" The stress in his tone as he releases the word is heavy with frustration and defeat. A tone he's often used with me but not with others because he wouldn't reveal his concern to anyone. But he lets his guard down with Marc.

Marc calmly says, "I do, but she comes back."

"If you walked away, she would too."

"Luke, we do not need to have this conversation, and you know that is not true." The gravelly tone of his voice mixed with his rasp makes his statement sound angered. But that's just Marc.

There's a constant knocking on the floor, likely Luke warding off his irritation. "I'm adding in my thoughts and opinions. I understand you know, but I'm giving you another perspective. I think Ky has, um, certain restricted feelings toward you, and if she does and you hold the same type of fondness…Sean and I are out on a limb." Luke stands up. "Let's keep this family-oriented. We're cool, and I don't want to force you to stay away from Kylie."

Marc snickers. "Got it, Luke."

The door opens and closes.

"He's right," I say against Marc's neck.

"I know that." He adjusts, forcing me to move as he gets up from my bed. "I came in because you were miserable. I intended to leave when you got up."

I hug my knees to my chest and look away from him as I ask, "Why can't we shake this?"

"We can." He crosses the floor to the door.

"Hold on," I say when he grabs the doorknob.

Marc faces the door, head hung low. "No, Ky," he says in an apologetic tone. "Remove the temptations, overcome the obstacle, and eliminate the distraction. And you live." He breathes. "It's straightforward. Plain and simple."

I scoot to the foot of my bed and resist the urge to go to him because I don't want to battle with him pulling away from me. "I know you are right. I know Luke is right. And I agree. But we see each other every day and sleep in this small house with only a few feet separating our rooms."

He looks over his shoulder, staring at me with a hint of anger lingering in his solemn expression and a question in his eyes. "What were you doing with Cory earlier?" He looks away from me. "And if you don't mind, I would appreciate it if you told me the truth." He faces me, full-bodied, leaning his back against the door. His left hand is still clutched around the doorknob.

I rub my index finger over my lips, maybe wiping off the proof or clearing the lie I was preparing. "Why?"

He glares at me, eyes squinting into tight slits, lining their purple. My cheeks burn, and my neck grows hot from his scowl, the anger I can see boiling in him from my evasion. His shadowed eyes lower, matching his thick eyebrows, lips in a thin line, his nostrils flared.

I remain silent.

He scratches his beard with the bed of his nails and pulls his bottom lip between his teeth. He bites it hard before letting it go and crossing his arms in front of his chest. "Fine," he blurts. "I'm not playing this game with you, Kylie. Are you going to answer the question or not?"

I shake my head. "Not."

He twists the doorknob. "If you were trying to find a way to push me away and cause me not to trust you, you picked the right thing to do."

"What does that mean?"

He grumbles before saying, "I *asked* you not to do that with him. I'm not stupid, Ky. I don't get what you're doing, what this is you have with him and me. Or maybe you don't even know, and you just go after whichever one of us is available for your convenience."

I jump to my feet and fight the urge to shout. "Don't be rude, Marc. You know it's nothing like that."

"Whatever, Kylie. I'm done. This is stupid. And how I feel about you…you're not worth it, or my negligence in saving you over my brother."

My legs grow heavy, and an odd feeling attacks my chest. The knife of his words cut me deeper this time, jabbing me right into my spine. I think I just felt my heartbeat stop and stall before beating again.

"Marc, *that* is not fair," I mutter breathlessly. My throat closes tightly around the words.

"Whatever, Ky. If you were innocent, you'd say so." He shakes his head. "So if you are going to continue to do *that*, I can't continue to do *this*."

"*This*? Just earlier you were pushing me off on him, begging to have nothing to do with me. Now, we're what, breaking up? You wanted us to be apart. You wanted this."

"Right, Kylie. I don't argue." He opens the door. I rush to him as he's walking out. "You don't have to follow me," he says, looking over his shoulder, and he stops me in my tracks.

Dammit!

CHAPTER NINE

"The meteorologists have announced a heatwave for the next five days. We've been instructed to limit training until it has passed. Luckily, some of you will be heading out. The Guidance is requesting Creations for Citizen Management. I'll have the list of who will be leaving before dinner. The ones chosen will leave in forty-eight hours," Sir Jord states before leaving us.

He carries a notepad in place of the tablet he's been carrying around. The paper clipped down on the wooden plank is black. Maybe he has concerns of his information being hacked, so he's resorting to written notes.

Could it have been Jord who left the note on my bed?

The past three days have been quiet. The heat has been putting a damper on training, so we've been indoors. I've stuck to myself; the less contact and communication with the others, the better.

I sit quietly at the table in the rec hall. The others ramble, and I nod when addressed, but everything has felt wrong and out of place for the last couple of days. I know I'm to blame, but Marc really knows how to lay it on thick. For three days now, this pang has persisted in my chest and back. What would be a good name for this? Maybe, heartbreak? Yeah, that's a good tag I can put on this, because that's what it feels like.

Heartbreak: overwhelming distress.

Well, I'm not distressed, and the pangs aren't overwhelming. It just hurts. So maybe it's not heartbreak, but disappointment. Marc is back to ignoring me, but he looks at me like he's waiting on me to say something to him first. But I won't. I have to let him think whatever it is he's thinking and leave it be.

Everyone hangs out in the rec hall. The snacks are out, and the air is cool. But what I wouldn't give to lie around for a day. But that would lead to sleep, and sleep alone leads to nightmares. It's not like me to think like this, but if someone could grant me one wish, I would wish to be able to sleep by myself without my dilemmas. Just one night, I'd like to know what it feels like to sleep alone and be calm.

Collins rants on about how she wants to be picked for Citizen Management. Luke's out with Marc and Colonel Harold. Harold is quite mysterious, never allowing his face to be seen, stealthily walking the grounds as though he's waiting for something to occur. He rarely speaks, but when he does, the information he reveals is always useful, as though he cherishes his words.

"Hey," Sean sits next to me.

"Hi."

He runs his hands through his hair. "You two give me a headache."

"Me too."

He dissolves into a fit of giggles. "How long is it going to last this time?" he chaffs.

"Forever, I hope." I mean it, but then I don't mean it too.

Looking away from me, he says, "Me too." I knit my brows. "Or until I don't need him anymore. Or until you're sixty-five."

That's out of the question. With this destruction that's to come, I doubt any of us will be seeing our next year's date of birth. "I doubt that either of us will make it that long. And even if we do, we'll probably want to continue fighting after. Or maybe we'll forget about each other."

"Yeah, maybe." He looks around. "Aren't you tired of hearing Collins blabber? I don't see how anyone could enjoy listening to her with her constant nagging. Collins," he yells. "Shut up!"

"You shut up," she shouts back.

"There is an announcement from the Guidance," a robotic voice calls over the speakers of the mess hall.

The back wall of the rec hall blacks out, revealing its screen. It flickers on, and a woman's avatar face presents itself, a smile making the animated figure more cryptic than friendly. "Thank you for being available for this announcement," the woman states in a kind voice. "It has come to the Guidance's attention that there are banned actions taking place, involving Creations of Separation." The woman's head looks left, then right, as though it were looking the crowd over. "These actions that display attractions and affection with others are not permitted in Creations. Creations should not become fond of one another or involve themselves in actions that demonstrate fondness. If you are not aware of these restrictions, please locate your nearest *Live by Creation Guide*." The head looks us over again. "I am sorry to have to remind you of this. I am sure many of you exceptional Creations are aware of the restrictions. We are very proud to have amazing Creations such as yourselves fighting for our country. Thank you for your dedication and your understanding of the restrictions placed upon your kind to keep each of you safe." The woman smiles happily, stretching her lips up to her cheekbones. "As you were. Please excuse the interruption." The screen flickers before turning back into the windowed wall.

"Blood over love!" A group of girls sing, laughing.

"Hey Collins," Sean laughs. "I guess that means you need to stop dunking."

She jumps up and punches him in his chest.

I can only imagine what *dunking* is, and I don't ask. "What do you think they'll do to us if they find out? Lock us away in a dungeon?" I ask Fein and Sean.

"They bring us to a secluded area with the opposite sex and expect for us not to be attracted to them." Sean moves from the bench to sit on the table. "If that was really the way they wanted it, they should have created us without hormones and the things that attract us to each other," he complains.

"They could only do so much. It's how they made us," Fein adds. "They put these things on our hands." She raises her left hand, looking at her embellishment.

Sean and I look at ours. "If they could strip us of fear and guilt, they should have been able to strip us of attractions and affections," he says, pulling my hand next to his. He looks back and forth between them.

"Then why do you think they didn't?" I ask, snatching my hand from him when he sniffs my palm. I shove him away from me with my forearm. "If we are only supposed to be here for our twins, why wouldn't they strip us of *all* feelings, saving our need to have our twin?"

"I think," Cecilia starts, "they need us to also *care* about our twin in order for us to want to keep them first. So without that feeling, we would be selfish and only care about ourselves. We have to love our twins, you know? They couldn't strip us of *all* our feelings. It would be inhuman."

"Are you human?" Fein asks.

"I am a Creation," Sean proclaims. "I am more than human, and I keep my brother at my right hand and my gun in my left. And we are better than all of you puny affection-possessing humans."

Gia comes behind him and yanks him off the table. "No, you're not!"

He hits the floor, taking her with him.

We laugh, watching them scrap. Gia tries to get up, and Sean keeps her pinned down. Watching Sean is always entertaining. Danielle, Marshal, Cory, Fein, Gia, and I sit around a table in the rec hall chatting as we try to stay cool. Danielle and Gia have been in Separation for two years, and like all Creations, they look comfortable with their position. They take orders and do as they're told, only breaking their character when in the confines of the rec hall around other Creations. We know our secrets, we know we're not mindless or affectionless robots, we know we have these flaws. But we know the Guidance doesn't want to know that because to them it means we are defective. It could mean, just maybe, they made us wrong.

"When was the last time you all were called for Citizen Management?" Fein asks the group of us.

"It's been a while for me," Marshal says. "Almost a year, not including the time we've been here."

"Yeah," Fein adds.

"It's been eight months for me," says Danielle. "I don't like Citizen Management. It's malicious, and we have to act like we are radioactive and have no cares. As if we really *aren't* human. Those people, they see us as humans. Only the position separates us from them in their eyes. The Waulers, no wonder they resent us. I'm not saying I actually care if they live or die, I'm just saying there should be a more humane way to do the Guidance's dirty work."

"I agree," Gia states. "They act like we are supposed to like doing things like this. And most people are innocent and have no other choice than to live the way they do."

Cory snorts. "We aren't obligated to like it. But we were born for that purpose. To do as they ask and not question it or feel bad about doing it before or while we do it. Not even after. They think they made us without feelings and emotions. I don't think they care or consider that most of us may feel guilty after we do it."

"Have you ever felt guilty before and during?" Gia asks him.

Cory's gaze darkens as he looks out to nothing. "I don't discuss my Citizen Management experiences," he says with a shrug.

"Oh, come on, Cory. It's not that serious," says Marshal.

Danielle wobbles her head left and right as she says to Marshal, "Well if it's not that serious, why don't you share yours? The one that changed you and brought on your first pinch of guilt before you did it. The one that made you realize you were not just a Creation, but also human?"

"Yeah, and add in where," Fein adds.

Marshal thinks for a minute. His eyes seem to shrink in his skull as the thought likely takes him back to that moment. He rubs his hand over his short hair. "I guess when I was in Houston," he starts slowly. "There were Waulers, seemed like everywhere. They were ruthless raiders. They burned down small towns and carried out countless murders. That's the simple part though, why we went down there. The guilty part was the order of execution. They lined them up. And like everything else, women and children were first." He shrugs and leaves his story unfinished. "What about you?" he asks Danielle.

Danielle sits forward, ready to release the goods of her story. Her hands move with her words as she begins with suspense in her voice. "We were in Detroit. Terrorists from the other side of the world had come in with threats of bombs and destruction. They threatened to take out the *entire* city," she says. Her arms spread out, and she brings them back in slowly. "They said that they placed this bomb in an elementary school, and it would go off at a certain time. We were near the school for Citizen Management. Our order was to go into the school and get out as many people as we could while the others located and did away with the terrorists." Her light mood shifts to sorrow, relaxing the muscles in her face, and her cheeks sag as she frowns. "In and out, I ran in the school, trying to help get everyone out. The call came through, saying there were only two minutes left. We were instructed to get out, and if we couldn't get them…to leave them. Out of obligation, I walked out on six kids…" She rubs her cheeks before her hands fall lamely in her lap.

"What about you, Ky?" Gia asks.

The first time I felt guilty about handling a citizen situation in Citizen Management? What Citizen Management situation *doesn't* bring on guilt? We may be obligated to accommodate every request, but there is always a second of hesitation. I don't have to think long about it, one has stuck with me. "Yes, I've had my experience. We were back home. We needed to round up Waulers. There were too many of them, the Guidance said, and they needed to be diminished. We were ordered for street cleaning. Our maximum number to maintain for this specific area was fifty-two. That order went to sixteen Creations, and it was fifty-two Normals and Waulers total. We hit our number quickly, and everyone else was to go. Fifty-two people are *not* a lot. I came upon a dark street, and something told me there were people down there. It made sense with it being so dark and a perfect hideaway. But I came upon two Waulers that were quietly fighting. I shot them both, and I would have left after if there wasn't a gasp. Behind a dumpster were an older woman and three children. The oldest was a girl, and she started crying and begging me with her eyes not to kill them.

"I thought for sixty-seven seconds. I decided I was going to let them live. Who would know if I did or didn't? I was the only one there, or so I thought, until I turned around and saw a council leader of the Guidance standing in the street's opening with a group of trainee Creations. 'What's the problem?' she asked in a strong tone that seemed like I couldn't be trusted or was hesitant.

Or maybe I just felt guilty. 'Go on then,' she hurried me with a wave of her hand, and the faces of the young Creations standing behind her were anxious. They were maybe ten years old. I turned back to the family and executed them, youngest to oldest."

"Damn, Ky," Marshal sings.

"That's somewhat like how mine was too," says Gia. "I know how you feel." She pats Cory's back. "You going to share?"

He shakes his head.

"Come on, Cory, we won't judge you," encourages Fein.

"Yeah, Cory, tell yours," I say, moving past the discomfort of my story.

He looks at me. "I think you take the cake, Ky."

"We'll know for sure after you tell yours," Danielle pushes.

Cory drags in an even breath. He looks us over and shrugs once. "I was sixteen and on my first Citizen Management for Waulers." He breathes heavily, a tone of discomfort steals his assertive voice. "It wouldn't have been so bad if we were actually containing Waulers, but we weren't. Residential citizens. We were instructed to execute them." His gaze meets mine. "Execute those they thought were invaders from outside our world and country. Implants." He looks away from me. "I'm certain everyone wasn't an implant, but it didn't matter. Entire families were up for execution, pets included. I only felt guilty when the woman, maybe the mother, groveled and begged me to stop. She kissed my boots then wrapped her arms around my legs and said, 'This isn't right, you're too young to have this kind of sin weigh you down for the rest of your life.' She kept begging me to spare her life. As she was yanked from me, I shot her, three times, without a second thought. Then one head shot for every one of her ten children." He rubs his hand over his face. "Shit was crazy."

"Wow..." Fein says. "She was right, huh?"

"She was only right because she said it. If she had not said it, he probably wouldn't have thought twice about it," Gia states.

"Do any of you regret it?" asks Fein. "I haven't been. I could have, but they needed me for training instead, so I missed out."

"More so, lucked out," Marshal corrects.

"Right," Fein drags.

"We aren't supposed to hold regrets. We aren't supposed to feel guilty," Cory states, face going red with anger. "We are given orders, and we are to follow those orders with no remorse. It's how they created us!" He stands up from the table and stalks off.

"Looks like you all upset him." Danielle slides her bright pink colored eyes over us. Her brother, Marshal's eyes are the same, and with his blond hair and deep red strawberry lips, he looks a little weird with neon pink eyes.

"I'll go check on him. Make sure he's okay."

"Okay, Ky," Fein responds.

"Wait up, Cory." Even with the sun setting, it's still blazing hot out here. We're approaching one-hundred-fifteen.

Cory slows. "What's up, Ky?"

"Don't walk out here. It's too hot out."

"I'm going to my house. You want to come?"

No way I'm going to go into Cory's house with him. "No. I wanted to make sure you were okay. You seem upset."

"The woman I killed?" I nod for him to continue. "She was my own."

I pull him to a stop. "Hold on, Cory."

"We can't talk about this outside, Ky."

"Okay, don't get into details. But I thought your mom was alive," I whisper.

"That's not our real mom." His head falls forward. "I mean, she is our real mom for being here as a Creation, but not my birth mom," he whispers.

"What about the other kids?"

He shrugs, rubbing his neck. "I assume implants too."

I look him over and must ask, "Why are you so comfortable telling me this stuff?"

Looking at me with hopeful eyes, he asks, "I've always been able to talk to you. I can trust you, right?"

"Yes. I wouldn't tell anyone what you tell me." I rub his shoulder and use the techniques I've been learning when training the Normals. "I understand what you're experiencing...an emotional discomfort. I'm...here for you if you'd like to talk."

He shrugs my hand from his shoulder and hisses, "Don't use those bullshit comforting tactics on me, Ky. I don't need that."

I drop my gaze to the ground and rub my boot over the dirt. "Sorry."

"I'm going to go sleep it off."

"The general is going to be announcing who's going off in an hour. Don't sleep too long."

"It's not going to be me, so I don't care." Cory has changed since he was demoted. What was once chin held high, 'I'm the leader of Separation' Cory, is now crybaby Cory. He's always moping around. I'd think he was doing it on purpose, a way to reel me in, but insecurity and a person's soft side does not make me want to go to their home and comfort them.

I leave to go back to the rec hall and spend more time chatting with the others.

CHAPTER TEN

JORD ENTERS the rec hall with Seits behind him. "They called for Citizen Management. Some states have gotten out of control. Their Creations are occupied with minimizing the undead, along with maintaining order and trying not to *become* the undead. The job as a Creation does not stop. As you all know, we have postponed some training because of the heat. I know you all don't think so, but they do care about you." He looks around at everyone, and no one comments. Seits hands him a clipboard. "Leaving from this division the day after tomorrow will be: Floyd and Feiney, Marcain and Seanabe, Joyce and Jace, Collins and Cecilia, Yolanda and Donald, Lester and Samuel, and Kendal and Kandis. Each of you and the Creations of your groups will head out at twelve hundred hours tomorrow. Where you will be going will be provided on the day of departure." He looks around the room then nods saying, "Respond."

In unison, everyone says, "We understand."

"It will be your responsibility to inform the Creations of your groups that they will be leaving with you. What your job will be for Citizen Management will be provided upon landing in your designated sites."

I should have known I wouldn't get picked to leave. All because Luke is now a captain. If I'm not on Zombie duty, I'm on training duty. I want to go out for Citizen Management. Get out of the desert for a few days.

"Kylie," Jord calls. "My office."

I give a silent grumble as I rise to my feet.

"Sorry you weren't picked, Ky," Collins states as I get up. "That has to suck."

I ignore her. Collins likes to get under my skin. I've come to the conclusion she does these things to annoy me on purpose.

I run into Luke on my way to General Jord's office. "You're done for the day?"

"No, I have to go check on the Normals, then I'll be done. Sir Jord just requested I meet him in his office, though."

I frown. "Me too."

"Why?"

"I don't know, but I hope he has the air on."

Luke drops his arm down on my shoulder. "You ready to talk about me walking in your room when Marc was in your bed with you?" Here he goes again, wanting to talk about Marc. He should stop caring. I am trying not to care. It's time he jumped on my bandwagon and gave up on these talks.

"Nope. I do not want to talk about it, and I was asleep like I told you. I think I dropped a bomb on a bulldozed building, though. Destroying the remaining rubble." Also known as Kylie and Marc's complicated friendship.

"How do you mean?" Luke tilts his head a bit to the right. "Why do you say that?"

I pull Luke to a stop and tell him every word of Marc's and my conversation from earlier. I watch his expression shift from uninterested, to shock, and remorseful, but he doesn't interrupt me. "His words made me feel, um," I snap my fingers as I try to recall the word. "Worthless: having no good qualities. I felt his contempt. And I've never felt like I wasn't good enough."

Luke sighs and purses his lips.

"I know this is better this way," I say rolling my eyes. "To let him stay angry and us stay separated. I get that. That's why I've been staying away. Ignoring you when you want to talk about it and ignoring him when he looks at me, but that doesn't make the way I feel go away." I shrug. "I don't know. I thought me saying it all out loud would fix it. But that didn't help either." I walk off.

Luke catches up with me. "You don't want to hear what I have to say?"

"Is it going to be what I said?"

"A little."

I smooth my hands over my ponytail and shove my emotional state in a low place. "Let's go see what the general wants, Luke. No, I don't want to hear it. And yes, I can stay away. I just wish we could be friends, I guess. Can we be around each other without the attraction and confusing feelings?"

"It's because of the attraction and the feelings that you want to be around him. So I guess you can't. Stop feeling the way you do, stop liking him, stop being attracted. See if that works."

"That isn't helpful."

We travel the quick walk to the general's office, and Luke opens the door. "Sir?" Luke says, and I nod.

Seits and Jord sit at his desk. "Kylie, you will be responsible for checking in on the captains and groups who are leaving. Luke, make sure you follow up with the groups of the captains. You all cannot train outside, so there will be all day training in the training hall. Lunch will be brought to you. Luke, you will be there as well. You all will be responsible for the entrances of Non-Creations and the remaining Creations of this draft for Separation. Numbers should be fine with the Creations leaving with their leaders. Do either of you have any questions?"

"No, sir."

"Okay, Luke. Ace and Stacey will be leaving as well, so any and all responsibilities will fall on you. Everyone who is supposed to be here for this draft's Separation has arrived, and our area is managed properly, so things should not be difficult to maintain."

"Kylie," Seits begins. "You and I will ride to the hole in the morning to check on the preparation of the labs. Luke will stay here and help Jord prepare for the Creations' departure. Respond," she demands softly.

"We understand."

"Do either of you have any questions before you leave this office?" Jord asks.

"No sir," we respond.

"As you were. We will meet you both in the morning."

As we walk out of the general's office, the howl of a coyote calls loud in the distance.

Our gazes meet. Ignoring it, we walk to our house.

When I'm in my room, getting changed, I hear two more coyotes howl louder. Peeking out my window to see how close or far they are, I catch Floyd and Fein running off from behind another house, leaving the base for the hills a couple miles out.

They are going out there to see the coyotes? Is it this easy to see us when we are running off?

I push away from the window, charging for Luke's room, hoping they aren't that fast so he can see them too. Without knocking, I burst in. He's changing and looks at me suspiciously as I rush through the room. "Sorry, but look." I point to the window that faces the same direction as mine.

He helps me pull back the curtain.

We watch Fein and Floyd run toward the hills and hear another coyote howl. "Looks like Floyd by the wonky way he runs."

"It is." We close the curtain. "Are you thinking what I'm thinking?"

"Yes."

We hurry to put on our suits and run from the house in the direction Floyd and Fein ran. When we make it to the hills, we quiet our footsteps to a silent jog.

Around the corner of the hill, there are whispers.

We throw out our arms, stopping each other from moving closer. Raising our index fingers to our lips, we tell each other to stay quiet as we prepare to peek around the corner.

Two Vojin males stand before Floyd and Fein. They look angry, displaying a hint of red in their swirling blue and green color. Like Talock did the day he strangled me in the borrow. I can just barely hear them, but I can make out the one on the left speaking in angry, hushed tones about someone trying to overthrow their plan back at their home.

Floyd raises his hand and asks, "What do they want us to do if things are back home and we are not affected down here?"

"We have never been to the *home* you speak of," Fein chimes in.

"That does not matter. It is where you are from and what your second priority is beyond your twin. We cannot afford to be overthrown; there is too much at stake for this and our plan to overtake this planet. You are either with us or against us. We need you two to get multiples to side with us when the time comes to enforce our better living upon the humans." He sounds exactly like Talock's domineering nature.

"This is not going beyond what we were implanted here to accomplish?" Fein asks. "This is strictly for a better living instructed by the Maker?"

The male Vojin on the left takes a step toward her. "Are you questioning us, Feiney? Have we done something for our word to *not* be good enough for you or followed without question or a second guess? Or is it the Creation in you rebelling against what you know is right?" He stops when he makes it in front of Fein. The blue and green hue of him reflects off her face. She stands strong, nostrils flaring. "Should we now question your motives?"

The explanation these Vojin are giving Fein and Floyd is different from the two stories we have already heard. We can't believe any of them.

"No. She wasn't questioning you. We will do as instructed," Floyd states.

The two Vojin nod and sink into pits of glowing particles before zipping back to the sky.

Luke pulls me back, and we press against the side of the mountain. He holds his hand out, saying we will stay. I chunk my thumb toward the corner of the mountain, asking if we will wait for them. He nods, and I nod, confirming.

Their ordered footsteps pound the dirt as they head in our direction. Luke and I wait for them to spot us.

We're cloaked by shadows with dusk falling over the hills. I doubt they will see us or that they are worried about someone being here if they didn't think they were followed. Slowly, they round the corner. If we were snakes, we could bite them multiple times and kill them before they even noticed us.

Luke and I step out, strolling behind them, waiting for them to notice we're here. They don't discuss the recent events. Their stroll is silent. So silent it keeps them from being aware of their surroundings.

I look around us, making sure *we* were not followed. Although we aren't typical Creations, these actions are normal for Luke and me. Floyd and Fein's aren't.

We've almost reached the fields when Luke kicks a rock.

They both halt, shoulders hitched near their ears, backs tight. They don't turn around as they stand in shock and silence.

"Who is it?" Floyd asks, shoulder slowly lowering, hand creeping to his gun.

"Luke and Ky," Luke says.

Floyd and Fein face us, both with their right hands drawn behind their backs, likely clutched around their M17. "We can explain," Fein says.

Luke shakes his head, and I gesture with a quick point to their arms. "Lift them up."

Muttering a slur under their breaths, they lift their hands in surrender. "It's not what it looks like, Ky." The muscles in Floyd's jaw twitches. "You need to hear us out."

Luke and I separate and walk in opposite directions around them. They keep us in their sights, turning their heads to watch our movements. Luke says, "Ky?"

"Yes?" I say in a hard tone, matching the way he called my name.

Luke scrapes his nails across the scruff on his chin. "It looks like we have a couple of traitors in our midst."

"It does…"

Fein drops her arms and faces me. "Kylie, really, we can explain."

Luke and I cross paths as we circle them again, staring them down. We don't have any intentions to take action, not right now, but we will let them know we know their secrets. And as Creations, we will treat them as traitors, to keep our own footing in this world. We also need them to know they dropped the ball, allowing themselves to get caught.

"No explanation needed, Feiney."

Luke and I meet back up and head for base, leaving them to ponder our next move.

They don't call out or follow us.

We jog back through the winding hills, over the dried, crack dirt, to the base and passing the fields and courses to our empty house. When we make it back to Luke's room, I push his door closed, asking, "What do you think?"

Luke throws his hands on his hips as he paces the floor. "Why would they run off when people could see them?"

I sit on his bed and lean over on my knees. That would be the million-credit question. "Maybe they wanted to be seen?"

"And you don't check your surroundings while you're out risking your life?"

"Not a mistake Creations as good as Floyd and Fein would make." I lower my voice to a whisper. "Why would the Vojin call in the day? You think they set them up?"

"How do the Vojin know who they are calling?"

I waggle my finger. "How do *we* know who they are calling? It's not like the coyote howls come with a name associated with them, or the little marble balls have our name carved into them."

Luke stops and meets my gaze, eyes wide with awe. "What if it's a test for us?"

I wince. "Like to see who's willing to risk their lives when they call? Or testing to see if they have any rebellious hosts like that Vojin mentioned."

"That would be it. Knowing Creation hosts have had their implants removed and we're really thinking on our own, not controlled by the Vojin anymore. That would pose a problem to their plan." Luke halts in his tracks and rubs his hand back and forth over his low-cut hair that's starting to grow out. "I don't know, Ky. But does what just happened make any sense to you?"

Someone knocks on the door.

I stand from Luke's bed to answer it. "I think we should talk." Cory stands on the other side of the door, fingernails tapping against the door panel.

I was not expecting him. "About what?"

"I saw you and Luke run after Floyd and Fein. I know what you saw. We should talk."

I look over my shoulder and back. "We'll be talking with Luke."

"I don't trust Luke."

Luke comes to the door, ripping it from my hand as he yanks it wider. "I don't trust you either, snake."

"How do you know what you tell me, I won't tell Luke?" I ask.

Cory looks back and forth from me to Luke, over and over again. "I don't know. Will you?"

"I tell Luke what he hears, when it comes to things you have said to me. If he doesn't hear it, he doesn't know." But he'll definitely hear it, from me that is. I hold in my chuckle.

"What do you know?" Cory asks Luke.

Luke's upper lip curls upward, revolted by Cory standing in his doorway. "I know you are a snake," he states matter-of-factly.

Cory steps in without an invitation. He walks over to the window and looks around outside. "If you do not mind, Luke, can you stay by the door to ensure we are not heard?"

"Just say what you need to say, speak quietly, and we won't be heard." Luke closes the door and stands with his back to it.

I lean against Luke's dresser.

"The night you saw me leaving from Jord's office, I was retrieving a list that revealed names of Vojin-implanted Creations. Their names were on that list."

"Are you working with Floyd and Fein?" I ask. I don't think every mixed Creation is on the same side. I don't know if there *is* a side. I can't help but think everyone is lying. And if they are not, we all may end up fighting against each other. We may be better off if we take out all the Vojin, regardless of what the greater good is.

"Yes. I'm working with them," Cory answers without hesitating. "They sent me here to talk to you two, to request your silence."

"Why should we trust any of you?" Luke asks. "What is our silence buying them or us?"

"Their lives and your friendship. For you, nothing. It may make you feel better as a person, a remedy for you being such a dick," Cory says. He crosses his arms and takes an unbreakable stance, but the twitch of his right brow gives away his insecurity.

Luke glowers at him.

Our names must not be on this list Cory had. The way Luke treats him, he would have called him out long ago. Maybe not in front of everyone, but he would have let it slip that he knows Luke is mixed and would have blackmailed him for sure. Cory looks humiliated to be asking Luke for anything.

Luke flicks his gaze from me to Cory, also noticing his distress. He looks back at me and slightly nods, then shakes his head, asking me whether or not we should go with it. I shrug my right shoulder that's out of Cory's view. He raises his brows up and down quickly, indecisive.

Another coyote howls in the night.

Cory looks to the window. "What made you follow Floyd and Fein out there anyway?" He turns his attention to Luke.

I snort a laugh, acknowledging his Creation-like way of interrogation. He's trying to get something on us, so we will give him our silence.

"I saw them sneaking off. We *do not* sneak. And if we do, we are up to something corrupt. Luke and I hold positions that allow us to follow up on anything we interpret as questionable. With or without permission from the person taking part in those mischievous actions."

"Like the ones you know all too well," Luke chimes in.

I follow quickly, before Cory and Luke go back and forth again. "They ran off, and I came here to get Luke so we could find out what they were running off to. We all have been complaining of the heat, yet you would run out to the hills, in the heat that has brought you discomfort all day. They deserved to be followed and questioned."

"We didn't question them," Luke interjects. "So there is no reason for you to question us. Tell them they have our silence like Kylie has granted you. Now get out of my room." Luke opens the door, inviting Cory to leave.

As Cory passes, he says, "Can you come talk to me after breakfast in the morning? I think you believe I mean something that I don't."

"You asked me for my silence, Cory. Let's not get comfortable in our disputes by discussing them or trying to come to a common ground that will never get established. How dare you question *us* about *our* actions for following up as leaders on more of your *kind* to keep our sector and our people safe? This is what we were born and trained for!"

He quickly defends, "I wasn't questioning you like–"

I throw up my hand, stopping him. "It may seem like I care, Cory. But if you look me in the eyes, you'll see that I don't."

Cory lowers his head and glares at me through his lashes. "That's not what your lips said the other day, Ky."

"It's what they are saying today," Luke chimes in. "You might want to listen to them. I don't want my sister to have to repeat herself."

Cory turns to Luke. "I can't wait until I'm able to get some dirt on you. I know you are not as good as you try to make yourself out to be. You're hiding something worse than all of us, and when I find out what that is, I am going to make sure I watch you crumble, and it will be *you* begging *me* for silence," he snarls, inches away from Luke's face.

Luke smiles, looking at Cory through hate-filled eyes. "Keep your fingers crossed," he encourages. "I'll be waiting for that day right along with you. But for now, I like to watch *you* beg...and crumble."

Cory balls his fist then un-balls it before he leaves, eyeing Luke all the way to the door.

Luke closes the door behind Cory's departure. He turns around and rubs his hand over his buzzed head, grumbling. "Do you need to shower? I am going to shower."

"Yes, I do. I'll meet you back here after." I approach his door, doorknob in hand. *Please don't let me open this door to Marc. Please don't let Marc be in the hallway. Please don't let me run into Marc as I go to the shower stalls.* I open the door to an empty hallway. *Phew.*

I rush to my room and grab my nightwear. *Don't run into Marc. Please don't run into Marc* sings through my head. I'm in the clear all the way to the shower.

Luke and I can't be the only ones oblivious to the invaders here. There's no identifier that reveals them, but Cory has built a close enough relationship with Fein and Floyd that they trust him. Or maybe Cory has used the knowledge provided to him by having that list, and he's recruiting or blackmailing them. What side is Cory working on? Based on what he said the day we were outside, it's *reconstruction.*

He is on the side of the ones I met in the burrow that coyote led me to. They're all wrong. I remember their message, *In order to reconstruct, you must first destruct.* And the destruction is what we are trying to avoid. Anyone who is for this world's destruction is against this world's survival. Though their intentions may be reconstruction, the ruler would establish this world in their view, to their liking. And while this place may need some changes, it doesn't need any more control.

CHAPTER ELEVEN

I sit by myself in the rec hall, watching everyone prepare to leave for their Citizen Management tasks. Correction: I sit by myself in the rec hall, watching *Marc* prepare to leave. They don't have a time span for the length of days they will be gone. Jord says they're to return once the job is done.

Marc and Sean are coming in my direction.

"Hug me, Ky," Sean says with a smile, mocking Marc's deep voice, "so we can go." Marc motions for me to come to him with a slow rise of his left brow.

I hug Marc hard.

"Don't miss me," he says, holding me tight.

"No problem," I whisper as he kisses my cheek and moves from our hug.

I sit back down and watch him leave the rec hall.

This will be perfect. Marc being gone may give my stupid attraction for him a break. He'll come back, and I'll be over him, back to the old me, the person I was before I ever laid eyes on him.

I run into Fein when I leave the rec hall. She avoids my eyes though she stops and says, "Thank you, Ky."

I pinch my lips to the side, quizzically staring at her. I never suspected Fein to be an implant, and I never thought she and Floyd would be so negligent to leave their back open to be followed or found out.

"You are welcome," I say strongly with a nod, and leave her.

At the training room, all the captains and privates' groups of Normals are hanging out with my group. There was no specific instruction given for what they need to work on or train in, so I fill their day with battle techniques I've discovered are effective against the Zombies.

"Danny," I call him to help me demonstrate my next technique. He comes over, standing in front of me. "Take my back, and I'll take yours. This way," I say loudly to the room. "You have eyes in the front and back. The undead are unpredictable. You never know which way they are going to come from, when they are going to come, or how fast they are going to attack. Implementing this simple maneuver may help keep you and your group members safe. You walk in step with them to limit tripping over each other's feet. Use their body language; if they halt and they're stiff, you know something is unexpected. If they are placid and stop instantly, you know a gun may be pointed at them. If they tap you, your first instinct should not be to turn around, but listen, wait, respond low, questioning what it could be. You all are each other's protection."

Moving from Danny's back, I retreat a few steps. "Okay Danny, face me." He turns. "Now take a few steps back." He follows orders. "Okay, you have to trust your group members. In an open field at night, your vision is limited. Facing Danny, I acknowledge the surrounding space. If they approach him from behind, what is the first thing you do?" I look out toward the large group.

"Tell him," someone yells.

"Get him out of the way," someone else follows.

"No, you shoot the Zombie. Don't warn him. He'll get it when you shoot. If you tell him, he may panic and make the wrong move, making himself more vulnerable," another with a boyish voice relays.

"Right. Who said that?"

A tall boy with shaggy hair that falls around the top of his head stands up. "I did," he states proudly.

"What's your name and what are you?"

He looks around at everyone before answering. "Today!" a girl from my group prods. I recognize the sound of Amber's voice.

"Cool it," I order. "But it would be nice if you could answer today," I tell the new face.

"I'm Christian, I'm a…human." He scratches the back of his head. "If that's what you're asking."

"Whose group are you from?" I ask.

"Seanabe."

"Okay. You can sit down if you want." I scratch the end of my eyebrow. "Christian is right." I turn back to Danny. "If Danny is about to get attacked, I don't want to panic him. He might make the wrong move, putting himself at jeopardy of getting attacked. I want to handle it, and Danny must have trust in me and believe if I'm pointing a gun in his direction, there is a good reason.

"Already, getting a gun pointed at you is intimidating. For some of you, it may raise panic at this moment, seeing me with it." I hold up my handgun in my left hand. "So now we will test your trust. Danny and I will go first, only as an example." Pointing my weapon at Danny, I ask, "Do you trust me, Danny?"

Danny pushes his long hair back, stretches, and then cracks his knuckles. "If I hadn't known you before this and how good of a shooter you are, I would say no."

I lower my gun. "You are supposed to just say yes, Danny." He taps his leg with his fingers. "And don't seem nervous," I gesture toward his anxious tell, "you'll scare them."

"Okay, Gabriel and Fredrick, can you bring the silicone dummies over here and place them behind Danny with their heads over his shoulders?"

"Sure," Fredrick responds as they get up.

"Danny, I promise I won't shoot you."

He wipes the sweat from his chin with his sleeve. "I believe you, Ky."

Once the dummies are in place and Danny is facing me, I fire my pistol twice, blasting two holes in the heads of the dummies. After the first shot, Danny jumps to his left where my second shot is headed.

I miss him by an inch only because the bullet is faster than he can move.

"Rule number two," I shout, gaze angrily pinned on Danny. "*Do not* dodge a bullet that is not aimed at you. Your trust is with the person who is saving your life. They see what you don't. So you don't see what they do. My bullet was an inch away from meeting your skull. You almost killed yourself jumping out of the way of non-danger."

"A warning would have been nice."

My trigger finger twitches. As calmly as I can, I say, "When you are out there, in it, there is no warning. There is no time to think. There are only threats and execution. You react off your first instinct. Your first instinct should not be endangering yourself or your team members." I motion my gun toward the people sitting. "Go sit down," I say, disappointed.

"Trust exercise!" I shout. "Creations, come forward. Good thing you all are great shooters," I tease with a smile, proud of my team's improvements. "Everyone will not do this, there are honestly too many of you."

"You should see how many brave Normals we have in our sector, Ky," Jesail says, grinning, a thrill filling her bright eyes with joy.

She's on to something. And I will probably get in trouble for this later, but…I shrug. "Okay, do we have any brave humans?"

A few stand.

There is a loud shrill outside, followed by three more. A few humans screech in fear and crowd together. *Yeah, like that would save them.*

I check my holster, hoping I brought my other gun. I didn't. I could stay here and let someone else handle it, but as I think and the seconds pass, I don't hear any gunshots.

Using these guns, we'll have five seconds or fewer, maybe a little more before the undead rise.

Come on Ky, think of a plan. What can we do?

I look at my group of Creations. "Okay, got it." I think out loud. "Creations, come with me." I talk fast. "I can only say this once so listen up. The guns we have will only falter them temporarily. Me and five of you will go after them. The others will race to the general's office. He has handguns and shotguns by his door that will kill them. Get the weapons and find us quickly. Remember what I've taught you. Do not get bitten or scratched. Try to keep them away from you. And look out for each other."

I run to the door, yelling, "Everyone else stay here! Creations, fall out!"

The heat smacks me hard when I run outside. I stand still, waiting for the shrill or sound of sluggish or fast approaching footsteps, someone yelling…something.

It's silent, nothing but the sound of the air conditioners running.

"What's wrong?" Joe asks.

"Shh." I listen more closely. They don't make a sound. "Quietly follow me," I tell them. "You all heard that shrill, right?"

"Yes," they say.

Okay, I'm not losing my mind.

We walk the dirt road toward Jord's office, running into Luke and his group of Creations. "You heard that too?" he asks, handing me a gun.

I take it, putting away the one that will do nothing to these Zombies. "Yes."

"You want to attract them? I don't get why we don't hear them anymore. Or why we don't hear anything."

"Me either."

I pull back out my other gun, preparing to hit them together. "My team doesn't have any of the guns we need."

Luke checks his mags and puts a bullet in the chamber. "Only some of mine have them. If there are a lot of Zombies, this may get ugly."

I nod. "For those of you who do not have the heavier guns, you can shoot them, but because they are not affected by our guns, you may need to fight and use what you can to sever their heads from their bodies. Everyone ready?" I ask. "Respond."

"Yes, we understand," they all say.

I raise my guns over my head and clap them together twice. "Watch your backs."

In no time, we are surrounded. Their approach is quiet until they snarl and charge. We fight and shoot until our guns fire empty. It reminds me of being in Chicago when we were outnumbered by the undead.

A few Normals scream in terror as I punch a Zombie back far enough to snatch my knife from my pocket. I plunge it into the Zombie's neck and sever the head from its body.

I hear a sound from the Normals. Not a good one.

Where is the general?

Their numbers are not reducing. I can't leave to check on them. We fight the Zombies until our guns are empty. The heat has no impact on the Zombies, but Creations pant. These monsters are strong and stable.

Creations smash the Zombies' heads with their guns. Brains

and blood cover everyone. Fighting these things takes so long. In the time it takes to keep one down, another advances on us.

We aren't prepared for this. A guy near me screams, and I'm sick. Shortly, we'll be fighting Creation-made Zombies. *Our team members.*

"Luke," I yell, ramming my gun into a Zombie's head until its skull becomes mush.

"What?" he answers, sounding like he's throwing a punch.

"We have to get out of here. We are losing, and they are going to start changing."

"Plan?"

No. No, I don't have a plan. *Run.* Get the ones who are left away from here and run to the nearest house, office, or hall.

Trucks screech to a stop, kicking up dust. Shots ring out, and it's music to my ears. The Zombies drop like pouring rain. While I'm thrilled he's come to our rescue, I want to ram my blood-smeared gun into the general's head for just now showing up and for having so few guns available when he knows there may be a chance of a Zombie attack.

It's quiet, but only for a second. Growling and the sharp sound of cracking bones alert me to something coming from behind us. I slowly turn around, taking in deep breaths of the scorching desert air. I raise my hand to my forehead, distressed and short of breath.

Three from my group are transforming and two from Luke's. Their twins are standing over them, trying to heal them. Their efforts do nothing.

I clench my fists so tightly my knuckles go white. Looking them over, I know there's no help. Joe and Anthony are both hurt, and they lie next to each other, holding hands. Neither of them is healing. Megan is kneeling on the ground next to Alex, holding his hand as he growls and his eyes turn red. Robert is the worst off. His lips are darkening, and his eyes are bloodshot. Edward nods, accepting he's changing. He stands and turns to me.

I look to Jord, hand extended. He places the heavier gun on my palm. "They haven't figured out any other options, sir?" I ask low.

"No."

I nod, turning to Edward. He's in front of me now. Edward surveys me with vibrant green eyes filled with hurt. "I'm sorry," I tell him, handing him the gun.

He turns on his heels, head hanging low as he walks back to his brother's side. He kneels beside him and whispers something in his ear. Robert snaps at Edward, and he jumps back, avoiding his bite. Edward's chest swells as he stands, aims, and fires.

His brother goes limp.

Edward looks away from him and walks to me. His warm, brown skin is flushed red, and his chin is trembling. I open my hand for the gun, but he slams it against my chest. I catch it before it falls to the ground as he continues past me. I hold back the urge to punch him; his anger is with the situation, not with me, and for this moment, I will allow that disrespect. I look away from him when he runs off.

"Megan?" I call.

She shakes her head as she cries, rubbing her brother's trembling head. He stares up at her, tears streaming from his eyes, the fear of death keeping him from blinking. Megan isn't ready to do what must be done. I look at Joe and Anthony. Both are growling, and their limbs are jerking and crack as they fight the change. With them both being under, it's up to me as their leader to end them.

I won't draw this out. I won't speak or give an apologetic face. This has always been a possibility since we found out about the

Zombies. Approaching Joe and Anthony, I stand over their heads, aiming my gun between Joe's eyes first. I fire. His head lifts from the ground, and it hits it, followed by his body going lifeless. Anthony's next, doing the same.

Alex is getting unruly. "Megan," I start. "If you can't do this, I'll do it for you," I tell her, rubbing her shoulder.

"I can't do it," she cries.

"Someone, take her away," I say, looking down at Alex. He finally closes his eyes.

Foster from Luke's group picks Megan up from the ground and carries her away as she wails.

I liked Alex. He was nice and tried his best at everything. Aiming my gun at him, I remember his boyish voice saying, "We don't suck rocks." I shoot and turn away.

Luke and his group take care of their fallen soldiers too.

"You all can go," I tell my group. "I know they were your friends and family, I'm sorry about what happened." They walk off without replying.

"My team is dismissed as well," Luke says, and they go too.

"Get someone to clean up the bodies," Jord tells Seits. She leaves, calling the others. Those who came out of the trucks get back in them, and they drive away. "What happened?" Jord asks.

"It was an attack!" I snap. "The Zombies were here, and we all came out to defend our base, outnumbered and with no firearms."

"Lower your tone, Ky," Luke warns.

Lower my tone?! I lost three of my group members, and we aren't even in a war! If we'd had the required firearms and all the Creations had been trained equally, this could have ended better.

"What happened to your units are unfortunate." Jord looks back and forth from Luke to me. "It's about time for you all to wrap up for the lunch break. Get yourselves something to eat and meet me in my office. Tell everyone else the day is done." He turns his back to us and heads off toward his office.

W-What? All we get is a "that's it for now" and he walks away? I stifle the emotional imbalance passing through my heart and mind. My heart wants me to scream at the top of my lungs and shoot a round through his back, but my mind knows I must find an appropriate way to express the burn of anger that makes it feel like something is melting in my chest. At the moment, neither can I give in to.

I sulk all the way to the training room with Luke striding tall at my side, unfazed by the event. I must be broken. He's so good at hiding his emotions, making it seem like nothing is bothering him. I want that. Losing four of my team members and knowing the distress put on the twins who are now, well, no longer twins. It's kind of hard to fight the way I'm affected by it all. Their life-lines, only family, best friends are gone forever, and they will never be the same. They're…normal. While Luke over here, even after losing two of his, hasn't batted an eye.

I pull Luke to a halt, stopping on the dirt road a quarter mile to the training room, between the mess hall of the leaders and the lecture hall. I step in front of him and lift my gaze to his.

Luke squints and arches a brow. "What is it now, Ky?"

"How aren't you affected by this?" I lift my shaky hand between us. "This is how angry I am."

"Bury it, Ky. Bury it in a deep place, and when it's time to see red, that's when you let it go." He walks around me and continues to the training room.

I sigh angrily, pursing my lips. If I bring up our parents or the Vojin, he blows a gasket. But this stuff? Nothing. After I revealed Jord possibly being in cahoots with Cory, he didn't blink twice about that either, which makes me believe I'm being left out of a bigger puzzle.

I turn on my heels to follow him and look to the west, seeing a storm far in the distance over the mountains. The clouds are thick, hovering near the peaks, lightning striking between the two. I can't hear the roar of the thunder, and the breeze doesn't make it this far over. But the blur of the storm is clear. Much like what's going on in my heart. So like Luke said, I bury it, muffling the roar of my thunder and just letting the rain pour inside me.

CHAPTER TWELVE

LUKE and I enter the training room. The chatter is loud, like transport vehicles rushing down an interstate. When the doors whine closed behind us, a hush falls over the room. Everyone's attention is eagerly drawn to us. Their faces are relaxed, mirroring the perfect lack of emotions expected in Creations.

Luke's voice booms through the quiet as he says, "You all are done for the day. You can stay here until you are finished with your lunch." He looks at his watch. "Lunch will be delivered here at thirteen hundred hours. Do not leave here and bombard the Creations that were once here with your questions. If anyone wants to discuss what happened, they will offer the information and should not be questioned about it."

He turns to leave, and I follow him, heading to Jord's office.

Luke's had this impassive demeanor for a while now. Maybe it's his additional workload weighing on him too. Or maybe we're being watched even more closely, and not by just the Guidance or the Trade, but by others around our camp. Like Seits so subtly mentioned the other day she and I visited the hole.

She showed a great interest in my relationship with Cory, and warned I should be careful around him. She said Cory is being watched. That he knows the implants of the invaders and will reveal who they are without tipping off the individual but will notify Seits and Jord. And although Cory and I appeared to have a close friendship prior to his exposure, and even while she and Jord are doubtful that I'm an invader implant, others may not be. Seits thinks Cory's closeness may be interpreted as a telling, and she warned me to keep my distance.

It was in that moment something occurred to me that has skated by since the night Cory revealed what he was doing in Jord's office. Jord has already known who the implants are... Cory was stealing the list *from* him, and if Jord had the list, keeping this information from the Trade would make Jord the hoarder which is frowned upon. Cory would've not only taken down our commander, but himself. And if he's picking off implanted Creations one by one by simply speaking with them, that would explain why they welcomed him back to the leaders' group and didn't kill him.

He made a deal. But that doesn't explain why Cory would need to reveal what Jord may already know. I still doubt Cory or Jord knows anything about Luke and I, but the conversation with Seits is making me reconsider Cory's intentions.

I look at Luke again. He keeps every step in line; the scarf pulled over his mouth, rim wet with sweat. We've discussed my discoveries, and this must be why he's keeping a lid on his bottled-up emotions. He and I are the exact same, and I know he feels the pain of losing his team mates too.

We make it to Jord's office, climbing the couple of steps to his porch and crossing the creaking wood to the whining screen door. I close the main door behind me. I pull off my helmet and tug down my sweat drenched scarf as I turn my attention to Jord.

He backs away from a file cabinet stuffed in a corner, saying, "We're moving Cory to a captain position. He'll no longer be following training orders. He is working on building his trust with us, and we are giving him the opportunity to prove himself." Jord takes the seat behind his desk, slapping a pile of papers on its center. Seits leans against the edge of the desk, arms crossed.

The news is far from shocking. There's definitely something deeper going on here. I can tell Luke wants to question Jord's decision, but he is in no position to do so. His helmet is tucked under his arm, and he's drawn down his scarf as well. There's the tiniest twitch to the corner of his mouth that hints at his anger, but the composed look he maintains is admirable.

Jord continues, "Just because he's trying to regain our trust, this does not mean he has it or that he will have it."

"You, the both of you, will keep an eye on him," Seits informs, picking up a packet of paper.

"Kylie, Cory seems to have taken a liking to you. Find out what you can if he's willing to release information. Specifically, uncover what he meant by *'destruction being reconstruction,'*" Jord says.

"Reconstruction?" Luke questions.

"That was our reaction," Jord responds. "And none of us can make sense of it. There is no reconstruction after things are destroyed. Who and what would reconstruct?"

"What will *destruct*? Should be your question, Jord." Seits corrects. She is right, and the only beings who would know the answer to that are the ones who originally said it, and maybe the implants from the Vojin.

Jord changes the topic. "Things have gotten out of control in some of the states of the America. Some of the Creations will be gone longer than others, and with over fifty Creations gone to other countries, our numbers here are minimal. We cannot afford to lose any more like we did today. The humans are not ready to fight, but we need to push them to get ready," he says, index finger pressing against the table. "Those Zombies don't stop, and I don't know if you all noticed, maybe you didn't have the time to, but—" he points toward the window. "—it is daytime."

The sun's slicing through the vertical blinds, casting lines of sun rays on the floor. I lift my wrist, as if the sun wasn't proof enough, to check the time. "Twelve thirteen PM." We now have day-walking Zombies. "Why is that?" I ask.

"There was an accident with an experiment. A Creation's blood was mixed with a vaccination that was administered to a few Zombies. They thought they were testing a cure. Things went haywire." Jord looks away from us. He turns the papers on his desk face down as he soberly admits, "We wouldn't have been able to fight our way out if they had come after us. There had been too many of them." He shrugs. "We left the old and new Zombies, the doctors, and the scientists."

I nod, looking away from him. *This is getting good.* We are Creations designed to manage and maintain order in the America, fight in the wars, and some of us are to train and control the citizens. But now, this battle against Zombies is trying to take over everything. Like Chicago. Without us, the Zombies would have taken over their entire city.

"Is there anything else?" I ask, ready to leave. Luke and I have plenty to discuss.

"No, you two are done for the day. Luke, check in with me in three hours."

"Yes, sir," Luke responds as we leave the office. It's easy to ignore the scorch with my anger still raising my temperature. We march across the vacant roads to the houses and enter our silent home. We're the only two here. "You want to lie in the den and watch a movie?" Luke asks.

"Sure. Was it Jord's idea to leave the people there with the Zombies?"

"Harold's." Luke snatches off his vest and plops down on the couch. "He can't be a Creation. Creations would have fought our way out even knowing we were outnumbered, but he said it would be better for us to leave than try to kill all of them."

"What'd Jord say?"

Kicking off his boots and propping his feet on the table, Luke says, "Nothing. I was surprised by that."

"If you go off and become Captain–"

"You are captain too, and either way, we wouldn't have gone to Citizen Management." Throwing up his hands, he gripes, "I already know where you're going with this."

"How do you know I was going to say that?"

"You are always complaining about something, Kylie."

I roll my eyes. "I'm going to change." I run upstairs and go to my room. As soon as I enter, I hear a scraping sound coming from my dresser. I rip open the top drawer to find the marbles loose, rolling around. They request us, but we won't answer. I grab a few pairs of socks and stuff the marbles into one sock, tie the top into a knot and stuff that packed sock into another. Just in case they want to continue rolling around, they won't be heard.

CHAPTER THIRTEEN

I LIE ON THE SOFA, resting my head on Luke's legs and propping my feet on the arm of the sofa. He speaks before I can. "Did you make sure we were the only ones here?"

"Yes. If the door has not opened, it's just us." I use the remote to hit play on a movie Luke paused for me. It starts, suspenseful music welcoming a dark, creepy building into view. "If this movie has kissing and the words 'I love you' I'm taking it out." I crack open a bag of baked chips and rest it on my stomach. Cramming a couple in my mouth, I grumble.

"Ky. If you're going to miss Marc and keep me from watching a movie when there is nothing to do here but talk to you, I'm going to someone else's house."

"Booo," I sing, throwing a chip at him.

He catches it in his mouth. "Get over it."

"You can be so heartless sometimes, Luke." I eat another chip and hand him the bag.

He snorts. "Don't point the finger at me, Ky. If anything, you would be the one who is heartless. We were created heartless, not to love. And do not comment on that."

I chew on my bottom lip. I'm not a child, I know the things

we aren't supposed to discuss or think about, but Luke knows we're different. He knows the things that make us different, and emotions and these feelings matter to me. He may just be trying to persuade himself more than to convince me. "Well," I sigh, "I used to think the most I wanted out of life was to go off to Separation and get away from our aunt. Maybe even fight for our purpose and become the highest-ranking female here. But it's deeper than that now." I lower my voice and continue, "And it's been being here at Separation and the Zombies that have shown me this. I still want the fight. But I want to fight for life, for growth, for the freedom to feel and revel in those feelings without worrying about consequences." I lift my gaze to Luke, and he keeps his attention tuned into the movie.

He flicks his gaze down at me for a sliver of a second. I encourage him to say something with a quick rise to my brows. He takes in a sharp breath. "I've recently had the urge to want to fight harder to survive after finding out about the Vojin's Zombie threat too. I want to have the opportunity to murder those glow in the dark turds." Cracking his neck, he sniffs, and I watch the anger fade from his eyes and be replaced by uncertainty. "Being among the secrets and yet still being in the dark has made me even more uncomfortable. There's definitely something going on with our general, maybe even the entire camp. I don't know who to trust anymore."

Maybe we shouldn't trust anyone. "Seits said Cory is signaling to whoever is watching him who the implants are by constantly talking to them and being around them."

Luke adjusts, sitting up from being slouched. "Think about this, Ky. Cory had the list when he was coming out of that office."

"Right."

"He had the list going back into that office too."

"Right..."

Luke cocks his head left, and whispers, *"They* have seen the list and also know whose names are on it. So who are these *people* who are watching him? And if they want to know the names, why don't they just go to Jord, *the general*, the head of our division, and ask? Since he's the one who had the list first."

I lick my lips and nod. "I was thinking that earlier."

"Unless *their* names are on the list." Luke leans back on the sofa and starts back in the bag of chips, shoving a handful in his mouth. "And that would explain why Cory is still here and moving back up. Bullshit they don't trust him, but they are moving him back to captain."

I think his words over. "Cory may be blackmailing them. But why wouldn't they just kill him?"

"I think it's because Cory isn't the only person who knows. And this third party knows Cory's *and* their names are on there."

"How long have you been contemplating this?"

"Since Cory came here and talked to you that night. We don't leave traitors alive. And even *us* doing so raises suspicions. If we're ever questioned about it, we can't admit we knew what they were doing."

Jord and Seits's names being on that list would change everything. "Which conversation with the Vojin do you take as the truth?"

In a monotone, Luke says, "All of them."

"Hmm. Because everyone can lie and be lied to?"

"And because... One," he throws up his index finger, "the way your neck looked that day you came home, it was a threat." He lifts his middle finger, "Two. Because they killed our parents for trying to stop them, likely because they wanted to destroy this planet. And three," he throws up the third finger, "because this wasn't the way when it was first introduced to us, and people seemed happy about peace. I believe the story about them stopping the destruction. Now, to keep the mixed Creations on their side, they're covering up the real truth with all these stories."

He passes me the bag of chips back. "They cover up the truth with the story of us being here to implement peace, but we *have* to know that's the major lie. What are we supposed to do?"

"Sit back and watch it unfold, let the mixed Creations present themselves to us, even if that means monitoring–" Luke stops talking mid-sentence. I eat a few chips, watching the movie, waiting for him to continue. When he gets an idea while he's talking, he'll just stop, leaving me hanging. When we were younger, I used to shake him until he snapped out of his thoughtful trance. Now I'm used to it.

"Seits wants you to stay away from Cory because the people he's signaling to, whoever they are, expect him to reveal the implants. Jord wants us to keep an eye on Cory as he reveals the implants. He also wants us to see who the implants are." Luke jolts forward, jumping to his feet, and I nearly topple off the sofa. "Has Cory told you yet if our names were on there?"

I readjust myself to sitting beside him as I say, "No, and I don't think they are. He would have said something, or at least used his knowledge to get to you."

He aggressively rubs his hand over his short hair. "You have a point." His blazing ambition sizzles out. He sits back down, brows drawing in tightly, as he thinks. "Who are the people watching Cory?"

"Maybe the Trade. Remember, they never got the list."

"And Jord likely wouldn't tell them because their names are on it."

"That's what Cory said that one night, remember."

"I can't figure out why we would need to keep an eye on Cory. The only thing I'm getting is to show us who the implants are. But why would they want us to know unless they wanted us to do something about it?"

"Why would Jord care if Cory is an implant if he is too?" I lie back down.

"Unless he's trying to throw us off. He may only be doing this to make us think Cory still shouldn't be trusted and make it seem like he's only using Cory to get information. A misdirect."

I nod. "Now that makes sense."

"Seriously, Ky, think about it. Seits told you to stay away from Cory not five days ago. Now, they want us to keep an eye on him. Putting you *around* him." Luke bumps his fist against his thigh. "Maybe it's a setup."

"Like you said, no one can be trusted." Everyone has their own game plan. "Hold on, Luke." I sit up and look at him dead on. "What if the generals don't trust us, and they are trying to see if *we* are the implants? What if they are using Cory to lead them to us and that is why they are telling us *now* to keep an eye on him? Jord and Seits have both been telling me to keep my distance. What if it's a test for *us*, not him?"

"Shit, Ky, you may be on to something. If that's true, Cory is setting you up."

Shaking my head, I say, "I won't leave myself open to be set up."

"Stay away from him. Every twin for themselves. If we all turn on each other, I want to come out on top."

"Me too." I ball up the empty bag of chips and toss it in the trash ben near the doorway. It goes right in. "If sports were still a big thing, I could be a football player. Did you see that shot?"

Luke's silent for a second. "Yeah, and I don't think the name of that sport was football. Football was the one with the eye-shaped ball. They still play sports in a lot of places. Like a pastime."

Shrugging, I say, "I know, but before the first destruction, they played it in the movies. When they made movies like these. They said those people used to be big like the Premier."

"That was a long time ago. Go get us another bag of chips and bring a can of soda."

I get up and go to the small fridge in the corner of the den.

"Okay." Grabbing his drink from the small fridge and a bag of chips from the top of it, I say, "Fein thanked me today."

"How did you respond?"

I hand him the can and open the chips before handing them to him too. "I told her she was welcome."

"Fein is nice, but like I said, no one can be trusted." He drinks from the can and finishes with a refreshing hiss. "You unscramble that letter yet?"

Pursing my lips, I shake my head. "Looking at that letter makes my head hurt. I think it's saying Mom and Dad were implants to the Vojin from the Trade."

"Then what? The Vojin implanted them in Separation...to kill them?" he asks.

"The Vojin found out they were implants from the Trade, and that's why they killed them?" I question back.

I watch the wheels spin in his head as he stares at me. "What would have been the Trade's reason for inserting Creation Breeders or even a Creation into the Vojin's plan? Did they intend for their implants to be placed into Separation as mixed Creations? And why wouldn't they inform their children?"

I think on that: a spy in a spy's court. "Okay, Luke, if I followed you correctly, it would be to keep it from happening again?" I shrug, throwing my arms out at my sides.

"We only have one mission. We are dedicated to one thing." He's said this our entire life, but he knows he's wrong. Especially now.

"That's not one hundred percent true, Luke." He knows our mission is beyond Vojin and beyond Creation.

He nods. "Let's not discuss that detail here." He's right. We can't be sure we aren't being heard, even in our homes, by something beyond the Vojin and the Guidance. "It's getting dark. You want to do a sweep before night falls? After the attack today, there shouldn't be many Zombies out now."

I cross my arms and throw my weight on my left foot. "They need to get control over this stuff."

"I agree. That's what the labs they are building are supposed to help with."

———

Luke and I go to Jord's empty office for reloads. As we're leaving, we run into Jord coming up the porch. "Where are you two off to?"

"A sweep before night falls, Sir Jord," I say.

"Three miles out and back is all. Take Cory and Hanley with you." I bite back my grumble. We don't need Cory and his puny sister.

"We were going out, Luke and I," I say. The last thing I want is to go out with Cory and Hanley, putting a target on our backs, after being told to watch out for him.

"It is not safe if you all become outnumbered." Jord continues into his office. "Do a sweep, taking Cory and Hanley with you. You should run into them on your way out," he states sternly, dismissing us.

"Yes, sir." We step off the porch and head away from his office to look for Cory and Hanley.

"Cory," I call when they cross our path. "You and Hanley are doing a sweep with us. Are you armed?"

"We can't sweep." Cory continues past us, adding, "We have something we need to take care of."

"General's orders, Cory," Luke states.

Hanley grabs Cory's shoulder as a coyote howls far off in the distance. Hanley and Cory immediately look out to their right.

"What's wrong?" Luke asks, eyeing them shadily.

Hanley faces us. "Nothing. We will go on the sweep with you. Give us an extra mag. We have guns."

It's an evil thought, but as we clear the ground, I'm hoping for a Zombie attack so we can see how they'd save themselves. If they'd risk revealing themselves in front of us. Something in my gut tells me they would. Hanley doesn't know Cory's trusting me with his most deadly secret. And with the way I've treated him, why he even trusts me is bizarre. What's even more mind-boggling, which I've not even mentioned to Luke because I don't want to panic him, is what Cory must think of me for not telling.

The sun sinks behind the hills, and the sky fades from blue to violet. We clear our third mile, and as we turn to head back, a coyote charges for us.

These Vojin are bold. Luke and I aim our gun at the wild animal, and Cory throws out his arms. "Wait!"

Luke and I look at each other as we lower our weapons.

"I think it is all clear. We are going to stay outside for a while. Can I talk to you later, Ky?" Cory asks, turning to me.

"No, Cory." I pull Luke to walk. "Have fun with your wolf." I don't know why I said that. It just seemed like I needed to say something that wouldn't give away what we know about the coyote.

I'm soaked with sweat and in desperate need of hydration. We head for our home, and I can hear the shower calling my name.

"You're not tired yet, right Ky?" Luke asks.

"Why?"

"I need to go check on something."

"Does that something have long hair and curves?"

Giving me a smug smile, Luke admits, "It might."

"Bye, Luke."

This would be a great opportunity for me to work on sleeping without nightmares. After my shower, I go to Luke's room and lie on his bed. One step at a time. My room doesn't feel safe yet.

Closing my eyes, I see Zombies, the dead bodies of my group members, dead bodies that I've caused, then the dead bodies of my parents. I open my eyes and think of something else before closing them again. I force myself to think of a white shake. A thick, creamy shake, topped with two cherries. The freezing glass wrapped in my hands. I drink it and lift my gaze from the glass cup to my right. Marc. He grabs my free hand and leads me to a booth in the diner. We laugh and share my shake and a basket of fries. I'm reminded of an old TV show I used to watch back home where people would go on dates at a diner and be...normal.

That's what this is, a date. Marc and I are on a date like the Normals and Breeders. I want to go on a date. Sit with Marc and laugh about nothing. Watch him open up and uncover himself for me.

No Ky, you want to leave Marc alone and not miss him like these thoughts are forcing you to do.

I try to change my thoughts, but they persist. Marc and me laughing and enjoying my fantasies of events that could never happen in either of our lifetimes.

CHAPTER FOURTEEN

"Wake up, Ky."

I part my lids, surveying Luke, fully suited. "Why are you dressed? You didn't wake me."

Luke rubs the back of his neck and tilts his head to the right. "Well, Ky. I came back last night, and you were asleep, peacefully, by yourself. I didn't want to disturb you, so I stayed out."

"Crap," I yell, throwing the covers off me as I climb out of bed.

"What's wrong?" he asks abruptly. "This is great, Ky! I'm so proud of you!" He spreads his arms to hug me, but I refuse.

I throw my hands in my face, mumbling, "I fell asleep thinking about Marc."

"He kept your nightmares at bay again? And no contact?"

"*Yes,*" I whine sorrowfully.

"Good, do that tonight too. In *your* room." He points over his shoulder at the closed bedroom door.

"No, it's not good, Luke. It's bad." And where is the horn this morning? *Please don't tell me it was such a great sleep I slept through the morning horn.* "What time is it?"

Luke checks his watch. "Nine in the morning. The horn blew hours ago."

I throw my head back and sigh long and hard. *Just great.* The fix to my biggest flaw is the one thing in this life that I can't have.

"Let's go so we can do a sweep and get to indoor training."

I drag my feet. How can he not see how this great achievement is equally tragic? "Is there anyone else here that can do the sweep? I'm tired of fighting the undead. I want to do something else like go drink shakes at the diner."

"You can when you retire, but for now, since the wars with the other countries are at a standstill and we are now at war with the Vojin and these Zombies, this is your life, this is what you will do, and being born to do it, you shouldn't be tired or whining about it. This is no different from what you were expecting. We put ourselves in this position. We bust our asses to get where we are and have the responsibilities that we hold. There is no need to wish anything different from what we have now and where we are now."

I grimace, faltered by the hostility in his tone. "Did I just make you mad or something?"

"No, Ky." Luke bows his head and rubs his temples. "It's not you. It's everything else. Get dressed so we can go. I'll find someone else to do the morning sweep, now that we have day-walking Zombies. I'll find you a shake too." He leaves.

I dress quickly, seeing as I'm late starting the day. Opening my door to leave my room, I hear Cory calling me from downstairs. I walk down the stairs and lean against the wall. He looks me over and just stands there, staring. So I stare back.

"What?" he asks.

"You are in my home, you called me, and you are staring at me not saying anything. Then you tell me *what*?"

"I don't want Luke to know about me."

Luke already knows about you, idiot. "Tell me the real reason Jord let you back. And why they're letting you move back up the ladder."

He scowls. "You tell me what you think."

I quietly reveal, "I think anyone who is not only here as a Creation should get shot in their head for being an implant. Along with anyone who is willing to reveal our secrets to our enemies."

"That's not what I'm here for."

"Then what are you here for, you and others like you?" I hold my breath, anxiously waiting to hear if his answer uncovers which Vojin's side he's on.

"I'm here to establish a better life amongst the humans. Not Creations. Creations are to be terminated."

Thankfully, the wall is at my back. His words nearly knock me off my feet. Though he says it calmly, it's in his eyes. Their somber expression reveals how much he agrees with that garbage. My brows furrow, and my nostrils flare. "What do you mean?" I snap.

"If they make a better life, what would Creations be needed for? Creations were created to manage and enforce order. If the humans on this world are ordered and civilized, we don't need to exist. There is no reason for Creations. We," he points to himself and me, "are not peaceful. We are not manageable. We follow orders, yes, but if we were to disobey and go against the Trade, the Premier, and the Guidance, we would triumph over them, and possibly, if we wanted, destroy them. We could take over this place. But instead, we—and when I say we, I mean the Creations who are implants and are here and around other areas of the America *and* the world—*we* will show *them*," he points up, "that we do not need to be destroyed and that we can help enforce peace."

I stare in awe. None of his words are those of a Creation, and because this has never showed in him before, I'm baffled. "Who are you?" I blurt in distaste. "Less than a year ago, you shot a girl in the face because she didn't belong here, and now you're talking about *peace* and better living." I take a step back from him. I, too, have thought of not fighting in the wars for the rest of our lives. But triumphing over the Trade and the Premier, what we've known our entire lives? Working with the Vojin, who probably put this crap in his head and made him believe they would implement peace, when really, they are trying to take over our planet? Trying to rule over us, destroy us, and then reconstruct us? No way!

What he's saying doesn't add up or match the other things he has said. If this is a fact, he would have never considered the thought of reconstruction. "I don't believe you," I tell him, squinting my eyes. He disgusts me. I don't know him at all. And the person I did know was more of him than he is right now. Something has changed in him. Cory would never say this.

Sadness makes his eyes droop. He frowns. "Why not?"

Oh. He's trying to convince me to side with him. Like the Vojin requested for Luke and me to do. He's making himself sound vulnerable so that I will give in, because he's telling the truth and puts his trust in me. But I know for a fact *that* is not truth. I don't know what the truth is, but it isn't this.

"Kylie, fight with me against them."

"Them who?"

"Who do you want to see fall?"

Luke walks in. "See what fall?" He stands next to Cory, and his face of disgust mirrors mine. "This is a snake-free zone, serpent. Because you are working your scaly way back up doesn't give you a pass to my sister. Stay away from her."

Cory shifts his gaze from Luke to me. "Think about what I said, Ky." He marches from our house, closing the door behind him.

"What did he say?"

"I don't know, Luke. He wants me to trust and believe him about him working for the Vojin to implement peace. Then maybe, he wants us to overpower everyone as Creations. He was talking a whole lot of crazy, nothing like a Creation, nothing like he's mixed, nothing like a human even." I rake my fingers through my hair to pull it into a ponytail. "Are we still going on the sweep?"

"No. Cory and Hanley will go. And I convinced the cooks to round us up a couple of shakes." He flashes his big brother smile and pats my shoulder.

"Good." We head outside, and I pull the door closed behind me. "Let's go drink them."

———

Gia sits with us in the rec hall. "I hate Separation on days like this. It's too hot to go outside."

Luke and I drink the shakes he managed to get us. Mine tastes okay, but I'm still missing the diner, the basket of fries, and Marc. I shake my head. What I *mean* to say is, I'm missing the diner and the basket of fries...

"It's boring, and with everyone gone, it's empty," I say, observing the quiet space. "What's on your schedule for today, Luke?"

"Thankfully, nothing, until the afternoon when I have to follow up with the captains and privates that left to check in on how things are going with Citizen Management and when they expect to return."

"That should deliver some good news," I say and take a sip of my shake.

"Good morning." Seits takes a seat.

"Good morning," we respond.

"You all are trying to stay out of the heat?"

"*Yes,*" Gia says loudly.

"Luke, I need your assistance. Cory and Hanley seem to have

disappeared. They went out for the morning sweep and are not responding to their radios. You will accompany Jord to look for them. Respond," she orders kindly.

"I understand," Luke says, rising.

"Excuse me, Gia. I would like to talk to Kylie." I am not accustomed to these private and personal talks with women of an older age. They make me uncomfortable because they always want to get a little too personal.

Gia nods and leaves, and I cringe at the thought of being left alone with Seits. She's been wanting to discuss Cory recently when no one is within earshot. When we are not talking about Cory, she uses the time to teach me ways I can be more like her. That's fine, but I do not want to be like the next person. I want to be better than them. Tell me your failures, your weaknesses, this way I can learn from your mistakes and avoid them. Tell me ways I can be *better* than you.

Long story short, I don't want to hear what she has to talk to me about right now.

"Kylie, how has everything been going? After our talk?"

I look her in her eyes and nod once. "I've kept my distance as you suggested."

"He hasn't kept his."

I'm short. "He's persistent."

"Would you be opposed to a few tests? Suspected implants are required to undergo a few we have set aside to weed them out."

"Is there some reason that I cannot be trusted?" Undergo a few tests? You can't test for mixed Creations. Our blood is the same. The only way they could find out is if we admit to it or show them. My blood, however, is not the same as that of a mixed Creation. I'm a rebellious host, and my blood will give Luke and me away.

"Should there be?"

I take the last sip of my shake as the straw hits the bottom of

CHAPTER FOURTEEN | 135

the Styrofoam cup. Looking at her, I say, "Test me. I wouldn't want there to be an issue. I've worked too hard to get to where I am and where I want to go. I am in support of your requirements." I don't have a choice...

Seits nods as she stands. "There will be a truck arriving in thirty minutes. You and I will go to the labs. Don't take this the wrong way, Kylie. We trust you, but there are instructions for us to test you."

I nod. When Cory gets back, I'm taking him to a training room, and I'm going to beat the life out of him. That son of a bitch set me up. He knows he's being watched by everyone. This was purposely done. Maybe our names *are* on the list, and his way of chopping down my brother is getting me out of the way first.

CHAPTER FIFTEEN

THE SCIENTIST SITS me in a chair in a metal room. Metal floor, metal table, metal walls, and a metal chair. I was stripped of my weapons, vest, and shirt. I sit in a white tank, my black pants, and boots untied, watching the doctor approach me.

My insides are boiling with anger, and I can feel my pulse jump in my arm as the doctor wraps a rubber tie around it. It looks like the one the nurse used on me when she gave us the vaccination that made our eyes change colors.

I'm quiet. As a Creation would be. I sit here and let them do what is needed. A Creation wouldn't fight back; they do as they're told all the way to death. We don't beg or give in. It's not in our nature.

"Kylie, they will take your blood." The walls speak with Seits's voice. I don't see a speaker from where it's coming from.

The doctor sticks a needle in my arm and draws three tubes of blood. It's dark red as it fills the tube, as it has always been.

"Kylie, they will check your blood pressure," Seits's voice informs me as the doctor wraps my arm with a black band that stays in place with Velcro. She squeezes the attached pump, and the wrap expands and tightly squeezes my arm. My circulation cuts off. She turns a small metal nob on the black pump and looks at her watch. Seconds later, she turns the same nob counterclockwise, and the band loosens, deflating. My blood rushes, pumping the pulse in my left arm faster.

"Kylie, they will inject you with a substance that may show a change in you." My heart rate kicks up, but I try to keep my breaths even. This, I am worried about. The last time, it made me sick, and I regurgitated on the side of the rec hall. But I can't object.

The doctor wraps another rubber band around my arm and ties it tight. She thumps the vein in the crux of my arm twice with her middle finger, causing my trigger finger to twitch. She brings forth a syringe with black liquid in the tube. In the black liquid are tiny yellow balls that move around, becoming more visible as they swirl inside the glass syringe.

I take in a breath as the big needle pinches my skin upon insertion. "Your vein may change colors. In most Creations, it will change the color of your eyes," the scientist informs me.

The liquid burns as it's pumped into me. My vein turns ice blue, the color of my eyes. I squeeze my right hand, handling the pain so I don't let it show.

The scientist pulls out the needle. She shines a flashlight in my eyes as she asks, "How do you feel?"

"I feel like I want you to take whatever you put in my arm out," I growl through my teeth.

"Good. It is supposed to feel like that." She grabs her supplies. "We will be back to check on you in an hour."

"Why an hour?"

"That's how long it takes."

"How long *what* takes?"

"For you to change."

I sit forward in an attempt to get up. Abruptly, restraints

shoot out of the metal chair and over my wrists and ankles. "Change into what?" I shout angrily.

"One of the undead."

What? Silenced, I stare at her as she leaves the room. Why would they want to change me into one of them? There is no cure to be changed back! What about my brother? What about me?

What can I do now?

Nothing.

Only wait for them to get what they want. Seits could have at least warned me, let me tell Luke goodbye, and kill Cory, and tell Marc that what I felt for him was love. And thanks to Separation, it doesn't mean anything.

I grow nauseous and have to swallow hard to keep down the hurl. Fire is coursing through my veins, and I ball my hands into tight fists, trying to fight the discomfort.

It's no use.

My brain is melting, and it becomes hard to focus. My eyesight blurs, and no matter how hard I try, I can't think clearly.

There's a sound, "The transformation is taking effect. Remove the shackles and observe."

Foam forms in my mouth.

I slither from the chair, crouched and ready. I'm alone. A growl that starts in my chest escapes from my slowly drooling mouth.

My fingers move. I look down at my hands. My flesh looks appetizing. I force myself not to bite into it. I want to, but I don't want to inflict pain upon myself.

I growl again, growing hungry and impatient. I'm frustrated and sick of being alone. I can smell fresh flesh, and my mouth waters. I smell warm blood, and my throat itches to swallow it.

Angrily, I flip the table and kick the chair I stood from as I snarl through my teeth. White fog is sinking down on me from the ceiling.

I cough, hurling up tar as I crumple over, blacking out.

———

I squint against the blinding light. A chilly breeze rustles my loose-fitting shirt.

I'm lifted off my feet and slammed to the ground. Dirt clouds around me, briefly shading me from the sun. It hovers before settling slowly.

Dropping into a crouch, I scan my surroundings. Nothing but land. I growl, hunger ratcheting up my anger.

I stride across the red ground, heels dragging with each step, until something catches my senses. In the cool breeze, heat wafts past my knees. Its iron aroma carries me toward the tantalizing scent. A soft thumping sound propels me forward and makes my mouth water.

I'm running, chasing the pleasure. A howl sounds behind me, something of a warning, but it means nothing to me now.

The source of the smell and sound reveals itself in the short distance. A snarl erupts from my throat as I race toward it.

"Kylie," the flesh says as it tries to escape me.

I run after the body with blond hair and green eyes, mouth foaming, watering, and thirsting for a taste. I leap in the air and land on top of the flesh I'm dying to sink my teeth into. I growl as I claw at the arms that are restricting me from attacking it.

"Ky, stop! Let me help you!"

I screech again, bowing to take a bite out of the hand holding back my arm. I'm punched in my face. I fall and have to scramble to my feet.

"What happened to you?" it hisses.

I growl and charge. There are two blaring snaps. I hit the ground.

A sharp pain attacks my legs, but I stand against it. The flesh holds an object, two blaring snaps echo the open land again, and two bolts of lightning blasts from the object in its hand. I stumble back, the effects of something thrashing against my chest. I drop to the ground, growling.

My arms are moved, and I am dragged backward, scrambling to get up. It's impossible.

CHAPTER SIXTEEN

I HEAVE, taking a lungful of dusty oxygen. When I part my lids, I'm looking up at the arms of a Vojin leaning away from me. Before they notice I'm conscious, I shut my eyes.

"She's still bleeding," Cory says.

"We can remove the infection, but we can do nothing to heal her wounds. It was not an infection created by a bite or by us. I would be careful if I were you, Cory."

Behind my closed lids, the sun beams down directly on top of me. It's baking my exposed flesh. I am lifted and carried, presumably by Cory, who walks us away. Tires screech to a stop and a few doors open and close. I'm gently laid upon on the ground.

Luke grabs my hand, squeezing it far too tightly. The kneecaps of my left and right knees and center of my chest radiates with heat as the wounds heal. The pain alleviates, and though I was already awake, so as not to tip off anyone watching, I allow my eyes to flutter and my lips to part as I exhale in relief. We stand in open desert land, not covered by hills or any structures. Luke pulls me from the ground, and I feel normal, thankfully no longer wanting to eat myself or anyone else.

Looking me over, Luke snaps, "Shit! Are you okay, Ky? What

happened to you?" I see worry in his eyes. Fighting back the tears lining his lower lids, he wipes his nose with the back of his hand. Luke's not one to show his soft side publicly, and he's resisting the urge to throw his arms around me and exhale in relief. I rub his shoulder to reassure him that I'm okay.

Another truck pulls up beside us. Seits jumps out. Too focused on Luke, I didn't notice Jord standing next to Cory. *Maybe he got out with Luke.* Seits walks to his side, and with her back to me, she whispers to him. Twisting around to face me, she urgently says, "Kylie, you are fine! It was a part of the test and proved nothing but what you've confirmed."

"What fucking tests?" Luke shouts, partly charging at the twin generals.

I grab his shoulder. While we all understand his anger, it wouldn't be in our best interest to take on the generals. "Luke," I go to explain to prevent his assault. "After you left—" I cough once. It feels like sandpaper is scraping my throat. I'm thirsty. "—Seits informed me that because Cory practically *stalks* me, I was suspected of being an implant, and I needed to undergo tests to ensure I was not. They took my blood and pumped me with this black and yellow stuff that turned me into a Zombie. It was very odd, Luke. But I don't know how I am no longer one. I woke up after you healed me." I point to the ground that still has the slight imprint of my body where I was sprawled. "I remember changing. I remember trying to attack Cory. I remember him shooting me and blacking out." I look at Seits. As I replay the events, anger boils in my gut. "Am I finished being tested?" I ask, keeping myself from shouting. "Or," I continue, partly hissing through my teeth, "must I continue to leave myself open to being turned into a Zombie and getting killed?"

Seits clasps her hands behind her back, looks me dead in the eyes, and says, "You are clear, Kylie. You, Luke, and Cory can take the truck back to the corridors. Jord and I will ride back in the others."

"Luke," Jord begins, "have everyone in before dark. We are going to bomb the hole and sweep the surrounding area to minimize our threat. We don't want any more casualties. Respond."

"I understand," Luke says, and we get in the truck Seits got out of.

The ride back is awkwardly silent. All three of us likely have several things we'd like to shout. Luke keeps his eyes peeled, still fuming. We're far from the base, driving over nothing but dirt, periodically passing a shrub or tumbleweed. Mountains in the distance line the land and slice the cloudless sky in half. Just beyond the mountains to the west is a wide stretch of deserted land that goes on for miles, valleys of dirt and scattered grass, minimal trees for shade stretch thousands of miles to the Ocean where an entire state resides miles beneath the surface. We've been there once. But it wasn't a pleasure, knowing the millions of people who must've lived in that state before it was drowned by the flood.

The air is blasting through the truck; the wind whipping my loose strands of hair. It feels amazing to my still burning skin, hot from both the blazing sun and whatever they injected me with. I relax on the seat and kick my boots up on the dash, using the toe of my boot to adjust the vent. Cory is a total asshole for what he did. Seits too. The two of them, though having different motives, set me up. And I won't stand for being used or targeted.

I begin to make out the base in the heatwaves, but it's hard to judge how near or far it is.

When we make it back to base, Luke parks in front of Jord's office, and we jump out and walk to our home with Cory following us all the way through the door. Once he closes it, I whirl on him. Shifting my weight, I put all my might in every punch. Elbow spiked high over my head, I drive down every blow fast and steady, landing solid jabs in his face. I do my best to shatter his cheekbones and knock out a few teeth.

Luke yanks me off him. I shove Luke away from me, shouting, "Back off!" And I'm back at Cory like a magnet. On my next punch, I knock Cory off his feet, and I resort to kicking him, shoving the toe of my boot into his ribcage and neck. Thankfully, one lands on his face.

"Stop, Ky!" he shouts, spluttering blood. "Let me explain!" I bend down and throw another jab in his mouth, wanting to shut him up forever.

Luke tugs me back again. I'm shaking out my fist; it's pouring blood by what seems like the pint. I rip the bottom half of my shirt off and wrap it around my knuckles. I see Cory stand in my periphery.

Once he's on his feet, I point, yelling, "You set me up, you son of a bitch! I should kill you right now!" I reach around to my rear holster, finding it empty, forgetting I was stripped of all my weapons.

"I didn't do anything," Cory shouts, arms splayed at his sides.

"You're a liar! You knew you were being watched. You told them you would show them who the implants were by always being around them. And you are *always* trying to be around me! You tried to set me up," I accuse angrily. "Just because you are a snake, a traitor, a manipulator, a terrorist," I yell, "doesn't mean I am." I step toward him, and Luke holds me back.

Cory dabs at his busted lip and swollen eye. Looking over his blood-smeared hand, he fires back, "I did tell them that, Ky! Sheesh, what the hell is wrong with you? What I was doing didn't include you. Sir Jord and Madam Seits know that."

"Just because they know doesn't mean whoever else is watching you knows, you idiot!" I lunge at Cory, but Luke keeps me back. I grunt and jerk against his hold. "*Agh!* Think about it, Cory. When the Trade steps in, the generals are obligated to follow the Trade's orders. They see you around me, that's showing the Trade I'm an implant, and they will want me to prove I am not."

"I'm sorry, Ky," he says, pressing his palms together. "I swear."

Luke throws a glance at me, one that questions if I'm okay. I give him a quick nod, and he releases me, taking a step toward Cory. "You saw her when she was a Zombie and shot her? How'd she turn back?" Luke asks.

"I snuck one of their syringes with the Creation cure and used it."

He's a liar! But I blurt, "Okay. You can leave now." I'm losing a lot of blood and need Luke to heal me before I grow too light-headed. I'm also dying of thirst and need to rest.

Cory leaves, taking his exit with a nod. I grab Luke's hand and encourage him with a rise of my bloody hand to heal it. Before doing so, he plucks out a piece of Cory's tooth. "I'm keeping this as a souvenir," he says with a smug grin.

I roll my eyes. "Just heal my damn hand, Luke." He heals me in seconds. I ball and un-ball my fists, testing it out. Taking off my vest, I reveal, "He's lying. There is no cure, and we all know that. I woke to a Vojin, only I pretended I was sleeping. They took out the infection and warned him I was not infected by a Zombie but by an injection."

"You think he set you up?"

"No, I think they set *him* up. And he is a negligent idiot, and he needed to taste his own blood because of it. I'm angry because they used me as bait."

Luke hugs me, patting my back. "You scared the shit out of me, Ky. The call came in from Cory saying you'd been turned into a Zombie, and he had to take you down. You look worn. Go clean up and get some rest. I'm going to tell everyone to wrap up and let them know to be in before night falls."

I grab his shoulder as he pivots. "They took my blood."

Gaze cast on his boots, he doesn't turn around fully. "I heard you mention that. I guess we'll find out what they know, if anything, soon enough."

"What do you think they'll do to us?"

One shoulder shrugs. "Depends. If they were truly using you as bait, they wouldn't care to test your blood, but maybe they also wouldn't have taken it in the first place. I don't know, Ky. We'll just wait and see."

I let him go, and he continues out of the house. I'm not afraid of them finding out our secret. If I die, let me die, but I do care about being tortured and tested on. The scientist would love to get their hands on Creations like Luke and I, who've removed our implants. They are interested in seeing how the Vojin cells bind with the Creation's DNA. How two entities can merge and primary control can be the Creation's. They may actually be considering a new species of Creations, finding great value in Vojin-infused Creations; our minds are wired differently, our bodies function differently. Even I don't know the depth of our physics and structure, but the scientists will definitely find out.

But they won't find out with me.

I clean my blood from the floor and toss the towels in the trash. I'm drained and need to sleep. My body has been through more than it can handle today.

I go to my room. The marbles I placed in the sock are clinking against each other. They shouldn't want anything right now. *Why would they be calling us?*

I take out the sock with the marbles and walk to my bed to empty the contents. Red-colored marbles topple out of the sock. They were previously the colors of the Vojin. This must mean something is wrong, but without speaking to them or going there —neither of which will I be doing—I won't find out what it is.

It might be a good thing for something to be wrong.

I pick up one of the marbles and hold it between my thumb

and index finger. A dim light appears as the marble whispers, "The time is coming soon. Be ready to undergo the ending of the current species of mankind. What is destroyed, we hope can be reconstructed. With your help, we can stop the destruction and maintain an understanding." The marbles shift back to their original blue and green shade and stop moving on their own.

I put them back in the sock, and I put the sock back in the drawer.

CHAPTER SEVENTEEN

As much as I would like to lounge around after being turned into a cannibal…it's not an off day. After I clean up and eat a protein bar, I shove on my helmet and head outside to finish the day.

"Kylie Alexander," I'm called by a light, male voice as I'm leaving the stoop of our corridors.

I look out to see a man marching in my direction.

I halt, acknowledging the slicked back black hair, beige slacks, collared navy-blue shirt with a fancy stitched *T* on the pocket, and a silver and black plastic and metal earpiece on his ear that looks artificial. All the Trade affiliates have one. They all wear the same uniform, and they all have their hair smoothed back and short, stopping at the nape of their neck. Females included.

At attention, I stand, shoulders back, chest out, back straight, in silence. You speak to the Trade after they have requested you to speak.

Looking straight forward, I wait and avoid eye contact.

He stops in front of me, stepping twice, spacing his feet evenly apart, shoulder width. "Kylie Alexander. I am Trade Officer Audrey Grandin. I'd like to speak with you. Reply."

"Yes, sir."

"In your home," he says, directing me toward the front door of the house.

I turn on my heels, heading back inside.

"There has been a lot of talk about the actions involving the Creations and humans within this sector. As you are aware, we keep watch on all sectors and all Creations. There is an understanding put forth in every Creation. The rules and laws for Creations to follow are not complicated. These actions go against your required roles as Creations. No Creation was designed to engage in relations with another. It will prevent you all from undergoing the task you were created for: War, to fight for the America. To protect the America. To stand for the America is the entire point of every Creation's life. The protection and priority of keeping your twin first is where your relation to another being should stand." *Being?* "If this should change, you not only risk your own life, but the life of your twin. No Creation wants to see their twin die."

"I was turned into a Zombie. Ordered by the Trade." I change the subject. Speaking out of turn may get me a fine, but I can't ignore this. I need an explanation.

Trade Officer Grandin removes his earpiece that someone is speaking loudly into. They never remove their earpieces. Could it be that the person at the other end is a distraction, or has he muted it? "There was discussion that you were a possible implant from the Vojin, the outsiders labeled as protectors of the Earth." I dare not cut in to explain I know the Vojin's relationship to the America. "You have proved yourself not to be. However, in order for us to be sure, you and others needed to undergo some tests." Tests. It's plural. "You are aware of the persisting threat that has been placed by them. This is not a recent threat. This is a threat that was issued years ago. Near the first destruction. We are not sure what they are after, but we have been putting forth more..." he stalls, tapping his thumb on his knee, "*research* to understand them, which will probably help to defeat them."

"If you don't mind me asking, what kind of research?"

"That is above your Creation level of clearance."

I do not appreciate his response. I have the right to know what's going on. Especially because of that note about my parents being implants from the Trade to the Vojin. Would *that* happen to be the research? Could his research be code for implanting Creations in the homes of the Vojin to understand them? I can't say anything about the letter, but I wonder. "With all due respect, Trade Officer Grandin, every day my twin Luke and I go outside and put our lives on the line for you, for the citizens of the America, and for our country as a land. We deserve to know something. We need more information."

He sits forward, his face twisting oddly, his scowl conveying insult. "You were not created to question our decisions. We understand you have your own mind, your own thought processes." He points his finger at me, elbow rested on his knee. "That does not mean you need to use it. You were created to fight for us, our land and our freedom. It is what you were designed for. *Deserve*," he hisses with disgust. "There isn't even a need to thank you for what you are supposed to do. We do not owe you anything special for doing what you were *created* to do. Your monthly payments to your depository and families are reimbursement enough."

I'm insulted. We are nothing to them. To anyone. Not the Vojin, not our country, not the Trade. "As told by the Guidance, we are the best of what the America has to offer."

"The best the America has. There was a requirement for the Trade. Things have changed, lives have changed, and people have changed. With the Vojin, more and more people are dying every day, including Creations." I peep a word, and he shuts me up with the flick of his hand. "Your parents would be glad to know their child, unlike other Creations, has a voice. You are different from a lot of the other Creations. You and Luke. Which was expected."

I scoot to the edge of the sofa. "What do you mean by that? *Expected?*"

He stands, grabbing his earpiece from the table. "Do not engage in relations with Cory Braden, the previous captain of this sector. A watch was placed, and he is the eye of many, not only the Trade." He hits a button on his earpiece as he slides it back on his ear. "I am to return," he says to whoever speaks to him. "Kylie Alexander has been spoken with. And warned." He looks me in my eyes. "Do we have an understanding?"

Hell no! Absolutely not. We do not have any understanding! I stand, snap my boots together, and draw my arms behind my back. Holding my head high, I nod once. "Yes, sir."

"Escort me to the door."

"Yes, sir." Grandin is a skinny man with blond eyebrows, showing his actual hair color is not the black he wears. His clothes are tailored to fit his body as all Trade members are. Usually, the Trade does not speak directly to soldiers. They usually do not address any of us. Messages, orders, and instructions are passed through the Guidance, from the Guidance to our general, and from the general to us.

He knows something; his insinuation revealed a lot, but too little. Everything and everyone keep bringing up our parents. Separation is supposed to be simple, like the life of a Creation. I shouldn't have to deal with jigsaw puzzles, word problems, and pop-up visits. I'm getting all these questions with no way of answering them.

I stay in and wait for Luke to return. With everyone in our home gone for Citizen Management, it makes the house the perfect meeting spot.

The door opens and Luke says, "Luke."

"I'm in the den," I call. "You will never guess what just happened to me."

He comes around the corner, eyebrows high and eyes wide, ready for me to tell the story. "You had even more of a day? After being turned into a Zombie," he asks with knit brows.

"Trade Officer Grandin stopped by."

"What?" his voice rises an octave. "I didn't see anyone."

"Well…" I roll my eyes. "He was here. It was pretty weird too, because the things he said didn't seem important enough to bring them down from the island." I throw up a finger, starting with my thumb, as I list off his topics, "Warning against relations, telling me to stay away from Cory. They know his secrets and must be using him. But forget about that," I say, waving my hands as I sit up from the sofa. "In a light voice, he said, 'You are different from a lot of the other Creations. You and Luke. Which was *expected*.' That our parents would be proud I have a voice unlike other Creations."

Luke grumbles, dramatically shaking his head. "Don't tell me you spoke out of turn to the Trade."

I purse my lips, shrugging. "He said we don't mean anything to them."

"Bullshit. We mean everything to them, or they would let us have lives and do what the hell we want to do. So…we are *expected* to be different…Do you feel any different?"

I shake my head.

"Did he happen to hint to you anything about that note? Did he mention our parents?"

"The only thing he said about our parents was what I just told you. But my *voice*, which I'm assuming he was implying I was *expressive*, effectively conveying thought or feeling."

"I know what expressive means, Ky," he drones.

"Right, well. He said I shouldn't use it. The only other thing was he mentioned they were researching the Vojin, giving me even more reason to think that letter is connecting our parents with the Vojin *and* the Trade. We just need to find out how."

Luke rubs his hand over his shaggy hair. He's in desperate need of a haircut. Sean usually cuts it for him, but Sean is gone and there's no telling when he'll be back. "Are you, too, getting the feeling everyone else knows something about us we don't?"

"More and more every day. And I think Seits is lying." I lower my voice to a whisper, "When they turned me into a Zombie, they filled three vials with my blood, Luke. They know…"

Luke's eyes narrow. He leans his shoulder against the door-frame of the den, drawling, "Questions will draw suspicion."

"How do we get answers to questions we can't ask?"

"We don't. They'll reveal it like they've been doing. Slowly? Maybe. But we'll find out soon enough. Anything hiding in the dark is sure to come to light. Even us."

"You're talking crazy, Luke. If we're discovered, it'll be worse than death."

Luke shrugs one shoulder. "Just be ready to fight, Ky. Because if you're right, and Seits knows, there's only a matter of time before they come for us."

CHAPTER EIGHTEEN

TIME DRAGS as we train and wait for the return of the Creations who departed for Citizen Management around the America and those who left to call a truce with the other countries. A month is too long for them to be gone and Luke won't give me any updates except, "everyone is doing fine and getting their jobs done."

I'm stuck here, training the Normals on how to fight Zombies. I wish I could tell them about the Vojin so I can hear their ideas on how they would take down such creatures. But the generals haven't given us the okay for that yet.

In order for us to go against the Vojin, we'd need to side with them so we'd get the opportunity to learn their weaknesses. The Vojin are intelligent beings, never allowing us to travel to their home. They limit the information provided about their kind, only keeping us privy to the *plan*. Our training material has taught us to know our enemy, be an insurgent if needed. The Vojin never gave us that opportunity. And it's sad we're just now realizing they've been dragging us along with empty promises and misleading orders.

The excessive heat warnings continue for another week. We're seeing temperatures as high as one hundred and twenty.

Without the obstacle course, track, and target course, I'm running out of things to teach the Normals. They need to get dirty, lose their breath, fight in the field until someone draws blood. They're getting bored too. Honestly, we should be gone by now, off to fight for the America. But the Zombies have changed everything.

Since they bombed the hole, there haven't been any daytime Zombie attacks, and the constant day and night sweeps have been successful in keeping them away from the base.

It's so safe, the Trade made an appearance. I am in awe that a Trade Officer stopped by. They never leave their sky towers in Highrum where their base-sized island hovers over the busiest city in the America where the wealthy and gifted reside.

Scientists, doctors, and educators roam their crowded streets, smiles washing their neighborhood as they carry out their daily tasks without a care in the world. Their children are raised without a concern of Separation or fear of death. They *have* children, the normal way. These Normals have the privilege of caring for their offspring from birth to adulthood, and those privileged ticks live a life that more than half of this world could never dream of. They hug their parents, relax their shoulders as they stroll the streets, laugh freely, don't care about being watched or seen doing something restricted, they *love...* They love their person of interest freely and forever if they want.

A freedom such as that is too far out of my reach.

I sigh, looking over the crowd of privates staring up at me. "Review?" I ask them.

"No," Christian says. "Can you tell us what you expected when you came to Separation?"

A lot of chatter erupts following his request, agreeing with his query. They've been training all day, hand to hand combat and target practice here in the training hall. Most of them are drenched in sweat, others are ready for another round, getting a little antsy as they encourage me to answer Christian's question.

"Okay, calm down," I say loudly. "I will discuss it." Once they quiet, I offer, "It was expected that we would train and then fight in the wars. The wars are against the other countries so we can keep our land and our power. It never stops. As the sea water continues to rise, citizens of the country continue to destroy their towns, and population increase, land is becoming sparse. The other countries are greedy, and if the America lets up for a second, our country will be wiped right out from under us. We didn't know about the Zombies until weeks after we arrived to Separation."

"What was your first reaction to the Zombies?" asks a girl wearing a big puffy ponytail.

"Shock," I say wide-eyed, rubbing the front of my neck. "They were like nothing I've ever seen before. They're monsters I don't understand," I add, an edge of uneasiness creeping in my tone and raising my voice an octave.

"What do you think will come of us if we go against them?" Renae is her name, I think. She's from Sean's group. Sitting on her knees, she crosses her arms. "After what happened with the Zombies on base, we've all been wondering."

I ask, "Us? You mean you? Non-Creations?"

"Yes," Multiple people respond.

"The same as Creations. If you are scratched, bitten, spit on, or infected by them in any way, you turn into one of them."

"And you kill us?"

A large black figure in my periphery catches my eye from the only window in the training hall. A bus is pulling in. Turning back to the impatient faces, I say, "Yes, we will kill. And you shouldn't feel bad about that. Because if it were our own twin... we would kill them too." Another bus pulls up behind the first.

My friends and the other Creations are back! It's going to be so nice to get rid of this large team. There are too many people to keep up with.

Although Fein thinks I hate her for being a traitor, she's missed too.

A slender boy with draping blond hair raises his hand, asking, "If you lose your twin, then you are like us, right?"

Uncontrollably, my gaze flicks to Edward. Though his eyes are still blue, where they were once as vibrant as a bright blue sky, they're now cloudy—in pain. I swallow hard and force myself to answer, "Yes." Sweeping my hand from left to right, I instruct, "Talk amongst yourselves. I'll be back."

Creations are pouring out of three buses, filling the air with red dust and crowding the open roads. I scan the faces, spotting Fein as she spots me. I smile, waving to her. She runs over. "Hey," she hugs me quickly.

"How was it?" I ask.

Nodding, an indifferent smile smooths her lips into a thin line. "It was bad. But we took care of it."

"Where were you drafted?"

Fein's orange eyes grow brighter as she smiles wider. "We went to Oregon. It was practically burned to the ground."

"The entire state?"

"Yes. It wasn't as bad as I may be making it seem, but the humans there were out of control." Oregon is—was—an average state. Only five males resided there with the females. Like the Dakotas, the Carolinas, and Oklahoma, they bred for workers whose occupation would be to construct and build. "It's nonexistent. There was nothing to save. The remaining citizens who showed no signs of the infection and who didn't go against management were transferred to California. After that, we had an emergency evacuation of Nevada. The undead had taken over. We dropped in, saved the remaining citizens, and burned it down. They haven't said if they will keep that state or not."

I shrug. "They may not."

"How's it been here?"

"Things have been quite interesting around here. We can get into details later. Come get your group so they can get away from me." I turn on my heels, heading back to the training room.

"You had everyone's Normals while we were gone?"

"Yes, I did. Who else is back?"

"Um, I'm not sure. Look, Ky," she pulls me to a stop. "Thank you for what you are doing. I mean it."

I turn away from her, continuing onward. "I don't know what you're talking about, Fein." I keep my back to her as I mention, "If I were you, I would stay away from Cory."

She clears her throat, letting me know I was heard, but she doesn't question it.

We walk into the training hall, and her group jumps to their feet, cheering as they run to her. She joins in, pumping her fists in the air as they hoot her name. Without waiting for my dismissal, they leave, and I couldn't care less.

Two more buses pull in as Luke enters the training hall. With five long strides to the center of the room, he steals everyone's attention. He announces, "The last of today's Leader and Creation arrivals are coming in. If you are a member of Floyd's team, he will meet you in here. He should be here shortly. If you are on Marc or Sean's team, they will meet you in your recreation hall. Head there now. Joyce and Jace will meet in the rec hall too. Those of their groups can stick around for thirty minutes and then head over."

Those instructed slowly climb to their feet but rush from the room. I'm relieved the pressure is off my shoulders. The twenty-some-odd group members of my own are enough, and I've fallen behind on checking in on their emotional states and strengthening progress.

Floyd comes in, and his group cheers as they go to him. Seems they were happy to get away from me as well.

"My group," I call over the chatter, "is done for the day." Turning to Luke, I ask, "What are you about to do?"

"I have to check in with the captains who are still gone to see when they will return. Then I'll go out with Harold to check the new labs. *Then* I'll follow up with the captains and privates. You'll be in attendance for it. We have to discuss the game plan for the threat with Jord."

"Cool. I'm going to lunch. Come find me later."

CHAPTER NINETEEN

SITTING on the floor with my knees propped up, I look up at Jord as he discusses the Vojin's threat, and finally, what we plan to do about it. For years, living uneducated, I've taken everyone for their word. Now, I'll study facial expressions. I'll work harder to read between the lines. I'm tired of having this wool pulled over my eyes.

"We have confirmation the outsiders will attempt to go to war against us. No one is prepared for this yet." Sir Jord takes a pause and looks over the unfazed faces of the captains and privates of our division. We sit among each other in the leader rec hall, each eagerly awaiting the 'go,' we've been itching to hear since we arrived. "Many other countries have agreed to fight with us against them. Over the next few weeks, we will strategize and come up with ways to defeat this enemy who was once our ally."

Before continuing, he makes direct eye contact with a few Creations. His eyes narrow slightly when he does this, but I cannot look to see who they are without giving myself away that I noticed this brief gesture.

"The Trade believes there may be implants from the outsiders among us." His voice rises an octave, grudgingly stating,

"*Creations* who stand *with* us but not *for* us. And these *implants*," he spits the word, "who wear our numbers and spoke our vows, will fight *against* us at the time of war." He bows his head, and his next words start as a murmur then rise with such triumph, it pumps adrenaline through my veins. "Here is a warning that will only be stated once. If there are any implants in this sector, and you are found out, the rules for a Creation's protection won't apply here. You will be executed publicly so everyone knows you will never come in our house, pretend to be one of us, all to turn against us! We do not tolerate traitors. Respond!"

"We understand!"

"As you were." Jord leaves, and chatter erupts through the rec hall.

I move from the floor to the table as we all space out and return to our activities.

Collins is the first at our table to speak, as expected. "Implants with us?" she asks, staggered.

"Unbelievable," Cecilia seconds her.

"Kylie," Seits calls, standing behind me. "I'd like to speak with you after dinner."

An uneasy feeling makes me queasy. "Okay," I agree in a strong tone. Tonight, she might make me do a sweep with her, Cory, Hanley, and Jord. The four of them may hold me down while a Zombie comes to bite me, and they'll leave me stranded in the desert as I turn into a monster until the Vojin come to save me. All so they can prove I'm an implant. "I will meet you in your office."

She nods once and walks away. Luke, Sean, and Marc enter as she exits. They sit, lunch trays smacking the table. Marc sits next to me, and finally, the sun comes out and brightens the dreariness of my last few weeks. I suck in a lungful of this fresh air, and I hope. I don't look at him or noticeably acknowledge his presence. I simply find his hand resting on the bench. He moves his fingers between mine and holds my hand tightly. I let out the breath I held and allow my shoulders to relax.

"How was Citizen Management?" Gia asks. I've missed most of the conversation, but Collins doesn't appear too happy to have been cut off.

"Deadly," Sean answers.

"Waulers had taken over our state," Marc adds. "They had run many people from their homes and taken up the vacancies."

"At first it was hard to tell everyone apart," Sean cuts in. "And a lot of innocent people might have died."

"Where were you?" Collins asks, stuffing her soup-soaked bread into her mouth.

Marc answers, "Maine. I don't think it will be lasting much longer."

Fein mentioned earlier how her state, Oregon, was diminished too. Acre by acre, they're already taking our land from us. We've just been too blind to see it until now. "Why do you say that?" I ask Marc, finally looking at him.

He meets my eyes but says nothing. He only stares. Seconds pass before he lets go of my hand, gets up, and leaves.

As usual, I stare at him walking away, hearing Sean ask, "What did you do, Ky?"

I shrug, turning back around. *What didn't I do?*

Cory sits next to me, and the air that was once fresh is now full of smut. "You should not sit here," I tell him.

"Let me talk to you, Ky." His face is healed, and this bothers me. I wish he could have worn those bruises longer. He's done well staying out of my sight since our last altercation. Why he's popping up now, I don't care enough to ask.

"She's not talking to you. Leave." Luke stands up quickly, fuming.

Cory stands. "Just for a minute, Kylie."

I rise to my feet. "Stay away from me, Cory. I mean it," I

threaten in a low voice. I don't want to do this in front of everyone, but I will.

He grabs my arm, and I yank back from him before my free hand balls to a fist and jabs him in his nose. His head whips back once and then again from another quick blow I didn't intend to execute. Sean grabs me. I've grown familiar with the feel of his arms because they're like his brother's. They're both quite muscular and strong, a clear indication of their years in boxing rings and weight training.

Luke moves in front of me, punching Cory again. He hits the floor.

Hanley races over and helps her brother up. "What is your problem, Luke?"

"Don't question him," I tell her. "Question your brother."

Cory shakes himself out and jabs a point at me. "You are tripping, Ky! What you think is wrong. It wasn't like that at all."

Sean's still holding me back, keeping my arms pinned behind me. "I don't care, Cory. I'm only going to warn you once. The next time you speak to me, upon your approach, I will draw blood. Give me fifty feet at all times!"

"I saved you, Kylie," he loudly defends as I'm turning around.

Twisting back around, I shout, "Saved me? If it wasn't for you," I express with the harsh point of my finger, "I wouldn't have needed saving."

"What did he save you from?" Sean asks near my ear.

"I can't say." I grab Luke's arm. "Let's go before the snake strikes us." This isn't the time or the place, and while I hate Cory, his circumstances aren't the onlookers' business. Plus, if they knew what I know, I'd be just as guilty.

We leave the rec hall, and I remember Seits requested I stop by. "I'll catch up to you two later. Going to check in with Seits."

"I'm coming with you," Luke informs, giving a nod to Sean as he jogs toward our home.

Sean calls, "Include me in later tonight." Likely wanting to know the details about the fuss with Cory.

Luke and I head for Jord's office. Shaking his head, Luke states, "You're not meeting with Seits alone anymore. Not after she turned you into one of those walking dead. I still think they are in this together."

"I know."

"Madam?" I call when we walk into the general's office.

"I called for Kylie, Luke," Seits says, looking at Luke with annoyance.

Luke crosses his arms and stands with his chest pushed out. "I'm standing in to ensure my twin doesn't get turned into the walking dead." He's slowly losing his respect, and that's a bad sign.

"It wasn't my order, Luke. The Trade required Kylie be tested to confirm she was not an implant. My assurance was not enough. The turning was the last of her tests to see if the outsiders would try to save her. She was out there for hours before she was found."

"You wanted to speak with me?" I change the subject. Luke will go on and on, expressing his disapproval about the way I was treated, and I appreciate he has my back.

"To thank you and apologize." Seits wants to apologize…? Weeks have passed, and *now* she wants to apologize. She has spoken with me several times since then. She's sitting forward on the chair, hands clasped, resting on the desk. The corners of her mouth are slightly turned upward in a smug smile, giving off the slightest hint of security. But I don't believe it. To hell with her apology!

"I'm fine. Is there anything else?"

"The labs are about finished. A group of you will check on them after they have built the bridges for crossing over the hole."

"I understand. If there isn't anything else, we'll dismiss ourselves," I say.

"You two can leave."

We leave the office for our house. Luke whispers, "Later tonight, I'll tell you how we're going to go to war against the outsiders."

"Cool," I sing with a nod. "I want to hear all about it."

When we make it to our home, I rush through a shower and get dressed. On my way back to my room, Marc's door calls to me. I put my clothes away and go to it, opening the door without knocking.

He's not here.

I pace the floor until my legs get tired, then sit on his bed and wait for him. Soon, I'm lying down, thinking about what I'm going to say. It's been a while since we've seen each other, and it seems silly to apologize for past events. But maybe that's what I'm supposed to do. Maybe I should even say I miss him or show I miss him. Unless he doesn't miss me...

This is a weird feeling.

Anticipation. This is what I must be feeling; an emotional state of anxiety awaiting a private reunion with Marc.

I stuff his pillow beneath my head and pull the blanket up to my shoulders, getting comfortable as I wait on his return. With my back to the door, I hear it open.

"No, Collins, not tonight," Marc says, following her request to be welcomed in his room. I remain quiet, likely unnoticed.

"Why not?" she flirts. There's a bit of shuffling.

"I'm not with that."

"Not with me, but you are with Ky. I saw the way you looked at her earlier."

"What I do with Ky is my business. Not yours." I gently turn over to see where they are while trying not to make the bed sound. When I rest on my right side, facing the door, the bed makes a slight creak.

Oops.

Collins asks, "Can I become your business?" as Marc looks over his shoulder.

He stands in the doorway with the door half closed. I can't see her because he's blocking her from his room. But the light from the hall cuts in, slicing over the bottom half of the bed, though I stay in the darkness.

He looks back at me and back quickly at Collins. "Goodnight Collins. I'll see you in the AM."

"Hugs?"

"No," he says, but not harshly. He probably would hug her if I wasn't here.

"Okay, Marc. Night," she says sweetly, and he closes the door.

I watch him walk to his rack and hang his vest and take off his guns and boots. "I'm going to get in the shower. Will you be in here when I return?"

"Yes."

He grabs some clothes from his top drawer. "I'll be back."

He doesn't take long showering, and when he throws his towel on his rack, I ask, "Collins, huh?"

"Collins and I are none of your business, Ky."

Hearing that makes me nauseous. I wait before I get up from his bed and walk to him leaning against his dresser. "I am sorry, Marc." I pondered it enough and decided this would be the best start.

"Sorry for what?" he asks, uncovering me with his shadowed purple eyes.

I swallow hard. "For making you feel you mean less to me than you do. For..." I carry on, "...making you feel like I'm leading you on. For making it seem like I'm juggling you and Cory. And for not being honest with you," I admit in a voice softer than I've ever spoken. The jitters attack my stomach and make my voice and hands shake.

He looks me over, leaning his weight on his elbows, which are propped up against the dresser. "You're weak for me, Kylie?" he asks.

"I'm not proud of it. But yes."

Marc rakes his hand through his hair and leaves it cuffed around the back of his neck. He gazes at me for a second. "You didn't do what I asked you to do."

"Dreaming about you takes away my nightmares," I admit, looking away from him to the floor.

He turns my head to face him. "I don't have an interest in Collins."

I hold back my smile. "And me?"

"I don't hate you, but I don't like you either."

I grumble, rolling my eyes as I turn away from him. "Your rejection is worse than being turned into a Zombie and craving flesh."

His eyebrows furrow. "How would you know that?"

"Word got through to the Trade that I was an implant, and they required me to go through some tests. One of those tests was to have me turned into a Zombie to see if the outsiders would help me by removing the infection."

"And they helped you?"

Lowering my voice, I say, "Cory helped me by calling them. He claimed he healed me by using a cure." I lift my brows high and grin, anticipating his bewildered response.

But Marc doesn't allow the shock to show on his face, though he gasps and says, "Cory's an implant?"

"As well as Floyd, Fein, and, we suspect, Jord and Seits."

He leans from the dresser and rubs his hand over his beard. "Are you sure, Ky?"

"No."

He shrugs and holds his shoulders near his ears as he asks, "Why would they suspect you of being an implant?"

"Something Cory said."

Crossing his arms, he leans back against the dresser. "So he knows."

"No," I hurry to say. "He knows nothing. I was proven to not be one. He said he never meant to lead them to me. He didn't mean for them to misinterpret him being around me as him telling them I was an implant."

"Wow." He leans over, and as he rises, he shoves his long hair from his face. He needs a haircut too, but I like its shaggy waves and how untamed it is.

I step closer to him, grabbing him by his sides. "Can we talk about that later?"

Marc tucks my hair behind my ears and holds me gently by my neck. "I think I should still be mad at you."

"Once someone says sorry, they are to be forgiven. It's law." I crack a small smile, but furrow my brows to forgo my seriousness.

"I forgive you, but that doesn't mean I have to accept you." I step back and he tugs me back to him. "But I do. So please don't kiss him."

"Kiss you?"

"Nope. You're leaving me alone. It's law," he seductively drawls with a smile that melts my spine.

"Stop it, Marc. Kiss me already."

He follows suit, mending what I've broken. I halt our kiss to hug him.

"You're about to leave?" he asks.

"You won't let me sleep in here anymore." I move away from him to his door.

"I haven't seen you in a while. Tonight, I might make an exception."

Happy, I try not to let it show. "Don't let Collins take my spot. I'm going to talk to Luke about something."

"You don't have to worry about that."

Leaving Marc's room, I run into Collins, who is dumbstruck by my exit. "Is there a problem?" I ask her, crossing my arms in front of my chest.

She glares at me. "You know what, Ky–"

I wave my hand dismissively. "Let me tell you something. The both of them, Marc," I throw my thumb toward his door behind me, "*and* Luke are mine." I point to my chest. "Back off."

Her evil glower remains intact as she says, "We'll see, Ky."

"Challenge me, and we will."

Luke comes up the stairs, catching our exchange. "What's going on?"

"Nothing. Collins was just walking away from this door." She is trying to get under my skin, and it's working.

Collins looks between me and Luke before she pushes past us, heading for the stairs. Her bedroom is downstairs, and there is no reason she should even be up here.

"You want to finish our talk? Or were you about to go in there?" Luke points to Marc's door.

"I was coming to find you. I ran into her preparing to go in there." I look at the door for a second too long, considering what could've happened if I hadn't been here.

"Why?"

I shrug. "I'm tired of Collins. Maybe she's growing bored. Creations need to stay busy, and they aren't using us for much, so relationships are the next best thing I suppose." We walk into Luke's room and push the door closed. "What were you able to find out?"

"We won't be able to accomplish this on our own, but I figure if we explain to a few Creations we are going in for destruction, they'll be willing to help."

I squint my eyes. "What are you talking about, Luke?"

"You have two marbles, one to get there and another to get back." He walks to his window and looks out before he says, "We will go there unannounced. Shoot up a few, no, a lot of them with the Creation Zombie bullets and come back the same night." A light takes his eyes as he talks downright crazy.

"How would we separate the good from the bad?"

His eyes narrow as he says, "They are all bad, Ky. How can you believe any of them are good?"

"I see where you are going with this. But take a minute and think about it." Crossing the floor to him, I gesture with my hands as I urgently say, "We are going to jump through a pit of colored particles with no idea where we'd arrive, and just shoot up some place in *hopes* the Zombie bullets work? Have you completely thought this through?"

"Yes," he states simply, quickly nodding his head.

I throw my hand in my face, disappointed. "Luke, please tell me you have put more thought into this."

"Ky, what do you suggest we do? Wait for them to come here through *their* pits of particles and shoot *us* up?"

I plop down on his bed. "If they come here, we are better prepared, and we have more that will fight with us."

"We hope. What's saying these Creations here aren't working with them? I hate to say it, but I agree with Cory about General Jord holding on to that list for a reason, and it is by no mistake there are implants in his division. Even if our effects are minimal, our rebellion will show them we aren't toys and we're not going to stand by while they threaten our planet."

Luke is going crazy. He wants to ambush the Vojin's base. That's a one-way trip, and he knows it. "Hold on, Luke, let's take a step back here. Why did you suggest using the Creation Zombie bullets?"

"We saw them work on killing a Vojin."

Now he has my undivided attention. "What? When? How? Why didn't you start with that?" Excitement builds in me at the thought of new possibilities.

"Harold discovered the bullets worked one day in the labs. Two mixed Creations are being held prisoner in the underground lab. The mixed Creations called the Vojin for the scientists. The Vojin came, and Harold was the first to pull out his gun, packed with the special bullets, and shot both of them. Instantly. It was like he had planned the entire thing out. No one was expecting it. Once they solidified, he pulled his goggles from his face and shot them each twice in the chest." Luke imitates Harold shooting with his arm out and trigger finger pulling back an invisible trigger. "They didn't turn into goo. Their bodies' color faded out, and they dropped to the floor. They turned a dark gray as we witnessed the life literally drain from their bodies. It was the coolest thing I've ever seen."

I bounce on my toes, hands clasped in front of my chest. "Did they bleed?"

"Yes." He smiles. "They leaked that colorful dust stuff, like smoke. The dust they leak after their bodies die still stays active. The scientist took samples."

"Wow."

"Okay. So what do you think?" He looks to me expectantly, already assuming I'm in.

I sit on his bed and lie back. "I think you're onto something. I have an idea. When the others come back, we should find out the exact time they plan to attack. Doing so will give us an upper hand, and maybe we could go there before they plan to come here. We'll shoot up the joint with our massive guns and explosives, taking down everything and anyone we see. And just before their reinforcements come, we'll jet."

He lies next to me. "Good idea. Because if they come here, it's all over for us, humans and Creations."

"I don't know. They'll still come here, especially after we attack. They'll just think about it first. They'll start thinking their implants have changed sides, and they are really relying on the implants to hold up their side of the bargain." I sit up. "If they have confirmed an attack, why do you think the Trade hasn't stepped in? When Trade member Grandin visited, he said they were researching them. *Not* trying to find a way to stop them."

"Good question."

"They seem to be more interested in finding out the implants."

Luke shrugs. "The heat wave is over. I want to hit the course in the morning. They put the bridges in today, the ones that Seits was telling us about, so a group of us will check them out tomorrow afternoon."

I stand. "I'll run with you in the morning. I'm going."

"Your boyfriend's back, and you leave your big brother, huh?"

I smile brightly. "Yes. That's how that works." I frown as I realize the term Luke used. "But I don't think he'd call me his girlfriend. '*We are only hugs and kisses, Ky,*'" I mock Marc.

"Right. And stop hugging and kissing," Luke orders, but he goes ignored as I leave his room.

The house has calmed. There are a couple of voices downstairs in the den, Sean and Fein. The projector light shines into the living room. They must be hanging out in there for the evening.

I cross the hall to Marc's room and tap before opening the door. He's lying on his back, watching me enter. "Sorry I walk in your room without an invitation."

"You're comfortable."

"I don't think that's it." I lean my back against the door. "I did that before I became comfortable with you."

"Are you going to hold up the door or come over here?"

Jitters sink into my stomach, making my legs shake.

Nervously, I cross the floor and lie beside him. "Um, I don't know if this is appropriate or not. But I missed you. A lot."

"It's not, but I'll share that with you." He pulls me closer to him.

"That's good."

He holds me as he rests his head against my neck. "You were turned into a Zombie, huh?"

I adjust to meet his tired gaze. For the second that I stare, I come to terms that this will never end, and it's pointless for me to continue to try, knowing I'll always come back here. To his arms. "I don't really want to talk."

He touches up my back. "Then what?"

It's a little tough to breathe as I fight my nerves. I bite the inside of my cheek before deciding to kiss him. Oxygen pushes itself easily through my lungs as we indulge in the contact.

He sits up, and my kiss grows greedy as I climb onto his lap, knees bent at his sides. We lock eyes, and I find serenity in the lighter hue of his purple eyes as he relaxes with me. His relaxation always takes me aback because Creations never relax, and though many will let their hair down sometimes, Marc's is always tied as tight as a knot.

I look him over and stroke his loose, soft hair. The world slows down as I stare at him, looking back and forth at each of his eyes. I even breathe slower, matching the passing of time.

It remains slow when I return his kiss, and tingles burst throughout my entire body. A sensation I've never experienced. It makes me more nervous. But I think I know this feeling. "Marc, I…" I take a slow breath that takes all of me. It's so hard to breathe, preparing to say this. "I…I'm sure, I mean, I know…I love you," I utter slowly.

His hooded eyebrows rise a centimeter, but his mouth doesn't move. He breathes, distressed, "Ky."

"Just, don't say anything." The world takes back its normal

rotation of time, and I'm not ready for Marc's rejection. "I just needed to...to tell you that." I clear my throat. I needed to say it aloud, at least once, to see if it made more sense coming out of my mouth than staying trapped in my head. It doesn't. It still sounds ludicrous. I should've kept it in. *Is it too late to take it back?*

"I know, Ky."

That wasn't the feedback I was expecting, and it makes me sick. I look him over again, growing more and more uncomfortable by the second. "I'm going to go."

When I move, he holds me still. "Hold up, Ky. I don't want you to go."

"I don't want to make you uncomfortable."

"Don't worry about that." He lies back down and turns us so he's over me. "You don't make me uncomfortable. Are you?"

I'm nervous. More nervous than I've ever been. But I think it's because I admitted my feelings that I'm not supposed to acknowledge. I don't expect him to feel the same as me, but I hoped he would. I swallow hard. "No," I say quietly.

"You're okay if I kiss you?"

"Yes. Kiss me." And take this insecurity away.

Leaning down, he kisses me, holding my affection on his lips and, as I'd hoped, my doubts wash away.

His gentle kisses make me want more, and I can't take it. I drag him closer to me, and as he kisses my neck, I tell him, "Touch me."

Against my skin, he asks, "Where?"

I sigh when his tongue slides over my collarbone. *"Everywhere,"* I purr.

Under my shirt, his hands are icy, sliding over my rib cage to my hips, making me shiver. Electric pricks are on his fingertips and palms, and the tingle in my body makes my legs tighten at his sides and my breaths shake. I sigh again as he continues to explore my body and kiss against me.

He's doing nothing, but doing *everything* to me, and I can't get enough.

Coming back, he places a kiss to my mouth, and his hips rock against mine. It makes my trembling legs quake. I love it and hate it. Hating that I can't get a grip on myself when I'm with him.

"Ky," he mutters, "holding back is getting complicated."

"Holding back from what?"

"Nothing, I'll be right back. Don't leave." He leaves his room.

I count the seconds he's gone as I snap myself out of this trance, getting rid of my jitters, nerves and other feelings I can't explain.

Five minutes later, he returns to lie next to me. "Are you okay?" I ask.

"Yes." He pushes his arm under and around me, and I lie on his shoulder. "I don't mean to make you uncomfortable, Ky."

Well, those tables turned quickly. I'm slightly disappointed. It was getting kind of hot. "I don't want to talk about it. I'll work on it tomorrow."

"Don't take it the wrong way."

I ignore him, moving my arm over his stomach and hugging his side. It's comfortable, and because I'm so tired, I doze off quickly.

CHAPTER TWENTY

THE WIND IS HEAVY, blowing the morning dew, as Luke and I race across the obstacle course. It's not as hot as it's been, and the breeze is refreshing. I left my hair down, and the freedom from allowing the light brown strands to whip around and enjoy the breeze is stimulating.

I hit the wall, quickly climbing it. Luke and I are on each other's tails, gaining inches on each other.

The ground is hard, despite the moisture in the air. I jump from the wall, landing hard, feeling the shock rack my legs. Up and over or down and under, I clear the six sets of logs and quickly come upon the barbed wire. Relief hits me on the third run when we are crawling through the tunnel.

Finish line in sight, it's only three feet away from me, but Luke's zipping past me. I didn't even see him coming. I bend over on my knees, catching my breath. "I'm done," I say through heaving breaths. "That's four laps of this course."

Luke slaps my back, and I jerk from the abruptness of the strike. "Let's go eat breakfast, Ky."

"As long as we've been out here," I start, straightening, "breakfast is over."

"We haven't been out that long. Can you run back?"

If I tell him no, he'll force me to run anyway. "Yes." He takes off. Shaking my head, I force myself to run after him.

He was right. We grab our food and sit at our usual table. I'm talking myself out of stabbing Collins with my fork, juggling it between my fingers. Her presence has begun to annoy me. She must know what she's doing, and she has to be doing this stuff on purpose. One day she's flirting with Luke; another day she's flirting with Marc.

Sir Jord clears his throat, grabbing everyone's attention. "The bridges have been placed, and the labs are finished. Luke, Kylie, Cory, Hanley, Collins, Cecilia, Marc, and Sean will go out for a final sweep. Respond!"

"We understand!"

Hands drawn behind his back and head bowed, Jord strides out into the morning. Lately, he's seemed a little detached from everyone. He gives direct orders; he doesn't check in on anyone, requiring Luke to do it instead, and he hangs his head with every departure. He hasn't been himself.

The group of us called to sweep the new area for the labs head out at noonday. We drive the Humvees ten miles from base, across open desert land to the hole. The sun sparkles against the platinum beams that make up the bridge. We exit the vehicles.

Sean says, "Looks like they went all out on this garbage." He slams his door and draws his M27 IAR to his chest, one hand gripped around the handle and the other near the barrel. The magazine of his firearm holds fifty rounds of the Creation Zombie bullets. Sean is an excellent shot. He prefers landing two in the body, one in the heart and one in the head. "For good measure," he always says. I've not yet seen him waste a bullet, so it's comforting, knowing he's with us.

The Zombies are peaceful as we cross the sturdy bridges they've built over the hole. The bridge extends a half mile on to the land, directly to the entrance of the labs. They're single level but well over thirty-two-hundred square feet. The well-constructed silver, oval-shaped building is placed in the middle of the desert. Windows make up the majority of the walls, making it easy for onlookers to view their experiments. It's likely, though, there are lower levels where more in-depth experimenting goes on.

The objective here is to make it such a popular landing, the Zombies will no longer flock over here, and any remaining will be shot down. If they were to fill this hole, that may work, but as long as there is dwelling for the Zombies, they'll remain here. I peer over the railing, down into the twenty-foot hole. Once the Zombies are under control in our area, they'll give the word for us to move out throughout the country to the highest populations of infestations. I'm more than happy to join that fight.

We'll sweep the labs now to make sure they're clear for the scientists to take up residence by this evening.

The two bridges stretch fifty-three yards over the hole. They were dropped down by choppers, evenly spaced apart and drilled into the ground by the ground workers. The posts built into the hole are made of steel and concrete and are a convenient feature for the Zombies to climb and attack the labs.

It's not my job to judge their architectural ability. I just protect it.

"There is no coming back from falling down there," Sean says. "They may look dormant now, with the sun up, but I bet if one of us was to go down there, they would tear us to shreds."

"While they eat us," I say, remembering what it felt like to be one. "They can bomb this hole a million times, and there would still be Zombies."

"Why do you think they are like cannibals anyway?"

I shrug, and Luke responds, "That may be how they process what is food. Like a wolf and a dog. A wolf and a dog aren't the same, but they are both a part of the canine family. You bring a dog to a pack of wolves, they will tear it to shreds. We aren't like them but look like them, like the dog and the wolves."

I survey him, processing his explanation. Seems logical. "What would make you think of that?"

Luke shrugs. "It makes sense, the same with a lion and a tiger."

"If you put a tiger with a lion," Sean begins. "The tiger would win."

"The tiger would never win against a lion," Marc says in a condescending tone. "Lions dominate tigers."

"I agree," I say.

Luke says, "Lions would win because they attack in packs, but tigers are loners. Give them a one-on-one brawl, male against male, that would be worth watching."

"It *would* be interesting to watch," Sean says in amusement.

I bump Sean's shoulder and give him an eager nod.

Cory clears his throat. "Are you all focused on the task at hand or worried about lions and tigers?"

If Cory didn't resent us, he would include himself in this conversation too.

We make it to the other end of the bridge, and the eight of us look at each other and then to the second bridge. We laugh, realizing we should have split up to test the sturdiness of both bridges at once.

The lab is surrounded by nothing but land. A few cacti and desert plants bring a little life to the area, but there are no sights but the mountains and hills in the distance. They are like a backdrop to this bright, silver and glass structure. We split up in twos. Luke and I walk to the far end of the lab. From the outside, it looks empty, and it's quiet, apart from the gusty winds.

"Ready?" I ask Luke, loading my gun. I raise my arm, waiting for him to meet it, confirming he's ready.

He loads his gun before bumping my arm and the side of my fist. "Ready."

Upon our approach, the glass doors part. We enter, smacked with the scent of chemical-based cleaners and fresh paint. The air is hot and still. We could hear a pin drop.

Though we entered through different entry doors, our group meets in the middle of the open room. The matte metal floor and white columns brighten up the open area. On the right side of the room are sectioned off stalls, the size of small bedrooms, with white beds. On the outer sides of the stalls are two closed off rooms. Blue doors lead into them. They're closed. In the back of the building are two white doors that lead to offset rooms, attached to the building on the outside. Inside the room, it's dark; maybe the last stop.

There are two glass rooms to our left. I take one, and Luke takes the other. Nothing but examination tables and a few chairs occupy the room. A couple of small refrigerators with glass doors line a far wall, and multiple monitors are mounted on the wall in the corners.

No Zombies.

"Clear," I say, my voice echoing through the building.

"Clear," the rest follow.

"That was quick," I say to Luke, meeting him back in the center of the room.

He nods. "That's why they sent eight people. They didn't want this to take all day."

"Exactly," Cory says, coming over. "Now, let's clear out. Head back before dinner."

"Yeah, we wouldn't want to be caught out here when those Zombies wake up," Sean says, laughing. "We'll be the dog in a pack of wolves." He and Marc laugh.

I never get his jokes, but I'm inclined to agree.

We head back, this time splitting up to cross both bridges.

Collins and Cory walk with Marc and me across the bridge we all crossed on our way to the labs. Luke, Sean, Hanley, and Cecilia take the other. The two bridges are spaced about five hundred feet apart. The wind has picked up and shakes the structure slightly. I make a mental note to report this to Jord when we return.

Collins and Cory are far ahead of Marc and me, already halfway across, racing against each other for the end.

"I would say he and I hate each other equally," Marc says.

"I would have to agree with you." I chuckle. "That may have happened after the whole kiss in the rec hall, then the fight when you repeatedly expressed your dislike for him by punching him in the face."

Marc's brows knit. "You think that's what gave it away?"

I laugh.

He walks ahead, giving the bridge a closer look.

It's the length of the bridge that makes it so easy for the wind to rattle it. They're going to need more posts in order to support the stretch of heavy metal and steel to make it more stable. Cory and Collins jumping and flipping at the bridge's end isn't helping. Collins is flipping from the floor or the railings while Cory, with his arms long enough to reach both on the left and right, balances himself, swinging his legs back and forth and into a backflip. Every time either of them lands on the bridge, it sends a vibration all the way down, and the rattling echoes through the hole.

I'm a mile from them, with Marc pretty far ahead of me. He stalls, examining the floor of the bridge, noticing the excessive shaking as I have. He throws a glance behind him to me. "Looks like a sandstorm is rolling in, Ky. Let's hurry across." He waves me on.

North of us, a thick orange cloud is crawling toward us. A heavy gust of wind causes the bridge to lean slightly. I grab hold of the railing, catching Marc throw his rifle strap over his shoulder.

At the same moment, Collins flips, accidently kicking Cory in the back. He shoves the railings further apart, causing one to snap off. I watch it break, clink by clink, and I try to break away from it before it breaks where I'm standing, but I'm too late.

I fall over, just catching the bottom of the railing by the tips of my fingers. I pant, adjusting to get a better grip.

"Ky!" Marc calls, echoing Luke. He asks, "You okay?" as he also holds on for dear life.

My stomach is calming from the fall, and I've lost my gun. It's now down there with the Zombies and the fence.

"I got it," I call, maneuvering to get a better grip of the bar. Marc is less than a half mile from me, and we have so far to go before we make it to the end. The bottom railing is made up of multiple linked bars as one long one may not have been able to securely stretch the length of the bridge.

I need to shuffle my grip from one section to the next. My shoulders are already sore, and my back is screaming for me to release the bar from which I hang and relax. It wouldn't be so bad if I didn't go four rounds on the course with Luke this morning. The wind isn't helping, shifting my dangling body as I figure out a plan of execution.

Marc's not moved, appearing to be waiting on me. "Go," I urge. "I'll make it."

He nods and begins swinging from one bar to another as if they were monkey bars.

I nod to myself. That's a good idea. I throw my weight to reach the next bar. Grabbing it, the steel snaps off. I hold it in my hand, studying it as if it would give me an answer as to why it broke off. I drop it and watch it plummet to the group of moseying Zombies beneath me.

Fine...

I try again, throwing myself to reach the next bar. Grasping it, I can tell it's sturdy, and I sigh with relief. I swing from one bar to the next, yelling to Luke. After he asks me for the third time if I have it, I yell, "Shut up! I got it! Give me a break, Luke!" He doesn't hear me, though I do my best to shout over the wind.

The bar snaps in my hand, hanging on by one side. Gravity yanks me down, and I hurry to grip the skinny steel in both my hands. My heart's pounding, and my ears are ringing. Palms growing sweaty, I struggle to hold on.

Luke screams, "Ky! Hold on!"

Marc whips around, swinging back in my direction. "Stop," I shout. "These bars are unpredictable!" We'll both be in my place if he grabs a weak bar like I did. "I can get myself out of this," I assure them. Though I'm not sure.

My shoulders sting, and the burn is too much to keep holding on.

"I'm coming for you, Ky," he says.

The bar's shaking, the other end ready to give at any moment.

I yank myself up like climbing a rope, gritting my teeth as I work against the pain. I reach for the next bar, screaming out in irritation as I realize I can't reach it. I grunt, relaxing my shoulder, getting so tired of hanging. I'll need to throw myself to the next bar, but what if it's weak too?

We don't live off what if, Ky. I hear Luke tell me. *If you get the chance, take it.*

With all my might, I yank myself upward as hard as I can and throw my weight to the bar above me. I catch it with the tip of my fingers crooked around the bar.

It breaks.

I'm plummeting. It's the fall that'll kill me, and hopefully, I hit the ground hard enough to avoid being eaten to death by the Zombies. Closing my eyes, I accept my fate.

I jerk. Something snatches my forearm, yanking my arm out of its socket. I cry through my teeth.

"I got you, Ky," Marc says, voice strained. I squint my eyes. He's hanging on to a bar with one hand, the other saving my life. "I got you…"

I look down, feeling his arm shaking, likely either from the bar or me being too heavy for him to hold.

"Grab hold of me, Ky."

I try to move my fingers, but the movement sends pain striking through my back. Turning my attention back to Marc, I look past him, to the bar in his loosening grasp. It's definitely shaking, ready to give at any second.

I shake my head. We're both not going to make it.

"Don't do that, Ky. I can get you, just try to grab hold of me."

Again, I shake my head, accepting my time is up. "It's okay, Marc. You can let me go. I'm not afraid. Let me go before the bar breaks, and we both fall. I'm not scared." I meet his eyes, reassuring him with a look of confidence. But he looks back at me, fear and worry causing his eyes to shake and his chin to tremble. An expression I'd resent if anyone else wore it.

"I am, Ky. Please grab hold. I can't let you go." His grip tightens on me as I slowly slip from his grasp. "*I am scared, Kylie. I won't let you go. Please?*" he begs, despair in his voice and shadowed orchid eyes.

I look away from him as my breath catches and my legs dangle in the wind. My heart fires up, pounding loudly in my ears, and over it, Luke's begging me to hold on. His shouts echo loudly.

Another gust of wind smacks into my dangling body, forcing me to slip through Marc's grip. I try to hold on with everything I have, our nails scraping our palms as we dig for a grip. We catch each other by crooked fingers, our blood making it hard to keep holding on.

"*Thank you,*" he mouths, looking out to nothing before he looks back down at me. "I got you." He carefully tugs me upward, grunting as he supports my weight with one arm. When I reach his waist, he says, "Wrap your arm around my legs." I do as he asks, releasing his hand, and he grips me between his legs, holding me in place. He shakes his hand out before swinging to a new bar. "Alright, Ky. Get up here."

I tug myself up his body, gripping his belt and vest, as he keeps his legs tightly wrapped around me. When I make it, I wrap my good arm around his neck and wind my legs around his waist. "Thanks," I say in his ear.

He exhales a relieved breath and makes it across the remaining distance of the broken bridge. We make it to the edge of the cliff, and Luke, Sean, and Collins pull us up onto firm ground. While still in Marc's arms, he whispers, "You are heavy, girl. And never tell me you can't save yourself for me. I need you, okay?" before I'm ripped from his grasp.

Luke hugs me for a split second before shoving me. I stumble as I'm holding him back from another attack and clutching my dislocated arm. "What the hell, Kylie! You didn't want to save yourself?" he shouts at the top of his lungs. Voice drenched in unnecessary anger, he blusters on about how I shouldn't have hesitated.

I heave a lungful of air so I can throw a few choice words at him, but Marc comes up behind me, wrapping his arm around my shoulders. "It's okay, Luke. I got her. You're good." His heavy rasp and the lightness of his reassurance settles Luke's anxiety.

I shuffle from Marc's hold and cross the ground to Luke. Throwing my arm around his neck, I say, "I'm sorry, Luke."

"That was not okay, Ky." He breaks away from me, snatches his helmet off the ground, and shoves it down on his head.

I snatch his arm. "Hey! Don't turn your back on me. I mean it.

I'm sorry." I force another hug. "I realize it was a bad move, but I am okay." *My arm is busted, but I'm alive.*

Luke returns my hug, head falling onto my good shoulder. I return his hug with my good arm and lay my head next to his. "You don't just give up," he tells me in our small huddle.

"At the time, it seemed better to lose one than two."

"If we had to return without the two of you, it would have been four. It was better for you to try than for you to want to fall."

"You are right, Luke." I don't want to argue. "I might've scared you. And I'm sorry for forcing you to experience that emotion."

"You did," he admits. "And that is not a feeling I'm used to or ever want to experience again."

"I agree," I say, leaning back. "Would you mind popping my shoulder back in place? That catch was rough."

I brace myself when he grabs my shoulder and arm, and without warning yanks it back in place. The crack is loud. I drop to my knees from the pain. "Thanks," I grunt.

"Want me to heal your hand?"

"No," I say quickly. "I'll clean it, and I'll be fine." These are scars I want to keep.

Once I'm on my feet, Cory comes to my side, throws his arm around me, quickly hugs me to him, and mutters, "Glad you're okay," before heading to the Humvee.

As we head for the Humvee, I look back at Marc talking to Sean, calming him down. Sean's not going to be happy that Marc, once again, risked his life to save mine, but though I originally denied his help, I'm grateful he offered it.

CHAPTER TWENTY-ONE

"The bridge broke," Luke calmly informs the general.

Sean scoffs. "That bridge didn't just break. It busted. It was poorly structured."

"How?" Jord's eyes bug out of his head, and his voice booms even louder than usual.

"We can't be sure," Luke answers, glowering at Cory and Collins. He relaxes the muscles in his face before Jord catches him. "It wasn't sturdy. Ky and Marc almost went over, but they made it back safely." He gestures to Marc at his left and me on his right. "The other bridge is fine, and the labs are clear, but the Zombies have crowded the hole again."

"So soon...?" Jord murmurs contemplatively. He flicks a curious gaze to Marc and me. "You two were trying to be the walking dead's dinner?"

"More accurately, I think someone was trying to feed us to them." I throw an infuriated glance at Cory.

Jord sits back down and crosses his arms. "I'll make a call to inform the engineering team the bridge needs repairs. Head in. The storm will be here soon."

"Yes, sir," we say.

We march home and gather in the den. Cory and Hanley have no reason to be here, and they should've gone home with the weather that's rolling in.

"Why did you two try to kill Marc and Ky, Collins?"

Collins shoves Sean. "We did not try to kill them. It was an accident. Who knew the bridge wasn't sturdy?"

Fein comes in and sits next to Sean. She leans over to whisper something that puts a smile on his face, but when he catches me noticing, he quickly erases it. "Why are all of you gathered in the den?" Fein asks.

"Ky and Marc almost died today," Sean tells her.

"We were fine, Fein. The bridge just collapsed, but Marc saved us, and we made it."

"Woo! Go Marc!" She puts her hand out to high five him, and he meets her.

"Shouldn't you be heading to your own corridors, Cory," Luke unkindly suggests.

Cory stands. "Is there something you'd like to say to me, Luke?"

I jump to my feet at the same time as Luke. "There's a lot I'd like to say to you, but I doubt you'd want me to say it in front of all of them." Luke gestures out to everyone. Nodding, he adds, "But I could."

Cory eyeballs him, turning up his nose. "Watch your back, Luke. You aren't the only one who knows things."

I step to Luke's side. "Watch *your* back, Cory. You're right. He's not the only one who knows things. And if I were you, I would find the door before my fist finds your nose."

"Don't threaten my brother, Kylie." Hanley takes her brother's side.

Luke loosely wraps his arm around my neck. Laughing, he says, "Let them go, Ky. Cory knows he and his sister are no match for us. Isn't that right, Cory?"

"Fuck you, Luke."

"Ooo," Luke sings, shaking his shoulders, "feisty." He fakes a shiver. "Get out, Cory, before my sister cracks another tooth." Cory looks back and forth from Luke and me, Hanley at his side doing the same. "Goodbye, snake," Luke says hard with disgust.

"Watch your mouth, Luke."

"Watch yours. Hurry and go, so you can help them weed out the implants in our sector. Isn't that your job now?"

A heavy hush falls over the room, I can practically hear eyelids stretching over bugged-out eyeballs.

Cory's eyes widen as they quickly shift around the room. His sister whispers in his ear before pulling him away.

I turn to Luke after the front door closes and punch him lightly on his chest. "You know how to hit him where it hurts."

"He's a snake. No one cares where they hurt."

Chuckling, I leave the den, heading for my room so I can change for a shower. Footsteps follow behind me, and when I open the door to my room, I turn around. "Thank you for saving me."

"No problem."

I back into my room. "You could have let me fall and got what you want."

Marc shuts the door behind him. "My wants don't matter."

"They do if you want me."

"You scared me today. I've never felt anything like that before. And it's making me uncomfortable to admit it."

"I saw it in your eyes." I shake my head. "I don't want to die. Not like that. I can go in battle, getting shot down, something with pride, something that shows strength. Not plummeting to my death in a hole full of Zombies."

Tugging me to his front, he cuffs my cheek with one hand as the other grips my waist. "You made me realize something today."

"What was that?"

"I don't want to lose you."

"Then let me stay with you."

He nods and kisses me before leaving.

I lie across my bed, feeling light, like I did the first time Marc kissed me in the alley, and I walked on mattresses instead of concrete.

Someone knocks on my door. "It's Fein, Ky. Can I talk to you?"

"Yes," I say, sitting up.

She comes in, closing the door behind her. Dressed in sweat-pants and a t-shirt, her arms hang loosely at her sides, and her orange gaze reminds me of the rising sun. She blinks. "Cory is weeding out the implants?"

"That's why I warned you. Don't trust him."

She sits beside me. "But he's no different from us."

I play shocked, asking, "Can *you* be trusted?"

She looks away from me, brows knit as it seems a thought crosses her mind. "I guess I can't be. I'm as bad as him, but I don't throw people under the bus."

"That means you're not a snake, but you are still a traitor. How do you know what those aliens say to you is true anyway?" *Here is my chance to try to turn her against them.*

"I was born knowing. They're all I know."

"But are they? You were raised with us, lived with us, fought with us, *we* are what you know. More than them. You've spent your entire life with us, Fein. And not to mention, they didn't look happy with you. Family doesn't treat you like that." I honestly can't comment on the family topic with my past, but Luke has shown me enough to know family shouldn't hurt us.

"Are you trying to turn me against them?"

Insulted, I state, "What Creation wouldn't, knowing what I do about you? They sent these *Zombies* here as a threat! A threat against us makes them an enemy. I don't see how you can choose them over us, when we've been there for you forever. You said you were born knowing them, but how much time did you actually spend with them versus the time you spent with us Creations? Who and what we are was instilled in us when we were born. We go against what goes against us. Not help it. They sounded like they wanted to go against us. If they go against us, they will be going against you too, Fein." I throw up my hands, done with the conversation. "Just remember how you were trained, what you have seen, and what we are. Would you prefer to be on their side or ours?" I stand from the bed and take off my vest, knives, and boots. "I'm going to shower. I'll see you in the morning."

She leaves without a word. *Maybe I got to her.*

Back home, before she died, this old lady used to tell me, "All you have to do is plant the seed, just provide the idea. It will manifest on its own, but as long as you plant the seed, that thought is within them." I planted the seed, and the thought is manifesting. That's what counts.

CHAPTER TWENTY-TWO

I DREAM of Marc kissing his lips. My lips press against smooth skin instead of soft lips. I open my eyes to Luke's arm. "Eww!" *How...disgusting!*

I move my head out of his arm and scoot out of his bed. With my thoughts and this seductive feeling of Marc on me, I can*not* lie here next to my brother. It's too weird.

I quietly pull Luke's door open, catching Collins sneaking out of Marc's room. *What is she doing coming out of there at this time of night?* What is she doing coming out of there, period?

She descends the stairs, perkily bouncing on her toes. My throat's closing around a breath. It sends a burning feeling coursing up to my cheeks and down to my stomach. I clench my teeth, waiting on the feeling to pass. When it does, I gently pull open Luke's door and try my hardest not to stomp across the hall, but my steps sound.

I try my damnedest not to swing open Marc's door, but it whines open and knocks off the wall. I *try*—very hard—not to slam it behind me, but it closes loudly.

Marc's on his feet, standing near the bed, shirtless. "Ky," he says.

I whip around, hiding my watery eyes. I swallow hard, hoping to remove the rock that landed in my throat, but it doesn't budge. This is a bad place to be and a worse way to feel. I bite down on my lip, but it's not enough to suppress these stupid feelings. It's not nearly enough to stop me from crying.

He pulls my arm, turning me around. I yank away from him. "It just looks bad," he says, grabbing me again.

"Why was she in your room?" I snarl through my teeth, trying to control my weakness and keep it from displaying through the falling of my tears or the shaking of my voice.

"She came and left, I did nothing with her, Ky." He wipes my face. "I'd never want to. I wouldn't."

I shove him away from me. "Then why don't you have any clothes on, Marc?"

"It's late, Kylie. What do you expect for me to sleep in? A sweatshirt and jeans? I only wear a shirt when you're in here, so you're not uncomfortable."

I turn back to face the door, allowing the burning tears to fall in private. Releasing it makes it hurt less. I even out my breaths so I don't huff or puff. I want to slam my fist against the door, but it will be too loud. Keeping my words even, I state, "She left too happy to have been rejected. And any time I come by, you're always dressed."

"Well she was, Ky. It's late. After a certain hour, if you don't come, this is how I sleep."

I wipe my face even though I don't have any intentions on turning back to him. "It's fine, Marc. I'm wrong to overreact." *Walk away, Kylie.*

Someone knocks on his door softly. I scrape the tears from my face before whipping it open. "What?" I snap in a whisper.

Collins jumps back. Her robe is clutched so tightly in her hand it protrudes through the cracks of her fingers. Its tie hangs from her other hand. Her bare feet scrape the floor as she recoils.

"Nothing," she mumbles, turning, headed back down the hall toward the stairs.

I face Marc, biting my tongue. *Literally.* I press my teeth down into my tongue, drawing pain to keep me silent. Anger dries the tears I regret letting fall. I turn around and head out of his room. I pull the door closed behind me, and he pulls it back open.

His hand wraps around my arm, tugging me back. I stumble backward, trying to free my arm from him.

"Kylie," he demands as the door closes in front of me. His chest presses against my back as his tight grip holds me in place by the crook of my arms. "She showed up like you do some nights, without knocking or saying anything. She climbed in my bed, and I was half sleep, briefly thinking she was you until she touched me. The second I acknowledged it was her and not you, I told her to leave. She was probably coming back to convince me, but how many times do I have to tell you I only give myself to you." He pushes his arms around my waist and hugs my middle. Kissing my neck, he adds, "Only you get this."

I huff. "I don't like that."

"Jealousy burns, doesn't it?" He moves us toward his bed. "You've got nothing to be jealous about. Believe me."

I turn, facing him. "And why not?" My gaze dances over his body before meeting his eyes.

"Why do you think?" he questions, gaze soft and compassionate.

"I don't know," I utter, sitting. I'm slowed by the feeling of affection, the all-consuming passion I feel for this boy that draws feelings from me I never felt, that I never knew I possessed until him. Feelings that I still don't understand.

"You know," he insists. "You told me first."

I scoot back, and he leans forward. I'm lying back on his bed, contemplating, "What have I said first."

"Affection."

I look away from him to the ceiling, mumbling, "You... Love me?"

"Me saving you over my brother, ignoring my better judgment, knowing you work for the enemy, not letting you fall into a pit of Zombies by risking my life to save yours... Didn't that say enough without me actually using the words?"

I study his eyes, their lightness, the softness of his gaze. "I love you."

"I know," he says, leaning in to kiss me.

I move back across the bed so my feet aren't on the edge when I bend my knees at his sides. Saying it confidently makes my feelings make sense. It's like admitting it brings these feelings reason and now they can calm down and not overreact and keep me nervous or jealous or angry or expecting the worst.

I touch his back, distracted for a second by his scars.

His touch is more confident. He no longer pauses before meeting his targets. His graze moves over my curves and under my shirt before it comes off. We move too quickly. Our kisses are eager, and our touches are aggressive. He moves against me. I'm expecting it and accepting of it, I want to feel it...him. I'm hoping he'll do it, kiss and touch me in places I'll allow no one else to.

Marc removes my bra, exposing me to his eyes, hands, and his tongue and lips. I bite my cheek, quietly sighing through my nose. "Talk to me, Ky," he requests. "Tell me what you feel. Tell me how you feel." He grabs my hands, pushing them over my head.

I cannot explain what I feel, but whatever it is, I feel it everywhere. I grasp onto his hands, moving my fingers between his, holding him tightly as they shake.

He kisses me after covering different areas of my upper body. I arch my body against him and release a soft sigh against his mouth.

"I can't hear you, Ky."

"I feel..." He slides down, kissing my stomach, hands slipping from mine. As his fingertips slide over my arms, I sense them in other places he's not made it to yet. "You're touching me everywhere all at once," I whisper, my voice breathy.

"What does it feel like?"

"Smooth. Electric." I gasp for the air being sucked out of his room. "It's suffocating but refreshing."

"What does it make you feel like?"

I breathe deep. Pressure is building in my chest, compressing my lungs, pushing me to the verge of hyperventilating. "I don't know, I can't explain it."

"Good?" He kisses my navel. "Bad?" He gently takes my breasts in both hands, mildly caressing them.

"Good." *Amazing.*

He dips to my abdomen, but I feel him kissing me somewhere else.

"Now?" he questions.

I breathe deep again. My legs tremble. My hands shake as I push them over the bundle of sheets under me. "I'm excited, nervous. It feels nice," I whisper through deep breaths. "You're kissing my stomach, but I feel you other places, and it makes my legs shake."

"Where do you feel me?"

Oh God, I can't say it. I clutch the sheets tightly in my fingers as he dips a little further down.

"Here?" he firmly presses his lips against me, over the waistband of my tight-fitting sweats.

I breathe out through my mouth. My nails dig into my hands through the sheets, as I clench my fists tightly against the pleasure.

"No?"

His body dipping further down spreads my legs wider. His shoulders brush my thighs. "Tell me, Ky."

No, no, I can't tell you.

"Here..."

Pleasure stabs me in the back, causing my middle to rise then fall against his bed. A sigh erupts from my throat as I fall back against the mattress.

He lies against me, chest to chest. "Shh, Ky," he says in my ear. Breathing heavily, I nod. His bare chest is pressed to mine. My body is a pack of jitters, tremors constantly scattering just beneath my flesh. My hands are shaking so badly, I can't control it.

I like it...I love it.

I kiss his lips. I don't know what to do with this pressure he built in me. It's an odd adrenaline that makes me want to be aggressive. I try to suppress it, try to push it down with deep breaths, but they increase the pressure, heightening my excitement.

Marc's thumb slips under my waistband and eases my pants downward. Slowly, I lift. He stops. "You–"

I hurry to cut him off. "I wouldn't," I say, knowing where he was going. "Just close enough to not fall over."

He draws back. "I would, so I'll stop."

I cover my chest with my arms. It's suddenly cold. "Wait. I don't want you to stop, but I don't want you to go that far."

"I can't." I have to move my arms to pull him back, and I don't want to do that with my chest bare. It feels different just exposing myself than him exposing me.

I lie back, looking at the ceiling. I'm not ready to go *that* far. "Close enough...?" I suggest, not wanting to stop this. Not yet. Whatever he just did to me was like bait. And though I'm not ready to get caught and have him reel me in, I want to keep nibbling.

His hands glide over my stomach to the band of my sweats. I breathe deep, grabbing my shoulders as I slowly lift when his fingertips slide along the band to my hips. He pulls down my pants as a couple of his fingers slide down my legs after them, then over my feet.

The last garment of clothing on me is my panties. I plan on leaving those on, and my nerves are going crazy from being this raw and open.

He hovers over me, still clothed. "Can you uncover down to your last too?" I'd be more comfortable if he did.

"You might not like that," he states.

"Why?"

He moves back with a smirk stealing his serious look. "I'll show you." He drops his pants and comes back over me. "Don't run away."

"Why would–" I'm cut off, jabbed by, well... I quickly back away, no longer concerned with exposing myself. "What is that?" I ask, shocked and high pitched.

"Shh. What do you think?" he snorts, pursing his lips.

"Oh." Right... "Um," I just made this awkward. "Don't do that like that."

He shrugs slowly. "It's going to feel the same either way."

"Why?"

He smiles, revealing his teeth. "Because Ky, it's supposed to go in you, not against you."

Oohh...Right...Um...I'm not ready for that. "I'm being weird about this."

"You asked me to take them off, and I warned you."

"Okay, are you going to put them back *on*?"

He shakes his head. "Nope." And he leans in to kiss me, but I'm not...*poked* again.

I smile against his lips and push my hands through his hair. It falls between my fingers as I seize it. As I pull him closer, he wraps an arm around my back and holds me against him.

Time slows again, and my legs and hands shake, wanting more. *What more could I want? How much more can he give me?* My legs wrap around each of his thighs, and I slowly pull him to me. Or he might just be moving slowly.

Someone knocks on his door.

"Oh, no."

It's Luke. I just know it's Luke, and if he had a cow because of Cory and me only kissing, I'm pretty sure he is going to shit a blue whale if he sees me like this...and Marc like that.

"Put your clothes on," Marc whispers, getting up and pulling his pants on. He asks, "Who is it?" as he looks for a shirt. I search the bed for my things.

"Luke," Luke says, causing me to search faster.

I get on my bra and look for my shirt. Marc throws me my pants as he says, "What?" He points behind me, showing me where my shirt is.

I nod as I slide on my pants and then slip on my shirt as Luke asks, "Is Kylie in there?" I see a shirt lying across Marc's rack. I snatch it off and throw it to him.

Marc coughs to stall as I climb back onto his bed without making a noise. "Yeah," he finally answers. He opens the door, and I shut my eyes, playing possum. "She's asleep. Everything okay?"

Luke must have awoken and seen I wasn't there. So my big brother needed to check on me and knows if I'm not with him, I'm in here. "What, Luke?" I whisper.

"Checking where you were."

"I'm here," I say, opening my eyes into slits.

Leaning against the wall, Marc mouths, "He is going to kill us." I laugh, turning into his pillow to smother it.

"Be gone before everyone wakes up, Ky. And don't enjoy yourself with my sister, Marc."

"Bye, Luke," I say dismissively, lifting my head from the pillow so I can see him leave. Marc closes the door and sits on the bed. "You're scared of my brother?"

"No." He smiles. "I was joking."

I lean up, grabbing his shirt to pull him to me. "I like it when you smile."

He leans back on his elbow and scoots up on the bed. "You make me smile." He smirks brightly, warming my heart. "You and all your alien mojo."

I lean away from him when he gets extremely close. "I don't have mojo."

He lies down on his back, asking, "What is it, smoke?"

I pinch my nose, thinking. "It's more like dust."

"Let me see," he says, buzzing with interest.

"See what?" I sit up on my elbow, surveying him.

Nodding, his hand gestures in a circle, pointing at me. "What you look like," he states in an obvious tone.

"I look no different. They're just a part of my DNA. My mouth may glow a little when I activate the glittering particles, but my appearance doesn't change." I shrug as I continue, "I was born a Creation. Not a Vojin."

"Let me see you release some *glittering particles.*"

I lie down and clear my throat. There's no harm as long as it doesn't escape the room. I move my hands into a cuff over my mouth and extended out about ten inches. I look at him. "Don't go ballistic when my mouth glows blue and green. It looks off, not normal."

"I won't," he says casually.

I turn back, facing the ceiling, and from my chest, I blow. Shortly, the particles start tickling my throat, and they escape, brushing past my lips. I see the glow reflect off my hands before they start filling with the fusing blue and green particles.

Momentarily, I stare at them circling slowly in my hands, wanting to be set free. "I hate it," I say out loud, although I only meant to think it.

"Now what are you going to do with it?" Marc asks.

"I wish I could shoot it. I wish I could shoot all of them." I bring my hand close to my mouth and suck in the particles until they're gone.

I want to cough from the tickle, but instead I roughly clear my throat.

Marc pushes his arm behind me and pulls me closer. "How is it you're infused with them? How did they infuse you?"

"Okay, so this part of your throat," I touch where his trachea is, "Ours are lined with this coating. It's *their* coating. When we were children, they stuck this tube down our throats, and stabbed us with a lot of miniature needles throughout that area, pushing this disgusting kind of organism that was about two inches in length, thin with legs or tentacles. It was the color of the dust stuff, like the particles they're fused with. They call it our implant. They inserted a piece of them within us." I want to tell him the entire truth about Luke's and my implants, but I stop myself. I hate that I'm still a part of them. I don't want to have any of them in me.

Marc pokes the skin beneath my right ear where a scar from years ago still feels raw. "You've got this scar here, does that have something to do with them too?"

I wince at the mention of it. This scar isn't a secret I'm prepared to reveal, so I change the subject. "They want to control us and it's something I don't want to be associated with." I lay my head on his shoulder and Marc looks down at me through his lashes.

"You hate them because they lied to you?"

"No, I don't care about them lying. It's because they killed my mother and father. It's because I don't understand what they are trying to prove."

"*Hmm.*" He pauses and then asks, "But you will continue to put in work for them?"

"Not at all. We're against them, and apparently, we're not the only ones." I sit up.

"What is it?" he asks, pushing back my hair that has fallen around my face.

"This may all be over soon, our world and our way of living."

He turns down the corners of his mouth, questioning me.

I adjust so my arms are propped on his chest. "I'll tell you. But don't judge me because of it. It's not my reason, and you can't say anything."

He rubs his hands over my shoulders and slides them to my elbows. "If I wanted to say something, you would be dead."

I nod and say, "They want to destroy the world, and after they destroy it, they want to reconstruct it. Starting with four. When I was talking to Cory a couple of months ago, he used their words after I asked if he thought the wars would ever end. He didn't respond in the way a Creation would; he said the world would be a better place after it's destroyed and reconstructed."

"Reconstructed?" Marc questions.

"The general heard him and asked the same question. We told Luke, and he had the same response."

Marc's brows knit. "But the general doesn't treat him any different if he knows."

"Exactly." I sit up. "So one group of the outsiders has a plan of destruction, and another group has a plan to stop them." I take his hands. "Like *we* wouldn't want this, *our* planet destroyed... Some of them don't either. They want us to help stop them."

He sits up, and I sit on his legs. "Us, like you all, or *us*, like Creations?"

"Us, like Creations and humans, who do not want th–*our* planet destroyed." I move away from him, feeling uneasy about not being able to positively claim this planet. "I don't know what they want us to do. And even if I did, I don't know if I could do it."

"Okay, so are you and others supposed to make us go with you or something?"

"Yes. Convince you to side with them. Before, it was for their domination, and now, it's to reserve our planet and fight against the ones that want to destroy it."

"That's not going to happen, Ky. I'll never side with the Vojin."

"I know, Marc. Could I convince you to fight with me? To side with me and fight against them?"

He's silent as he lies beside me, looking up at the ceiling. "I wouldn't. I don't believe them."

"But you believe me?"

Hesitantly, he says, "Yes."

"If instead, I ask you to help me destroy them and save our home, will you?"

"If that were possible...yes."

CHAPTER TWENTY-THREE

THE HORN BLARES THIS MORNING, louder than usual. I'm still in Marc's bed, snuggled up against him. He scoots off the bed. "I'll leave first, with everyone." Cracking his neck, he stretches his arms, adding, "Luke will probably come get you once the hall clears."

I rub my eyes and stretch my arms over my head. "Cool."

Marc puts a knee on his bed and leans over. He kisses me once. "Stay with you?"

I nod. "And let me stay with you."

He nods and leaves his room. I release a heavy exhale, accepting our confirming seal that we're together now. No more back and forth or avoidance. He loves me. He hasn't said it, but he does. Smiling to myself, I lie back on his bed, throwing his pillow over my red turning face to hide my oversized, girlish grin.

His door opens. "Come on, Ky." Luke pulls on my leg, quickly letting it go.

"Okay."

———

The roads are full of buses with the last of the Creations returning. A large, all white SUV is parked out front of the general's office. Maybe someone from the Guidance or the Premier making an appearance. "Why are they here?" I ask Luke.

"Don't know." Sir Jord's office door opens. "But I have a feeling we are about to find out. Let's smile for the people who don't give a shit about us," he quickly whispers.

Luke and I stop, watching two well-built, adult Creations stomp out of the office. With their shoulders straight and chests pushed out, they stand tall, wearing no facial blocking or headgear. One has medium-length hair, and the other is bald, but they resemble one another.

A woman dressed in a dark brown suit exits Jord's office. Her straight black hair hangs loosely around her shoulders. A man with jeans and a buttoned black shirt isn't far behind her. The two of them stand there on the porch, surveying the base as they exchange words. After she nods, they walk forward, and an older man walks from the office, hunched at the back, heels dragging. The wind tousles his thin gray hair, and a salt and pepper beard spots his chin and cheeks. He wears a black suit and shiny black shoes that are sprinkled with dust from the dirt roads.

The general comes out after him, hands on his hips, expression stoic. Jord looks our direction and waves us over.

"You were right," I say to Luke as we head over.

Jord extends his arms as Luke and I approach. "Lukahn, Kylie, meet Premier Norman Stelloh and the leaders of the Guidance, Richard Majewski, and Arletta Fett."

They salute as we do, dropping our hands after the Premier has. "We hear you two came in and obtained leader positions rather quickly, a reflection of your general and his twin." Arletta says, admiring us with a smile, hands clasped in front of her belt buckle. Her nose is straight, and her sharp gray eyes make her expression daunting. "What an honor," she adds. Her eyelids, smoothed with deep red eyeshadow, blink over her eyes as her gaze sweeps from one side of our line to the other. Her smile widens. The red lipstick flawlessly spread across her lips brightens her perfect smile, but a tiny twitch in the right corner of her mouth draws a falter to her beauty.

"We work hard and put our efforts into being better than the next man or woman," Luke responds strongly.

"That sounds worthy. What do you think of there being implants in this division?" she asks.

"They should be executed," I state.

"Could you perform that execution, Kylie?"

"Without question," I state the way they would want a Creation to respond.

The four of them nod. "Can I meet your team?" The Premier asks. He attempts to straighten his hunched posture when addressing us. It looks uncomfortable, but I appreciate his effort. Unlike the Trade, his address shows we *do* mean something to them, and he appreciates us.

Besides fighting for him, per his requests, our teams hold no importance. His request to meet them is odd. Luke and I look at Jord, seeing if it is okay.

"There is no problem in greeting their teams. Gather your groups and bring them here. Quickly, they are preparing to leave. Respond."

"We understand." We run toward the rec hall to find our groups. We go to the Creations' hall first. Upon entering, Luke speaks loudly, "Creations of Ky and myself, the Premier has requested to meet you. Here now, do not lollygag, present yourselves as Creations. Do not slouch or slack. Face forward unless instructed to do otherwise. Remain at attention. Fall out." Luke and I turn, leaving for the Normals' hall.

As I walk in, I say, loud and demanding, "Non-Creations of Luke's and my team, stand to leave." I repeat to them Luke's instruction, and they are slower leaving than the Creations. Because of that, they will be trained hard today.

We run back to the Premier and stand at attention. Our groups gather behind us.

The Premier looks everyone over with Arletta and Richard behind him, doing the same. "How long have the Non-Creations been here?" he asks Jord.

"So far, three months," Jord answers.

The Premier nods. "Training is too light on them. Their faces are at ease. They are too comfortable, not alert. The Creations in each group look great. Good job with their training, Kylie and Lukahn." He stalls, looking each face over. "Why is there an uneven number of Creations?" he asks Jord.

"During a daytime attack of the undead, both groups were fighting, outnumbered. Kylie lost three Creations, and Lukahn lost two. It was unfortunate."

The Premier slowly nods. "We will get a handle on these dead infestations. We are losing so many citizens and Creations to them, it's unbelievable. We need to destroy the head, and the tail will follow in death," he says, smashing his shaky fist to his palm.

I flick my gaze left and right. That is an odd implication.

"Let me go!" Someone yells from behind us. Everyone looks.

Fein is being dragged by her neck by Marshal hurrying in our direction. When they make it to Jord, he throws her on the ground. In his other hand, he holds a coyote that looks like its neck is broken. It's dead.

"What is this?" Jord asks, brows furrowed and eyes wide. He seems embarrassed by such a display in front of the most important people in the world.

Marshal throws the coyote next to Fein as she starts to stand. He cocks his gun back, saying, "You better not get up. Stay on your knees." He looks at Jord. "I saw her contacting the outsiders.

Colorful mists left her mouth, her mouth was glowing. Shortly after, that thing howled and showed up."

She didn't learn when Luke and I caught her? Marshal's actions should have been ours, but we let her go.

"Get her twin and bring him here," Jord tells Marshal. He nods, running toward our rec hall.

Fein keeps her head down. I try to not look at Luke and instead look over my group to make sure the faces of the Creations have not faltered or been affected by this scene. This couldn't have happened at a worse time, and in front of the Guidance, of all people. Sir Jord won't be able to write this off like he's done Cory or anyone else he's discovered is on that list.

Arletta drags her red painted nails down her long neck as she looks Fein over. She asks, "What do you all do when you find an implant?"

Jord says, "The first two that were found are being held captive and tested on."

She glides her index and middle finger back and forth over her mouth without smudging her lipstick. "Hmm." She taps her bottom lip twice as she slightly nods. "Do you need any more for testing?"

Everyone looks at Jord for his answer, even Fein, her eyes begging him to say yes. He could save her, spare her and Floyd's life by taking them to the labs. If he says no, Arletta will demand execution for them both right now.

It's oddly silent as we wait for Jord's answer. He avoids looking down at Fein. Right before he speaks, he quickly flicks his gaze to her and back up. I wouldn't have seen him do it if I wasn't staring him in his eyes. There's a relationship there, and I think it's their connection with the Vojin.

"No," he says hard, looking at Arletta. I unnoticeably release a shocked breath.

I'm sorry, Fein.

"Good to hear," Arletta says as Marshal comes back with Floyd, walking cheerfully at his side.

Floyd spots Fein on the ground on her knees. "Fuck!" He expresses his anger, throwing his head back. He turns to make a run for it, or he may be checking his surroundings, but Marshal stops him.

With her brother here, Fein straightens her spine and holds her head high.

"Kylie," Richard calls. I pull my eyes from Fein to him, keeping my face strong. "Execute," he orders.

Why me?

Marshal grabs Floyd's neck and shoves him to his knees so he's in the same position as his sister. I look at Luke when everyone's eyes lock on me. Luke's stare reads I have no choice but to follow orders.

I draw my gun and walk to the backs of Fein and Floyd.

I cock it back.

Floyd says, "Me first, Ky." Floyd and Fein are my friends. I don't want to do this. If I did, I would have turned them in myself. Why did they have to be so stupid, so negligent to get caught? You *never* make the same mistake twice. Now, I'm forced to kill my good friend and her brother.

Fein clears her throat and says, "Thank you, Ky."

My heart's thumping roughly, but my breaths remain steady. I aim at Floyd first, take in a deep breath, and slowly let it out. I pull back the trigger. He falls forward, and Fein wails, looking away from him. I cock my gun back again, wanting to end her misery as fast as I can. A heat of remorse washes over me as I aim it at her.

"Wait," Arletta presses her index finger against the back of my hand, pushing it aside. I look at it, glossy fingernail polish matching her eyeshadow and lipstick. Having no choice, I wait, shifting my gaze from her hand to her face.

She holds her hand out at her side and listens. Fein's cries seem to echo through the base, and I realize *that* is what she is listening to, with her eyes looking up at the sky and a smirk on her mouth—pleased by the tormented sound. Fein sobs, and Arletta lowers her hand. "Okay...now." She gently pulls my wrist back in place and taps the barrel of my gun. Smiling, she steps back and nods.

I'm sorry, Fein. I pull the trigger. She falls like her brother. I lower my gun. Before I stand at attention, I look back and forth to Floyd and Fein, giving them a moment of silence.

Richard, Arletta, and the Premier pat my back, saying, "Good job, Kylie," as they pass me and walk to their white truck. Their hands are like weights smacking down on my body. I don't acknowledge them, keeping my gaze pinned on the peak of a mountain in the distance.

I finally look away when Richard orders the Creations standing at attention by the general's door to get the bodies and throw them in the back of their truck, and then informs us they will be leaving.

Jord steps to my side, grabbing my shoulder. "You did what you had to do." He squeezes my shoulder before he walks away.

I replace my gun. My movements are slow, but I keep my stance strong while still in everyone's presence. Luke comes to me, grabbing my head and places his forehead to the side of mine. He says in my ear, "Ky, don't let your discomfort show." He lets me go and turns to our groups. "As you all were." Most of them quickly disperse, but some take a minute out of shock.

With my head held high, I wipe the sweat from my brows. Marshal runs to me as I head for the rec hall. "It sucks we had to get rid of a friend," he says. "If they were working for them, they weren't our friends anyway."

"Right," I say with a plastered smile, rubbing my hands over my head. We walk into the mess hall, and he goes to his table. I find mine, accompanied by Luke, shortly thereafter.

I sit next to Marc and lay my head against his shoulder. *Deep breaths*, I tell myself. I take four before the discomfort is gone. He grabs my hand and pulls me to leave with him.

We stroll away, and by the time he speaks, I'm feeling better. "What's wrong?" he asks.

"How can you tell something is wrong?"

"This feeling you're giving off, and you're quiet and resting against me with everyone around." He shrugs. "You're sad."

"I had to execute Fein and Floyd."

He stops abruptly. "Why?" he asks with an edge of surprise raising his voice an octave.

I suck in a jagged breath. "The Premier and Guidance were here while Marshal caught her reaching out to the outsiders."

Marc's head droops forward. "Damn."

"Exactly." I grab the shoulder straps of my vest as I throw a glance to the sky. "They told me *good job*."

He crinkles his nose. "I mean. If they weren't your friends, you would feel the same way, Ky."

"Yeah." I shrug. "I guess. But I'm fine now. It's just that I didn't want to be the one tasked with killing them."

He pulls me in front of him when we get behind a house. "You want me to hug you?"

I hug him, hating that our vests separate us.

"Let's go. We have training," he says, pulling me with him to head back. "Sean may be pretty upset, but we don't have a choice in anything, Ky. Anyone willing to risk being caught didn't deserve your mercy."

"Okay, *Luke*. I don't need the big brother talk right now. I just needed a minute."

Marc pats my back. "You don't have time to take a moment.

Get back to work. Pretend it doesn't bother you." He brushes his knuckles across my cheek and says, "We'll talk it out later tonight," before jogging off to his responsibilities.

CHAPTER TWENTY-FOUR

"WORK ON YOUR POSTURE, Non-Creations. Shoulders back, spine straight, head held high, face even," I yell to my group while they charge through the open field, warming up by running suicides.

They're all too afraid to address me, and each of them are quick to follow orders without complaining. They know how close Fein and I were, and some of them are probably scared I'll shoot them since I didn't hesitate to execute a friend.

"Now practice combat, turn to the person beside you, left to right." I'm deflated; I can't take anymore. "Practice that, combat moves in war against other humans." I sit on the floor. Fein falling to the ground replays in my mind like a scene from a movie. It would have been better if it were Collins. I could put a bullet through her head without a second thought.

Danny comes over. "I don't have a partner. Come on." He extends his hand to help me from the floor. I take it.

Time flies, and before I know it, the lunch bell's ringing.

"Floyd and Fein were implants?" Collins says, shocked, stirring her soup. "Serves them right to get shot down."

"Shut up, Collins," Sean orders in a stern tone.

"Don't get upset with me for expressing my feelings because your *girlfriend* got shot down by Kylie."

"He said shut up, Collins," I snap. I will have no problem stabbing her with my fork today.

"You shut up, Kylie. You're the one who shot them. Wasn't she *your* friend?"

"Ky, you try to break her nose this time," Sean begins. "I won't stop you."

She smiles. "Marc will stop her."

"No, I won't." Marc responds, stuffing a piece of bread into his mouth.

"No one at this table will stop her, but your sister," Luke adds. "And she'll only be able to stop her if she can make it through us."

I drop my fork, ready to throw my fist across the table. "I'm just playing, Kylie." Collins laughs me off. "I'm not serious, Sean. Fein was a nice friend to all of us, but her being an implant voids that. Each of you should feel the same way."

Seits comes in and clears her throat. "We are taking volunteers for tonight's sweep." Collins stands along with a few others. They gather by Seits, and the bell dongs, calling the end of lunch.

After lunch, I make my group run the obstacle course. They go four against Gia's group until everyone has run it. Because my group is oddly numbered, Danny sits out of training. He requested to show his improvement in combat. He's been working hard to get my recommendation for the male leadership position of our division. I make myself available when he wants to practice or wants extra training.

"Like this." He maneuvers himself, grabbing my arm, pulling it roughly around my neck.

I quickly get out of his maneuver, spinning around and getting him in a headlock with his arm pinned behind his back. I knee him in his spine, dropping him to his knees.

"I guess not," he utters.

I let him go. "Nope."

He stands, stretching his arms. "I know how to street fight. Not all these combat moves."

"The combat moves help you when going against a street fighter. You know things they don't. Understanding pressure points, smaller bones that, when broken, can affect your enemy as if they were bigger ones. It gives you an upper hand in a brawl."

He nods and swings at me. I block it, not catching him swiping his leg under mine, knocking me off my feet. With his hands around my throat, he holds me down. "I got you, right?" He smiles.

I could get out of this easily by using a number of maneuvers with my legs or my free arms, which he's neglected to hold down, but I'll give him this one because he did catch me off guard. "Yes." He lets me go. "Remember, when you pin someone down, you want to make sure you block off their defenses too. What if I'd have a knife in my hand? My hands were free to stab you."

"I see," he thinks. "Let's go again."

Fighting with Danny, Gia, and the rest of our group, racing each other on the course, takes up the rest of the day. My group has grown to enjoy the course, and I love ending a day without hearing their complaining. "Great job today, everybody. Get some rest, and we'll pick it back up tomorrow."

After dinner and a shower, I go to Luke's room. "You're sleeping here?"

"Yeah, I'll let Marc miss me. And keep you company."

"You found a way to get rid of your nightmares, and you still won't sleep by yourself."

I shrug. "That was only once. I don't know if that will work all the time, or if all time, I'll dream about him. And maybe I'm not comfortable sleeping by myself. I had to perform an execution today for two of my friends. I might dream of fighting the Guidance, yelling at them for making me kill them."

"They were stupid for contacting them here, right now, and having knowledge of the suspicions circling the Creations. You warned her, right?"

"Of course. How are we going to find out when the Vojin will attack if we won't be able to reach out to them?"

"We won't. They may have extra security now. We can't call out to them."

"No, we can't."

"I'm going to address the general tomorrow. I could be risking it, but I think I'll have a good approach. I'm going to ask when we are with Harold. I know for a fact Harold is mixed. But like us, he's turned from them."

I lie on my back, looking around Luke's dark room. "You want to hear something funny?"

"Sure."

"If we were to talk to them, and they knew our change of heart, they would call us the traitors and the snakes."

He snorts. "They would..."

I turn my head to Luke's arm, preparing to sleep. It hits me. "Harold? Why, specifically, ask Jord in front of him?"

"Because Jord seems to be less of a person around him. He's weak and abides by whatever Harold says. I might talk to Harold first, *then* I'll talk to Jord." His shoulder shrugs against my forehead. "I'll make up some story about why I assume, or how I found out."

"What if the Vojin's plan is to attack before we can?"

He shrugs again. "I don't think it is. With them, everything is strategic. They have to make sure everything is in order before execution."

"It would have been nice if we had found out why Fein was trying to contact them. What was so important she needed to reach out in the middle of the day?" A soft knock sounds against Luke's door as a girl's small voice calls his name. "Isn't it a little late for this, Luke?"

"It is, and they know not to come here after hours, or at night, with the Zombies walking around." He gets up and goes to his door.

I may as well leave because he's probably going to let her in. I sit up as she says, "They'll come for me," voice trembling. "They are going to find out about me and come for me." She shoves past him, barging into his room. Her gaze lands on me, and she clamps her hand over her mouth.

"You might want to check your surroundings before you speak," I tell her, lips pursed as I give her a lazy gaze. I don't know her name, but I've seen her around. "She's a dense one, Luke. There wasn't a riper tomato in the garden?"

"Hold on, Ky," Luke closes his door. "What are you talking about, Virginia?"

Her brown curls whip about with how aggressively she shakes her head and jabs a finger in my direction. "She's the one who will do it. Why is she in your room?"

"First of all, who doesn't know that she is my twin? Second, anything that you are going to tell me about, apart from our sex activities and intimate talks, I'm going to tell her anyway. Now, what is it? Or it can wait 'til tomorrow."

Nervously crossing her trembling arms in front of her chest, she sucks in a shaky breath. I've never seen someone so scared to talk in my life. It's almost comical. "They are coming after the implants," she whispers.

"You are saying you are one?" Luke asks carefully, words drawling out with an edge of skepticism.

"And she," she averts her gaze from me, "is going to kill me."

"As scared as you are about getting caught, how are you even an implant?" he questions, chuckling. "The two that got executed today went out with pride. They didn't whimper like you are doing. Not to mention you just revealed yourself to the female lead captain of this division."

She throws her hands over her mouth and says, "Don't tell anyone, please."

"What made you come and tell me?"

"I can trust you." She grabs his shirt and drops to her knees. "Please," she cries, "I *can* trust you, right? You and your twin? Please, Luke. Don't let them kill me."

I roll my eyes and scoot off the bed. "See you in the AM., Luke," I say. "Make sure she's dead before dawn," I order, walking to the door. "Or I'll become *her biggest fear*," I sing spookily, slowly pulling the door open. "I'll be back to kill her before the sun rises."

She gulps. "Huh?"

"She's not serious," Luke laughs, closing the door behind me.

I could go to my room and lie in my bed, but I won't. Not with Fein still on my mind. I cross the hall to Marc's room. I knock. There is no answer, and I knock again. Because Collins wants to just up and walk in his room now, I've started knocking.

Raspier than usual, Marc asks, "Who is it?" I tap on his door. "Come in." He's lying on his bed. When I walk in, he turns from his stomach to his back. "What's wrong?"

"Luke kicked me out for some girl."

"Are you going to go to sleep or hold the door and wait for him to be finished?"

"Finished with what?"

He chuckles manly-like. "*Talking,*" he says with a sly edge to his voice.

"No, I'm not going to hold the door."

He yawns loudly, turning back on to his stomach. "Lie down then." He scoots from the middle of his bed and pats the now empty space. "So we can sleep."

CHAPTER TWENTY-FIVE

"Okay, there are some things we need to work on today," I tell my group. "We will work on target practice. We will work on posture. We will work on your fighting skills. We will also work on your—for the Normals—ability to kill." We stand in the middle of the empty field, and I take in a large group of Normals and Creations, deciding how I'm going to divvy them up into smaller teams.

They stare at me, brows knit, corners of their mouths turned down, and remorse in their color-filled eyes. I hate these expressions they wear: concern, remorse, dejection. Everyone here has tormented me with these side-eye expressions today, and it's making me want to find a dark corner to escape them. "What?" I blurt. "What the hell is it?"

Many heads shake as they look away from me. Danny steps forward. "Everyone's a little intimidated by you, Ky."

I look around at them all. The thought of comforting them, offering kindness, and reassurance floats around in my mind. We must discuss their concerns. "Okay, is there something any of you would like to talk about? Something you all would like for me to address?"

"I do," says Brandy.

Brandy does not speak out, and I only pay attention to her when I give her direct instructions or training. Her brown skin compliments her amber eyes and ginger hair that reaches her butt. She's quite skinny and complains most when weight training. She does, however, take instructions well. "What's your question, Brandy?"

She clears her throat, and people move from standing in front of her. "Fein was your friend. You showed none of that when you were ordered to kill her. How were you able to do that?" she asks. She stalls before adding, "And can you teach me?"

Shocked, I stare at her momentarily. I knew this would be a discussion about what happened, but I was not expecting a request for training in how I was able to keep a straight face and boldly pull the trigger of my gun and watch Fein, my friend, fall lifeless.

I look over everyone before responding. No one is shaking their heads. No one is looking at Brandy like she has requested something out of the ordinary. They are all content with her request and seem to want the same. Loudly, I ask, "Is this something you all have discussed?"

"Yes," many say and others nod.

I'm struck silent, proud of my team. "I honestly cannot believe this is my team standing before me, requesting this." Enthused by my actions and wanting to copy me. My team is not that strong, and yet, here they are. "Okay," I agree, not yet sure of my next words, shock and joy stealing my thoughts. I bow my head to hide my smile. Looking back at them, I ask, "Who are you people?" I smile wider. "When did you all gain courage and dignity? This is something you *all* are seeking. You all want that strength?"

"Yes. Yeah. Uh-huh," they all respond with head nods and small shrugs.

Maybe the expressions I've been seeing today weren't resentment or dissatisfaction, but envy.

"Wow," I state profoundly, crossing my arms in front of my chest. "Seriously *wow*." I look them over again. I'm excited and proud. I've done a good job. "Okay, let's do this." I walk back and forth in front of them, deciding where we will start. "First, there's courage. What is courage?" I ask rhetorically. "Courage is the quality of mind or spirit that enables a person to face difficulties, dangers, pain...*anything* without fear. Courage is bravery, being able to stand against anything regardless of the outcome." I breathe, thinking of Edward. "Courage is being able to accept what has come upon you, weigh your options, and understand even if it is the worst option...it still must be followed through." I meet Edward's gaze. "Can you step forward, Edward?" He does. "Edward showed he has an abundant amount of courage the day I saw him end his twin. That," I shake my head in discomfort, not sure if even *I* could do that, "had to be hard for him. But for Edward, there was only one option. What made him courageous is not that he knew his twin had to die, but that he was able to take the gun and kill him himself." I gesture for him to step back with a sweeping motion. "How many of you can say you can end the life of someone you care about?" I ask, reflecting on this.

If Luke were to get infected, I *could* shoot him to end his misery. Luke would never want to be a Zombie, and I wouldn't want him to be either. It's only right to kill him. Then there is Marc. If Marc was to turn, thinking about it now... I *may* not be able to do it. I couldn't stand over him, look into his eyes, and pull my trigger.

I would, instead, take the bite, take his attack...and turn with him.

Rubbing my hand over my head, I shake away the thoughts. That sounds so stupid and ridiculous. "It is different for those of you who are not Creations. Those of us who *are* Creations, we appear to be bothered by nothing, but when it comes to our twins, believe me when I tell you, we can be weak." I stall, recalling the bridge and Luke's anger with me and his display of weakness. Then I think of Edward's display of strength compared to Megan's lack thereof. "If someone can hold their hurt and push out their pride when dealing with their twin, or with someone they care about, that is courageous. That is what you all need to learn how to do."

"How?" a female asks. I still don't know all their voices well enough.

"First, you have to remember fear is in your mind." I press my index finger to my temple. "If you don't think it, it doesn't exist."

"How do we eliminate fear?" Brandy asks.

"You have to change your way of thinking." That is easier said than done. I look for a better explanation. "It may not be simple, considering you all have gone seventeen to eighteen years conditioned in your current mindset. But if you can overcome your way of thinking when it comes to your fears, that is equally beneficial. Tell yourself that you are strong, convince yourself that you can do anything, and just...jump."

They nod. I try to think of ways to teach them to manage their fears and understand them. We would first need to discuss them and then work on ways to overcome them.

"Did you feel anything, Ky, when you did it?" Another girl asks.

"Who said that?" I ask.

"Me." Kendra steps forward. "Should I not have asked?" Her shoulders draw forward as her frame shrinks. "We just figured that since you are our leader, you would share things with us. To help us. Ky, a lot of us *are* scared. Maybe not the Creations, but Non-Creations. We fear what's out there: implants, walking dead, Creations dying. Our world is in danger. It's a lot for us to accept. We are supposed to fight in the war against other people like us, not things we know nothing about."

"I understand. This is why we are working so hard to train you. It's why we're *still* training you."

Kendra interjects. "How do you train for something like this? It seems like you all don't even fully understand what we're up against."

She is partially right. "They're conducting studies so we can better understand—"

She cuts me off again, quizzing, "Can Non-Creations be implants?"

This question triggers an accusatory thought. But maybe it's all still related to Fein. "Why do you ask?"

"Well, if Creations can be, why wouldn't Non-Creations be as well?"

I shrug. "I don't know what requirements outsiders look for in a Creation or Non-Creation."

Kendra's upper lip curls as she aggressively interrogates me. "What *do* you know, Kylie?" she says with a snarl.

My brows furrow. I move my hands behind my back, holding my anger together by clutching the handle of my pistol tightly between my hands. She's challenging me. But why? "Are you an implant, Kendra?" I ask calmly, then I straighten, stretching my neck left then right to remove the tension.

She glares at me as her left brow hitches. Her eyes narrow, and for some odd reason, I sense her telling me yes. I grow impatient waiting on her response. "No," she answers in a harsh tone.

I doubt it. I draw my gun and step to her. My barrel presses against her forehead, just between her eyebrows. She keeps eye contact with me, not a glimpse of fear in her eyes. I ask again, "*Are* you an implant, Kendra?" Her silence is revealing, and the group and I wait for her answer. I pull my gun away an inch to cock it back before pressing it back against her skin.

Her eyes widen and twitch, revealing a glimpse of fear. "N-No," she stutters.

"You better not be," I say low for only her to hear. "And the next time you're asked, being hesitant to answer may get you killed." I gently tap her temple with the barrel of the gun. "Never test me again, Kendra." Taking a few steps back, I order, "Enough Q and A. Get back to business. Creations, do your worst."

CHAPTER TWENTY-SIX

AFTER BATTLING ROUNDS, Normals versus Creations, my group closes the day in the weight room, building their strength and endurance. Both will help in the war against Zombies, may it be fighting or just running from them.

I head to Jord's office hoping, to get some answers to a few questions about Normals being implanted. Luke left with him earlier, and they should be back by now. I knock twice and wait for an answer. The lock turns, and Seits opens the door, "Hi Ky."

I keep my face even, but ever since she turned me into a Zombie, her presence has made me uncomfortable. "Hello. I was looking for General Jord, is he here?"

"He's out with a few of the leaders. Can I help you with something?"

I shake my head. "I'll come back later. Thank you." I pivot, and she grabs my shoulder. Looking at her hand first, then at her eyes, I ask, "Is there something you would like to discuss?"

"Can you step into the office?"

I move my arm from her hand, debating speaking with her or not. I'd prefer not. Though she may have been obligated to follow orders from the Trade, it would be fair to provide a warning. "I'm headed to the rec hall." I give her an ultimatum. "Would you like to walk with me there and speak?"

"You would prefer this?"

"I would. I'm not comfortable speaking with you." I'm not afraid of her. I just don't have respect for her. However, I don't want to be bad-mannered as I respect her position. I also know myself, and if she tries to do something to me again, I will kill her.

She nods slowly, agreeing. I turn on my heels and step off the stoop. At my side as we stroll, Seits says, "You can also speak with me, Ky, about any questions or concerns you may have. Both Jord and I are available."

"I understand." Is my simple response. "Have you seen Luke?"

"He left with Jord. Are you okay, Kylie? You performed an execution yesterday for one of your good friends here."

Responding as a Creation would, I say, "She was not my friend. Feiney was an implant, and that voids any relationship and concern I had for her. She got what was coming to her." But I would prefer to say, '*I did, and it upsets me she would leave herself exposed to get found out and force me to perform that execution,*' though I cannot.

"Do you *honestly* feel that way, Kylie?" She stops and grabs my arm, so I stop too.

I drop my gaze to my grasped arm and then meet her eyes. "Please." She releases me, and her hands fall at her sides. "Yes. I do *honestly,*" I mock the word as she spoke it quaintly, "feel this way. You don't?"

"I feel that we lost someone, and she may have deserved a better way to be expunged."

I turn to continue. "You should talk to Sir Jord about that. It was his choice for execution over saving her."

"Excuse me?" she gasps in a bewildered tone.

I wasn't looking at her before, but I am now. Her piercing

purple eyes radiate, brightening and dimming as though they beat with her heart. *Why is this news shocking?* "Arletta asked him if he needed any test subjects of implanted Creations. He declined and ordered Fein and Floyd's execution. What is the problem?"

She quickly shakes her head. "There...there is no problem. I thought the execution was the only option."

"After he said he didn't need them, it was. But I suppose if he'd said he would use them for tests, they may have let them leave and escorted them to the underground labs, which you are well acquainted with."

Slowly, she begins, "Kylie, I am sorry about what happened. I cannot stress that enough. I knew they were going to turn you into the walking dead. It is a part of the tests. But I could not warn you. They would have known by your reactions."

"Madam Seits, it no longer matters. If you will excuse me, I'm going to eat dinner."

"Yes, Ky. One more thing." She takes my shoulders in her strong grip, fingers pressed firmly against my muscles. Looking at me head on, she says, "A coyote doesn't just howl to call its pack...but to also warn them of intruders."

Though my lips are parted, my gasp is silent.

"Hey Ky!" Sean calls, distracting me from Seits's shocking reveal. She walks away and doesn't look back. "Ky," Sean calls again, now beside me.

We were right...

"Earth to, Ky!" Sean shoves me against my shoulder.

I blink. "What?"

"What's wrong?"

I shake my hands, trying to remove this disturbing sensation crawling over my flesh as though her words have legs. "Nothing."

"Have you seen Marc?"

"No, why?"

"I haven't seen him. I checked with his group. They haven't seen him for the past two hours." His arms splay out before falling limply at his sides as he says, "It's dinnertime, and no one seems to know where he is."

"He may be with Luke and Jord. They are checking on the other leaders of our sector."

He knits his brows. "How'd you find that out?"

"Seits told me. You're worried?"

He heads for the doors of the mess hall, and I follow behind him. "Yeah. He may have gotten eaten by a Zombie or turned into one."

I drop a pat on his shoulder. "Marc's a big boy. He can handle a few Zombies. He's fine."

Sean shoves the doors open. "We have to go in here and sit with annoying-ass Collins. I do not like her. You should have cracked her in the face last night."

"I wanted to. You know, since yesterday, everyone has been acting weird. They either fear or envy me. I don't know what to make of it."

"That has to be the Normals you're talking about. My group wanted to talk about it. I kept the conversation short and explained you did what was ordered. If you had refused that order, everyone would have assumed that you couldn't rid us of an implant because you are one, and you would have been lying there right along with them."

I nod, agreeing. "My team asked me to explain how I could effortlessly kill a friend. I told them they'd need courage in the face of fear. We tell our twins that if we get turned into one of those things to kill us, but do we mean that? We know that we would prefer there be a cure. But there is none, so our escape is death. Think of the pressure we are putting on our twin."

"I really meant for Marc to kill me."

"But instead..."

"Right. He found another option. But if there was no other option, I know he would do it. What about you? If it were you and Marc. Would you kill him?" Sean's question catches me by the legs, and I stumble forward. I grab Sean's arm to catch myself from falling.

Regaining my footing, I clear my throat. "Why do you ask?"

"He's my twin. He chose you over me. I'm trying not to feel uncomfortable about it." Sean rubs the back of his neck. "The way I cope is by talking about what bothers me. I don't understand you two. I get that you all feel a *way* about each other, but you can't feel for him what he feels for you. It's impossible."

"This isn't easy for me to discuss, Sean." I don't want to talk about Marc and me with him. Sometimes I don't want to talk about Marc and me with Luke. I actually *only* want to talk about Marc and me with Marc. He's the only one that matters.

Sean pulls me to a stop. I don't like the way it feels when someone forces me to do something. "Just let me know, Ky. You would still choose Luke over Marc? We know Marc's choice, but yours is still a mystery, so tell me. And don't lead my brother on. If you know there is a difference in your feelings and his, don't keep leading him on and making him think this is something that it's not. I'm not going to stand out on a plank with you and wonder which one of us he'll push or save." There's an edge to each word. His anger, though light, seems all the more violent because it's rarely ever displayed.

"Sean." I pry his hand from my left arm. "You know how I feel about him. You knew before he knew. There are things I am obligated to say. But we know–"

I'm slapped on the back. "Hey, what are you two talking about?" Luke asks.

"Luke, was Marc with you?" Sean asks him before I can answer Luke's question.

"Earlier, but not recently. When I left him, he was headed to the house."

"Couldn't have been? I just left there before meeting Ky. He wasn't there." He throws his head back and pulls his hair in a ponytail. "Where the hell is my brother?" he asks himself and leaves the mess hall.

"Hey," I say as I bump Luke's fist with mine. "We weren't talking about anything. He was trying to find Marc. What happened today?"

"Let's eat first, we'll talk later." Hopefully, Luke learned some things today too.

CHAPTER TWENTY-SEVEN

Luke and I sit at our usual table, preparing to eat when Jord loudly calls, "Kylie," from the door of the mess hall.

I jump up from my seat, startled by the aggressiveness of his call. "Sir?"

"I need to speak with you." I nod and cross the mess hall, Luke hot on my heels. "You are not needed, Luke. As you were," Jord says, dismissing him.

"Yes, I am." Luke says in a stern tone, glaring at Jord, daring to tell him no again. "When you are uncomfortable with tasks your sister is up against, do you accompany her?" Luke nods once, answering for Jord. "And I will do the same for mine."

Jord's jaw works, and he narrows his eyes as he glares at Luke. Luke doesn't bat an eye, meeting Jord's silent challenge by not backing down. I wince when Jord's lips part, expecting an accusing shout toward Luke. But he licks his lips, nods, and leads us from the mess hall.

I look at Luke and mouth, "What the heck was that?"

Luke widens his eyes and shrugs. A small smirk lifts the left corner of his mouth. It's gone by the time we make it outside and continue behind Jord to his office.

"You wanted to speak with me, Kylie?" Jord asks.

I sigh, happy he wasn't requesting me for something worse. "Yes, someone from my team said something odd today. I wanted to ask you about Normals being implants."

"Was this asked in front of your entire group?"

"Yes, sir."

Jord looks at Luke, then around us. "Let's talk about this in my office." Once we walk into his office, and he closes the door, he says, "Luke, would you like to inform Kylie of our talk today?"

I tug off my helmet and tuck it under my arm.

"I was going to later," Luke says. "But if you would like for me to do it now, I can." Jord nods. Luke faces me and easily says, "General Jord, Madam Seits, and Colonel Harold are implants. And yes, the Normals can also be implants."

I'm holding my breath as I bite back my words. First, I can't respond. I look at Jord, observing his straight face and relaxed disposition. He reclines on his chair with his left leg crossed over his right and clasped hands resting above his belt. Luke also wears a straight face. I'm silenced. *How should I respond?*

Luke continues, "They have this idea that the Vojin want to destroy the Earth, and they want to stop them." I nod. "They have asked if we will accompany them in overpowering the Vojin and fight for our world."

I purse my lips and narrow my eyes, asking, "What was your response?" I am unsure of what to say, not being able to ask the questions I want to, questions about us also having the same plan.

"I haven't responded yet."

I ask Jord, "Why tell him this? Why release to us the worst of your secrets?"

He stands from his chair, slowly walks around his desk, and leans his hip against it. "We need Creations who are strong and want to save the world." He looks between Luke and me. "We also need Creations who are mixed and may have a reason to go against the ones they previously worked for. To get revenge. Possibly for..." he carries the word in thought, "killing their parents."

What the hell did I walk into right now?

I flick my gaze to Luke. I think my facial expression has faltered; the poker face usually keeping my skin smooth has failed. My cheeks feel tight, and my eyebrows may have reached my hairline.

Jord continues, "I am not asking anything but for you all to fight with us, invade their realm, and assist us in defeating them. Can I rely on you two to do that?"

"We will be back with our response," Luke tells him. He nods his head toward the door, motioning for us to leave.

"Before you go, understand there are others here who are mixed. They do not know about the Vojin's deception, and they are still working toward gaining other Creations to fight with them to overcome this world."

We leave his office and the screen door slams behind us. Walking to our house, we hurry across the dirt road, kicking up dust with every step. "What just happened, Luke?"

"Ky...I don't know."

"Are we going to help?"

"Yes."

"Are you going to tell him?"

"Not yet." He opens the door to our home, and someone is talking from upstairs. Luke puts his finger to his lips.

I hear Cory saying, "They are planning to come in two weeks to take over this planet, and we need to have enough people on our side so that we can convince everyone else to welcome them here."

Luke and I creep toward the stairs to hear them better.

Collins says, "Cory, that's not a good idea. Who would we

convince? You saw what they did to Floyd and Fein. If we are found out, that will be us too."

Ooh... I am going to say something. I want to see the look on Collins face when she sees that I know her secret. Then, with my gun pointed between her eyes, I want her to beg me not to say anything.

Looking at Luke, I open my mouth to speak. He nods for me to go ahead.

I smile, stepping to the foot of the stairs, able to see Cory and Collins in the hallway upstairs. "Found out about what, Collins?" I ask loudly, slowly climbing the stairs with Luke behind me.

She sucks in her breath and glares at me. "How long have you been standing down there?"

"Long enough."

"Kylie–" Cory starts.

I quickly cut him off. "Don't you speak to me," I say, pointing my finger at him. "I will still break your nose." Dropping my hand, I look back at Collins. "You all can finish your talk. I'm going to talk to the general." I turn around, and my arm is yanked, turning me back.

"You better say nothing, Ky," Collins threatens.

I push her away from me. "And if I do? What are you going to do about it?"

"Kylie, you don't have to say anything." Cory adds in his two cents no one asked for.

I rush him and draw my fist back. Collins pulls me back. "You don't have to say anything, Kylie."

Luke pushes her back. "Don't touch my sister. No one cares about your life, Collins. We will bring forth all traitors and execute them. We can do it here or tell the general first, and if he has instructions, we'll follow those. You know the rules, there are no exceptions."

"After the things we've done, Luke, you will have me executed?"

"We did nothing, Collins. You were just a contender who wanted me to bone her. Don't use our history to save your life. It makes you sound pathetic."

That was disrespectful.

Collins smacks Luke across the face. What Luke said was mean, and he deserved to get smacked, but I will not allow *Collins* to hit my brother and have no reaction.

I punch her with my left fist. She quickly retaliates, and we brawl before we're pulled away from each other. "What is your problem, Kylie?" she shouts, trying to break out of Cory's hold on her.

I shake out my arm. "Come on, Luke," I grab his arm.

"Ky, don't do this," Cory says to our backs as we walk down the stairs. "If you two calm down for a minute, I know we can talk about this. You can't extend courtesy to one and not the other."

I look at Luke. "We'll talk when we get back outside," he tells me.

"Come on, Ky, don't be a bitch about this," Collins yells to us as we near the door. "And Luke, even though you are being a total dick in front of your sister, I know you don't want to do this."

"Shut up, Collins," I yell back.

They run down the stairs once we reach the door. "Wait! Seriously, Ky," Cory says.

Marc, Sean, Gia, and Cecilia walk through the door taking in the four of us. "What's happening?" Cecilia asks.

"Ky and Luke were just headed back to the rec hall with us, we're late for dinner and needed to talk," Cory responds.

Marc grabs my arms as he pushes me backward in the direction of the kitchen. "What were you and him going to talk about?" he asks once we make it out of hearing distance.

I shake my head. "He's just trying to cover something up." Roughly rubbing my hand across my forehead, I try to ease the forming headache. "Where were you at dinner?" I grab his forearms. His hands are still wrapped around my arms.

"I was with my group in their rec hall. Why?"

I hitch a brow, taken aback by his lie, but I won't dig into it as there are other pressing matters. "Just asking. I didn't see you is all."

He licks his lips, and a small smirk steals his serious expression. "And you expected to?"

I smile shyly. "Maybe."

"Um-hum." He leans forward and kisses me. Marc's kisses sink me into short-lived oblivion. Short-lived because he always breaks away too quickly, and my lips can't stay placed against his forever.

When he leans back, I lean forward, not letting his lips part from mine. His mouth smiles against mine. I break away, wanting to witness it. I match its brightness. "I wasn't ready for you to leave yet."

Going back in for another kiss, he stops, and his smile fades when he looks to the opening of the kitchen. Cory walks in. "Can we talk?" he asks.

"Never," I respond. "And if you continue to talk to me, I'm going to reintroduce my fist to your face."

"Get over yourself, Kylie," Collins comes to his side, standing in the doorway. "Hey Marc."

She's pushing her luck. Marc kisses my neck before he says, "I'll find you later." He leaves us and heads away to the shower stalls.

I cross my arms and ask, "What, Collins?"

"We are supposed to be friends, remember, Ky?" she whispers. "I am not what you think. He is," she points to Cory, "and he wants me to help convince others to help him."

I walk away from her to find Luke. He's standing by the front door, talking to Sean and Gia. "Luke, let's go on a sweep."

"Me and Collins will go with you," Cecilia says from behind me.

I shrug and pull Luke to leave the house. The night sweep is the last thing I want to do, but I also don't want to be crowded in our home with Cory and Collins trying to convince me of their lies.

CHAPTER TWENTY-EIGHT

LATELY, on my night sweeps, there haven't been any Zombie attacks. I'm not complaining. I hate Zombie-hunting in the sweltering desert for miles. My mind is bogged down with so much, though. I can't concentrate on even keeping my steps ordered.

"Let's head back," Luke says.

"Great," I cheer under my breath.

The four of us check our surroundings before heading for the base. "Ky," Collins calls.

She goes unanswered as I head back.

"Ky, we should talk about what happened. The four of us, before we get back to our corridors."

"Collins," Luke begins. "We heard what we heard. If this is your way of requesting our silence, you should try a little harder."

"I'm never begging Ky for anything. I deserve your respect and dammit, you're going to give it to me," she snaps, a demanding edge in her tone.

I stop. My gun weighs heavier in my hand. Without the thought crossing my mind, I twist around, gun raised. My barrel is at Collins's head. I'm not even aware I crossed the ground to her. "I could just execute you right now, Collins."

"You could, Ky, but then what will happen if they," she points to the sky, "find out you killed me? They'll come down here for you."

"I'll blow their heads off too," I say, never breaking eye contact. My finger twitches, and I'm itching to pull the trigger. *I want to put a hole in her head so badly.*

She pushes my gun from her face. "Ky, I'm not one of them, I promise. Me or Cecilia. We are full Creations. You know how much I hate traitors."

I survey her. "Why were you associating with one if you hate traitors?"

"Why were you?"

Oohh, she's got me.

Collins purses her lips and quips, "Cat got your tongue, Ky?"

I bite into my left cheek to manage my anger and not slap her with my pistol. Admitting defeat, I nod. "That is accurate. But we weren't siding with the enemy. Didn't you say something about convincing others to help? That sounds like something a snake would do."

"We could point the finger all night, Ky. Let's be adults and let bygones be bygones. I'm not a traitor, and I'm not a snake. I'm trying to find out what Cory's plan is because you have been ignoring his obvious signs of being a traitor."

I look at Luke. "How *not* true is that statement?"

"It's getting late. Let's head back. Besides, we have other things we need to discuss." Luke turns, and I follow. "And by the way, Collins, you may not be a snake or a traitor, but you are definitely a slut. Remember that."

I bump Luke's arm with my elbow. "Why are you being so vulgar tonight? You are usually a little more respectful than that."

A shotgun clicks and fires. Luke jolts forward, face-planting in the dirt. I lurch forward, searching his body, sighing with relief at finding the slug caught in his vest.

I fire at Collins before I look her direction. When I do turn to her, the shotgun is falling from her hands. My next shot hits Collins between the eyes. Her head jerks back as her body falls backward. Cecilia snatches up her hand as she falls. She shouts, "Ky! You could have killed her."

"Shit," I mutter, disappointed. *Apparently, I didn't kill her.* "I wanted to though, that's the reason I shot her in the face."

As she heals Collins, I turn back to Luke. "Are you okay?" He climbs to his feet.

"Yes. You think you shot her enough times?"

I kick dirt, grumping, "No. She's still alive."

He cracks his neck. "When she gets up, I'm going to bust her lip for shooting me. That shit hurt." His back likely has a bruise the size of a watermelon.

"Honestly, Luke, I don't like Collins, but you deserved to get shot because of what you said."

He blows me off, waving his hand in my face.

"Let it go, Luke. If someone had said that to me, they would have gotten shot too."

He reluctantly turns and walks away. "Okay, but when she comes back after you for shooting her in the head, don't expect me to say anything."

I scoff. "I can handle Collins without you. I'm not worried about her retaliation. Just if she shoots me, you better be as fast as Cecilia in healing me. Did you see how fast she jumped for her?"

Luke laughs. "Yeah. I'd grab you that fast too if you were about to die. Let's hurry back to let Jord know we've returned."

"Speaking of Jord, and now that no one is around…" I smack his arm with the back of my hand. "When were you going to tell me that he knows about us?"

He jumps from my attack. "When would I, Ky?"

"*We* know about *them*, and," I carry on, "we *all* want the same thing."

Luke nods. "The five of us seem to want the same thing. But everyone here doesn't."

"I need to know everything, Luke. Before we make it back to his office, tell me *everything*."

We stop before we make it back to the light of the base. "I said I would talk to Harold first, and I did. I told him up front there is something suspicious about him, and I think he and Jord are mixed Creations. He questioned me asking, 'Not implants?' I didn't refer to him as an implant. So I repeated, 'Are you all mixed Creations?' He took off his goggles. I've never seen him without his goggles."

"They're always tinted, and the majority of his face is always blocked off," I cut in.

"Right, so he took them off and stared at me with eyes the same color as ours. But his entire eye was this color and sparkling like the Vojin's particles. He said, 'Yes,' and put his goggles back on, then asked, 'What made you suspect that?' I told him about what we discussed the other night and how we suspected Jord and Seits because of Cory and because of the list and everything else. He nodded and agreed with me. Then he told me about how he, Jord, and Seits are mixed, but they do not work for the Vojin. They're rebellious hosts, and even the Vojin know they're against them. Without care, Harold released all this information.

"Harold is against them because they killed his twin. Like our parents, his brother found out that they had a plan bigger than domination, and he suspected it was only a matter of time before they executed that plan. Harold disagreed with his brother, and when his brother went to confront the Vojin, they murdered him. This was his proof. Jord and Seits are close to Harold. They all grew up together in New York. They were shipped to Arizona for Separation placement when they were younger. When Jord and Seits found out the

Vojin killed Harold's brother, they crossed too, removing their implants."

"How and when did they find out about us and our parents?"

"I don't know, Ky. When you heard it, it was the first time I heard it."

"He knows details."

"What do you want to do?"

"I don't know." I purse my lips. "You're the brains of this operation." I shrug. "I just know I want it to involve killing a lot of Vojin. Me having to reload over and over and over. And us not dying in the process."

"We are probably going to die, Ky. But as long as we go out with pride, avenging our parents, taking out more of them than they do us. Our deaths will count."

"We may make it out alive."

"I hope we do. But if we plan on raiding their home, we will be outnumbered. Logically, there's no way we make it out alive, but let's hope for the best."

"We'll tell Jord we will help but not confirm we're mixed. That'll open too many doors because, technically, that's not the truth. We, the generals, and Harold will raid the Vojin," I strategize, playing out the conversations and the event in my mind. I see Jord nodding and hours later Vojin falling.

Luke grabs his chin between his thumb and index finger, and rubs it before saying, "Jord wants you to convince Marc and Sean to fight against them with us, going up there with us," he says, pointing to the sky. "And I am supposed to be convincing Collins and Cecilia."

"You are off to a great start," I warble sarcastically, lifting my brows high and widening my eyes. There's no way Collins will listen to anything he says now.

Luke snorts. "If I tell Collins to jump off one of those bridges they built, she'll do it. There isn't much convincing needed, no matter how I treat her."

"Why?"

Luke rolls his eyes and starts back for the base. "The same reason Marc has you picking him over me."

Oohh, that is not nice. His words strike me in my back, and I tense from the pain. "I am not picking Marc over you, Luke. I'm–"

"Don't lie to me, Kylie. It's better for you to say nothing at all than to lie to me. We'll do this and succeed in clearing out these Vojin. Maybe the wars will stop now that we have set aside our differences as countries and are working together. Then maybe Separation won't be so intense, and you and him can have each other. Go on a date or something," he says dryly, looking over his shoulder for a second then turning away. He shrugs once.

I know Luke is pissed about Marc, but for some reason, he doesn't display it as I expect him to. When I think of the end of the wars, people coming together, I long to be laughing and talking with Marc at the diner with a shake and a basket of fries. But at what cost? Would it be worth it not to have Separation and war?

———

We walk into Jord's office, and Jord stands, asking, "Did you have enough time to think about it?"

"We did," Luke responds.

"You have decided?"

"Before I give you our answer." Luke pauses. "When we walked into our corridors, Cory was there talking to Collins about the Vojin planning to attack in two weeks. Would you know anything about that?"

Jord crosses his arms, brows knitting. "We were not sure

when they planned to attack. We only knew *we* wanted to attack them first."

"When *are* you planning to attack?" I ask.

He sits back down and looks at a couple of papers on his desk. "The four of us have to travel out to Highrum in the morning. We will set our mission on the Vojin destruction after we return."

"Were you going to wait until the last minute to tell us about this Highrum mission? Why are we going there?" I ask.

"You have *something* better to do than what you're told, Kylie?" he continues, and I zip my lips. "We are required by the Guidance to do so." *They are going to turn all of us into Zombies. I just know it.* "There is a party there in honor of the Premier. We were *cordially* invited. Whatever that means." Luke and I shrug. Why does it matter how you are invited, or what type of invite it is? I don't get it either. "They requested the heads of the sector, which is Seits and me, and my top incoming leaders, which are you two. Arletta seemed to be very impressed with you, Kylie, and when we spoke this morning, she wanted to confirm you and Luke will attend."

"I'm honored," I say with an edge of sarcasm, trying not to roll my eyes. "I mean no disrespect," I quickly follow. I have no problems with the Guidance. We've lived under them forever. If it weren't for their order and instruction, things in the America would probably be worse off. I should actually thank them for creating me. They are the reason Creations exist. But I'm not that generous. "I am honored she's shown a liking in me, sir. I performed as I was born to and deserved the praise I received following orders and executing the implants."

"You are correct, Ky. Be ready at eight hundred hours for our departure. By the way," he lowers his voice. "Ky, Luke is already aware of this. We will also need reinforcements when we go. Those who may not be mixed as well. I suspect you can convince

Marc and Sean to accompany us on this mission, and Luke is expected to convince Collins and Cecilia."

I nod, and we leave his office. When we're far enough away, I say, "Luke, I've already talked to Marc about him helping us."

"Great. What'd he say?" Luke asks, interest piquing as he looks at me with prominent brows.

I scratch my eyebrow and mutter, "I think he's undecided. I'll talk to him again tonight."

Luke grumbles, "Damn, Ky. Is there anything he doesn't know?"

"What's that supposed to mean?"

"Does he know everything that we found out?"

"Almost."

"What the hell, Ky. You'll just tell him everything?"

I shrug. "Yes. What's the problem? He risked his life for me, Luke."

He shakes his head. "Whatever, Kylie. Are you sleeping in my room or his?"

"Yours. I'm going to talk to him for a minute after I shower."

Luke opens the door to our house and walks in without waiting on me. He's disappointed, and I get that. But it's not necessary. I wouldn't pick Marc over Luke.

Correction, it's possible that I *will* pick Marc over Luke. I just hope that I'm never presented with the option.

CHAPTER TWENTY-NINE

AFTER I SHOWER and put my clothes away, I go to Marc's room. Sean is coming out as I'm preparing to knock. "Hey," he greets.

"Hi. Are you coming back?"

"No. I'll finish talking to him in the morning." He leaves the door open so I can walk in.

Closing the door behind me, I watch Marc sit on his bed. He drags his hand down his face and grumbles. "What's wrong?"

He meets my gaze and slightly brightens his expression with the hint of a smile. "Nothing, what's wrong with you?" I study his expression and can't place the feeling, but he lied earlier and is lying now.

"You sure everything is okay, Marc? You seem a little detached."

He nods. "I'm fine, Ky. The days are just weighing on me." He waves me over. "Want to help me out with that?"

Maybe that's true. Our days have been hard on us lately. But Marc's never really bothered by anything. I push past it and cross the floor to stand in front of him. "I'm leaving tomorrow. Maybe for a day or two." Maybe the break will be good. It could be me he's detached from.

"Why? Leaving where?"

I sit beside him. "Luke, Jord, Seits, and I were requested by the Guidance to go to this party for the Premier. Mandatory, something *cordially* invited." I shrug.

"Hmm. Sounds fancy. You're going to wear a dress?"

"Eww. I hope not."

Marc chuckles. "I bet you'd be hot in a dress, Ky."

"Well, thanks."

"Mmm." He lies back on his bed, and I go with him. "One day, we will run away. We'll come back. But we will run away so I can take you on a walk somewhere. I don't know where just yet, but somewhere pleasant, and we'll be uncovered for each other, holding hands and sharing one of your white shakes." I laugh. "Seriously, then we will go eat a Chicago-style hotdog. Though I doubt we'll be in Chicago."

I grab his hand, and he moves his fingers between mine, holding them in the air as he stares at our linked fist.

Smiling, I ask, "Then what?" picturing the event as he speaks.

"After we eat, and I get you smelling like grilled onions, we are going to find a park with trees, those big bushy trees, you know, and plush grass that we can lie on and stare at the sky at night when we can see the stars."

"Are you uncovered for me, Marcain?" I turn on my side to look at him.

"Something like that." He touches my cheek, rubbing his thumb back and forth over my cheekbone. "What did you come in here for?"

"Wanted to talk, to tell you I was leaving, ask you something."

He grazes his fingers from my cheek to my neck as he leans in, but not close enough for him to kiss me. It's not until his eyes shift to my lips that I realize he's waiting on me to meet him.

I lean forward and kiss him deep. The bed under me softens the instant our lips touch. The oxygen in his room thins out, and his hand on my neck becomes heavy. His touch and the feeling of his lips and tongue lightly brushing over mine are all that I am aware of. If I allowed myself to get completely lost in his kiss, I'd probably feel the breeze from the park he envisioned earlier. But I can't. There's a point to my being here, and it's not to indulge in his company. I lean back, touching his hand on my neck and removing it so he can't pull me back to him.

"What?" he asks, moving his hand from mine so it's resting on my waist. "What's wrong?"

I sigh and swallow hard. "I want to ask again...Um..." There's this feeling in the pit of my stomach that this is either going to lead to an argument or rejection. There's not a doubt in my mind that Marc is anything but a Creation and asking him of this didn't go so well last time.

"Spit it out, Ky." He lies on his back, scooting over a bit–away from me.

I sit up, crossing my legs and pulling my hair into a ponytail. My hair lies against my neck, and its weight comforts me. "I need you to go against *them* with me. They have–"

"They who?" he cuts in aggressively.

"Jord."

"Ky, I'm not doing anything with your extended kind. Something here, with you, I'm okay with. But you telling me the other day the general is with Cory and they are working on helping *them* come here and convince Creations to help them..."

I explain everything to Marc, telling him all about Seits and Jord and their plan to inflict damage on the Vojin. "I'm going to do it, but..." I wait for him to look at me. He doesn't, so I lean forward to grab his jaw and turn him to face me. "I've been tasked with asking you and Sean to come with us, and Luke needs to convince Collins and Cecilia."

Shaking his head, Marc grabs my wrist and tugs my hand down. "That's not going to happen, Ky."

"You won't help me?"

"How do you know what they say is true?"

"Honestly, if it is or isn't, Luke and I had that plan anyway. It was going to be the two of us, and we were going to go there and shoot up everything, live or die. But in order for us to be as effective as we want, we will need reinforcements. It took us by surprise to find out about Jord and Seits tonight."

"Why Collins?"

Why Collins, that's his takeaway? I shrug. "Why are we talking about Collins? Who cares why? Because she can shoot a gun, I guess, Marc. You have to trust me, okay? You know I couldn't let anyone cross you or anything hurt you. I would never walk you into danger. Trust me and do this with me."

"You don't have to make me blind promises, Ky. You don't even know what *you* are walking into. You're blinded by revenge, anything to get back at the beings who snatched your parents from you will sound good." He sits up on his elbows. "How do you know that once you get there, Jord and Seits won't ambush you in a setup?"

"I doubt it. But I can't say what will happen when I get there. I can only go off what they say."

"You are blinded by vengeance, Ky."

"So that's a no?"

He stares at me for a moment. "Kylie," he grumbles remorsefully, falling flat on his bed.

I get up, upset he's not as easy to convince as Luke thinks Collins will be. "Don't worry about it," I tell him.

He grabs my waist, pulling me to sit back down. "Don't leave," he says, scooting closer to me. "Okay. I'll talk to Sean. I'll get back to you when you come back."

I look down at him. He grabs my arm and lays a single kiss against it. My shoulders relax, and I sigh. He was great before, but now that we are together and not trying to push each other away, we feel...amazing. *He* feels amazing as he kisses me every few seconds–down my arm to my hand. I shiver; the feel of his soft lips is exhilarating.

Kissing my knuckles, he asks, "Are you staying or are you going?"

"What do you want?"

"We already know the answer to that."

"I don't. I need you to tell me."

"I want you to come here so I can kiss you. And I don't want you to go."

I lean down, close enough not to kiss him, but to feel his breaths wafting over my lips. "I'll kiss you when I come back. And I'm not staying in here. I have to go talk to my brother before we leave in the morning."

"I highly doubt that you will leave this room without kissing me."

I lean away from him and narrow my eyes. "Are you challenging me, Marc?"

"No, I'm stating facts."

"I think it's *you* who can't let me leave without kissing me."

He blinks, looking away from me, then back. "I can't let you leave...without me."

I'm left speechless. "You mean that?" I sound like such a girl. Gentle, feminine, and open with my feelings flooding out of me through my look, my touch, and my kiss. One that I'm sweetly placing against his lips after he nods, answering my question. "I love you so much."

He smiles against my mouth. "I told you, you were going to kiss me."

"Ooo, you're good. And I love your smile."

"I love you without guns, vests, and army suits."

"When we run away, maybe we can find me a dress that stops at my thighs, or a skirt with a shirt that doesn't cover my arms.

Then we can look like a girl and boy on a date. I can even leave my hair down." I could keep my hair down around Marc, knowing he'd look out for both of us, and I wouldn't need to.

"I would love to see you in a dress with your legs out." He pulls me down beside him.

"So a dress?"

"Yes."

"What color?"

"Um. Purple, like my eyes."

"And what will you wear?"

"I want to wear sneakers and whatever you'd prefer to see me in."

"A collared shirt and some fitted jeans that don't sag like I used to see boys wear back home when I saw their underwear."

"Okay. I can do that," he says quickly with a nod.

I smile wide, lying next to him. "Good." *I love this boy.*

Marc and I lie across his bed and stay up talking all night. Talking about everything, talking about nothing like we are regular teenagers. Not the Vojin, not Creations, not Separations, nothing relevant to why we are here. We make up perfect dates we could spend with each other and pretend to have conversations Creations wouldn't admit to having. Our future, the one that doesn't exist. He is completely uncovered. I am uncovered. Our laughter bounces off the walls of his room, and we're warm with comfort, thrilled by a fantasy I only wish would one day be ours.

Then reality strikes. Tomorrow I'll be visiting Highrum for the first time. It's a rarity for any Creation fighter to visit, and I'm nervous. I'll also be around Arletta's ominous demeanor again. I'm not sure yet what it is about her, besides her finding joy in other's suffering, but she gets under my skin.

CHAPTER THIRTY

"You two may want to act like you are excited about being here," Seits says as we get off the plane.

I yawn, dragging my feet to the transport vehicle. "Are we going to a hotel or something? When is the party? And how long do we have to stay there?"

"Stop whining, Ky. It's annoying," Luke says from behind me, walking down the stairs of the plane. "None of us want to be here."

"As I mentioned, you all may want to *at least* look happy about it. Even you, Jord." Jord shrugs. "We have two days here; we are going to a hotel; the party is tomorrow, and we will leave after it is over."

"Why are we here today if the party isn't until tomorrow?" I ask with less of a whine so I won't anger Luke.

Jord throws his duffle bag into the vehicle and crouches to get in. "They want to *talk*."

"Talk about what?" Luke asks, following him in. Seits and I are right behind them.

"We don't know yet," Jord answers.

"Something important," Seits seconds.

*Something important...*Everything here is important.

The moisture in the air is so thick, I try to swat it as I suck in a breath. Coughing, I pull the collar of my shirt over my nose to block off some of the moisture in the air. I'm so used to the dry heat; the oxygen here makes it hard to breathe.

The sun brightens the beauty of Highrum. The skyscrapers and glossy buildings some miles from the landing zone glisten and sparkle like new. If only the other states could be so lucky to look this way. The streets are paved with the country's finest asphalt and concrete—not a bump or pothole flaws the ride. Plush grass and thick trees are so bold and bright the greenery is tempting to eat. As we pass tall buildings and structures, we see Creations cascading from the roofs to clean the bulletproof, tinted windows and storm-gray concrete walls. All the buildings here in Highrum look the same. The only difference separating them is height and width. The exception is the Premier's home and the Guidance headquarters, which are both black. Black windows, black walls, black roof, but white doors. It's an off-putting contrast that makes me shudder as we drive by.

We are chauffeured to an Inn where we will be allowed to rest until two PM. At this time, we're required to sit in on a session with the Guidance where they will be discussing their plan against the threat. Today, we are required to wear our suits, but tomorrow we must formally dress up for the Premier's birthday celebration.

The car stops in front of a six-story building, dressed with balconies and an entry door that automatically slides open when someone approaches it. We exit, throwing our duffle bags over our shoulders.

"At least, we can relax while we are here," Jord says, following a yawn with an exaggerated grumble. "Get a couple of hours of shut eye and a glass of brandy."

"Jord, you will not be drinking while we are here," Seits quickly dismisses his plans.

He ignores her saying, "What do you say, Luke? Glass of dark liquor is good for the soul."

"I'll meet you at the bar after Ky and I get settled," Luke responds. I turn my attention to him, ready to shoot down his plan, but on the other side of the street, a boutique with purple dresses in the window catches my eye, and I muster my own plan. "You'll be okay with me leaving you later, Ky?"

"Go ahead. Treat these two days like it's a vacation."

"Great idea, Kylie," Jord cheers with a clap. "Treat this like it's a vacation."

The three of us enter the Inn, and the air is dry and warm. I inhale deeply, grateful for the change. The indoors, unlike the bathed silver city, from floor to ceiling, are dressed in gold. Black petunias circle around tall gold pillars posted in every corner and line the junction of the wall and ceiling. They make the gold not so harsh on the eyes.

As we cross the glossy floor to the front desk, we're greeted with pleasantries and sincere smiles. A few passersby pat my back, and I must remind myself the gesture is one of endearment and is normal in Highrum.

Jord gives the tall, pale-skinned lady standing behind the desk his name, and she slowly taps away on her keyboard. Her non-urgency annoys me. Being places where people lug around without care of other's time is infuriating.

"Excuse me," Jord adjusts to look at the pale lady's name tag. "Johanne, are you able to find it?"

"Have some patience, Jord Austin. I've found it." She cracks an indulgent smile that warms her green eyes. "Creations such as yourselves have never stayed in our Inn before. It's quite the honor to be in your presence. One minute, and I'll have your keys for the two rooms."

"Thank you," he states with a nod. He looks down at me through his lashes, explaining, "The only Creations these people have ever seen were workers."

"The soft ones," Seits cuts in.

"They've never seen fighters." There's a pause. "Killers."

I shrug, unconcerned by the Normals' enthusiasm.

"Is there something you'd like to do while the guys go to the bar, Ky?" Seits grabs the keys from the receptionist and hands one to Luke and me. "The doors aren't monitored, and nothing is timed here."

"After a couple of hours of sleep, I'm going to a couple of those boutiques across the street."

"Would you mind if I accompanied you?"

I purse my lips, take a breath, and subtly release it. "No, Seits. I'll be okay."

"I'm not coming as a chaperone, just company."

Fine. "Okay, Seits. Sure."

We take an elevator to the third floor and head for our rooms, number thirty-four for Luke and me. Luke kicks the door open and throws his duffel bag on the first bed he finds. Sighing, he charges for the knee-high refrigerator and snatches up a protein bar from its door. He practically gobbles the thing up in one breath.

"Are you okay?" I survey him carefully.

"Did you talk to Marc last night?"

Passing him to get to the bed by the window, I answer, "Yeah. He, um, didn't give me an answer. He actually shot me down, then I pouted, and he told me he would let me know when I get back."

"Damn. Collins wasn't that easy to convince either."

"You were with her last night? I thought you said she would be simple."

"She was supposed to be, but she took some persuading."

"But she agreed to help?"

"She did."

I go to the bathroom to clean off the four-hour flight. "Don't get drunk, Luke." The door opens and closes without him responding. I shed my suit, shower, and wash my face and brush my teeth at the sink. Staring in the mirror, I smooth my fingers over my thick eyebrows and pop a pimple on my crooked chin. I dress in my spare suit, strap on my black vest and boots, and pull my black shoestrings tight.

The Inn's beds, topped with plush pillows and blankets, are bigger than the beds in Separation. I fall back on it, accidently falling asleep. My dreams of Marc are peaceful, and I calmly sleep alone.

I awake, refreshed, a couple hours later. Stretching, I stand from the bed and head for the bathroom to brush my teeth again before leaving for Seits's room.

I knock, and she answers. "Hey, Ky, you ready to go?"

"Yes."

"Where are we off to?" She gleams with confidence and joy for our ventures.

"Dress shopping," I admit. "At the boutique with the purple dress in the window." I wish I knew what size Marc wears so that I can also find his collared shirt and fitted jeans. But I'd need to find a boutique that sold those things, and I didn't see one on our way in.

"Ky, you would look really cute in this dress." Seits holds out a glittering navy-blue dress with long sleeves and a turtleneck. "It will complement your eyes."

"I'm looking for something that will complement *your* eyes," I tell her, brushing off the dress she holds out in front of me. I scan racks of dresses.

"Ky," Seits calls again, holding up a gorgeous orchid purple, waffle-textured, sleeveless dress that flares at the bottom. I take it to try it on.

Before a tall silver-edged mirror, I stare at myself, starting at my bare toes and moving up my long, muscular legs. Carrying my gaze from the dress's ruffled bottom, starting mid-thigh, past the lacy fabric hugging my middle and chest, I skip over my manly arms and rest my eyes on my face. I take in the dress and then my studious expression. I crack a crooked smile, tug the band from my hair, and shake my head. Sandy brown locks waterfall past my shoulders and brush my cheeks, making my look more feminine. My smile grows wider and more comfortable with my appearance. "It's better like this. Less like a man in a dress."

"Give yourself more credit, Kylie. You're beautiful!" Seits surveys me from my left, out of the mirror's reflecting range.

"So he says," I mutter under my breath. "It's amazing," I say. Flicking my gaze from the dress to Seits's warm lilac eyes, I conclude, *'It'll match Marc's eyes beautifully.'*

"Do you like heels or no?"

"No heels." I don't know how to walk in heels. I've always worn boots or sneakers. I change out of the dress, walking into Seits when I exit the dressing room. She holds up a pair of black and purple plaid shoes. They match perfectly. "I'll take them," I cheer, bouncing on my toes. Darting my gaze away from her, I clear my throat, hating myself for just doing that. "Excuse me."

"It's actually beneficial to allow the people in Highrum to see us shopping and laughing," she whispers. "They may begin looking at us as more than mindless killing machines."

I scoff, "I guess they'll see us as *happy* mindless killing machines." I take the shoes, and with the dress slung over my arm, I go to the counter. "Hi," I greet the cashier.

"Hello, is this all for you?" The cashier flips her chestnut colored hair over her shoulder. I nod. "Creation number for the account I can charge your purchase to?"

"Two six seven. Kylie Alexander."

"Do you have your identifier?"

Obviously. But maybe she asked to be polite. I lift my arm and show her the three embellishment lines circled around my wrist, allowing her to scan it. It beeps twice, and my name shows across her computer screen.

"Thank you, Kylie. You have made an excellent purchase today. You are all set, come again soon." She smiles. It twitches, likely from discomfort.

"Thank you." I grab my bag. We're leaving the boutique, and since Seits has opened herself up, I risk asking, "What size do you think Marc wears?"

She thinks momentarily, strolling at my side. "He's about five-eleven, maybe six-foot, in height. I know his weight is one hundred ninety-five pounds. If you're looking to purchase clothing for him, you can provide that information along with his body type to an associate, and they may be able to figure his sizes for you."

"Thank you." I test the boutique two stores down. Luckily, I've made the right choice. A slim girl, standing about my height, with deep red hair cut like Luke's greets, "Welcome to News Crews! Can I help you find your next purchase today?"

I describe Marc's body to a *T*, slightly embarrassed that I know it so well.

"Okay," the associate says. "I think I can help, and maybe you can try a couple of sizes just in case."

"Thank you," I tell her. She returns with a few different colored shirts and jeans in different sizes. This must be the best way to shop. Tell someone what you're looking for, and they gather it and bring it to you to take your pick. Stress free, swiping through fabrics. Shopping is not an activity I usually like to partake in. "I'll take the collared black shirt with dark blue jeans." I'm falling short on his outfit wish, missing the sneakers, but I don't know what size shoe he wears. I'm not that well acquainted with his feet to guess at it.

The associate grins. "Okay, I'll get a few sizes that may work and bring them to the counter."

"Thank you," I say, pleased with her speed. She quickly bags my items, and we're out the door.

Shopping with Seits isn't as bad as I thought it'd be. She keeps up a pleasant conversation, and I walk beside her, holding my bags. We go back to our rooms, splitting up at the hall where she turns off to head to her own room.

I enter, seeing Luke lie across the bed, face down. He snores, seeming dead to the world.

Idiot got drunk. I told this silly boy not to do that!

"Luke," I call loudly after I've packed the new clothes in my bag. "Luke," I call again. He doesn't flinch—out cold. We have another hour before we must go, and he is not going to be ready.

"Luke!" I smack his shoulder.

"What is it, Ky?" he grunts. "Shut up."

"You need to start getting ready. It's almost two."

"I don't feel like it, Kylie."

"Come on, Luke, don't be a baby." I pull his leg. "Get in the shower so you can sober up. I'll put it on for you."

CHAPTER THIRTY-ONE

IN A LARGE, oval-shaped room in the center of the Guidance headquarters, the Premier and primary Guidance leaders of the America sit, gazing at the podium, awaiting its speaker. Richard strides in through a door on the opposite end of the room. A black robe drapes his shoulders, and his stoic expression makes him unreadable.

He approaches the podium and says, "As most of you know, there has been a threat put forth against Earth from the Vojin. We have discovered there are implants amongst Creations that are slowly being weeded out. Because of how difficult it is to crack a Creation, you may imagine the challenge our Creation leaders are encountering. There have been tests extended to suspected Creations. These tests have revealed several Creations who were implanted by the Vojin. However, what we are trying to figure out is *how* they were implanted by them. Creations are created by *our* scientists," he shouts, slamming his hand on the glass structure. "*This* must mean they are being implanted after birth, and our suspicions should start with the Breeder!"

"Start with the Breeder?" A young man with a pointy chin and small, pecan-shaped eyes folds his hands on top of the black twenty-foot table.

All the Guidance leaders wear black robes, and before them, on the table, sits a black tablet with images of a Creation boy next to one of the Vojin.

Richard says, "Breeders may be welcoming the invaders and offering Creation infants to the Vojin as willing implants. Possibly like the Non-Creations offer their children to Separation. It's possible they, too, may be implants."

The same young man lifts his hand as he asks, "What will they gain by offering their children to the invaders to be implanted in Separation?" I try to catch a glimpse of his name tag, but with his current angle, it's impossible.

"That is a question we would also like answered." Richard takes a sip from a glass filled to the rim with water, and he carefully sets it back down without spilling a drop. A large screen behind him that stretches from one side of the wall to the other reads, *We are the BETTER*. And they honestly believe this. "We designed Creations for their longevity, to live without fear of death or uncertain outcomes, to achieve what someone like you and me would consider impossible. We fight today to keep our creation of the specimen a secret from the other countries who try to get their hands on the Creation blueprint. There are a number of reasons why others would want to use Creations. Why would you, Mr. Conroy?" he asks the young man. "And please introduce yourself to the room."

Mr. Conroy stands with a soft smile that makes him appear friendly, arms resting at his sides. "Good afternoon," he greets, looking from one end of the table to the other. We are *lucky* enough to stand. We must stand the entire time as proud Creations while they discuss us as if we are things and not people. "I am Peter Conroy, Breeder Guidance Leader, first in the America. I would think the Vojin would want the Creations because of their strength and because they manage the citizens of the America. If you are a leader, people will follow you, may this be by trust or fear. Creations are looked upon as leaders, either respected or feared. Either way, people do what they say, and *that* is what matters. That must be why they want Creations."

"I agree with you, Peter Conroy," Richard says with a nod in his direction, and Peter sits. "This assumption would also scare us into destroying the Creations. If they are a threat to us and possibly a gold mine for our enemies, we would need to eliminate them." Luke, Jord, Seits, and I stand, unfazed by the conversation, although they must be thinking the same thing I am. *You stupid Normals, we're right here, stop being assholes!*

A woman with dark, straight hair chuckles at the statement. "We couldn't eliminate the Creations. Number one, that would leave us defenseless. Secondly, there are reasons behind why they were created. Their influence on the America and the citizens is extraordinary," she says. She sits at the head of the table, facing away from us. Because we are standing at Richard's feet, I can't see her face. Her shiny black hair is slicked back and almost camouflaged by her black robe. "The problem is not the Creations," she continues. "The issue is the threat. We have no need to fix what is not broken. We need to fix what poses as our destruction and holds a threat to us *and* the Creations. Should their intent be to make Creations our enemies in hopes we would eliminate them, their greater motive may be for us to eliminate our defense. So let's stop talking about Breeders and Creations and begin finding out how to fix the problem."

"How do you suppose we do that?" Peter asks.

The woman nods. "They have come *here* often. Should we go there?"

Peter scoffs, and a few around the table match the dismissive sound. "We couldn't go there. We have no idea where they live or how they are equipped."

"What we should be focusing on, besides the Creations being implanted by the Vojin or figuring out how we are even going to get there," Arletta begins, "is why they have put forth this threat and what it is they think they possess that's better than what we have already implemented." She takes a deep breath and carries on. "Everything we have done is by the book. When they came before, they mentioned something about our way of living and mindset. With them posing a threat to the world by turning humans into the undead, they are worse than us in every way. We've followed their rules in taking care of our land; we've done right by their requests, but we will not stand by while some alien forces their way on us. We never agreed to this, and this is invasive. They are turning into the beings they swore they'd protect us from."

I agree with her. The Vojin do not have the right to suggest what should be destroyed or kept intact. I would also like more information about their plan of reconstruction. They said something about needing four. I know they will need humans, and Luke and I were considered two of the four. If they destroyed the world, the Earth's population would be destroyed. Which means they would try to reestablish it, to rebuild the land and maybe the population. Luke and I along with two others would be responsible for doing that? Why? Why choose us? I would prefer to go down in the destruction.

Chatter grows into ruckus as everyone tries to talk over one another. Richard has joined in, shouting from his podium to someone on the far end of the table, whose idea is to deploy missiles into the sky and hope they hit the Vojin. People stand up at the table, shoving their fingers at one another, getting rowdy. I can't understand any of them at this point.

"Hey," I shout. A hush falls over the room, and all their gazes pin on me. "Sit down! Only one person can talk at once!"

"Thank you, Kylie Alexander," Richard says, looking down

from the podium. He gives me a nod. I'm grateful he approved, and I'm not reprimanded for speaking out of turn. They were getting out of hand. "We all have questions that do not yet have answers. We can't–" He gasps. Others follow as we all take notice of the green and blue lines of particles quickly blowing into the room through the doors and windows. My hand flies to my gun, like the others. We retrieve our weapons as the thick dust-like particles circle near the ceiling before diving to the floor, separating into five pits.

The Vojin rise and solidify. One says, "When we are the topic of discussion, we would like to be present." The five Vojin, all male, look toward the podium, three feet away from Richard.

They are lined up, side by side, and the third Vojin from the left speaks. "It is courtesy," he states.

Richard says, "If you were giving answers to questions and not threatening humanity as a whole, you may have been offered the proposition. Please excuse yourselves so we may continue our discussion." Unlike many faces around the table, Richard stands at his podium, fearless as he speaks to the Vojin. A stern tone makes his voice hard and assertive, and the stoic expression is a clear indication he's been trained well.

"When have any of your beings tried to contact us?" The Vojin asks. "No one has tried to make contact with us. We've waited."

Richard nods. The Vojin must be right. "Answer a few questions today then."

"We are willing to answer any and all questions you may have." Just because the Vojin agree to answer their questions, this doesn't mean the questions will be answered truthfully.

Arletta walks onto the stage and stands at the podium next to Richard. Her petite frame straightens as she draws her shoulders back. She licks her red painted lips and says, "Why have you all threatened humanity?"

"You all have threatened your own humanity. You murder

your own kind, destroy your life source, and treat the ground you walk upon like the trash you burn. The atmosphere of your Earth is crumbling, and there is no care for it. Your people run about murdering, stealing, and enduring the evil of your land. Why not have it destroyed so we can bring forth a better living?"

"What gives you the right to take out an entire planet?" Arletta asks.

"We have received acceptance of our proposal from the Maker. He provided permission to enforce our change."

"No one speaks to the Maker!" Richard shouts angrily.

"*We* speak to the Maker," The Vojin on the far right states. Unlike the other Vojin we've encountered, they don't introduce themselves and they don't sound familiar.

Arletta whispers in Richard's ear. He nods. "What will you do after your *change*?" he asks calmly, making air quotes as he utters the word.

"We will reconstruct it. Teach the new occupants a better way to live."

They will rule the world and have the humans be their slaves as they're taking over another planet. That's what I believe.

"What are you gaining from this?" Arletta asks dryly, a bored expression causing her once furrowed brows to relax. It seems she doesn't believe them either.

"We have been protecting Earth for years. You all need a change. We are gaining nothing but the title of being the reason why the Earth will be better than what it is today."

"Why have you implanted Creations with your misty residue?" Arletta asks.

The Vojin look at each other, heads turning as their bodies remain still. "They will help convince the humans to side with us when we implement our plan. You all have created an amazing type of human that we happen to need at our disposal. However,

they will not be needed in the future of the Earth's reconstruction."

"I see," Richard says with a nod. "Is there any way we can get
you to change your mind about the destruction? Anything we can
offer you?"

The Vojin doing most of the talking steps out of their line.
"Remember my name. Soval. I am leader of the Vojin race. Here
this from my mouth." He pauses and turns around, looking at
everyone in the room. Each Guidance leader he makes eye
contact with jumps, except Arletta and Richard, who remain
unfazed by his intimidation. To Richard he says, "We want to
enforce a new set of laws. To enforce a better order that does not
involve the loss of life lessening the already lowered population.
We will institute a better way to resolve issues that does not
involve wars and loss of lives. If we cannot have order over the
humans, there is nothing you can offer us, and nothing to
discuss."

Richard and Arletta whisper back and forth to each other for
a few minutes, then they turn back to Soval saying, "Then it is
settled. You all can leave."

The Vojin sink into their pits of fusing particles and blow out
of the room the same way they blew in.

"Protectors of Earth," a man blurts out. "That is
preposterous!"

"We can't stand for this," another man says louder.

Everyone's yelling again, expressing their disapproval for the
Vojin.

Richard raises his hands and slowly lowers them as though to
decrease the volume of the angry Guidance leaders. "We will not
stand for this. We will fight back as we have fought back anything
and anyone who has posed a threat toward us."

"How?" a woman shouts. "How will we fight back?"

Personally, I doubt any of the people in this room will be

fighting anything. The loosely used *we* is upsetting. They should be asking how *they*–the Creations–will fight back. Because it will be *us* who will be fighting the Vojin. The humans, they are too afraid to fight. They fear what they don't know and what they cannot understand. They fear what they don't believe they can defeat. For us, even if we cannot defeat *all* of them, we will defeat most of them. That is why I'm going. I don't need to murder them all, but enough to compensate for the death of my parents.

"We will get back to you about that. For now, peace amongst each other for peace within our citizens. Enjoy your evening, and we will see you tomorrow evening for the Premier's birthday celebration." Slowly, everyone stands and leaves. We wait around for them to exit the room and be dismissed by Richard.

Richard and Arletta walk to us. "Would you all like to accompany us to dinner?"

We nod, and Jord responds, "We would."

"Great," Richard says with a smile. "We will have someone bring your clothing to your rooms. Give you a break from your suits." He pats Luke's shoulder.

"Tonight?" I ask. "Isn't it unsafe to go out after dark, Guidance Leader, sir?"

Arletta shakes her head. "Highrum doesn't have this issue. There have been no walking dead in our city. But if we did, we have a brutal set of Creations just waiting for the opportunity to take them out."

CHAPTER THIRTY-TWO

LUKE LIES next to me on the bed nearest the window. "I'm stuffed, Ky." He belches.

I rub my stomach. "Me too. I haven't eaten like that since before we left for Separation."

"Too bad we were only born as Creations."

"Yeah, if we could have been born anything else, we could enjoy this kind of life every day."

"Yep." He belches again. "Why do you think they don't have Zombies here?"

"I was wondering about that earlier, before we left for dinner. You think they even know about them?"

"These snobs, no way. The Guidance wouldn't even allow Highrum citizens to experience that kind of fear. They monitor everything these people eat, watch, and read. Notice how the Creations stay separated from the Normals? *We've never had a Creation here before,*" Luke mocks the receptionist from earlier. "Creations know too much, and they don't want them sharing it with the Normals."

"I didn't notice that. But I did notice how skinny their Creations are."

"These Creations here are useless in a fight. They're just for show and city maintenance." Luke yawns and stretches his arms over his head. "What'd you and Seits do when you went out?"

"Shopped. What are we supposed to do tomorrow?"

"They are going to show us effective ways to kill the Vojin. Well, they will show us ideas they believe may be effective in killing the Vojin."

"Do they have any Vojin?"

"Supposedly."

"Oh," I sing, shocked. "This oughta be good."

———

We receive a wake up call at 7:35 AM. Sleeping in feels luxurious, and I've missed it. "Luke, wake up. We need to go find out how to kill the Vojin." I shove his arm.

"I know how to kill the Vojin. We shoot them." He turns over on his stomach, throws a pillow over his head, and snores.

I kick the side of the bed. "Come on, Luke."

"Yeah. Yeah. Yeah." he grumbles groggily, pulling himself from the bed.

I make sure he's at least sitting up before heading to the bathroom.

I shower, dress, and leave the room to roam the halls while I wait for everyone to get ready. The halls on this level of the Inn have pictures on the walls, and the floor has white tile instead of gold. The pictures, in black and white, are events from before the world's first destruction. The collages cover the entire wall. The one I pass is of a group standing among debris, holding hands with the American flag hanging over their heads.

"Excuse me."

I turn around to face a tall, teenage boy with blond hair that stops at his shoulders. He has a strong jawline and sharp light brown eyes. Smiling brightly, he gazes at me.

"Yes?" I answer skeptically. Luke was right. We don't see the Normals speaking with Creations here, so this boy speaking to me is throwing me off.

He slowly crosses the hall. "I couldn't help but notice I've never seen you before. And from the light in your eyes, I can tell you are not from around here."

"No, I am not," I answer, turning to finish my walk down the hall, interested in studying the remaining pictures.

The boy jogs to my side and looks at the walls. "Where are you from?"

I cross the hall and observe the collage on this side where the pictures depict happier events. A marathon of some sort, people smiling with their fists raised in the air. "Arizona Separation. Why?"

"Just curious. I keep up with newcomers in this area."

"Who are you?" What authority does he have to keep up with people here?

"Carden. I'm in line for Citizen Guidance Leader, second in rule. Because I'm only nineteen, I can't have the title as a Guidance Leader yet."

I nod. "Not until you're twenty-one can you become a leader of the Guidance."

"Exactly. What's your name?"

"Kylie. If you would excuse me, I'd like to finish looking at these pictures."

"I could explain them to you. By the look on your face, you don't seem to recognize the events."

I do not recognize these events. I'm not very familiar with the history of the America before its partial destruction. The picture I'm looking at is of a burning building and another that resembles it, but it's standing tall. Not too far from the building, however, is a plane and by the way its path is headed, it may hit the building still intact. "What happened here?" I ask, touching the part of the picture with the undamaged building. "Did this aircraft collide with the building?"

He raises his hand and places it on the wall and walks, gliding his hand over the picture from one end to the other, saying, "Thiiiisssss." He inhales. "*All* of this is an event labeled as nine eleven." From the end of the hall, he walks back to my side. "Terrorists attacked the America back on September eleventh, two-thousand-one. They took over two planes and flew them into these buildings," he points to each building, "in the middle of the day. Many lives were lost. It happened in New York City, and these were called the Twin Towers."

"New York City?" I ask with highbrows and wide eyes. "New York was big enough to be its own city?"

"It was, believe it or not. That's how it got its name. It affected everyone in the America, and even some other countries. Stories say that for once, everyone who lived here actually got along. People joined together and were unified."

"That must've not lasted long."

"Of course not." Carden chuckles. "But this moment made history because of its destruction and reconstruction."

I stammer, "What?" Taken aback, I repeat skeptically, "*Destruction and reconstruction.* There is no reconstruction after things are destroyed," I tell him. Cory and the Vojin instantly crowd my mind. Maybe Carden's no different.

"You *must* be a Creation," he articulates with a wide smile. I look back to the wall as he says, "This moment proves that after destruction, things can be reconstructed. Maybe not what was destroyed." He waves for me to follow him down the hall, and we stop where people are hugging, holding hands, crying, sad and happy with gray faces where no one is separated by eye color, skin color, or hair color. "See," he says. "These two buildings were destroyed, thousands of people died, and look what came from it. People were brought *together*, regardless of who they were or what they presented. Even if just for the short time it took for these pictures to be taken. It shows reconstruction in mankind. It shows we can come together." He looks at me to see my reaction before he continues. "What's sad about it is that something tragic had to happen in order for it to occur." He strides down the hall and points at the wall at different times when people are not covered in ash, and they are holding hands with raised candles, signs that state the event and flags that represent the America. "The gatherings didn't last long, but this moment was always remembered. And I hope that when they did remember it, it continued to bring people together and made the America a better place back then."

I cross my arms, keeping my gaze on the picture as I ask, "You believe that in tragedy lies good?"

"And in hate lies love."

"And things of bad nature can hold destruction in order to implant a reconstruction of happiness to make it a better place?"

He nods once. "Just about, but it's not the same beliefs as what you might think. I don't believe the *whole* world needs to be destroyed, just a part of it. It's the reason why the world is this way. It's the reason why we have turmoil and tragedies, why there is death, why there is hate. As humans, we have to see the difference, which gives a choice in what life we are to partake in. The hate or the love."

I flick my gaze to the wall on the other side of the hall. A couple is laughing, hugging. "Some of us don't get that choice."

"It doesn't seem like it right now because of how humans are born into factions with instructions and meanings and requirements of life, but any human with a brain can choose what they want to do. Doing as you were *made* or not."

"So if I wanted to be in construction though I was born a

Creation, you are saying, I could leave being a Creation and go into construction?"

"Yes," he states simply with a nod, and his blond locks brush his cheeks.

I scoff, "And get myself killed for going against the Guidance."

"If that's what you choose. Do you fear death, Kylie the Creation?"

My lips twist, disgusted by the word. "I fear nothing."

"Good. You sound like a respected Creation. Born for what they created her to live by." *That sounds insulting.* He looks past me. "And this must be your twin? Hi," he says cheerfully. "I'm Carden. Soon to be Citizen Guidance Leader."

"Hello," Luke greets dryly. "Let's go, Ky."

I turn as he turns. "Bye, Kylie the Creation."

Luke knits his brows and crinkles his nose.

"I don't know, Luke, he's weird," I say for only Luke to hear as we head for Jord and Seits's room.

"How long have you two been talking?" Luke asks as he knocks on their door.

"However long it took you to get dressed. He was telling me about the pictures on the walls." I gesture around us at more pictures plastered around the hall.

Seits opens the door. "Good morning," Seits greets us as she and Jord exit the room.

"Good morning," I say.

We head for the elevator, and Luke asks, "You left and got a history lesson from that guy?"

"That's exactly what happened. He was telling me about this event called nine eleven. Said it was tragic and killed thousands of people, but it also brought them together. I was into it until he mentioned destruction and reconstruction. I don't understand how people can think what's destroyed can be reconstructed. It's like trying to iron out a wrinkled sheet of paper—impossible. But then he made this point by saying, everything doesn't need to be destroyed in order for reconstruction to take place."

"Like saying," Seits begins, "destroying the tree but keeping the seed. Then planting the seed to grow a new tree from the base of the old one."

"Great analogy, General Seits, leader of 23rd base, division section 245." Carden welcomes himself to our small discussion as we're waiting for the elevator.

"This is Carden Fett," Jord introduces, "He is in line as leader for the Guidance."

"Hi," Carden greets cheerfully. I've taken that his cheerful attitude is a reflection of his entire personality. It goes along with being a part of the Guidance; their motto is "One must appear happy to make the citizens feel there are no worries so they can also be happy." Our motto as Creations is "Appear fearless and manage the fearful."

"Are you attending the Premier's birthday celebration this evening?" Carden asks, clasping his hands gleefully in front of his chest.

"Yes," Jord responds as the elevator opens.

"Great! I'll see you all there. Have a great day." He smiles brightly before walking away.

"That is too much joy for one person," Luke complains.

CHAPTER THIRTY-THREE

WE STAND in a glass box extended above a lab where they are conducting science experiments. They have samples of the fusing particles that make the Vojin and other concoctions that are mixed with it, trying to find out what will make it combustible. A Vojin replica, likely made by the scientists, is laid on an examination table.

"We have come to find the particles the Vojin seem to use," which assists them in travel. They bleed and are not as indestructible as we originally believed," a woman in a white lab coat with goggles pulled over her eyes says. We sit in a skybox ten feet above their heads. Most sit, but as Creations, we stand. I don't mind; I'm interested in knowing what they come up with.

"What have you all concluded to be the source of *their* destruction?" Richard asks in a doubtful tone.

"It seems the Vojin are made with a self-relative material. An element our Earth does not create. When testing it, it compares to a mixture of elements, two metals; magnesium and zinc, textiles, and the beneficial material...coal." She smiles behind her white face mask. I can tell because her cheekbones rise. "We have found a specialized radioactive bullet that is effective with the right amount of fuel, oxygen–that our Earth provides plenty of–and heat, when shot in the right place on their bodies from a measurable distance. Once said bullet penetrates the Vojin's body, it explodes, resulting in a deflagration within the Vojin." Her smile grows wider as she looks at her nodding colleagues. "The best part about this is, once the Vojin's outer layer bursts, it will be effective to start combustibility in the surrounding Vojin by overtaking the oxygen source."

"Keep in mind," a brown-skinned man in a white suit that's covered by a lab coat cuts in as he sets his beaker down, "the hazardous material held within the bullets mixed with the Vojin's matter can also be dangerous to anyone in the area. Take into consideration gas masks and facial protection."

Everyone claps, except for us. I don't know yet if it is the bullets that blow them up, or if it's what the Vojin are already mixed with that does the job. I did pick up that us killing them can be risky, so we'll need to strap up and wear gas masks.

Arletta presses the microphone button in the corner of the box. Speaking into it, she asks, "Can you show us an illustration of how it works? When will these bullets be ready to deploy?"

"We will gladly show you," a bronze-skinned woman, possibly from too much sun, says, stepping toward the Vojin dummy. "It will be our pleasure, actually." The three scientists surround the body. It's fusing with the green and blue particles like the Vojin.

The man pulls out a black pistol with a long barrel. He instructs, "Standing at least a three-foot distance away from them will provide the time the bullet needs to meet the maximum required temperature. After penetrating the Vojin's solid frame, it will explode within them." He shoots. It's quiet...silent. No pop and spark.

The bullet hits the fake Vojin's body in the chest. There's a small spark from the bullet before the inside of the dummy clouds with a gray fog. It builds, and the body expands like a balloon before popping. As it explodes, a glass dome encases it, keeping the explosive matter from spreading.

Murmurs of excitement fill the room with a low hum. The shift in energy is almost palpable.

"Of course, a rush can be put on making the bullets," the male scientist states. "We can design them to fit the guns everyone already has to kill the Zombies."

Speaking of killing the Zombies, I thought Luke said Harold shot a Vojin, and the bullets used to kill the Creation Zombies were effective in killing them. I tap Luke's shoulder and mention it.

"You have a point," Luke says and passes along the detail to Jord.

Jord goes to Arletta and Richard to share the news. They talk, and then Richard presses the button to speak into the mic. "What is the difference in these bullets compared to the bullets used to kill the Creations that were infected by the threat?"

The three scientists exchange glances before the tanned woman says, "The pink infused bullets." She picks one up from a table behind her, stocked with items of all sorts. "These can effectively kill a Vojin; however, after being shot, their infused particles are still alive. This will call out to more of them. That's what the material does. It informs other Vojin if they are needed, when they are needed, so they can track each other, as well as check in on those who are infused with their particles. By using these bullets," she raises a slim black round, "they penetrate the flesh without leaving an opening for the particles to leak out and contact others. As you noticed, the dummy Vojin did not leak."

That *is* beneficial. I imagine us raiding the Vojin's realm and using those bullets.

"Excuse me," I say to Richard. "Is it the gun that makes the shot silent? The barrel on that gun is much smaller than the silencer that we would attach to our guns, and the butt on the gun she used is larger and slightly wider than what I have seen."

"Brilliant observation, Kylie Alexander," Arletta states. Finger still on the microphone button, she asks, "Did you all hear her question?"

The scientists look up at us. I assume they are trying to see me, so I walk to the glass. "Hello," they all greet. I nod, letting them know I acknowledge them. "These bullets we are making work specifically with these guns." The man shows me his pistol. I nod, letting him know I see it. "They fit the bullet precisely to provide the needed friction to heat the bullet and get the combustible components warmed to the right temperature as it glides through the air toward your target."

"How many of those guns do you have today?" I ask loudly.

He raises his hand to his ear, shaking his head. "I'm sorry," Arletta states. "I wasn't pressing the button." She hits the mic and repeats, "How many of those guns do you all have today."

"Currently, we have twelve that have recently passed testing," the man informs.

I look to make sure Arletta is pressing the button. She is, and I look back to them, saying, "We need sixteen, today. Before we leave. And as many of those bullets you have and can be made prior to our departure."

Luke goes to the microphone, adding, "We will actually need over three hundred bullets tonight. And a follow-up of three hundred to be expedited to us the moment they are ready."

The scientists look at each other, concern narrowing their eyes.

"Will that be a problem?" Richard asks.

They shake their heads. The tanned woman confirms, "Three hundred *tonight?*"

"Yes," Arletta responds. "Looks like you all should get to work."

The scientists shuffle around each other, racking up their equipment and hustling from the room.

"Kylie Alexander, Lukahn Alexander, lunch?" Arletta asks.

———

We leave the lab, going back to the Inn for lunch. "You two are very demanding," Richard says.

"They know how to take charge," Jord responds.

"I want to ensure that when we leave here tonight, we will be leaving with the required ammunition and artilleries that will help us kill the Vojin if they intend to attack," Luke says.

"Great," Arletta states. "Do you all have a big problem with Vojin in Arizona?"

"Not yet, but we have been threatened and would like to be prepared if they come."

She strolls with her hands tucked in the pockets of her white suit. "We will make sure you all are well equipped with what you need before you leave tonight."

"Thank you," Seits says.

We sit at a table in the dining area of the Inn. Carden has graced us with his joyful presence. Through my observation of an exchange between him and Arletta, where she greeted him with a hug and kiss to his cheek, he is her son. He also calls her Mom. The two do not resemble one another. Arletta is assertive, direct, and seemingly heartless. Her olive skin is pulled perfectly over high cheekbones and a narrow jaw. Gray eyes add to the intensity of her face while her perfectly plucked eyebrows lighten the fierceness she must know she has.

Carden's hair is blond while his mother's is black. His boyish face is bright from the overbearing smiling, and his natural blue irises add to the easiness he has on the eyes. His mother has likely spent a ton of money to get his teeth perfectly straight and to keep his hair this blond color. I suspect it's treated from his dark, also plucked eyebrows. "After the celebration this evening, you all are going home, Kylie the Creation?" he asks.

"Yes, we are," Luke answers.

Carden looks at me. I look at Luke, and he shakes his head. What is this Carden boy playing at? A small girl walks up and sits next to Luke. She has dark orange hair and a petite shape.

"Hi," she chirps. "I'm Sandy." She turns to Luke. "I'm your escort for tonight, Lukahn. Carden," she points to him, "is Kylie's escort, and Andel," she points across the room to an older lady with short red hair and a wide butt. "Is Jord's escort." She then points to the other side of the room, now to our left to a tall, slim bald man. "Greg, there, is Seits's escort."

"Why do we need escorts?" I'm okay with going by myself.

"It is a formal event with a date required," Sandy says, smiling at Luke. Is there any girl on this planet who won't try to flirt with my brother?

I nod at her and finish my food. Drinking from my glass, I look over its rim at Luke doing that gazing thing with his eyes as he beams at Sandy. "Cut it out, Luke," I tell him.

"Stop it, Ky. Because as soon as we get home, we know where you're going."

I place the glass down a little more aggressively than I intend. "What's that supposed to mean?"

"You want to talk about this now, Kylie, or enjoy this lunch?" Luke asks with a plastered smile.

I glare at him. That was a low blow, even for him. "We'll eat lunch."

"Ky, I'm going," Luke tells me with a nudge to my side. "What time should we be ready for tonight's celebration?"

"We have three hours before we need to get ready," Sandy responds.

"Thank you," Luke says as he gets up, leaving his plate behind. We were instructed to not lift a finger.

"Kylie, would you like to go out and find a dress you'd like to wear tonight?" Seits asks.

"You all don't have to worry about that. There will be clothes placed for you in your rooms," Arletta happily informs us.

"That's good to know," Jord says, scraping his plate clean. He stuffs the last forkful in his mouth and wipes his chin.

"Should I remove my plate from the table before I leave?" I ask. It's killing me to walk away and not clean up after myself.

Arletta stands and drops her napkin on her empty plate. "Leave it. The waitress will clean it."

Leaving the table, I'm followed by Carden. "Can you explain to me, Kylie the Creation, where would you be going when you get home if you are already at home?"

Striding to the elevator, I say, "I think you should mind your business."

"I just thought we could get to know each other before our date this evening."

"You are my escort. This is not a date." He's at my side, his consistent bright smile making my stomach turn. "Is there something I can help you with, Carden?"

"Kylie the Creation—"

"Just Kylie."

"Kylie?"

"Yes?"

He presses the up button for the elevator and takes a step back. His hair sways loosely around his skinny shoulders. Carden has likely never worked out a day in his life; I bet he needs help to open a pickle jar. Or he has servants who do that for him. "I think you should visit us here in Highrum more often. Maybe get comfortable exploring your other talents apart from being a Creation."

"I am only interested in being a Creation, Carden."

"What about when things change?"

The elevator dings, but the distraction isn't enough, and I question, "What is going to change?"

He pinches his lips to the left, the right, then forward. Time ticks by as he studies me, before saying, "You would have to be around to find out, Kylie the Creation." He smiles wider. "I will be at your door in less than three hours to escort you to this evening's celebration."

I ignore him as I step onto the elevator.

Carden throws his hand between the elevator doors, preventing them from closing. "Just a minute, Kylie. If you will, can I show you something?"

"Like what?"

"A few things that we keep ourselves entertained with here in Highrum before we are required to strictly care about our nation and the citizens of the America." He steps onto the elevator and calls, "Floor six." There's a soft chime before the elevator lifts. "Would I be right in assuming you've been consumed with duties as a Creation your entire life? Fought forever, marched even as you strolled. I'd like to show you the softer side of life. You'll like it," he insists, smoothly turning his attention away from me and to our reflections in the gold-plated elevator doors.

They part.

I say, "We do not have time to explore, Carden." Plus, there is no softer side of life. There is managing, control, and reliance. Dominating the weak, managing the poor, and eliminating the useless. This is what we've been conditioned to believe, and apart from that, I've learned there is love and intimacy. These two things are the softer sides of life, but Carden isn't going to show *this* to me.

He flashes a welcoming grin at me and heads down the hall. "If you prefer to march rather than casually stroll," he calls back.

"I can march instead." He stomps his feet against the floor, pounds echoing down the hall.

I laugh at his arms, angrily swiping his sides and his knees, lifting high past his hips. "Will you stop this obscure dance move if I come with you?"

"Is this not how you march?"

"No, it's not. We do not march; we order our steps. And you're pushing your fists back and forth; we do not do that either." I walk at his side as he leads me to the "softer side of life."

"You referred to it as a dance move. It was not; I know this," he imitates his version of marching, "is not how you move. I could show you a dance move, but it will involve touching you."

I drop my hands on my hips and look ahead. "I'd rather we do not try the dance move unless required."

"Understandable." He picks up his speed. "Let's add some pep to our step. We only have three hours." He grins brightly. His cheeks ought to be sore with how frequently he smiles. And if his cheeks aren't sore, the wrinkles that form around his eyes should at least be permanent. When the muscles in his face relax, and he looks at me without expression, the wrinkles are invisible. Carden isn't hard to look at, but this continuous observation makes me uncomfortable. I'm not used to someone smiling every minute of the hour.

I follow Carden to a ballroom full of wall-sized pictures like those I saw in the hall on our room's floor. These pictures, though, are of different events, and the people look incredibly happy.

"Hey," I sing, hurrying across the slippery black-tiled floor. "I recognize this instrument." I point to a large pearl table with four legs and a bench. Its top is lifted by a thin post and the slim bars are black. "It makes music, right? I saw it on a movie once!" I reach out my hand to graze its beauty, but retract it, afraid I'll break it.

"It does. It's a piano. It can make soothing tunes. Come, sit." He adjusts himself on the bench and glides his fingers over the black keys. "I'm playing the keys of the piano." It's like magic, the way his fingers glide over the keys, and the soft rhythmic melody echoes throughout the ballroom.

My lids fall over my eyes, and I exhale.

Softly, he sings the lyrics long and flowing with the melody of his song. It's relaxing as he croons of feelings and pleasantries.

"This is one of the softer sides of life in our world." He speaks. My eyes shoot open, and I jump to my feet, straightening my stance. I clear my throat.

"Interesting," he utters, no longer playing.

I pull my arms behind my back and look ahead, gaze falling on nothing specific. "It looks easier than it is."

"I bet."

"You sing?"

"No."

Carden licks his lips before drawing them between his teeth. Nodding, he stands. "Let me show you something else I know you'd never experience as a Creation."

"Well, I think I should head back."

He throws his palms together and pokes out his bottom lip. "One more thing. Please?"

I chuckle. "Okay, fine. *Then* we depart and prepare for this evening."

"Yes. *God forbid* a Creation of your stature and high influence is late for the Premier's Grand Celebration that he has *every year* on this *same* date."

"I'm sensing sarcasm in your statement."

He hitches a brow. The smile fades, and Carden fixes me with his studious gaze. "You are cute and smart, Just Kylie." Looking away from me, he asks, "Now what would be your response to this statement?"

"Thanks for your observation of my appearance and intelligence."

He scoffs, "They're right. You are a well-trained Creation."

"Thank you."

I follow Carden back through the door we entered, and he leads us to another room of the Inn. "Okay, Just Kylie, there are Breeders here in Highrum. The scientists have crafted Creations of a different nature that I can't really get into detail about. Before the babies can be released to their placement parents, they stay here and are monitored for specific behavior patterns or any irregular growth." I follow him through a door. "Can I have your word that what you see will remain between you and me?"

"Yes." As if I would answer any other way.

He opens a door to a room painted light green. The air is warm and sticky and smells of an odd chemical. Six posts protrude from the floor, and on their tops are domes inclosing infants. Carden goes to one of them, and on a screen connected to the post, he taps it. The glass of the dome opens, exposing the infant. Carden picks up the child and cradles it close to his chest, staining his black shirt with the slimy clear fluid dripping from the baby.

I grab the nearest gloves available when he nears me with it.

"No. Put the gloves down," Carden orders.

"I can't touch that," I say, shaking my head as I retract a step. I'm overcome with nervousness at just the thought of holding something so fragile. I'd break it or drop it or something.

He wraps the baby in a blanket he grabs from a shelf on the post. "Here." He cautiously passes me the baby.

I'm hesitant taking it, cupping my arm around its tiny body as its head rests against my muscle. The baby yawns, and its tiny fist rises, breaking out of the blanket. The green-colored embellishment on its wrist glistens in the light above us. I gently brush my index finger over it.

"It's soft and smells like recycled oxygen," I mutter. I've held a baby, but this baby is not normal. Its fist opens, and I take it, examining its unusual palm. It has the same large circle with the smaller ones scattered throughout its middle, like mine, but the color throws me off. "Why are this baby's hands green?"

"Are you being a Creation, examining the soft side of life when you are supposed to just accept it?"

"I believe I should take that as an insult," I say, watching the baby yawn again. I try to look down its throat, but its mouth closes too fast.

"Are you comfortable holding the child?"

"No, I'd like to understand more about it."

"He is a boy."

"Okay." I hold its hand in mine, comparing our palms. "It's a Creation?"

"*He* is a Creation." Carden takes the baby from me. I go to the dome beside me and cautiously take the baby from it like he did, using a blanket I take from the shelf. This Creation child is a girl. Her embellishments are colored yellow.

"I didn't bring you here to examine the babies. But I guess some things are not easy for a Creation to adapt or adjust to."

I put the baby back in the dome, and it seals shut. All six babies are calm, eyes closed, sleeping. "Excuse me," I say, acknowledging his discomfort. "I don't do well with things I don't understand."

Carden presses his lips together and glances at the infants. He sucks in a breath and loudly releases it. "We should go. There is minimal time left for us to prepare for the celebration."

I soften my expression, asking, "Have I made you uncomfortable, Carden?"

He goes to a sink and scrubs his hands clean. I do the same, looking for him to answer. "I guess I expected another reaction from you. Creations, they look like everyone else. Why can't they *be* like everyone else?"

Offended, I say, "What? You want us to embrace all the terrible stuff that goes on in this country? You want us to awe and be jolly? Do you want me to see these infants and wonder about their future or swoon over how cute they are? Because that's what Normals do?"

"No," he snaps, crossing the floor to me. "I want you to see that everything isn't structured. That everything doesn't end in a period or a question mark. That everything is greater than this moment."

I snatch a towel from a nearby shelf and dry my wet hands. "Well, if you have a problem with the way we were created, then maybe you should change it."

He utters under his breath, "I did." Speaking louder, he continues, "These beautiful boys and girls will not only protect and serve our country, but they will consider life. They will look upon babies and acknowledge their innocence and beauty because they'll know they'll have bright futures. When they see Waulers lying in the street, they won't dispose of them, but build them a home and get them off the streets."

I throw my hand up, silencing his stupidity. "Have you ever thought, for a moment, that Creations follow orders? We don't make the calls for population demolition. Those come from *your* people. If the order came for us to build houses and get every Wauler off the street, we'd do that. If the order came for us to feed the hungry, we'd do that too. If they trained us to look at babies and people as flesh and heartbeats instead of occupants of a falling country, we'd do that too. But your mother has desired the opposite. So don't turn your lip up at me because I am the way I am. I was created this way, and they," I point to his science projects, "will be this way too." I stalk out of the room, breathing away my anger. I'm not the bad guy. They are. The Guidance, the

Trade, the Vojin. I only follow orders. I only do as I'm told. All of them are the enemy.

I march down the hall to the elevators. The doors part as soon as I smash the down button. I step in, still feeling the infant cradled against my arms. "Lobby," I say, and the elevator descends. *The softer side of life?* I guess this is really moments that makes someone happy, that slows them down and makes them embrace the experience. That, for me, isn't holding infants. Carden playing the piano, though. This took me out of the havoc of this world to a place of peace, if only for a second. *Tranquil: free from disturbance; calm.* But like everything else that brings me joy, it couldn't last.

CHAPTER THIRTY-FOUR

"I CANNOT BELIEVE the Premier got that intoxicated," Seits laughs, plopping down onto her seat of the jet that's flying us back home tonight. She's had five glasses of wine too many.

I am the only sober one on this flight besides the pilots.

"Shh, Seits," Jord hushes her. She giggles. "That is the last time you will be taking a drink."

"I think you should say," Luke belches, "that is the last time you will consume any alcoholic beverages."

We were cordially invited to a charade of music and drinking. Minimal dancing, and I was happy for it because it reduced the opportunity for Carden to touch me. The party started off calm and informal. The music was peaceful, and if it had played in my bedroom, I would have fallen asleep to it. A sinless melody of pianos and violins, which Carden assisted in playing. I thought it was going to be a nice relaxing event with swaying dancing and pleasant greetings. It wasn't.

Carden and I walked through the oversized double doors of the ballroom after Luke and Sandy. Everyone made it their business to speak to us, expressing kind words, constantly touching my exposed arms, hugging and kissing me after mentioning how beautiful Carden and I were together and how phenomenal I looked *out of my suit.*

They were constantly in Luke's face, and my cheeks burned with extreme embarrassment. When I wouldn't change from the color of Jord's date's hair, people finally thought it would be a good idea to relax. Carden constantly rubbed my arm or my back as Arletta instructed him to do so, and he wasn't opposed to it.

It was when everyone started drinking that things went haywire. I don't know what was in the punch, but it had them acting like wild animals. They were dancing on the tables, stripping, singing off-key to wordless music, gyrating on their dance partners. I've never seen adults act this way. I'm blaming it on the alcohol.

After the heated discussion with Carden, I thought the evening would be awkward with him, but it was kind of fun. We laughed together, making fun of the crazies and sharing snacks. He talked more about some of the pictures on the walls and discussed his upcoming role as Citizen Guidance Leader, where he will be required to maintain and keep track of the citizens of the America. He would have power over how they're managed and protected.

Carden was good company; he just has an unusual way of thinking. He is passionate about his idea of minimal destruction to have people establish their own reconstruction, where the America will bring itself together as he'd seen it done in the past. If it does work, the past has also shown those moments are only temporary. So what will he do, destroy something else?

It's late now, a couple hours after the ending of the Premiers party.

Highrum's helper Creations finish loading the last few crates packed with the new guns and bullets that we'll need to kill the Vojin. We'll soon be preparing for takeoff and will land back in Desert Hills at the butt crack of dawn. Jord will call a meeting tomorrow to discuss our mission, and my adrenaline is pumping with anticipation to take out the Vojin.

"Did you all enjoy yourselves?" Jord asks as the jet starts to move.

"I did," Luke says calmly. "I may have..." his words slur into jumbles that I can't make out.

"Um-humph," Jord says. "Me too." We sit in sets of two, Jord and Seits sitting across from Luke and me.

Luke's head hits the window. I lift and gently adjust him to lean against my shoulder.

I can't wait to get back and see Marc's face when he sees my dress and the outfit I got him. I have this crazy idea that maybe we can sneak out to one of the smaller rec halls and have dinner, then we'll go to the hall for a movie, then climb to the roof of one of the buildings to lie back and look at the stars. All with Seits's help, which she agreed to.

She's siding with me so that I'll side with her on the Vojin thing, or maybe she's just this nice. The dinner and movie were her suggestions, and she made sure to warn me to be careful of the Zombies and the cameras. I appreciate her help because I want the night to be perfect for him.

———

I lug Luke into the house, trying to keep it quiet because it's so late. We enter noiselessly. The horn may blow in the next five hours, and I am aching to get some sleep. My feet hurt from the heeled shoes I was obligated to wear. I was more than happy to trade them for my boots after the party, but hauling Luke's two hundred and ten pounds brings back the sore memory.

Dragging Luke to his room, I take off his vest and boots after I've laid him on his bed. He turns over on his stomach and breathes deeply, out like a light. I shed my vest, outer shirt, and boots before lying next to him and placing my head against his shoulder.

The instant I close my eyes and drift, the horns blare.

Luke groans loudly in my ear. I match his irritation. "Come on, Luke." I pry his arm from my head. "Let's go."

He grumbles indistinct words.

"I don't understand, Luke. Get up." I pull his leg after I've moved from the bed.

He sits up, holding his head with one hand and rubbing his eye with the other. "What's today?"

"Monday."

"Not Wednesday?"

I shake my head. "And not Thursday. Get up. We have work to do."

After I shower and dress, I head back to Luke's room to make sure he's up. He's sitting on his bed and has changed at least.

"Are you ready?" I ask. We have training today.

"No," Luke says, standing.

"This is what you get for drinking and making me help the four of us off the jet, into the truck, drive us to the base, and carry your heavy ass up those stairs." I shove him from his room and down the stairs to the front door.

"Thanks for all that, Ky." He's sluggish, and I want to slap him across the face to wake him up.

We walk to the mess hall, and he goes straight for a table, laying his head down. I gather him some food and two bottled waters. "Here, Luke," I say when I sit. "This should help with your hangover." He takes the contents. Getting back up to get my own food, I run into Seits.

"Kylie," she says cheerfully. "I wanted to let you know the Guidance will be away tonight." She raises her eyebrows and tips her head down a bit. "You still wanted to *go out*?" she asks slowly before looking away. I follow her gaze, and it lands on Marc. He's sitting, talking to Sean.

We turn back to each other. I get it. *Tonight* is the night to go on my 'date.' I nod, smiling. "Okay."

"Do you know when?"

I pinch my nose. "I'm not sure. Haven't talked to him yet."

She nods quickly. "Tell him nine. Everyone will start winding down by then, and you can sneak out," she whispers.

I fight my smile, but I can feel my cheeks blush. "Okay. Thanks."

"You're welcome. I'll see you later. Oh, I've added a little twist in the movie room. No roof." She leaves the mess hall, humming to herself.

I have a well-thought-out plan for this evening, and with Seits's help, I hope it will be perfect. I pile my breakfast on my plate and squeeze between Marc and Sean at their table.

Marc wraps his arm around my shoulders and pulls me to him while turning me in to his hug. I hug him as he says in my ear, "Hey. I missed you."

I kiss his neck and say, "I missed you too." I lean away slightly so I can speak near his ear. "Don't get weird about it, but I got you something."

He leans back, holding my eye contact. "What?"

I can't fight the smile, so I look away from him, whispering, "I'll give it to you at a quarter to nine, then we are going to leave the house." I look back at him. "Just say okay."

He licks his lips, and after gazing at me for too long, he says, "Okay."

I eat as the jitters in my stomach make me aware of their presence.

"You were gone, Ky," Collins says, pointing her fork at me.

"I know," I tell her, drinking my milk. Blinking, I hold back my smart remark.

"Well, where'd you go?"

"Don't talk to me." I don't like her. She shot my brother, she's disrespectful, and she purposely tries to push my buttons.

Collins smacks her lips. "Kylie, what happened was like three days ago. Stop holding grudges. I'm not holding a grudge against you after you tried to kill me. I didn't even retaliate."

"When did you try to kill her?" Sean asks excitedly, fork dropping to his plate.

"Before we left," I tell him. "She shot Luke, so I shot her."

"The bitch didn't *just* shoot me. She shot me in my head and almost killed me!"

"And if you don't watch your mouth," I warn, "I just may do it again." I leave the table as the horn calls the end of breakfast.

My group is already walking to the fields. Today I want them to work out and include jumping rope and mountain climbing in their cardio routines. I run to them. "Hey! Weight room," I tell them. We jog the half mile to the weight room and enter, immediately relishing the blasting air conditioning.

"Who helped you all while I was gone?" I ask.

"Collins," Jesail tells me.

"What'd she teach you?"

"Nothing. Fought against Sean's team all day," Jesail says, rolling her eyes. "Collins didn't care about what we did. She was barely paying us any attention as her team fought Marc's, and she flirted with him."

"You should've kicked her teeth out. Bet that would've grabbed her attention," I say under my breath.

Jesail chuckles. "I hate her too." She preps a barbell, and I stand behind the bench to spot her.

Danny jogs over. "I think I'm ready to go out for the male leader position." Danny has picked up a few pounds of muscle since he arrived; he sounds more confident and has won every battle I put him up against.

I survey him and really consider if he's ready for this role. "You look physically ready, but what's your mental state? How bad do you want it? What are your fears? What's keeping you from accomplishing your goals, and who or what is your priority? The reason for the last question is because you don't have a twin. So the answer should be yourself." He nods, and I continue, "Creations are all about our twins, but we are also arrogant, not self-centered but twin-centered. My twin and I are the best at what we do. Nothing and no one is stronger than us, and nothing and no one can overcome us."

He stretches his arms, watching Jesail press one hundred-sixty pounds. "And I would say, I am the best at what I do, nothing and no one is stronger than me, and nothing can overcome me."

"Exactly. How strong are you?" He shrugs. "Strong enough to conquer any and all things should be your answer." I tap my head. "Remember, as you think, so you are."

"Stronger than what I should be." He tries his answer again.

"That works too."

"Can you fight?"

"Anything."

"Good response. How do you feel about implants?"

He stalls. "Kill them," he says with uncertainty.

"They should be disposed of," I correct. "You may be challenged to fight. They may want to make sure you aren't afraid to shoot someone."

"I can do that."

"Good. Our general is not the easiest to persuade. I'll put in a word for you the next time we have a meeting. There has been a lot going on with these Zombies and implants and the Guidance popping up, but once I'm able to talk to him, I'll let you know. If there is someone else in line for the same position, you may have to fight for it." Danny nods. "Okay, go convince one of the Creations to let you use them for target practice."

I pat Jesail's shoulder, letting her know that's enough. "Go jump rope for thirty minutes."

I spot Edward going a few rounds with a punching bag. Rounding the bag, I hold it for him. "You okay?"

"No. But I will be. I don't want your pity." He jabs and jabs, throwing bone-breaking blows against the bag.

"I'm not here to pity you. I'm being a friend. Here to let you let it out if you need someone to talk to."

He grabs the bag by its sides and rests his sweaty forehead to its ripped leather. "I miss my brother is all. I feel half empty."

"Sorry, Edward," I say. I try to think of something else. Maybe I could tell him his brother was a hero, but that would be a lie. I could tell him he's in a better place, like they do in movies, but I don't know that for sure. Maybe I could tell him to focus on being alive, but that seems heartless as he mourns his brother's death. Coming up with nothing, I rub his back. My touch doesn't seem soothing. It's rough at first, but I lighten it by letting my hand somewhat caress his back. "You'll be fine. You're strong and a fighter. He went in battle; he was strong and will not be forgotten."

"Thank you," he says, lifting his head, looking at me.

"No problem. You want me to help you lift some weights?"

"Sure," he says. His tone is more cheerful, but it doesn't reflect in his mourning eyes.

CHAPTER THIRTY-FIVE

AFTER DINNER, I head home to shower. I'm happy. Really happy. *Too* happy. I feel like skipping to my room, but I repress that urge and casually walk there with a smile. *Please let this be perfect, and please don't let any Zombies be present or coyotes or anything to ruin our moods. And let him be willing to do what I ask him to blindly walk into.*

It's seven, *not* nine. The minutes are taking too long to pass. I sit on my bed after throwing on a plain white shirt and blue jeans.

"Ky?" Collins knocks on my door.

No, not tonight. "Not right now, Collins. I'm not in the mood for you right now." My happiness slowly dwindles, being replaced with disgust.

"Come on, Ky."

I open the door. "I'm serious Collins, not tonight. Talk to me tomorrow."

"I just wanted to let you know that I talked to Luke, Jord, and Seits. I'm in."

I purse my lips and question, "What are you talking about?"

She shoves past me, entering my room. I roll my eyes, closing the door. She is out to ruin my life. Has to be.

"Invading the enemy's realm," she whispers and shrugs. "I'm in."

Oh, yeah. I'm supposed to be convincing Marc of that too. I wanted to talk about everything *but* Vojin tonight. I don't want to make it seem like I'm doing all of this to try to persuade him to fight with me. I do want him to, but that's not why I've set up tonight.

"Okay, Collins. Thanks for telling me." I grab the doorknob. "Now can you leave?"

"You know, Ky," she starts with a mischievous smile. "If you aren't able to convince Marc to come with us, I can."

"Saying things like that, Collins, is what gets you shot in your face," I say with a plastered smile. Pulling the door open, I add, "Now please get out."

She laughs. "I'm just letting it be known. If *you* can't handle Marc, *I* can definitely tame that beast."

I kick my foot against her ass, shoving her the rest of the way out of my room. She twists around, and I slam the door in her face. I hear her giggle, trotting down the hall.

My door's ripped open, and Luke barges in. "If you are going to say words that start with *V*, *C*, or *S*, I don't want to hear it."

He gives me a contemplative side-eye. "I think one of my words has an *S*." He shrugs. "Maybe another has a *C*."

I laugh. "What Luke? And close the door."

He does and says, "I talked to Collins. That's the one with the *C*. And she, that's the one with the *S*, is in."

"I know. She told me. And I don't want to talk about that right now. You feel better?"

He rubs the back of his head and nods. "A little. That was a nice couple of days off."

"It was. The beds were fantastic, and the hot water lasted longer than it does here."

"Carden offered you placement there?"

"I think that's what he was doing. But that's not how he said it. He said it like I had a choice between being a Creation and something else. I told him that was impossible, and he responded there was going to be a change. Maybe something he'll implement."

"Yeah, when he gets his position, he's going to make an offer to the leaders of Separation. Oh, sorry, that's another *S*. But he wants them to have a choice after they reach the age of twenty-one or thirty to choose if they want to stay in Separation or not. Look, I'm sorry. I can't, see, I can't not say," he shakes his head, rolling his eyes, "a word with a *S*, *C* and uh..."

"A *V*. It's okay. I broke my own rule. What are you about to do? This conversation can be talked about later because who knows if we are even going to see nineteen."

"Nothing. Go check on a couple of things. You?"

"Nothing. Go talk to Marc in a bit."

"Don't forget you need to get his answer as soon as possible. We have the weapons, ammunition, and we need those two to complete us. After we get their okay, we plan our mission."

I hold in my grumble. "I got it, Luke." I'll ask him tomorrow, unless *he* brings it up. "Oh!" I get up and check the hall before I say, "Carden is creating new Creations." I lift my palm before him. "Their circles were colored green."

"Why?"

"He wants to bring them up differently than us. Make them more human than *mindless killing machines*. But I think he now knows that we aren't mindless killing machines of our own accord."

"Were their eyes black like ours before we got the vaccine?"

"Don't know. They were sleeping."

A strange look comes over Luke's face. "Oh shit, Ky! I spaced, too much booze! Don't leave. I'll be right back." Luke races from my room and quickly returns. "Look." He closes the door behind him.

He holds a torn sheet of paper with the same scribbled handwriting as the letter I received months ago. I slap my hand against the side of his head. "How could you forget to tell me about this?"

"Ow!" He punches my arm. "Too much to drink, I said! Check it out." He points as he reads. *"They were inserted as result in further experimentation. Unexpectedly, they were accepted as part of the Vojin's plan. Being brought back to earth as implants for Breeders in Separation. The experiment brought forth unknown information of the Vojin's threat before the threat was initiated..."*

"Hold on." I lift my gaze to the empty wall of my bedroom, recalling, "That's what that Trade member said."

"Check this out." He points further down where the words are clearer. *"The more concrete question is who implanted them in the Trade..."*

"What...?" I ask, jumping to my feet.

Tapping the paper, Luke nods. "This is bigger than we thought, Ky."

"Who were our parents?"

"What were our parents?"

"What are we?" Not exactly Vojin? Not exactly human? Not exactly Creations?

Luke rubs the back of his neck. "Last time I checked, I was a Creation."

"Me too." I nod. "But by how much?"

"Every ounce of us is Creation. Don't think anything different."

"What if they know about us? What if that light thing mom mentioned once actually means something?"

Luke's hand clamps down over my mouth. "Shut up. Don't speak about that. Don't think it. You know better," he hushes me.

I roll my eyes, pushing him away from me. "I wanted a night where I didn't need to focus on this! I wanted to stay away from words like Creations, Separation, Vojin, Trade, implant," I complain.

"Welcome to Separation, Kylie, where as a Creation, you are now obligated to battle against Vojin and implants as ordered by the Trade." He smiles. "Now watch your mouth and never bring up what Mom said again."

"Thanks for nothing, Luke." I punch his chest. It's not like he nor I know anything about it. Except one day when mom grabbed our hands, the night before she and dad were murdered, and said, "There's a light within you two that someone will want one day. Protect each other and let no one steal it away." We never heard another thing about it after that. So we never bring it up because we don't know if it's incriminating.

"Good. I'll see you later."

No, he won't, but I don't want to continue our talk. He leaves, and not thirty seconds after he closes the door, it opens.

"I'm not waiting until a quarter to nine," Marc says, closing the door behind him. He crosses the floor to me and stands near my bed.

I smile and push away all thoughts except this night I plan to experience with him. "Very impatient you are, Marcain."

"Yes, I am." He sits on my bed. "You were also gone for a while. I missed your voice." He waves me over.

Giddily, I go and kiss him without him asking or trying to kiss me first. He leans back, and we lie across my bed, me straddling his legs.

I clutch his shirt tightly in my fist, holding myself back from getting too deep into his kiss. Warmth blossoms in my chest, making my nerves erratic. His hand slips beneath my shirt and rubs over the part of my hips that dip in from my muscles. He tugs me closer.

I kiss his neck. "You are special."

"You too," he says as his rough hands scrape over my back, inching up to my neck and back down.

I lean away. "You want me to show you what I got?"

"Is it better than you?"

I smile. "Maybe."

"Nothing is better than you."

"If it enhances me, it might be."

He turns down the corners of his mouth and shrugs. "What've you got?"

I climb off the bed and gesture for him to do the same, saying. "Stand up and face the wall. Don't look until I say."

He gets up without question and faces the wall. I quickly shuffle through the drawer where the dress is neatly folded so it wouldn't wrinkle. I grab the dress and the shoes I put next to it. I quickly change and slip on the shoes. Going to the window in my room, I use the reflection as a mirror to see if I look okay. Today I wore my hair in two French braids so it will be wavy when I let it loose. I unbraid them and comb my fingers through my long hair. It waves past my shoulders to the middle of my back and came out just the way I hoped.

My hands shake as I stare at the beautiful girl looking back at me. I'm so far out of my comfort zone, trading my suit and boots for this gorgeous dress and flats. I hope he thinks it's cute.

Going back to the middle of the floor, I stand a few feet behind him. I breathe and say, "Okay, turn around."

He peeks over his shoulder, and his hooded eyes open wider as he turns around. He grins brightly. My dress is almost the same purple of his eyes, and it fits me perfectly.

"That dress is amazing, Kylie," he says in his heavy rasp.

I look down over the dress. "You like it?"

He crosses the floor, picks me up by my waist, and spins us around. "You look amazing." Placing me back down, he adds, "And your legs are phenomenal."

I swallow the giggle but can't stop blushing. "This is part one of three."

He's reaching up to grab me but stops midway. "Part one of *three?*"

Going back to the dresser, I pull out his clothes. "Okay, I didn't know what size you wear, so I got you three of the same things in different sizes." I lay the clothes out on my bed. "I had to describe you to the sales associate, and she said one of these should work."

He comes up behind me, first touching my sides, then wrapping his hands around my middle. "What made you do all this? And what's part three?"

"We were talking about it, so I went out to buy it. It's amazing, right?" I spin around on my toes and face him. My cheeks warm as my smile grows wider when I see the delight in his eyes.

He shoves his hand through his hair, smile growing wider than mine. "It is, Ky."

"Pick which one is your right size. And go change. You will, unfortunately, have to wear boots because there was no way I could guess the size of your feet."

"It's fine," he says, looking at the first outfit I laid out. "You wanted to get the things we talked about?"

"Especially the dress."

He picks up the second outfit and shows it to me. "This is my size."

"Great! Don't be seen because we can't let anyone see us leave in these clothes."

"Can you tell me how you plan on pulling all of this off?"

I bounce on my toes, and let my widest, brightest grin break through. "A lot of nervous jitters, some help from Seits, and your cooperation."

He kisses my cheek. "You have my cooperation. You have whatever you want from me as long as you're standing here in this dress."

I press my palms together and fight my overgrowing grin. "Even better."

"What are you going to do with the other clothes?"

I shrug. "I don't know yet, but it's not my concern right now."

He nods and leaves my room. I look back in the window to see what he sees when he looks at me. I'm blushing; even my arms are red. But he liked it. *Yay! He liked it!*

After ten minutes pass, I leave to his room. I knock and wait for an answer.

"Yeah?"

"It's just me," I tell him, walking in.

He spreads his arms out to his sides and does a three-sixty. "Do I look as nice as you?"

Marc looks phenomenal no matter what he has on. He could wear a chicken suit with feathers scattered about his head, and I'd think he'd look great. Nevertheless, he does look nice out of his suit, t-shirts, and hooded sweatshirts. "Yes. Handsome, with your long hair waving around like that." His hair sweeps his shoulders and blankets his neck. He shoves his fingers through it, pushing the strands from his face.

"You want to touch it?" he asks when he is closer to me.

"Yes." I push my hands past his ears. His hair's so soft, slipping between my fingers. As I make it to the back of his head, he moves in closer. I retract until my back is to the door, and his body is pressed to mine. Marc comes in for a kiss, but I press my index finger against his lips, holding him back. "This is not a part of our mission," I whisper, fighting the temptation.

"Right." He puts a little distance between us. "I'm excited to see what is. Go ahead, I'll be right behind you."

I leave his room.

The hall is quiet, and the lights are out. After he comes out, we sneak from the house, and I stop on our stoop, sickened by the red dirt covering every inch of everything.

"What's wrong?"

"My shoes will get dirty, and my feet will be covered in dirt."

He scoops me up in his arms. "No longer a problem. Now, where are we going?"

"You are awesome, Marc."

"And you are heavy. You want to tell me?"

"To the smaller rec hall, Prince Charming. I saw a princess say that in a movie once when a man held her like this."

"I bet." He starts forward, saving my shoes from the dirt. "I hope we don't get attacked by Zombies."

"Me too, because I'm not armed."

"I am, but I can't reach my gun."

"We'll be fine." *I hope.*

He walks us to the smaller rec hall, and Seits has our table set with plates and glasses. She's not in here, thankfully. "This is half of part three," I tell him. "You are really going to love this part." I pull him to the table, and we sit in front of a plate, silverware, and glasses. "Alright. I've never had a Chicago-style Polish, but Seits knew what I was talking about. We got everything, even the mustard. And white shakes!" I cheer.

Marc holds my hand resting atop the table. "You in the business of making dreams come true, Ky?"

"No." I frown. "I don't have grass, sneakers, or the path by the water."

"What you have is good enough. You made something out of nothing, and I wasn't expecting any of this in this dump."

One of the cooks sets a plate with the Chicago-style Polishes on the already placed plates, and from a pitcher, he pours our shake in only one of the glasses. He gives us two straws.

After he leaves, I say, "I'm happy you're enjoying it."

"What's the second half of part three?"

I smile. "You will see after you get me smelling like onions."

"If I didn't like surprises, I would have a problem with your secrets."

"Eat your food so we can move on. But don't rush, these moments can last all night."

"Are we sharing your vanilla shake?"

Laughing, I nod. "Yep! Our white shake is being shared." I separate the straws so one is face him too.

Again today, he gazes at me with brimming happiness. Marc's eyes are lighter, and his cheeks are lifted. "I really like seeing you this free and light-hearted."

He nods and looks away. We eat our food and drink our shake. The cook refills it, and we finish the second one over small talk and laughs.

Standing, I pull him from his seat. "I do not enjoy smelling like onions," I tell him.

He wipes his mouth, coming with me. "You'll be fine. It's just me."

"You need to pick me back up because we are leaving here."

"To where?"

"The auditorium hall."

"A movie?"

"*Something* like that."

He picks me up and quietly walks us to the hall. It's peaceful outside, no snarls or blazing gunshots.

As Seits advised, she removed the roof. On the stage are blankets and pillows Seits laid out earlier. We climb the stairs and walk to center stage.

"Wow, Ky," Marc admires Seits's work.

I pull him to sit with me, and I gesture up at the starlit sky. "Now," I begin, "we have to talk about birds and fish. Surfing and snowboarding. Hang gliding and skydiving. And hold hands while we sweep each other away from Separation."

Marc continues to admire our venue, tone awed and light as he asks, "Seits helped you do all this?"

"Yeah, she was really nice about it."

"That's so cool. Thank you for putting all this together."

"Anything you want to talk about?"

"No. I'm speechless."

"We can lie here in silence. I get the room for three hours. Then our date night is over, and we go home, back into our lives of Separation, where you don't date, or love, or have someone other than your twin you care about."

"Hmmm, Ky." I scoot closer to him, resting my head on his shoulder. "You are special."

"I only try with you."

"What did you all do while you were gone?"

Why does he want to talk about work? This is supposed to be a Creation-free zone. "Tonight, Marc, there's no talking about work or Separation. We're Normals on a date."

"Then you're not doing all this as an act of persuasion?"

And here we go. "No," I say, sitting up. "I did all this because I cared about making you happy. I wanted to make us comfortable for once."

"You sure?

"Yes." Waving my hand, I reject his accusation. "I don't want to talk about that. This was something I wanted to do for us. I promise one has nothing to do with the other."

"Collins came and asked me."

I prop up my knees and throw my hands in my face. "They didn't tell her to do that," I bemoan, muffled.

"I told her no."

"Okay." I drag my hands down my face and prop my elbows on my bare knees. "Like I said, I don't want to talk about that tonight."

He looks up at the sky. "But to answer your question..." he says, continuing to ruin the mood, "Sean and I will help."

I draw my lips to the side, not wanting to give off my relief and excitement and still not wanting him to think this topic is why I'm giving us tonight. "Okay. Thanks. But—"

"I heard you. You got dressed up and fed me onions because you love me." He flashes a Marcain smile my way, and I look away from him, fighting to prevent my cheeks from blushing.

"So what happened here while we were gone?"

"Nothing. A few Zombie attacks. They found out a few Normals were implants. Lady Helen, from the draft eight years ago, she was standing in for Jord. She ordered Cory to execute both of them."

"Ouch."

"They whimpered and cried until he got the nerve to pull the trigger. He was hesitant, and they noticed. He hasn't been around yesterday or today."

"Eh." I shrug.

I lean down and kiss him as he's speaking, but he pushes me back. "I think you should stop kissing me."

I knit my brows. "Why?" I thought things were going fine. The moment calls for a kiss.

"Because," he stalls. "I can't keep it that simple."

"Oh." I get it.

"I don't want to make you uncomfortable. Or go too far when I know it may not be something you want."

"I get it." I lie back against his chest, and he strokes my hair.

"What you did tonight was amazing, Kylie. I wish I would have thought of it.

"Thanks. Next date is on you."

CHAPTER THIRTY-SIX

"WERE you able to talk to Marc, Ky?" Jord asks me as he, Seits, Luke, and I stand around his office.

"I have. He and Sean will help."

"Good," Jord says with a clap. "We also have Collins and Cecilia on board. Tomorrow will be a good day. We will meet with everyone tonight to discuss the mission. To everyone, we are only Creations with a plan to invade the Vojin's realm, that's it."

Luke and I nod.

"Today, work on target practice. Remember where they told us to shoot them." He points to the center of his chest. "Your groups can also work on target practice."

We nod again.

"You are dismissed."

We leave, closing the door behind us. "I couldn't find you last night, Ky."

"I didn't know you were looking for me. How were you able to convince Collins so quickly?"

Luke shrugs "I kissed her cheek and asked her to fight with me. She said okay."

"And Cecilia?"

"I kissed her cheek too. And she said she wanted to fight with me."

I shake my head. "You are ridiculous, Luke."

"How'd you get Marc and Sean?"

"He told me he would. I didn't have to kiss his cheek."

"Good. You want to train together today?"

"Sure." We go to the group's rec hall and gather them for target practice in the fields. "You all have it easy today," I tell forty-plus people. "Shoot your targets, talk amongst yourselves, be civilized, and when they call for lunch, leave and come back to do the same thing." I look at Luke. "You okay with that?"

"No. But you've already told it to them now." Luke works his team to death. They deserve a day's break.

"Okay, don't shoot each other and enjoy target practice." Luke grumbles, resenting the cheerful faces of his team as they hurry to the field. We follow behind them. "Get over it, Luke. We've got more important things to focus on than shouting orders at our groups." I push Luke toward our gelatin targets. "Where are we supposed to shoot them again?"

"The chest, left side, eight inches down from the neck, five inches from the pit of their left arms." Luke lifts his gun, narrows his eyes as he lines the barrel with his target and fires.

"That's simple."

"Unless they're moving." Lowering his gun, he clips on the safety and stuffs it into the holster at his back.

Good point. "When we go," I begin as I load my regular hand-gun, "I want us to make it back. I'm not afraid of dying or anything, and if I go in action, I'm okay with that. But I'm not ready to die right now."

"I want us to make it back too." He pulls a black tablet from his back pocket and taps on the screen, turning on the moving targets only on our side. "We should go in quiet and undetectable. Be invaders on *their* turf and bring *them* inconvenience. We will turn their bodies into time-ticking explosives like they turned our brothers and sisters here into brain-eating Zombies." He fires at the targets, hitting a few and missing a couple. "Then we should try to make it to the headquarters, to whoever the guy is up there calling the shots, and we will shoot him in his head. Soval, I think was his name. At that point, who cares what his magical dust calls out to. We'll leave after we take out whatever comes after us. Everything we encounter, we kill. That way no one knows it was us." He reloads and shoots again, hitting all the moving targets in the perfect spots.

I nod. "I want to find the ones responsible for killing mom and dad." I aim, lining my barrel with the jolting targets moving one way and then the other. Firing, I miss.

"There is no way we'll be able to find that out, Ky. No one will admit it. And by us questioning it, they'll know it's us, and we'll probably end up dead the next morning."

I try again, firing three shots. Two hit. "You're right. I just want to know what's going on with them and the Trade and the Vojin. Aren't you the least bit curious about these letters that've been popping up in our rooms of all places?" I fire off three more shots, none hit. "Crap!"

"Come on, Ky. You got this. Remember, we can't waste bullets so every shot must count. Concentrate. By the time we get there, you're going to be under far more pressure than right now. Focus. Your mission is aim and fire. You will make every shot count. Say it."

I roll my eyes upward. "I will make every shot count."

"Damn right you will. Every shot missed is a bullet wasted, every bullet wasted means another Vojin gets the chance to live. I'm not having that shit. We need to show them we aren't playing. We have a plan too, and that plan is to stop the destruction they are so insistent on implementing. *Like*," he emphasizes, "our parents were trying to do."

"Speaking of their plan. You remember when I told you about the time in the burrow?"

"Yeah. What about it?"

"They said they would destruct the world, saving only four, and you and I were two of those four considered for the reconstruction."

He lowers his weapon, turning away from the targets. "I'm not following you, Ky."

"They also said they will get rid of all the—" I'm cut off by someone shouting. Three gunshots follow the disturbance.

We race over to the growing crowd, shoving people out of our way as we make it to the center. A girl from Luke's team, the one who came to his room some nights ago, is lying on the ground with a shot to her head, neck, and one in her vest.

Luke crouches down next to her. "Who shot her?" Luke asks calmly.

"I did." A boy, also from Luke's group, steps forward, standing proudly on the other side of her corpse. He crouches down too, strong shoulders and mighty frame shadowing Luke. "Her mouth was glowing. It was inhuman," he informs calmly.

"Okay, Charles. What was happening when her mouth started glowing?"

Charles drops one knee to the dirt and rests his arm on the one still propped up. "She was mad, arguing with Abel and Tamela. She was going to yell, and these weird colorful particles burst from her mouth."

Luke looks up and off to the right at twins who may be Abel and Tamela.

Abel is standing with his arms crossed, deep pink eyes peering through his lashes. "There has been talk about her being an implant. She was accused, and she became defensive. The dusty stuff circled up to the sky and Charles shot her."

Charles stands up. "She was a friend, but not good enough a friend that it could go ignored."

Luke stands. "No one is that good a friend to ignore them being an implant." They shake hands over her dead body. "You did what you were trained to do." Charles nods. "You are also privileged to carry her body to the general's office and explain her death."

A few laugh at Charles twisted face when he looks at her bullet-riddled body, blood pooling beneath her corpse. "I guess I don't have a choice."

"You do not," Luke says.

"Luke and Ky!" Cory is running in our direction, beelining through the group of onlookers. Nearly tripping, he stumbles to a stop, gaze locked on the body. "Who is that, and why is she dead?"

"She was an implant and got shot. What is it?" Luke asks.

"A shipment came in for you. Some heavy artillery the general thought you'd want to see asap."

Luke nods then says loudly, "Ky and I are going. If you all happen to find any more implants amongst yourselves, bring them to us or the general before you execute them. We'd like to keep up with them in case they can be used for testing. Come on, Charles. Pick up Virginia and let's go."

Charles scoops up Virginia. Her head dangles over his arm, dripping blood on the way to the general's office.

Jord throws his hand out when Luke opens the door. "No. Don't bring that in here. I won't be able to get the bloodstains or smell out of this wood for months. Take it back outside without leaking all over the porch." Jord follows us out of his office. "Implant?" he guesses.

Charles informs, "Yes," placing her on the ground. "I shot her, Sir Jord."

"Okay, return to your training and have Cory clean this up." Jord waves his hand in sweeping motions, and Charles nods and runs back to the field. "I have something you two would like to see." His smile wrinkles the chocolate skin around his eyes and mouth. Going back into his office, he goes through the mysterious door in the back corner. I've been wondering about it ever since the first time I stepped foot in here. The door leads to a bedroom-sized room full of bulky suitcases and boxes. Jord picks up one of the suitcases and sets it on top of a box. Opening it, he reveals a black handgun with a long barrel and bulky handle like the one from the lab back in Highrum.

I take it from him. "I've been waiting to get my hands on this." It's smooth as polished gold and light as a bottle of water. The metal warms in my hand as my grip gets comfortable around the trigger. I grab the mag from the packing cushion in the suitcase and stuff it into the gun. It clicks, and the sound is mouthwatering. I put the gun down to grab another mag and pop out a bullet.

The bullets are sterling silver with a clear line down the middle. A dark mist slowly moves inside of it. It flows like fog, almost unnoticeably if not being studied. The mag is also light, along with the bullets.

I hand the loaded gun to Luke. "You're going to like it."

He takes it from me, and I go back to the suitcase to move it from the box. I go to open the box and stop myself. "Can I look inside this?" I ask Jord.

"Yes."

In the box are face masks with breathing filters; they are thin and light as well. "These are air purifiers, right?" I ask, showing Jord a mask.

"Yes, they are supposed to be light on us and easy to use. They are to be soundless as we breathe through them and filter our air so we are not affected by the explosive particles." I nod, turning back. "Look at what they got for us. This is the best part." He picks up a bigger suitcase and cracks it open on the floor. "Check this one out." Between his hands, Jord cradles the most gorgeous shotgun to ever bless my eyes.

"Aww," I sigh. It takes my breath away.

"The only girl you'll ever meet that's left speechless by a piece of machinery," Luke jokes.

I scoff. "There are plenty of us out there." I can't tear my eyes away from its beauty. "Do you see this, Luke? Please let me hold it." Jord passes me the weapon. Black steel makes up a double-barrel, pump-action, twelve-gauge shotgun. It's the length of my arm, and the weight, though heavy, is comfortable. I press it to my shoulder and take the handles in my grips. The finger grooves are easy to align with, and the shot scope will make aiming a breeze. "What is it? Fifteen rounds?" I ask, lowering the weapon and leaving it to rest in my hands as I gaze upon its gorgeousness.

Luke comes to my side and rubs his hand over it. "Yes. It's nice." He takes it from me. "And the weight is perfect."

"This gun is ten rounds," Jord answers. "The best thing about that gun and its rounds is if there are Vojin in a line you can take them out with one bullet. It will enter them and, before exiting, release the poison, and plow through the flesh. It's a brilliant round. That thing will keep going until it runs out or until it meets a non-penetrable object." From another box sitting on the floor, Jord retrieves a narrow bullet with a sharp tip that ends in a point. "This would come in handy."

I smile. My adrenaline pumps just at the thought. "We're going to do some serious damage. I want to shoot this gun!"

"Let's go!" Jord says, waving me toward the door.

"There are multiple of these?" Luke asks. He moves it out of

my grasp as I reach for it. Jord nods and picks up another suitcase, setting it beside the first. "Stop, Ky." Luke swats my hand.
"Get your own."

"I had it first, Luke. Why must you be a jerk your *entire* life?" I
huff and pop open the new suitcase for the gun I am going to
carve my name into. "Do we have test bullets?"

"A few," Jord responds. He grabs a box of shotgun shells and a
handgun. I grab a handgun for the Zombies and stuff it into my
spare holster. Luke follows my lead. "Get the others and meet me
in the target hall."

"I'll get Marc and Sean, you get Collins and Cecilia," I tell
Luke, leaving, keeping the shotgun glued to my hands.

On my way to find Marc, I run into Sean running laps around
the base with his team.

"Two more laps then hit the showers," Sean shouts to his
team. He slows his run, and his eyes immediately admire my
shotgun. "What is that beauty?" he sings, reaching for it.

"It's nice, right?" I keep it out of his grasp. "It's new. Made for
a specific being." I wink twice. "Come on, we have orders to test
it out. Where's Marc?"

"This way," he says, turning on his heels and heading for the
weight room. "Can I hold it?"

I hand it to him. "Sure."

Gripping the barrel, he sings, "Whoa, it's not heavy. With how
bulky it is, it looks like it should be."

"It's incredible. We also got these." I pull my handgun with the
long barrel from my back holster and show it to him.

"Cool."

We enter the weight room, and Sean shouts, "Marc! Look at
Kylie's new gun." He holds it up with one hand and points to it
with the other.

Marc looks up from helping someone on the weight bench.
He leaves her and comes over to us. "Whoa." He snatches the gun

from Sean and feels it in his hands, testing its weight. "Hey," he greets me.

"Hey. You like my gun?"

He nods, examining the weapon. "I like your everything."

I blush and bite my cheeks to fight the smile. "Good. You both get one, and we're going to test them." I wave for them to follow me. "Let's go."

Marc passes the gun back to Sean and turns to his group, ordering, "Continue until lunch. I'll meet you all by the obstacle course after."

"We understand," his group says in unison.

We head for the indoor target range. Sean asks, "Would this happen to be for our vengeance on the outer world?"

"It would," I tell him. "I wish you could see what the bullets do."

"Ky," Marc puts his arm around my shoulders, "You are very attractive in a dress, breathtaking, but seeing you excited about guns...you are drop-dead gorgeous."

Blushing, I bump my elbow to his side. If we were back home or hidden from the world in his room, I'd kiss his cheek and whisper, "Thanks, handsome."

"Aw, you two are so cute," Sean teases. "Now, Ky, you should say, 'And Marc, you're remarkably hot when you hold my guns.'" He and Marc laugh, but it's over my head.

"Sean, I don't get it. But can I please have my gun back?"

"Here," he hands me the weapon. "Let me see your new pistol. I see the handle peeking from your holster, and it looks superb."

I take the shotgun and pass him the handgun. "Here. Wait 'til you all see the bullets for these things." We enter the target hall where Jord, Luke, Collins, and Cecilia wait for us. It's brightly lit with the recessed lights shining off the white bulletproof walls and tile floor.

"Close the doors behind you," Jord instructs.

Sean closes the door. "Is this some secret target practice operation where we're all going to strip to our socks and shoot guns? Because I'd like to be a part of something like that." He skips back to the line of us.

Jord throws his hand over his eyes and rubs his temples. Gesturing with his free hand, he orders, "Grab a gun from the table, one of each. We can't use the bullets we will be using in action because we have a limited number, but we'll use dummies because our targets must be on point. I planned to discuss our mission tonight, but since we are all here, let's go over it now. Then we can enjoy shooting these new weapons." He straightens his spine and crosses his arms. "In battle, I've fought with most of you in the past. We have all accomplished our missions and made it out alive. This will be nothing like that..."

I survey the room, and the reality of what we are about to do sinks in on the others' faces.

Jord continues, "We will be away from our home, on another's turf. We do not know where or what we are going into. Only that we are going. I cannot guarantee all of us will make it out alive. But I promise, you will be prepared and have the artillery we need to bust some alien ass."

I look over the weapon in my hand, eager to fire off a few shots. If he'd only wrap up his briefing quicker.

"You all are holding our new weapons made specially for this mission. These will allow us to abolish the enemy. And in an extraordinary way. Kylie and Lukahn have been witnesses to that. The bullets must be shot in a specific place on the enemy in order to be most effective. This is the left side of the chest." He points to the target point on his chest while his other hand digs in his pocket. "These." He holds up a blue and green marble. The particles on the inside slowly fuse like the ones the coyote threw up a few months back. "Are our form of transportation. Getting there and leaving. We are not the only ones leaving there, just the only ones in our Separation sector. Another group will leave with their own." He stuffs the marble back into his pocket. "Two groups from Chicago will go. One group from New York." He nods, and we follow with a nod. "Our mission," he continues in a more instructive, deep tone, "is to raid and invade as they have done to us. Destroy as they have destroyed. Kill as they have killed. We will shoot everything we see and anyone who is not our own. Look out for each other. They could be capable of things we aren't aware of, so do not let your guard down."

"Is there something we are trying to find out by going there? A message?" Collins asks.

"Yes," Jord answers. "Don't fuck with us," he states smoothly, without a blink or waver.

"What if it angers them, and our actions make them go through with this threat?"

"Seits and I will be looking for their Premier." *Their leader*, I correct mentally. They do not have a Premier. Jord likely knows this, but maybe he wants his ignorance to come off as though he knows little about the Vojin, so the others won't suspect him of being a double-dealer. "If they do not change their instruction, he will end up like the rest." Collins peeps like she's about to ask another question, but Jord talks over her. "Stay quiet when we arrive. These guns are silent. We will be like thieves in the night. We will come in, steal the lives of many, and escape without being noticed or erupting havoc. Respond."

"We understand," we say.

"Alright," he concludes. "Test your firearms. Kylie, I know you would like to go first."

I'd love to go first. Grinning ear to ear, I step in front of my target so it's ten feet in front of me. I load my shotgun with the dummy bullets Jord has in a box sat next to my feet. They're similar to the thick, black, pointed rounds without the center line of poison.

Pressing the butt of the shotgun to my shoulder, I click off the safety and pump two rounds into the chamber. I wrap my finger around the trigger and press my cheek to the cold metal to peer through the scope. Excited jitters tickle my stomach as I line up my target.

I have an idea.

I pull the gun down, looking at Jord. "Do you think if we shot the dummies with the other bullets they'd explode like the one did back in Highrum?"

"I doubt it. All the required components are not involved to make it explode."

"Ky," Luke barks, "can you just shoot the damn gun?"

"Yes, Luke." I raise the gun again. "Gosh. Have some patience." I aim and fire. There is no kickback, no jolt, no blast, just a quiet *pfft*. Like the sound of blowing air through a straw. I hit the dummy in the chest and look at the gun, amazed. "That is incredible." The gun is huge; the bullets are big, but it's so light and quiet.

"I didn't even hear it!" Collins states with annoying astonishment.

I take out the handgun and load it with a dummy bullet and shoot it. It's also quiet, like the ones they shot in the labs.

I step away from the target area in awe as I stare at my weapons. Walking to the table, I set them both down, and everyone takes turns shooting the new guns.

After the shock wears off, we practice hitting the targets in the appropriate place. Still targets are easy to hit, but moving targets, as Luke pointed out, are the hardest.

"This was a good exercise," Jord praises, wrapping practice up. "There are specific masks you will also be provided to protect us from the explosive matter and particles that will kill them and may be harmful to us. We will attack at twenty-one hundred hours tomorrow night."

"So soon," I overhear Collins say to her sister, but I ignore it. I may not trust her, but Jord's right; we do need her for this mission because she is an excellent shot and a great fighter.

We leave the target hall and head to our homes to put our guns away.

CHAPTER THIRTY-SEVEN

For DINNER, we gather together at our usual table, quietly discussing our new mission. "I personally think those guns are the most amazing things man could have invented," Collins says, spooning her soup.

"Good thing nobody cares about your opinion of man-made products," Sean retorts.

Luke is the only one not sitting with us. He had to follow up with the other leaders to discuss the other countries' infestation of Zombies.

Sean and Collins bicker back and forth, and a joke I recall Fein telling trickles into my mind. She must've been mad at me for pulling the trigger. That girl, Virginia, she was an implant and died. I'm a mixed Creation, and though one or two may know, it's a miracle I'm still alive. Marc should've wiped us clean off the Earth. Now, here we are, going on a suicide mission, and everything in my gut is telling me this is why my life was preserved, because with *this* one, we aren't making it out of there no matter how good our weapons are. Something is telling me Luke and I are going to be dead on the floor of the Vojin base, lying next to each other in a puddle of our own blood. And I'm comfortable with that as long as I can kill at least thirty-two of them. Shoot me down, fine! But I'm not going out without taking a few of them with me. They'll remember our names, and forever they will ring along with those of my parents.

Linder and Poppie Alexander.

Nevertheless, I'd still be dead, and nobody really wants to die at eighteen. At least I've gotten to go on a date. I've been kissed. I've shot the greatest gun in the America, and I made the highest rank as a Creation. The America will know me too. Carden will stand before the citizens and say, "Just Kylie was a badass, and she risked her life for every one of you."

Ha! Yeah, right.

I'll go down as another Creation they'll forget about two months after they discover the enemy murdered me.

"Ky," Collins calls. "You zoned out?"

I look my food over, sticking my potatoes with my fork. "Collins, I don't understand why you think you can just address me. We are not friends. Don't speak to me."

"You going to have to get over yourself, Ky. We have to look out for each other."

"I can look out for you and not like you. Just trust me to have your back, and I trust you to have mine."

"Whatever, Ky," she says. She rolls her eyes, and her gaze falls on Marc. "Marc, what are you doing after dinner on your last night alive?"

"Not you," Marc responds and takes a drink of his red soda.

She scolds him with a narrowed glance. "You don't need to be rude."

I feel a tickle attacking the back of my neck. I throw a glance over my shoulder and spot Luke staring a hole through me. He waves me to him. I go after throwing away my tray. "What's wrong?"

They call for the end of dinner after we leave the rec hall.

"I'll tell you when we get to my room. It's about tomorrow night."

"Give me a hint. I hate waiting."

"I just left a burrow, *forced* there by two Vojin coyotes, off in the hills."

"Were you followed?"

"I'm not stupid, Ky."

"Well, I have to ask."

A vein is popping out of his forehead, and steam is practically blowing from his ears. "Is it something that made you mad?"

"Not really."

Okay, I'm going to shut up because he's not giving me any answers. We reach our house and are the only ones here. Climbing the stairs to his room, my heart is racing, wondering what he could be about to tell me.

Stepping through the door, Luke says, "I need to grab a shower before we talk. After, I'm not going to leave my room." He heads for the stalls.

Since I'll have to wait for him anyway, I grab a shower too and head to my room after to dress. I'm out before him and looking out my open door for Luke to return. The instant he returns, I cross the hall to his room and push the door closed, demanding, "Okay, tell me."

Luke sits on the bed and rubs his hands over his head. He gives a long sigh. "They think we are going to raid their realm. They wanted me to find out who it is and talk them out of it because they plan to come here next week and implement their form of peace."

"What is their form of peace?"

"The Vojin I spoke to was Noranti, the one who once told us they did not want to destroy our planet or theirs. She wanted to come here as a warning and request we fight with them against the other Vojin who want to kill everyone. You want to know what I told her?"

"What?"

"I told her that I don't give a shit about her need for help or domination. They have all lied to me, and it would be my pleasure to fight *against* all of them." He meets my gaze. "You wanna know what she said?"

I sit, unable to look away from him. "What?"

"She said that if we plan to invade their realm, we can at least spare the lives of the blue and pink Vojin."

"Why?"

"That's what I asked. She said they are the ones whose true intentions are to protect the Earth and the outers of our planet. They are under an influence and are unaware of their actions as they have no control of their decisions."

"What else? Anything useful?"

"They want the important members of Vojin society to be abolished. The ones who are bigger, more silver than blue, bright. If we can get them, the instruction to destroy Earth could be terminated."

I nod, saying, "That's good news."

"Can you turn that light off? Are you sleeping in here?"

"Yes." I turn off the light and lie beside Luke. "If we don't make it out, Luke, or if you make it and I don't, know I love you."

"I love you too, Ky. And we are either both going to make it, or neither of us is going to make it."

"If the Vojin get what they want, if they convince the America to do away with Creations, we are out either way."

"As long as we go out together. What do you have to live for besides me?"

"Nothing," I say, and it comes out breathless and unsure.

"Kylie?"

"Hmm?"

"If we go in there, and it comes down to save me or Marc, don't choose to save Marc."

His request wraps around my neck and strangles me too tightly. I lose the feeling in my toes, but to keep him from sensing my doubt or hesitation, I shake my head. "I won't, Luke."

"Good." He wraps his arm around my head and pulls me to his shoulder.

There's a knock on his door.

"Now who is this?" Luke complains.

"Probably one of your girlfriends," I joke.

"I don't have those. Who is it?"

"Luke?" A girl calls. The voice sounds vaguely familiar.

"Aren't they supposed to stay in after nightfall? How do you not have this under control yet?" I say as he gets up.

"Yes. You'll leave or no?"

I curl my lip and gag. "You're about to be nasty?"

"I have to get it all out of my system before we die."

Pressing my lips into a thin line, I shake my head as I cross the floor to the door. "Fine." I pull open the door, and the girl is right on top of it. "Pardon me."

She moves aside. "Um, hi, Ky."

"Hi," I say gruffly, passing her to get to my room. I get here and lie down, but only for a second. Grumbling, I flip onto my left side and then my right. *I don't know why I came in here.*

I go to Marc's room and knock on the door. He returns with a triple knock against the wall. I go in. Closing the door, I keep the knob in my hand as I lean my shoulder against it. "You can't talk?"

"No."

"What if I wasn't me?"

He turns, facing the door. "You are you."

"Can I come in?"

"Isn't that why you came here?" He yawns and turns back over. "To come in?"

"Yes. It's not late, Marc. Why are you so tired?"

He makes a throaty chuckle. "Collins just left. She took a lot out of me."

My body turns to stone. Why would he tell me that? Drawn speechless, I chew on the inside of my bottom lip. He stares at me, hooded eyebrows rising, the purple in his eyes brightening. My shoulders slacken, and I exhale. "You're not being serious, right?"

"No. But you're still holding up the door."

I sit beside him, and he scoots over for me to lie down. But I remain sitting, leaned over on my knees. Building my courage, I prepare to ask something that's been sitting in the back of my mind for months now. I stretch the back of my neck and clutch my inner shoulders. "Would you, well, try that with me?"

He lifts his head. "What I was just joking about?"

I nod, but say, "If the question makes you uncomfortable, you don't have to answer it."

"Yes, I want to do that with you." I hold my breath, and my nerves kick in again with his unexpected response. "Why?"

Be brave, Ky. But I can't say.

"You want to do that with me?"

I look away from him to the window and nod, embarrassed I'm even considering it. My hands are shaking as the jitters jump around in my stomach and chest. They're creeping around to my back, and I feel uneasy.

"Just because you say it, doesn't mean it's about to happen right now, Ky. You don't have to be nervous."

I look back at him. He's propped up on his elbows, his gaze soft and heavy rasp gentle. "I do if I'm thinking about it happening right now." I press my hand to the mattress and lean over to kiss him as I move on top of him.

He pushes me back a little. "Mmm, Ky. You do not want to do this right now."

"You don't?"

He grabs my thighs, then he glides past my butt to my back. "I do, and for a while now. But that's intense."

That odd adrenaline takes me over, and my entire body tingles. I sigh as he touches me again. "The way your touch feels is what's intense," I say as my body turns electric. Meeting his eyes, compassion fills the empty spaces in my chest where the electric prickles can't reach. "Can you tell me you love me?"

He pushes my hair back from my face and silently looks at me for a long time. "Ky," the words pour from him slowly, "I love you."

If I were a cup, I'd be flowing over. My heartbeat pulses through every centimeter of me. "And I love you."

"And you want to do this, tonight?"

"If you do too. Before I die, or I'm discovered, or the world destructs and I never get the chance to be that close to you."

"Hold on, Ky. I'll be right back." He moves me from him and leaves the room. He might be giving me time to reconsider. But I won't. I want us to advance in this. I've wanted it for a while too; I've just never had the courage until now. Maybe it's because I'm facing death, maybe not. But if the option came, and I had to choose between him or Luke, I can make the choice knowing, at least, he and I held nothing back. We knew every bit of each other, and the memory of him will be good enough.

He returns, quietly shutting the door behind him. "Where did you go?" I ask when he sits on his bed.

He looks over his shoulder at me before turning around. "I had to get something."

"From who?"

"Sean."

I grab him to me and lie back on his bed. "Why?"

Kissing me once, he hovers over me. "It was important." He kisses me again. "You sure you want this?"

"Yes, just don't hurt me with that baseball bat in your pants."

He laughs, retorting, "What?"

"Nothing." My legs shake.

"I'll try not to hurt you. Um." He looks away from me. "You will be the first girl this happens with, so," he looks back at me, adding, "tell me if I hurt you."

I even my breaths and unintentionally whisper, "Okay."

His kisses to my lips are soft. So gentle I barely feel them. His graze against my skin is even softer, and while a part of me wants to question it, it may just be my nerves. Cautiously, we undress each other, and the heat beats between our bodies. It feels like we're moving in slow motion, slowly, heavy breaths move time forward. Every time our breaths stalls, so does time.

I push my hands over his back. "I wish I could heal away your scars."

Lips against mine, he whispers, "Don't. I often forget they're there when you're not touching my back." Marc leans back, and his eyes shine a unique purple I've never seen. "Remember what I said," he says.

I stop breathing when his hand grips my bare waist. He notices and whispers, "You can tell me to stop."

"Don't." I force the air from my lungs, and he draws near me, nothing separating us. My muscles tense, and I swallow a gasp.

"Stop?" he asks.

I breathe, saying, "No."

It started off uncomfortable, but it isn't lasting. We're losing ourselves when there's a knock on the door.

"Shit, I knew that was going to happen," Marc utters.

"It's probably my brother."

"Or mine. You want me to get it?"

"No way."

The door goes unanswered.

I finally relax, wrapping my arms around him, and it seems he's relaxed as well. Our breaths grow heavy, and an odd pressure builds in my chest until it feels like it explodes. A silverish light blasts out between us, beaming past his shoulders and onto the ceiling.

Marc jumps back and throws his blanket over me, dimming the sudden luminosity of my body. It's not enough. I scramble to pull the pillow over me, and it helps.

Panicked, he asks, "Is that supposed to happen?"

I shake my head, hugging the items to my body to hide myself. "I don't know. I've never done this before." I push my hand over my forehead to my hair and release a heavy sigh. My racing heart calms. *What the hell is wrong with me? I glow with light now?*

Marc cautiously peeks beneath the blanket, and to our relief, I've stopped glowing. We sigh, but I keep the blanket clutched in my hand, covering my body as I sit up.

Sitting at the edge of the bed, he rakes his fingers through his hair. "Whoa, Ky. You're mixed with Vojin, huh?"

"Yeah." Our breaths have evened out, but the shock is taking a bit to wear off for me. I push my hand across his back and scoot a little closer to him. "I'm sorry. Are you okay?"

His brows knit. "Don't be sorry. You're okay?" Looking away from me, he asks, "I didn't…break anything, did I?"

I look myself over. "No. Nothing is wrong." I smile and place a kiss to his shoulder. "Maybe it's a side effect to uh, pleasure."

He chuckles, turning to face me. "Yeah?" he asks with a seductive drawl.

I nod. "Can we try it again? I'll keep my *alien mojo* under control."

"Your alien mojo is likely going to call your cousins in here, and they'll see all your naked lady parts."

I hitch my finger for him to come closer. "We wouldn't want that."

Marc eases over me. His hands pressed to the mattress holds up his weight as he looks me over. As if he's doing a pushup, he sinks down on me and pecks my lips. "Tell me something." He drops to his elbows and inches separate us. His body is a comfortable weight on mine, and I lift my knees to his sides and push my arms around his back. Through a breath he asks, "Will you choose Luke over me?"

Nervousness shutters my flesh. He feels it. I can tell by the way he drops his gaze to the right. I suspect this has been a burning question for him ever since the night he nearly lost Sean, and I put my life on the line for them. It's a question I've been hoping to avoid. One I would prefer for time to tell while also hoping for the moment to never come. I'd like to think I wouldn't know what to do if I were put in such a situation. But I do. Slowly, letting my arms fall away from him, feeling as though I'm sinking into the firm mattress, I say, "I'd choose Luke."

Marc burns me to a crisp with his unrelenting stare. As if snapped out of my disloyal trance, he blinks as his brows bump together in a scowl. "Are you—." He takes a pause to clear the heavy rasp from his throat. And though it's not gone, his tone is clearer when he asks, "Ky, are you saying that because you were born to or because that's what you would do?"

My brows tremble as they meet in their center. I reach for his cheek, and he retracts, turning his head a bit to make it clear he doesn't want the contact. The pain in his narrowed eyes slowly darkens the purple hue of his gaze. I swallow hard. "I don't want to answer that."

My response seems to shove him away from me. He sits at the end of the bed, shoving his hands through his hair as he leans back, forcing his elbows to point to the ceiling and the muscles in his back to react to the movement. Nodding, he relaxes and says, "Okay."

"Okay?" So simple? After I could read the visible disappointment in his eyes, the regret forcing his chest to rise and fall with every harsh breath... Just, okay?

Marc nods and lies back beside me. "I'm not supposed to love you, Kylie. But I do. And I'm sorry."

With my arms bent at my chest, he wraps me in his. "Sorry about what?"

He kisses my forehead and breathes long and hard. "Tomorrow is going to be crazy. Maybe we should call it a night."

An uneasy feeling attacks my stomach. "Are you sorry for loving me?"

He shakes his head. "Not yet."

"Well, I love you back. I do." I swear it.

CHAPTER THIRTY-EIGHT

I RUB my shaking hands together and take deep breaths as I enter Jord's office. The day has flown by, and I've eagerly awaited this very moment. The base is quiet. An eerie quiet that makes me give the empty roads an onceover before I push the door closed behind me. I'm the last one to join the group. Marc and Sean, Collins and Cecelia, Jord and Seits, Harold, and Luke are already here, suited up and getting briefed for our mission.

Jord hands each of us one marble. "We will use one for all of us to get there. Each of you have one to get back if the person next to you doesn't make it. I don't expect us to stay together. When you need to come back, throw it against the ground. It will break, jump in, and have it already established when it's leaving your fingers *here* is where you want to return. If we all do end up staying together, the hole we jump through will still be here, and we can all jump back through and, of course, end up here. Any questions?"

"No."

I bump Luke. "Don't stop until we're out."

"Don't drop."

"Don't doubt."

"I got you." He lifts his arm vertically with his fist facing the ceiling.

I do the same with mine, saying, "I got you." Our arms align before we bump the sides of our fists together.

We've crowded around Jord's office. Harold, Seits, and Jord are lined up beside each other, and the rest of us stand twin by twin. I meet Marc's purple gaze and mouth, "I love you."

He hesitates before he mouths it back. I turn around to Jord handing out the face masks. They're black, matching our suits. Placing them over our faces, they cover our nose, mouth, and most of our chin. We strap it on with a plastic dual-sided release buckle. We load our guns with the proper bullets and stuff one into each holster; one's at my back, my front, my left thigh, and my right ankle. My shotgun is slung over my shoulder by a strap. Along my vest pockets and extra compartments of my suit, I've stashed extra ammunition, but Jord has also provided us with backpacks and belts that contain more.

We slip on our goggles and strap on our helmets.

"Okay," Jord slams the marble on the floor, and it shatters. A pit forms. It's big enough for us to jump two at a time. "Let's go!"

Harold's first, then Jord and Seits, and after is Luke and then me.

I dive through a tunnel made up of the Vojin green and blue particles. Moving at lightning speed, the colors rush past me. We fall out of the gateway, landing upright. Jumping to our feet, guns in hand, Luke and I find four Vojin, gray, expanding like balloons on the glass-like floor. The floor, wall, and ceiling are illuminated in a calming blue color, and there are green lines of light that surf up the walls. Maybe they're message or communication lines.

Jord waves toward an opening that's the shape of a doorway. He gestures for us to continue. Luke and I move to the opening as others fall in line behind us. Luke peeks out to the hall, then waves me forward. I hustle behind him, and we quietly make our way across the slick floor, one foot over the other. Every hall looks the same as the last, with the dim blue glass lighting our path. Checking our rear, down a side hallway we're passing, a faint glow grows brighter as it nears the distant corner.

I tap Luke and point down the hall. Flicking two fingers forward, we hustle in the direction of the hall. As we're nearing the corner, six bluish-silver Vojin leisurely round the corner. We fire six silent shots. The aliens crumple to the floor, bodies expanding, preparing to explode.

I nod toward the corner, wordlessly asking Luke if we should head this way. He nods once and looks behind him, waving our comrades on.

With Luke and I in front and Jord and Seits in the back, we follow the wall, creeping on alert, waiting to be caught off guard. Along this wall, where the green lines of light continue to scale upward, we come upon another opening. Luke stops at its edge and peeks in. Beyond the opening, I can barely make out a whispered exchange. Luke raises his fist. I copy his move, stopping Cecilia behind me.

Luke meets my eyes with his squinted, questioning if I can understand them. I shake my head. I don't think they're speaking English. He looks around me and points to him and me, then the room. We get a nod of approval from Jord.

Storming into the small space, before they can peep a word, Luke fires four shots before the rest of us can make it in. Cecilia and Collins watch the hall as the rest of us look over the screens taking up the top half of the room up to the ceiling.

I don't recognize any of the jumbles of symbols scattered over the gray screens. Luke taps my shoulder and nods for us to go.

We leave the room to find Marc and Sean waiting for us in the dimly lit blue hall. We follow the hallway, stepping over Vojin bodies that have expanded and will soon explode. They likely took them out while we were in the room. This shows the Vojin must have no idea we're here. The weapons work better than we expected.

We come upon a wide opening in a large area at the end of the hall. Its size reminds me of the ballroom in Highrum. A lot of Vojin mill around this open space. *This* is where the battle begins.

———

We reload our weapons, and Jord, Seits, and Harold rush in, guns blazing. They attack before the Vojin even know what's happening. Their silent shots don't even render screams. The Vojin, all pink, bluish-green, and gray drop from their perfect aim. Collins and Cecilia are next. Then Luke and me. By this point, as we charge from the opening of the hall, the Vojin have discovered us and fight back with strikes of light and acid burning gas spheres spurting from their hands. The light strikes off their fingers like lightning and dark orange gas balls form as they roll down their arms to their hands. The Vojin throw them off their flesh with much might.

One hits my leg, burning through the pant leg and stinging my skin, scorching like acid.

I push past the pain and trade my handgun for my shotgun. Blasting Vojin by twos and threes, I hit everything I see, targets precisely executed. I pump and fire quickly, dodging the Vojin attacks.

I fire empty and sling the shotgun back over my shoulder. I don't have time to reload. Grabbing one handgun from my front holster and another from the holster on my thigh, I'm back in the game.

Catching a break from the Vojin attacking in front of me, I spin on my heels to check my rear. I grab Collins out of the way of an oncoming Vojin sphere that is firing for her head. She nods to me as she hustles to the other side of the room.

We cautiously move around the room, shooting and conveniently avoiding their attacks. A deep gray fog erupts from the exploding Vojin and darkens the room. The other Vojin drop, attacks falling limp, havoc gone peaceful. The battle's over so quickly. If I'd blinked too long, I would have missed it.

I survey the room before the gray fog from the exploded Vojin makes it too hard to see. On the far end of the space are more screens that stretch from floor to ceiling, showing Earth with a large blue target dot on it. We keep close to the wall that rounds the room in the shape of an oval. One entry is behind us, and the other is on the other side of the room. The wall beside it holds a screen, depicting a video of our planet.

Jord taps his gun, grabbing our attention. He points to a glass staircase that circles the wall of this room to an upper floor. We nod, and he, Seits, and Harold jog up the stairs without waiting on us.

There's a slight *pfft* of air being released, followed by something squeaking over the floor. Luke and I turn around, and a door opens behind us. Two Vojin, seven feet tall, charge through, and I'm hit hard on the back of my neck, knocked out.

CHAPTER THIRTY-NINE

REGAINING CONSCIOUSNESS, I feel my head swaying. I swallow hard, trying to shake the dizzy feeling. I'm on my knees with my arms tied behind my back, execution style. Groaning from the pain in my neck and head, I open my eyes. It's black. I see stars as I fight for my sight to return. I blink. Boots appear in a darkened haze.

My sight clears the more I blink, and the dizziness lessens. I follow the boots up the body to the face. Collins is pointing her gun at me. I nod, accepting this. To my left, I spot Luke, still sluggishly awakening, also on his knees, slumped over with his arms tied behind his back. He shakes his head as his surroundings slowly come into focus and he looks at me. He looks at Collins and nods like I did.

"What's this?" he asks.

"You and Ky's execution. We thought it would be good to execute you in your own home."

He nods again and says to me, "You should've let me kill her, Ky."

"Yeah…" I say, annoyed, rolling my eyes. "I know."

Collins laughs. It rings through this small room and screeches through my ears.

The door slides open behind her.

Marc and Sean barge in, guns drawn and revenge in their eyes. Relief sweeps over me.

"Put your gun down, Collins," Sean demands.

She does as instructed as they continue forward. "Stand up," Sean kindly tells us, and we follow his request.

Three gray seven-foot Vojin fall in behind them. Marc and Sean pull out their shotguns, aiming them at us. Sean forces Luke to stare down his barrel, and Marc's is aimed at me. Aimed right in my face. "Any last words?" Sean asks.

"Ain't this a bitch," Luke snaps as their guns load.

To Be Continued in CULMINATED

Find out how it all ends.
Start reading the final installment of the Separation Trilogy,
CULMINATED!

CONTINUE IN CULMINATED

I hope you enjoyed reading CONTAMINATED.
Please take a moment to leave a rating or review and share your
experience with a friend. I greatly appreciate the support, and I
love hearing your thoughts on The Separation Trilogy. I'll see
you in book 3!

Keep turning to start the next book in the series,
CULMINATED.

ABOUT THE AUTHOR

Felisha Antonette writes heart-throbbing YA/NA fantasy where danger, found family, and faith collide—and hope refuses to back down. Her books (including The Sephlem Trials and its spin-off Shadows Because of Ashes) blend pulse-pounding stakes with emotionally grounded characters and a slightly lyrical edge. When she isn't drafting or studying the Word, she's with her teenager, her dogs, or her jungle of houseplants.

Hope is a weapon. She writes like it.

reach@felishaantonette.com • @FelishaAntonette on socials

ALSO BY FELISHA ANTONETTE

The Separation Trilogy

(YA-Science Fiction)

INCEPTION

CREATED

CONTAMINATED

CULMINATED

The Sephlem Trials

(YA-Dark Paranormal Romance)

Plight (Call of the Burning Feather)

Brazen (Thoughts of a Wicked Mind)

Cohere (Stains of the Fallen Tears)

Finite (Whisper from the Defining Silence)

Blind Trust Standalone Series

(NA-Romantic Suspense - 18+)

Blind Trust

Sign up for Felisha Antonette's Newsletter for exclusive updates and new releases!

CULMINATED SNEAK PEEK

KEEP READING FOR A LOOK
INTO BOOK 3, CULMINATED

CHAPTER 1

I SUCK IN AN EVEN BREATH, staring past the double-barrel shotgun to Marc's narrowed eyes. The heavy pounding of my heart causes every inch of my flesh to vibrate. Anger bubbles in my gut as I focus my gaze and peer into the barrel. Gunpowder burns my nostrils as the heat of the shotgun warms my face. Impatiently, I wait for the bullet to erupt.

The seven-foot Vojin with latex flesh the color of a storm cloud moves in my periphery. "Execute," he instructs.

I'm suddenly aware of how heavily I'm breathing. My breaths thrash past my parted lips and from my nose. My chest aggressively rises and falls. I can feel something working its way from my aching knees through my numbing chest to settle in my burning throat. *Heartbreak*. The feeling Marc may have experienced when he found out I was involved with the Vojin. *Betrayal*. And now he's turned the tables, and I experience it firsthand.

Marc doesn't break our eye contact. He loads the gun, and the sound stabs me in the chest. I clear the burn from my throat and blink away the tears. After everything we've done, the words we shared, the moments we wouldn't have given to anyone else, the only other person in this universe I'd spare my life for, Marc's betraying me. But why?

His index finger wraps around the trigger, and I swallow hard. I'm not afraid of dying. I expect death. I prepared for it. But to be killed by him? Not in a million years would I have guessed this.

The anticipation is killing me.

I take a step forward and press my head against the barrel so it's firmly placed between my brows.

"Just tell me this one thing before you kill my sister and me," Luke says. I dare not flick my gaze to him. My eyes are still locked on Marc's, waiting for him to falter. A glimpse of a wink, a smirk, a tremble to his chin, a twitch of his index finger pulling away from the trigger, a flare of one nostril, a hitch from his brow. I wait for something to indicate he's not a traitor. That he didn't use me. That everything between us wasn't just some sick trick, some sick game he played with me. But I find no lies in his sober stare.

"Speak, Lukahn," the Vojin says, granting him his request.

"Why?"

"You are—" the Vojin starts.

Luke cuts the Vojin off, throwing his hand up. "Not you. You two." He gestures to Marc and Sean with a nod.

"That is not of importance," the Vojin says.

"The hell it isn't!" Luke snaps. By the rage in his tone, anger is erupting inside him. He'll try to fight his way out of here and likely get himself killed in the process.

I shake my head, but I can't make out the words needed to talk him down.

The entrance behind our deceivers slides open. Smaller Vojin rush through, entering the dimly-lit blue hall we stand in. Urgently, bodies buzzing with their bluish green color infusing through them, they say, "We need you in the mainframe."

Gunshots go off from somewhere near us. It's music to my ears. I don't relax against the hope that thrashes through me, but I blink, letting my eyes remain closed for a full second before I open them and see the three Vojin race from the hall. The gray seven-foot Vojin rushes out behind them, movements fluid as their steps hurry across the glass floor flickering green at the sound of every gunshot.

The four of us are left alone.

I smack the shotgun from my face. "What the hell are you doing?"

"Don't talk to me, Kylie," Marc says, the rasp is so thick in his voice I clear my own throat.

"Marc," I whine and regret the weakness that's revealed from my doing so. "Just tell me. Why?"

His gaze flicks to the ground for a second. As it rises, so does his weapon, with me at the end of both.

A slow breath blows past my lips.

"Well, Ky," Collins sings, coming up behind me. She continues past me and takes Marc's side. "I bet you're upset, huh?" She grabs his shoulder in her skinny hands. Maybe due to my anger and rushing adrenaline, I see her moving in slow motion, rising on her toes and laying a long-lasting kiss to his cheek.

Before she breaks the connection, I look away from them and tilt my head back to swallow the tears. I won't allow this to tear me down. I'm stronger than the betrayal, than him and her.

The entrance slides open again, and three gray Vojin enter. One has Cory by the neck, forcing him to walk forward. He says, "Lead them to a cell."

At least, this means we won't be executed right now. Luke and I will have a little more time to figure this all out.

Marc and Sean jerk their guns to our right, and Luke and I quietly follow instructions. I go first, Marc behind me, and I suspect Sean's behind Luke with Collins somewhere following closely behind. This narrow hall is short. The walls and floor are a glass or a thick, glass-like plastic. They're matte and glow a bluish green, but it's not as bright as it was when we arrived. Likely to lessen visibility for the intruders as the Vojin try to get a handle on our invasion.

Cory, Luke, and I are forced into a cellar. A blue-tinted glass door closes behind Luke, and the small space becomes our holding cell. I find a corner in the rear of the cell to slide down in. I press my back to the wall and draw my knees to my chest.

Luke paces the floor. His heavy boots pound the glass, every step sounding like a slap and a thud. I'm tempted to beg him to sit the hell down, but I dare not get on his bad side.

Luke stops in his tracks and whips around. "What the hell are you doing here?" he asks, glaring at Cory with furrowed brows and wide eyes as if his presence represents a crime. "Why don't you need a mask to breathe?"

Cory leans against the wall to my right, shoulders pressed to the glass as his lower body is slightly extended away from it. Dressed in casual attire, a long-sleeve, dark-green t-shirt and black jeans, he had to be in his dwelling when he departed for here. He stuffs his thumbs into his pockets and stares at Luke. "Because I don't." His sigh rumbles. "I'm here because I needed to speak with someone about their plot for ruin. Apparently," he carries on, pulling himself from the wall and stepping to the center of the floor, "I'm a part of this plan to raid their territory. Unbeknownst to me," he shouts, throwing his arms up. More to himself, he mumbles, "Somehow, even when I do nothing, I'm here, held prisoner with you two dipshits."

Luke and Cory bicker, and I zone them out. The obnoxious pounding in my chest has not subsided. The breaking of my heart hasn't alleviated. It hurts so badly. I hug my knees to my chest to suppress it. I thought the feeling of jealousy was bad, or fear, which was absolutely traitorous. This, though... This feels like

I'm dying with every pulse and every pause I get to take a gulp of air for it only to be knocked out of me again.

"So..." Cory crosses the floor to me. He knocks the side of my boot with his twice. "Marc isn't the guy you thought he was, huh?"

With the heel of my palms pressed to my forehead, I utter, "Just because we are prisoners together, that does not mean I will not punch you in the face and chip another tooth."

Cory chuckles. "Sorry, Ky. But dude seriously played you."

"He did play you, Ky," Luke says, now at my side, leaning his shoulder against the wall as he looks down at me.

I flinch and glare up at him through my lashes. "You trusted him too, Luke!"

"Maybe. But you loved him, and I told you not to." He meets my gaze. My eyes continue to well with tears, frequently on the edge of rolling over, getting harder and harder to fight. I look away from him, shame keeping me from looking him in the eyes. There's no way I would tell him what Marc and I did. But somehow, he reads it on me. "Ky," he sings in a remorseful tone, shoulders slacking as he slides to the floor. "Tell me you didn't?"

I cross my arms and rest them against my propped-up knees. "No, Luke. I didn't. I'm just angry," I say, pressing my forehead to my forearm. I don't need his pity or his sympathy.

The door to our cell slides open. I sit up. A pink female Vojin stands in the entryway, large almond shaped eyes looking the three of us over. The pink Vojin were supposed to be the good ones who wanted to preserve the America and their kind. They had asked to be spared. I try to recall if I shot any pink Vojin, but everything happened so quickly. I don't know. "Lukahn? Kylie?" she says. Luke approaches her, but she doesn't move from blocking the doorway until I make it to his side. "Follow me please." Her body turns toward the exit, and she steps forward on her right foot, movement slow until her left foot falls in step, then she walks at a normal pace. Luke and I cautiously follow behind her. Her voice is vaguely familiar, but I can't place her name.

She leads us from the cell to a hall lit in soft forest green, providing just enough light to quietly maneuver behind the Vojin. She stops around a corner, and we wait behind her. Nearby, we hear the sound of a door sliding open and closed. A bright silver light engulfs the hall we wait to enter, likely one of the gray Vojin. It fades, heading the opposite direction of us.

The female Vojin rounds the corner. We follow behind her. She heads down the hall, stopping at a cloudy white glass door. Here, she presses her slender hand to the central panel, and the reader acknowledges her action by outlining the shape of her hand in pink. The door slides left, unlike the other doors that slid right. We cautiously enter the small space. The Vojin steps in, and the room takes on her pink hue. The door closes, and our surroundings shift, briefly tugging us toward the floor. The room ascends.

"You would call this an elevator," she says in a hushed voice, likely taking notice of my confused expression as I survey this contraption. "I visited you on Earth, in your home, pleading for you to consider rebelling with us."

I recall her and another warning us their leader had been overthrown by rebellious Vojin who are responsible for the threat on Earth.

"You all are now prisoners of the Vojin."

Luke snorts. I flick my gaze to his repulsed face before focusing back on the slinky frame of the Vojin.

She continues, "We will keep you from execution. Stay silent. You should avoid answering or asking any questions. Your associates called Jord, Seits, and Harold have also been captured. I have convinced them to move you all near them. In the night, when the passageway is clear and falls dark, this should be the preferred time to discuss your escape and how you will take down the Volones. Once they are out of the picture, the destruction of your planet as well as the takeover will end." Just as she finishes, the elevator stops and the door slides open.

Volones. This must be what they are calling the oversized gray Vojin. They look like a completely different species with their seven-foot height and gray fusing color, like storm clouds slowly churning beneath their flesh. They seem built to dominate the smaller Vojin. But their frames are the same: broad shoulders and a wide torso that slims down making their hips skinny to fall in line with their long legs.

I hold my questions, sensing the Vojin chose to finally speak in the elevator because she was safe from being heard. Luke and I follow her exit. The back of my head is throbbing from being knocked out by that gun, and my arm twitches for me to rub it. But I keep my hands to my sides so I don't draw attention to my discomfort. I don't think it's bleeding, but with every pulse, it feels like the knot is growing bigger.

The pink female Vojin approaches another door that slides open when she steps in front of it. The door opens to another hall that leads to a dead end, with walls and glass floor lit in a cloudy white that doesn't shine brightly but brings enough light to see. I see twelve prison-like cells, six on each side, small rooms enclosed by bars made up of thick glass tubes about the width of my wrist.

We continue down the hall until the Vojin stops in front of the third cell on the left. The clear glass bars lift into the ceiling at our approach. Within the cell, against the wall to the left is a floating, twin-size cot. There's no toilet or sink unlike the punishment lockups back on Earth. We better start planning our escape immediately. These conditions will not work for us. The Vojin points for Luke and me to walk in. "Here first," she tells us. "I'll move you later."

We follow orders. The bars quickly shoot down from the ceiling into the floor where a vacuum like sound continues until the bars stop moving. Once they do, she walks away.

I find a corner and sit with my back against the wall. Crossing my arms, I rest them on my propped-up knees and lay my forehead against them.

CHAPTER 2

HOW DIDN'T I see it?

Was it staring me in the face the entire time, and I was just blind?

The heat of regret warms over my flesh. I shiver.

How can I be so gullible? So...stupid?

Even now, after the recent events, I settle in the corner of this prison cell, headache persisting—a reminder—and regrettably...I think about Marc.

My regret isn't because of the time I dedicated to him or the amount of myself I gave to him, but because of how I wish the person betraying me wasn't him.

I whip my head back, and ram it against the wall over and over, worsening the knot from where I was clocked in the back of my head.

Luke sits beside me. He wraps his arm around my shoulders and pulls me to rest against him. "Shh," he soothes and rubs my arm. "I'm sorry, Ky," he whispers.

I cringe. It should be me apologizing to him for getting us into this whole mess. But peeping a word results in a gasp or whimper, and I will allow neither to escape. Ever.

"Pull it together, Ky. You'll be fine. Shake it off." Luke knows. He's too smart for me to ever hide anything from him, and though he likely has a million disapproving comments to beat me over the head with, I appreciate he's not being a jerk right now.

My tears stay back, but there's a pain in my chest, a constant fluttering that makes me aware of my heartbeat. It's pounding in my throat too. I sigh, "I can't believe I was so stupid."

"Don't talk about it." He shifts. "Get up. Somebody's coming."

We climb to our feet, watching the edge of the cell for whoever may be heading our direction. A gray Vojin—Volones—comes down the hall with Seits and Jord, hands strapped behind their backs. Marc and Sean are behind them, guns aimed at the backs of their heads. They approach the cell across from ours, and the bars shoot up into the ceiling. The two are shoved in, and the cell is sealed.

Turning around, the Volones crosses the hall to our cell, and it opens. He points to me as do Marc and Sean's guns. Luke and I walk forward, and the Volones shoves Luke back so hard he slams into the wall and falls onto the floor. He grunts. I whip around to aid him, and I'm snatched back by my arm, yanked out of the cell. The bars shoot down from the ceiling and quickly seal, separating me from my brother.

I don't turn away from Luke until he meets my eyes and gives me a nod. Now knowing he's okay, I turn my attention back to the Volones. He points down the hall. I march further down the hall until I'm ordered to stop. In the last cell on the left, I'm shoved forward through the opening, and the cell seals behind me. My trigger finger twitches, and I lean against the wall and remind myself to stay quiet.

"You," the Volones points to Sean. "Watch her. And you," he points to Marc. "Watch them." He gestures to Jord and Seits and leaves after stating he's going for Cory and Harold.

I keep my gaze on the floating bed, knowing if I were to avert it, I'd find myself staring at Sean's back and acting out three different events that would get me shot.

The cell across from me is empty, and the others are too far away to discreetly communicate with.

A thump sounds from the glass bars. I look their direction. Marc stands at my cell, shotgun lowered, slung over his shoulder. He gestures for me to come over. I shake my head. Marc places his forehead to the bars with his arms through them, both hands wave me over.

Again, I shake my head.

He mouths, "I'm sorry."

I flick my gaze away from his frown and lowered eyebrows to the cloudy white ceiling, trying to keep my tears from falling. This is such a stupid feature to this body. The tears burn my eyes but refrain from pouring over.

Marc taps the bar again.

Grumbling, I dart my gaze in his direction, and a tear skates down my cheek. He looks away from me. "What?" I harshly whisper.

"Come here," he mouths.

"No," I mouth back, slamming my fist against my leg. "Go away."

He extends his hand through the bars into my cell and opens his eyes a little wider. "Please," he begs, brows trembling and lips drawing inward.

Getting up, I go to him. At my approach, he grazes my neck and pushes his hand up through my messy ponytail to the knot protruding from my head. He gently massages the spot. The bars are wide enough apart for him to place his forehead to mine when he inches me forward. "I'm sorry." I try to pull away, but his free hand shoots out and grabs my waist. He keeps me close.

His body heat warms my neck and face. The comfort I get

from the contact stabs a knife in my back, as if the action is a betrayal to myself.

Marc turns my head to whisper in my ear, "I'd never turn on you. I do love you, Ky. I just…now…I know in the end you'll pick Luke, and I can't be with you knowing you are my first pick and I'm not yours. That's why I agreed to do things this way. So be mad at me, I can take it. I just wanted to explain and reassure you everything we did was one hundred percent authentic. My love in you was the most genuine emotion I've ever felt." He pauses. "I think I love you too much. And while I'm okay with that, my love isn't enough for you." He meets my eyes. "But trust I love you."

I grab the glass bars in my hands to keep myself from reaching for Marc and attacking him. "How can I trust you?" This close to him, I avoid looking into his eyes. "If everything was real for you, you would be behind these bars with me. Not on the other side."

"That's not true, Kylie."

I try to keep my voice low, but the burn building in my throat makes it rough. "You are a snake, and I stupidly fell into your deception." I push away, but his hands, still wrapped around my waist and the back of my head, force me to stay. "I'm through with you. Let me go."

His hold on me tightens. "Would you look at me?"

I shake my head.

"Then hear me." Marc's lips brush my ear as he whispers, "I can't explain right now what's going on. But you just need to trust me." He leans back a bit and begs, "Please, Ky. Trust me."

I can't. "As long as you're out there, and I'm in here, I'll never trust you." I step back, but my hands remain wrapped around the bars. His pleading eyes locked on mine make my sureties insecurities, and I begin to doubt I'm making the right decision.

I hold my breath and lean over, grip tightening around the glass. Sadness is working its way through me, but I will not break down. Not here. Not in front of him. I cough against the pain and wince to fight it off.

"Hey," Marc carries on in a whisper. "Come here, Ky." His rough palm rubs my neck. As I rise, he cuffs my cheek and swipes the tear from my eye. "I hate to see you cry."

I grab him by the shoulder straps of his vest. I shake him once. "I want to tell you I hate you so badly," I whisper, now understanding exactly what he meant when he said that to me. "I *want* to hate you."

He wraps me in his arms, bars separating our frames. An inch away from my lips, he utters, "But your wants don't matter." He kisses me, and I don't want it to feel as reassuring and perfectly perfect as it does. What is it about him, this boy I accidentally fell in love with at Separation? How did I get here?

Marc's lips move smoothly against mine, like we've known each other for years. In this uncomfortable situation, he makes it comfortable. Breaking away, he requests, "Now, tell me you love me, Kylie."

Though I may, I will not say those words. "Tell me now. What's going on?"

He sighs so low I barely hear it. "Why haven't you asked me yet?"

I roll my eyes at his change in subject. "What?"

"If I'm mixed."

I shrug. "I don't care. I wouldn't have cared. I didn't fall for you because of what you are. If you are still you, none of that even matters." Marc looks down, and I survey him, his dark hair, warm skin tone, his beard lining his jawline, and his neutral expression. Regrettably, I recall Collins kissing him, and an onslaught of memories pound against my already hurting head. A realization pulls a gasp from me.

Marc looks up, eyes squinting as he waits for me to reveal what's caused my shock.

"All this time. You'd been acting weird, sneaking away, and no one could find you, keeping secrets, and being standoffish at times." The pieces begin fitting together like a puzzle. "Then Collins always being around you, stopping by your room late at night. She may have been trying to get under my skin, but I had it wrong, didn't I? It wasn't romantic between you two. You've been working with her the entire time, haven't you? Planning this?"

"Yes," he answers in a matter-of-fact monotone that I interpret as truth.

"And you expect me to trust you!" I hiss, thrusting a jab at him that doesn't connect as he jumps out of the way of it. "You disloyal son of a bitch! I've given you everything," I whisper harshly.

Staggered, his brows furrow, and his orchid eyes darken. He stalks back to the bars. "You're so naive, Kylie. Me!" he snaps in a hushed tone. "I've given up everything for you. From the trust of my brother to my loyalty to myself. It's you who's betrayed me, from every night you'd lie with me to standing in my face yesterday and telling me I wasn't important enough for you to make the same sacrifices for me, Ky." He huffs angrily, looking away from me as he shakes his head. When he looks back up, I look away from him. He says, "Now sit the hell down and trust me to work this out." He steps away from the cell, warning, "Someone is coming."

I grit my teeth, taking three steps back from the bars. He won't get away with talking to me like that.

The Volones's silver illumination casts over the hall before he enters. The sound of rubber scraping glass screeches through the cellar. The Volones has Cory by his neck, dragging him as though his neck were a handle and his legs were wagon wheels. The toes of his boots scrape across the floor. The Volones throws Cory in the cell across from mine, and the bars quickly shut. Another seven-foot Volones is shoving Harold into the cell beside me, and then Jord's pushed into the cell across from him—next to Cory, but diagonal from me.

It's quiet.

At least for a minute, the silence swallows the prison in the way quiet follows an explosion after the eruption, which is Collins. The glass floor makes it easy to see the reflections of the traitors. The floor being glass also makes the sound of Collins's footsteps clear. They both draw my attention to her presence. She comes down the hall, one of her feet dragging after every third step, maybe her left. She glances in my direction before turning to Marc. "Why haven't we killed her yet?"

"They are not ready to kill any of them," he tells her.

I sit on the floor in the corner, back to the wall. She closes the distance between them, and I look away to the floating bed, wondering if I ripped it away from the wall and threw it at the bars, would it still have the ability to hover?

Collins utters to Marc, "Not them, just her."

I clench my fist and bite down on my lip to keep in my anger. But it comes out, though not explosively. "Collins," I say peacefully, yet low and sincere, "I can't wait to kill you."

She snickers. "You will never get that chance, Ky."

There's movement. "Don't taunt her," Marc warns.

"Get off me," she says, dismissing him.

I cut in. "The moment I get the chance, Collins. And oh, yes, I will definitely get that chance. I am going to watch you suffer. My hands will be wound around your neck, gripping you tighter and tighter the more bloodshot your eyes become, and when your face is burning red and your nails are digging into my wrist and the heels of your boots are scraping the ground, while the hope for mercy bleeds in your slowly beating heart, and inaudibly, your last breath is used to beg me to let you go. I'm going to revel in those words and say no just before I proudly prove it."

In my periphery, I see her approach my cell. Her hands wrap

around a couple of the bars. "Even in death, Ky. I will never beg you for anything."

Meeting her gaze, I nod. "We'll see," I say and drag my lazy gaze away from her. "When I'm out from behind these bars and not being threatened with a gun to my head, don't run."

"I won't," she promises.

"If she does run, Ky, I'll catch her." Luke's voice echoes from down the hall. "But only if you let me kill Sean's bitch of a brother and then his bitch ass."

Something hits against a glass bar. The clunk echoes and the glass vibrates. "You do realize we're the ones holding the guns while you sit locked up?" Sean says. His lighthearted perky tone is replaced by a seriousness that makes him sound more like his brother. I take a quick glance at Marc to make sure I've been speaking to the right twin. Meeting his gaze, I look away. *It's him.*

Pressing the heels of my hands against my forehead and my elbows to my knees, I agree with my brother. "Sure, Luke. You can kill Marc and Sean. *Pfft*, whether I catch Collins or not, you can kill them." I shrug.

"I got you, Ky," he concludes.

Cecilia comes to Collins, who is still standing in front of my cell. "Collins, if you shoot her right now, they won't find out until they come back. Worst that can happen is they get upset. But they need us now, so her premature death won't matter." Cecilia glares at me. She says through her teeth, "I'd like to see how long it will take you to bleed out before you pass out."

I sweep my hand through the air, not even caring enough to use my words against her. I've proven neither of them are a match for me. The only way they'll get the upper hand is with me behind bars.

"I'd like to know what type of Creations you four are to turn on your country and stand with the invaders." Harold's throaty voice, deep and a bit harsh, causes a slight rumbling echo in the hall.

"We are only Creations," Collins states. "We were offered an opportunity to be the first of our planet's reconstruction. Marc and I and Sean and Cecilia. We will breed a new life on Earth." She hits the butt of her shotgun against the bars of my cell. "You hear that, Ky? I'll get to lie with Marc over and over as we make babies to populate the earth. How does that make you feel?"

I hold my grumble but sigh as I lean my head against the wall and close my eyes. My leg twitches for me to jump to my feet, race across the small cell, snatch her by the collar of her vest and yank her forward so hard that when her head rams against the bar, the glass and her skull will shatter. Marc does not object to her derisive words, and while I wait for jealousy to churn in my stomach, I remain numb. I snort, but it turns into a chuckle. "I hope you've already gotten the chance to lie with Marc because there's no way you're making it out of here alive."

She laughs.

Jord clears his throat, and loudly states, "The four of you turned on us just to have the title of being the first on Earth for their reconstruction?"

Collins finally leaves, going to Jord's cell. "Yes," she says as if the answer is obvious and makes sense.

Cory grumbles a rough breath, causing his lips to make a vibrating sound. "You sound so dumb, Collins." Standing from the floating bed, he nears the bars of his cell. "They don't even like Creations, you dimwitted lunatic. They even hate humans and want to purge the Creations completely! Why would they use you four to reconstruct?"

Collins takes a couple of steps over to his cell. "Because we are strong, we manage, and have an understanding with them," she states sternly, throwing her hands on her hips.

"No. You are a fucking idiot. They chose you because you

could stand between whatever plan Jord had to go against them." Cory's the only one of us, seeming comfortable in this world, but disconnected because he looks more like us as a Creation than the Vojin, his origin. He glares down at Collins, his upper lip curled in disgust. "They created an ally, and you fail to realize that the only position you hold in this is to prove your disloyalty to your family. You really think, seeing how quickly you turned on your own people, they are going to bring you onboard with their plan? They see you can be bought Collins, all four of you! All you're good for is knowing the secrets of this mission, and keeping an eye on the others. Don't get this shit confused thinking the Vojin are your pals because they're not." Cory turns his back to her, goes back to the bed, and lies down. "The only way any of us will be making it out of here is by death. Period."

I expected to either be caught or die here. Last night, I mentally prepared myself for this. Being locked in a cell, likely staring death in the face, doesn't bother me. *He* bothers me.

Marc stares a hole through me until I dart my gaze to him. "What?" I mouth.

He turns a quarter of the way to me. "What she said. That's not true," he says, mouthing the words.

"I don't care," I mouth back, shrugging.

He inhales, chest swelling, shoulders rising high. The air rushes out of him as he exhales and looks away from me. "Sean," he calls. "Trade spots with me." He glances my way once more before being replaced by his brother.

Marc doesn't have the right to be upset with me for being angry at him or angry about this situation. They set us up, working with the Vojin for whatever reason. The four Creations least suspected to be mixed are the ones who took the Vojin side. How do they expect us to respond?

I'm with Cory. I know the Vojin have no interest in Creations. We're their enemy. Maybe not their greatest enemy, but we,

Creations, are the only ones who can give them a run for their money. Like they mentioned at the meeting in Highrum, the Zombies were a threat that would end if our government would eliminate Creations, which I believe might be a ploy to get the Guidance to take out the America's greatest defenses.

If the Guidance or the Trade believe them, Creations are done for.

Now, we're going to be left to watch as it all unfolds.

CHAPTER 3

FOR WHAT SEEMS LIKE HOURS, we wait for night to fall. Or something for us to interpret as night. My watch is distorted. The hands slowly wind counterclockwise constantly.

My eyes are dry, and my muscles cramp from sitting in the same position for too long. I fight a yawn and start to climb to my feet when I hear the door to the hall slide open.

Soft pink washes over the dimmed corridor. The glow grows brighter as the pink female Vojin makes her way to my cell. "Kylie?" she calls, voice the same as the Vojin from earlier.

I stand as the bars rise. The Vojin heads out of the hall, and I follow closely behind her, keeping my steps quiet and my guard up. Our *guards* watch me as I depart, but they say nothing.

Finally, something that shuts Collins up.

We pass Luke's cell, and I look in on him, seeing him sleeping like a baby. I smile to myself. It's a relief he's found comfort. He's not worried about us getting out of here, so I won't worry about it either. We clearly have this pink Vojin on our side, and maybe she's waiting for the right moment when the Volones let their guard down so she can really help us get out of here.

We quietly walk through the narrow halls. The glass floor is a dimly lit blueish green, and a green stream of lights runs up the walls, seemingly within the glass. Maybe it's their way of communication. By the way the floor and walls responded to the war and the Vojin's steps, it's connected to them in some way.

The female Vojin leads me to the elevator room. With the multiple turns we take, I get lost in this maze of halls, unable to determine my right from my left. Should we make it out of those cells, there's no way we would find our way back to the portals without help from a Vojin.

The elevator takes us down until the door slides open. She exits first and surveys the halls. With the coast clear, she waves me on. We walk three feet to the left, down a hall also made of a glasslike material. It's dimly lit in a stormy gray like the hall cellar with the jail cells.

We come up on our destination, another section in the glass that's a sliding door. It's so quiet I can hear myself breathe, but I don't hear a single move the pink Vojin makes, even as she lifts her right hand and presses it to the center of the door. The door slides to the left, opening to a small command center lit by a soft white hue. What I interpret as clear glass tables curve around half the room, facing a blank glass wall.

The pink Vojin approaches the tables, four feet from where we stand, and places her hand to the center of the one directly in front of us. The table tops glow pink as a switchboard reveals itself. Buttons and keys reflect in the glass as the wall beyond it presents eight rectangular screens from floor to ceiling, as though they were being projected onto the glass wall.

The room's white hue turns a greenish-blue that mixes with the Vojin's pink. The female Vojin presses her middle finger, the largest of the four that looks as though the two middle fingers of a normal hand were merged into one, against an outlined circle on the table. She says, "This is real time," as the screens on the wall begin showing videos. "It shows what's going on right now on your Earth."

I shrug a shoulder, unconcerned at the moment about the events on Earth. I need to get out of here. "Okay. Is this going to get us back home?"

The pink Vojin looks away from me, placing her hands on her hips. Her use of body language helps me recall her name, Noranti. "There." She points to the monitor in the middle. Waulers gang up on a man, kicking and stabbing him. "Death," she informs me. Pointing to another, she says, "Destruction." Fire is erupting along a forest. At another she gestures, saying, "Hate." People are marching, fists thrusting in the air as they hold up posters and sticks, raiding yet another city that may soon be swarmed with Creations for Citizen Management. She continues to go over the video, showing our dying planet from the pollution poisoning the air to the withering wildlife and forests. "This species is a virus to the planet Earth. Such a beautiful place." The screens change from the worst of scenes to open seas where large fish roam, to a rushing river deep in a forest where a deer drinks from the water, to snow falling on an empty, abandoned street untainted by human traffic.

The screens change again, back to the first scenes. Then Noranti says, "There is so much hate and death. So much destruction wreaks havoc on Earth already." On a few other screens are landmines of garbage and debris piled high on land or flooding the water supply, attacks on cities, and on the last is the ongoing war between the countries.

I nod slowly, saying, "This is why Creations are here."

She presses her hand to the switchboard again, and the screens blink as they change again. "Creations are the problem."

A string of cuss words gathers on my tongue. I bite them back when she gestures toward the screens. Creations march on the protest as I suspected they would. They take out all parties involved; a simple way to resolve the violence is to eliminate the cause of hate. The Waulers, they're also diminished. The mounds of trash are taken care of by a crew of Creations that has been working around the clock to minimize pollution and find preferred ways to dispose of trash overflow, composting it instead of burning it. Everything she reveals is exactly what Creations are instructed to do. There's no problem here.

"Like I said, Creations eliminate the problem," I say.

"The only benefit to Creations is that they follow instructions well, put aside their opinions, and run into the fire when ordered. However," she points to the middle screen now, which shows lines of dead bodies with Creations standing around them, adding more. "Death." On another monitor, Creations torch an entire town. "Destruction." On a final screen, she shows Creations fighting to the death with another country. "Hate." The screens disappear. Noranti takes a single step back from the switchboard and faces me. "Creations were not a resolution to this virus, but another strain. A development of a greater problem."

I meet her black, big almond-shaped eyes feeling attacked on both counts, human and Creation. Derision causes my upper lip to curl up and my nose to crinkle. "Creations do as they're told," I say, shoving a pointed finger toward the ground. "*We* have a job to do. We were created for this reason, and we will uphold our duty to the America. Questioning this, refusing to comply puts our lives at risk. You know this. The Vojin insisted their implants accommodate the rules imposed on Creations by the government of the America."

She blinks, a film-like eyelid falling down and slowly lifting, glossing the once dry-appearing eyes. "We are enemies of the Earth as you all are enemies of the Earth."

Shaking my head, I say, "We manage the citizens of the America. We were created to do so. We fight the other countries to maintain the America's top placement in the world's hierarchy. And we show the universe our country is able to face all things without fear."

"Creations were created to kill, to destroy—"

"We were created to protect, to enhance, and encourage!" I say through my teeth.

"They," she says with emphasis, flashing a shade of red, "were created to despise anyone and anything that goes against their government." She continues to gesture to the blank wall. "Creations are the destruction. You manage the citizens, maybe to maintain order, but you manage the citizens by making them afraid of you, by keeping their numbers down, keeping them in control, and eliminating their freedom."

"The America is the freest country on the planet Earth!" I fire back.

"You are not free, Kylie."

"I'm free," I say, pointing at my chest.

"You may be free to speak and walk. You are not free to change, to experience without sneaking or hiding, to bask in the real enjoyment of life."

I find myself shouting to defend myself and slightly rising up on my toes with every word I spit past my lips. "My life's enjoyment is being better than everyone else, fighting for my country, and applying myself."

Noranti turns away from me in a smooth motion, going back to the switchboard. She presses her hand to the center then climbs over the desk to the wall. She presses her finger to the second to last screen on the right... "This is your life's enjoyment."

My chest swells. I swallow hard and cross my arms to keep my hands from shaking. I'm two inches tall as I witness her reveal: Marc, carrying me dressed in my purple dress around the base. In this shot, I see a moment of that night I've wanted to keep private. On the screen, he stops beneath the moonlight, and in the middle of the road, he spins us around. We wear smiles the width of our shoulders, and our eyes are brighter than the moon. We shared our fictitious freedom and lived in it for a night, with each other, something we could never get from anyone else. They could release me as a Creation and tell me I'd never have to follow another order as long as I live, but I'd still feel captive without...*him*. The thought crashes around in my head, and I hate the stabbing sensation climbing up my spine.

That shouldn't be the case anymore.

"This doesn't matter!" I smash my palm down on the glass. The event continues to play and takes over every monitor. I slap my palm down again in a different area, but it doesn't stop. Over and over I slap the glass, trying to get the screens to change. "Shut this off. I was not free! I was fooled! I can't see this as freedom or enjoyment!"

She presses her elongated middle finger against the screen in the middle. "No?" she asks as the video playing changes. They caught us, here, talking through the bars. They noticed my slight tell when I melt for him. It boils my blood.

I slam my fist on the glass again, knowing full well I have no effect on it. I lean over, palms on the glass, shaking my head as my breaths grow heavy. My feelings burn my cheeks, and an ache wrenches through my chest. I breathe and say, "What is your point?"

"The Volones want the Creations terminated and Earth destroyed. They've taken out many planets before, and it was only a matter of time before they tried to take out Earth again."

Narrowing my eyes, I cross my arms. "Again?" To my knowledge, Earth has only been attacked once. "The Volones were responsible for the first destruction..."

She nods. It's impossible to read her facial expression because she lacks the necessary facial features. No eyelids, eyebrows, or skin to help express a wrinkle from a frown or the stretch of a smile. "They partially destroyed the Earth, and then saved it so the Earth's leaders would trust them. This not only implied their value, but also their strength."

"It was all a ploy for this?" I gesture around me and realize I'm not on Earth, and she can't see the herds of Zombies and their destruction on our planet. A thought trickles into my mind of the time we visited Highrum and the conversation came up about eliminating Creations. "It was all for the day they could make requests, such as destroy Creations?"

She nods. "Originally, we were to select four, you and Lukahn and two other humans. You four would establish a race of humans in which our values of order and control were already within the bloodline."

"By the blood of an inserted Creation."

She shakes her head and whispers almost too low for me to hear her, "By a rebellious Creation. Every offspring would have the DNA of a being that is of each of the parties. The human knows remorse and love, the Creation has the will to protect and heal, and the Vojin has the ability to latch and control. They would not only be able to care for each other, but care for the planet as well. Our hope is we can teach them, end the loss of life, end destruction, and eliminate hate."

Since being a Creation, since being a forged host to Vojin, and living on earth, I've learned a lot. I've studied emotions and experiences; I've tested ideas and broken limits. And there's one thing I've learned that I doubt will ever change. "Hate lies in people regardless. Blood has been shed on the land, there's no erasing that, and the evil that rises with the revenge of those departed souls will continue to haunt the land and spread the evil."

Her hands rise at her sides, palms up. "Understandable. This will take some practice. However, with strict observation and study of the mind, constant instruction, and induced behavior treatments, I doubt by the time we're finished that evil will be a concern within the new generation."

"Induced behavior treatments?" I lift my hand to my chin and take it between my fingers. "This is how you all created the Zombies?"

She makes an odd tittering sound, but her face can't express amusement. "It is simple to create humans who want to hurt and destroy other humans. Although, establishing a human who wants to care for, love, give, and understand is a task that not even the Maker could help us achieve. We tried that with you and Luke, encouraging you to focus in on your dormant emotions, your human anatomy, to make you a better species, but it was a failure. Instead, it brought you here, raiding our command module."

Wait, so this isn't even their home base? What a freaking bust this entire plan was! I hang my head and press my thumb and middle finger to my temples, trying to suppress the escalating headache that's traveling from the back of my head to the front. I shrug, replaying her statement in my head, how Luke and I were technically failed experiments. Looking back at her, I say, "No one is perfect. So what now? You're going to help us out of here?"

"The destruction of Creations has already begun. Bases are crumbling as we speak, from your leader's instruction to discontinue the Separation bases. Some Creations, however, are being reserved for the sake of protection, but it may not be for much longer. The Volones will continue their destruction, they're careless about what can become of the humans because the more fear they can create, the easier it will be for the planet's leaders to turn to them for help. Like the other planets they've taken over. Minimize population, set up homes, give Vojin free range to Earth's resources, and the inhabitants live indebted to them."

"Why me?" I ask. "Why are you telling me all this?"

"We need you, Kylie. You and Lukahn. Your mother and

father were so close to putting an end to their mission, but were caught before they could."

Easily piqued at the mention of my parents, I beg, "What can you tell me about them? I want to know everything. I demand to know the exact reason you all killed them." It wasn't a Volones who threatened me in that burrow or taunted me with the reveal of killing my mom and dad, it was a Vojin. A regular-sized blueish green Vojin.

Her hands grab my shoulders. The beds of her four fingers pressing against my flesh are firm and round like a coin. "We don't have the time for that right now. Assist in stopping them. Pick up where they left off."

Shoving her bright arms from me, I say, "I don't know if you've noticed this or not, but you all currently have me locked in a Vojin prison where I have to pee on the floor in front of everyone. I can't assist you in anything."

"The brothers will help you when the sisters and Volones are not around."

Pursing my lips, I murmur, "Sure they will."

"Put aside your anger with them. Your tarnished freedom with your friend will reconstruct." Noranti presses her hand against the glass on the switchboard again. The monitors turn on. "It was only partially destroyed, but the freedom that lives in your heart is long-lasting. You simply need to change your mind."

Partially destroyed. Carden's incredibly quirky smile flashes in my mind, and I remember him saying the same words.

"Things can be destroyed and reconstructed. It only takes a seed to grow a tree, even after you've burned down the entire forest." She turns for the entry door. "We will return to your cell now." She heads out of the room, and I follow behind her. Just before the door slides open, she adds, "They will execute their plan in two Earth days. Figure out your strategy quickly."

THE GLASS FLOOR is getting uncomfortable. I stand up from sitting in the corner and pace the floor. I'm tired, but I refuse to sleep. Anything can happen if I blink too long, and I don't want to miss it. We're still on day one, waiting on night, or at least for the hall to empty.

"Ky?" Sean whispers, gaze flicking back and forth from me to what's in front of him, down the hall. He may be keeping an eye on Collins or his brother.

I press my thumb and index finger against my closed lids. Rubbing hard, I try to draw some water to my dry eyes and wake myself up. "Yeah?"

"Rest. You'll need it. You're good."

Shaking my head, I say, "I prefer not."

Grumbling, Sean leaves from standing on this side of the hall and goes to his brother. "Let's go get some shut eye. Collins and Cecilia, you two. We've been up for hours. They'll be fine." I hear all four of their footsteps slap the glass floor before the door whishes open and closes behind them.

"Kylie?" Luke calls my name at the same time Jord says, "Pssst" to try and get my attention. "What'd that Vojin say?" Luke asks, four cells down. He's farther away from me than I'd like him to be and closer to the door. I worry about him being snatched out of the hall, should I accidentally fall asleep.

I explain everything Noranti and I discussed, leaving out Marc. But I do mention, "She and Marc have told me they are on our sides. I just don't know for sure."

"You know him better than all of us, Kylie," Seits starts. "Do you think he would turn on us? On you?"

"Or do you think they have something on him that would force his hand?" Jord adds.

I pinch my bottom lip and lift my gaze to the ceiling. "I...I don't know." Marc isn't the type to be suckered into doing something he doesn't want to do.

"You all need to accept your prince is a pauper and move on," Cory says in his typical grumpy tone, turning onto his side as he lays on the floating bed.

I roll my eyes and lean against the glass wall of my cell opposite the bed. I refuse to sit on that thing. A shudder crawls up my spine every time I look at it. This whole place makes me uncomfortable. Being in the enemy's camp, not knowing if anyone can be trusted. "We need to get out of here, guys. Any ideas?"

"Did you see anything on your walk with the pink one?" Jord asks.

"Nothing but hall after hall. No identifiers or anything that looked familiar. We'll need to take out the Volones first, the big gray ones. They're the cause of everything. And they plan on destroying our world in two days." I think over my words and correct myself. "Their partial destruction, but that pink Vojin, Noranti, didn't mention Earth being the problem." Maybe their plan is to recycle the world. If they intend to only cause disruptions on Earth by eliminating humans and Creations, why wouldn't they expect the Earth to be affected by their actions in some way? "But something can't be partially destroyed, right?" I wonder out loud. Maybe they actually plan not only to wipe out the inhabitants from Earth, but to destroy the planet like they tried to do last time.

Cory walks to his bars and leans his shoulder against them as he looks down the hall. "Sure it can. You take what you can salvage, destroy everything else, and in using what you have, make something new or better than what you had."

Enlightened, I push for more intel by giving more detail. Cory seems and has always seemed to know a lot about the Vojin's plan. "You terminate all the people on earth, save four—two guys and two girls—and use them to rebuild mankind."

"Train them up the way you please," Harold chimes in.

Jord says, "And you'll have their minds to mold and manipulate for an eternity."

Shaking my head, though he can't see me, I say, "Not if everyone is turned into Zombies. They aren't hurting the planet at all. They're only killing or changing people. The world's technically safe this way, and the dead bodies possibly help fertilize the land."

"Essentially, you destroy the people without hurting the planet," Cory says matter-of-factly. "But people make the world whole, without them that's destruction in itself. The only thing standing between them getting what they want is Creations. Creations will continue to fight as long as they exist. Once they're out of the way, the Vojin or Volones will hold the planet in their hands."

"Enough with the small talk," Harold nearly shouts. "We can try to figure out these things once we're back home. Kylie, that *thing* must have told you something we can use to get out of here."

I nod, though I know he can't see me. "Noranti will help us get out of here as long as we help them by taking out those Volones. Period."

"Help while you're behind bars, huh?" Cory scoffs. He goes to the floating bed and lies back down, throwing his arms behind his head.

"Then that's where Marc and Sean come in?" Luke asks.

I wrap my arms around my middle. The idea of asking Marc for something or relying on him turns my stomach. I snort and say, "Yep."

Luke asks, "Are you working on coming to terms with that?"

"No."

"Well, Ky. You need to suck that shit up. Woman up and do what you need to do so we can get out of here. We're all ready to go home, and if the only thing standing between us and getting out from behind these bars is you making nice with Marc, you'll do that."

I roll my eyes. I don't need him telling me what to do.

"After we're out, then what?" Cory asks.

"We fight without getting killed," Harold answers.

———

Snores echo through the hall.

I sit against the wall, staring at the bed, my eyelids growing heavy with every breath. My head droops, and I jerk up, repositioning myself, stretching my legs out and pressing my palms to the cold glass. I breathe.

"Hey Ky?" Cory calls.

Thank goodness. Something to keep me alert. "Yeah?" The gray light of the hall has warmed to where it's nearly hard to see. Nothing but a soft beam, like the glow of the moon on a cloudy day. This must be night.

"Remember when we would lay out blankets on my roof and watch the storm clouds blow in the wind? We'd have to keep our stuff from blowing away because the wind would be so strong." He chuckles. "Those nights with fewer responsibilities."

A small smile twitches at the left corner of my mouth. "I remember." Those nights looked just like the dreary setting in this depressing prison. "I could go for the fresh air and breeze right now."

Cory huffs a laugh. "Me too." He pauses. "Sorry about all the trouble I caused you. I was just trying to do my job."

"Un-huh." There's so much on my mind right now. The past isn't taking precedence at this moment. "Thanks for your apology."

"The list I was getting for the Trade, remember?"

I draw my knees to my chest to rest my head against them. Looking in his direction, I see him standing near his bars, bright green eyes looking my direction. "Of course I remember."

It's difficult to make out his face in the low light. But the low tone of his voice has a taut edge that makes my stomach squirm at the thought of his next words. "I knew you and Luke were mixed. I'd been undercover with the Trade. Something unconstitutional has been going on for years, and they needed someone age-appropriate to be in Separation. It's why I was shipped out early."

On my feet, I cross the floor to the bars.

"My placement mother, she was undercover with your parents." I wish I knew as much about my parent's dealings with the Vojin and the Trade as Cory does. All I have is what the crumbled letter told me, and it wasn't enough. "They were placed to identify the roles played by the Vojin and Guidance. They may be in cahoots, but no one has had the chance to report back or confirm this as fact. When the Vojin discover there's a traitor in the midst, they don't have as much kindness as someone like you. What you are is what can make this world a better place."

My brows draw taut. "In what way?"

The door slides open, and the hall lights up with the gray shine of a Volones entering. We back away from our bars and ease into the darkness of our cells. The snores once breaking the silence stop.

The Volones slowly strides down the hall to Cory's cell. "Step out," he orders, bars shooting up into the ceiling.

Cory steps into the hall, standing before the Volones with his spine straight and his shoulders drawn back. His face is even and not a glimmer of fear stains his eyes.

The Volones looks down on him. Almond eyes survey him as his arms hang at his sides and his fingers move fluidly as though he doesn't know what to do with them. He asks Cory, "What was the reason for your implant?"

Cory's brows furrow, confusion wiping over his face for a brief second before he sobers. "I was born Vojin. I am my implant."

The Volones lifts his hand, first finger extended and swipes across Cory's cheek as though he were wiping dust from a shelf. "Your flesh?" he asks.

Cory keeps his eye's locked on the Volones. The sudden contact doesn't faze him. "The way I was designed to blend in with the Creations from birth."

At seven feet tall, the Volones towers over Cory, looking down at him with no expression on his face. It's only by the deceptive tone of his voice that I realize this is an interrogation. "And you believe Creations do not need to be destroyed. Even though you are not a born Creation?"

Cory's left eye twitches, but he's yet to move. "I have lived this way for twenty years. It is what I am accustomed to."

The Volones raises his hand to Cory's face. His first and last fingers press to his temples, the middle one to his forehead, and thumb to his chin. Cory vibrates, along with the air around him, and he bursts with a soft *poof*. Blue and green particles sprinkle onto the floor and stick to the body of the Volones.

My heart pounds in my ears. Wide-eyed and slack-jawed, I stand as the world seems to expand and shrink with every beat. I hold my breath to slow my huffing and puffing.

The Volones wipes his hands over each other and turns on his heels to head for the cell beside mine. Harold hisses under his breath, daring the Volones's attack.

I hear the bars rise, a quick whiffing movement as they lift into the ceiling.

If Cory was one of them, and the Volones had no problem taking him out, what does that mean for the rest of us? I lean against the bars of my cell to peer into the hall.

Harold steps out of the cell, sizing up the Volones, glowering at him. Harold's usually covered from head to toe. They've taken his mask and helmet. Harold's ginger beard brushes his chest. Ice blue eyes peer at the alien giant towering over him.

"You once had a twin Creation?" the Volones asks.

"Yes," Harold responds simply.

"What was the reason for your implant?"

"Not to have my twin killed by the Vojin who we thought wanted to help the Earth, not destroy it!" Harold says through gritted teeth.

The Volones lifts his hand and Harold smacks it away. "Hell no! I'm not going out that easy!" he snaps. Harold throws a punch at the Volones's stomach, but it has no effect. The Volones doesn't move from the attack.

His hand shoots out, grabbing Harold around the neck, and in a blink, he erupts like Cory. There's a small *pop*, like a bubble bursting. Unlike Cory, there's no blue and green dust. Only flickering atoms that dissolve in thin air.

I swallow hard. Glancing over from my cell, I see Jord's wide eyes and knit brows. As he stands back from the bars, I can see the fight in his eyes. The second his bars rise, he's planning to fight to the death, and I understand. We've learned: avoid the touch.

I expect the Volones to come in my direction, but he heads the opposite way, down the hall.

My face is pressed to the bar as I watch the Volones stop in front of Luke's cell. "Step out," he orders once the bars rise.

I'm barely able to see Luke when he steps out of his cell, only hearing his steps cross the floor. There's a drumming in my ears that makes it hard to hear, my face is burning, and my hands shake. A feeling is sinking in my stomach that makes me heavy.

"What was the reason for your implant?" The Volones asks Luke.

"To replace my parents and enforce change on Earth at the point of the Vojin's takeover," Luke answers truthfully.

"Ah," the Volones says, understanding. "Your parents are diminished?" *Dead.*

"Yes. However, the—"

"Luke!" I shout, cutting him off. "Just *yes.*" *You cocky bastard, don't let your mouth get you killed.*

"Is that your Creation twin?" the Volones asks.

"Yes, I am," I answer for Luke. "How about you come down here and talk to me."

The Volones looks to be lifting his hand. He says, "We have no use for any of you."

"Hey!" I shout. "Wait!" I tug at the rigid bars that have grown warm from my sweaty palms. "Don't you lay a finger on my brother!" Ramming my fist against the glass, I shout, "You hear me?!" The glass doesn't budge or crack.

"Don't beg, Ky," Luke scolds.

"Shut up, Luke! I swear if you kill my brother, you lanky light pole, you're going to wish you took me first."

What feels like a sonic blast blinds me. A crack of thunder is quick to follow as a gust of wind smacks into me, and I fly back, hitting the floor. The glass bars of the cells are vibrating, causing a hollow ring to echo in the hall. It only lasts a second before a hush falls over the area.

The Volones stammers over his words, managing to say, "What kind of creature?"

I scramble to my hands and knees and crawl to the bars. "Luke?"

I try to shove my head through the bars, but I can't. I use the bars to pull myself to my feet, my knocking knees and numbing legs making it a chore. "Luke!" I shout. "Answer me. Please?"

I ram my fist against the glass again.

"Luke!" I scream. "Please answer me," I whisper but know he won't.

The door to the hallway slides open then whips closed. The lights dim. It's dark again.

Crumpling to my knees, hands sliding down the bars as I fall, I gasp for air. My chest caves, and my stomach tightens. I drop back down to the floor, legs giving out. "Luke?" comes out croaky. I tug myself onto my knees, short-winded. Looking to Jord, I ask in a hoarse voice, "Please tell me my brother's okay. That he's just passed out."

Jord's gaze drops to the floor, and his shoulder's slump inward. "I'm sorry, Kylie."

I turn my back to them and scream through my clenched teeth, wrapping my arms around my aching stomach. I wail and heave for air. "Dammit, Luke!"

CHAPTER 5

I PICK myself up from the floor when the door slides open again. My breaths are deep and slow, awaiting the gray shine of the Volones to brighten the hall, for him to come and finish the job.

A high-pitched chuckle escapes Collins. Sets of footsteps smack the glass floor as the others enter the hall.

Though my cheeks are streaked with tears, I turn around to see the four of them coming down the hall. I study each face, memorizing them and picturing how I'll murder each of them.

I clear my throat when Collins meets my gaze.

"What's wrong with you, Ky?" she asks with a nagging edge to her joyful tone. "You sad? Finally seeing the bigger picture?" she taunts, bottom lip poked out.

"Yes," I answer calmly. "Yes, I am sad." I drag the back of my hand across my tear-drenched chin.

She stares at me blankly for a second. Then she begins to shift her gaze up and down the hall. She rubs her right arm up and down and her chin trembles. "Why are you sad, Ky?" she asks with less sarcasm.

I ignore her.

Collins stomps her foot and shouts with more emphasis. "Why are you sad, Kylie?"

"Because," I start, as my tears return, skating down my face and falling onto my arm. Though I cry, I keep my facial expression calm, muscles remaining relaxed. "My brother is dead," I say peacefully, glaring at her.

Her gun hits the floor, and her mouth falls open. Raising her hands to her mouth, she lets out a wail that echoes off the walls. There's plenty I want to say, but I don't. Instead, I turn my back to her and lean against the bars. She goes on for a while, and when she finally quiets, I calmly inform her, "I'm going to kill all four of you." Turning around, my gaze instantly meets Marc's, and I say, "Especially you." Tears continue to fall from my eyes. "And I can't wait for that moment."

Collins cries again, falling to the floor. Her arms are splayed out at her sides, and her back arches inward as she wails for my brother's death.

"Shut up, Collins!" I shout. "You wanted this! You wanted all of us to die, remember? Why are you crying over him? You want Marc, don't you? He's alive. For now. Enjoy him, and don't weep over my brother like his death is some big damn deal to you, you fucking traitor! Every death that happened in here is on you four," I say, waving in their direction.

Marc takes a step toward my cell, and I warn, "Don't come near me. Ever."

He retracts.

The door slides open, and my stomach drops again, waiting for the gray hue to wash the hall. It's pink, but the relief never comes.

The female Vojin comes down to my cell. The bars rise and Noranti says to Marc, "Go in with her."

"No!" I shout, backing farther into my cell. Marc steps in, and I shove him out. "I said no!"

He pushes me back so hard I fall over, and in the time it takes me to regain my footing, the bars shut, and he hands his guns over to Sean.

We meet in the center of my cell. I wipe my eyes with the back of my hands, needing clear vision to knock him out. I charge forward. As I raise my arms for an attack, he snatches them by my wrists. I yank them from his grasp, forcing him to bend over, and I drive my knee into his chest.

He grunts and stands, keeping me tight in his grasp. Twisting me around, he has my arms crossed in front of my chest as my back is to his frame. His hold on me grows tighter now that his arms are wrapped around me.

I struggle to get loose, and realize all the times before, he wasn't using half of his strength in our fights. He starts forward, forcing me to walk to the other end of my cell. Once there, he loosens his constricting hold.

I break out of it and shove him away from me.

He grumbles, his face contorting into a scowl and his shaggy hair swaying around his head. Charging for me, he shoves me against the wall and pins me there. "Stop it, Ky."

I huff and puff, grunt and growl, all as I'm trying to break free. "Get away from me, Marc."

In a tranquil tone, with a soft, concerning knit to his brows, he says, "Kylie, stop and listen."

Droplets of sweat bead my forehead as anger raises my temperature and my hands and knees continue to shake. "If it wasn't for you turning on us, he wouldn't have been killed, Marc! What did you do?" I thrash forward, but he keeps me pinned. "Let me go!"

Marc's breaths rush harshly against my arms. He's using all his strength to hold me back, and the second he gets tired, I'm breaking through. He sandwiches me between his body and the wall. His head moves beside mine, and as he exhales, his even breaths brush across my neck. Gently, he sighs and drops his head. He whispers, "I'm so sorry, Ky." His beard scrapes my skin.

I bite my bottom lip and hate the tears for returning and the hurt that washes over me for being so mad at Marc. "I don't want your *I'm sorry*." This pain and the loss of Luke bombard me. "It feels like I'm being stabbed in my neck, my back, and my stomach. They killed my brother." I sniffle. "And it hurts, Marc. It hurts everywhere."

I sob. And all at once, it comes crashing down on me. I collapse against Marc's shoulder, crying because I'm imprisoned, because I lost my twin, and because even though I hate Marc I still love him and want him to hold me until it all passes.

Marc hugs me to him, squeezing me as though he's trying to soak up my sadness. We sink to the floor, and he finds a way to wrap every limb around me as I bawl against his chest. I release it, loosening the knot tightening my stomach.

This is my destruction.

CHAPTER 6

I ADJUST and find myself secured by warm arms wrapped around my chest and strong legs enveloped around mine. I blink. As if Marc knows I've awakened, he hugs me, saying, "I understand you're confused about me right now. But I'm here for you, and I love you. And I'm not allowing anything to convince you otherwise."

I crawl out of his grasp and climb to my weak legs. They've fallen asleep from the awkward position I was in for who knows how long. I turn my back to Marc and cross the cell to the bed. "Me leaning on you in that moment of weakness was an accident. Don't take this as an opportunity to speak to me and feed me more lies, Marc." I sit on the bed and lean over on my knees, taking my aching head between my palms. Every breath scratches my sore throat. Likely from the crying and the sore realization I'm solo forever now. They killed my brother, and it feels like I've lost the entire left side of my body. I can feel his presence no longer exists, and it slows me down. So many accomplishments left to me to achieve. I won't let him down. I won't let my parents down. I'll never let myself down. Our name will be upheld, and we'll be remembered for all our hard work and efforts. For Luke.

I push my hand over my messy hair, sighing. *I'll get through this. I can do this.*

Noranti remains outside of my cell, standing in the middle of the hall, facing the entrance. Her attention seems otherwise occupied. She may be using her telekinetic ability to tune into other things going on around her base. She may also be looking out while Marc takes up space in my cell.

"Kylie," Marc calls in a weak tone that causes his raspy voice to crack. I keep my back to him. "In order for us to get out of here, somebody had to remain outside of these cells. It was a dead cert we were caught. They were onto us days before we left the base. It was a whole thing, Ky. They threatened me and nearly killed Sean. My hands were tied. I. I," he stammers and sighs. "I needed to save *him* this time. And hurting you is tearing me apart, but my brother needed to know I had his back."

My back is to him. I prop up my right foot on the cot and draw my knee to my chest. I couldn't care less about his reasons for his deception. Whatever would have happened, I would've preferred to get caught and die before siding with our enemy, or shit-face Collins.

"Ky, can you listen to me?"

"I don't have a choice, Marc." I lean my shoulder against the gray glass wall and rest my head against its coolness. My muscles relax. *Gah, that's nice.*

"Trust me, Ky. When the time is right, we're getting out."

Calmly, I reply, "I know that, Marc." Facing him, I say, "That's not my concern. We were going to get out with or without you turning your backs on us. Now, my informant over there," I gesture in the direction of Noranti, "has let me know you're needed in order to do that, and that's fine. I accept it." I shrug and shake my head. "But I'm alone now." Narrowing my eyes, I stare at him. "Can you understand that? Forget everything else. I lost the most important piece of me. Now shut up about trusting you.

Okay?" I look away from him to the corner of my cell where the bars meet the floor. "Because a true friend, or whatever you call yourself, wouldn't have been standing on the outside of those bars looking back at me. He would've been inside, and we would've been working on a plan to get all nine of us out alive."

"I am sitting on the inside of these bars trying to talk to you about a plan to get us out," he states matter-of-factly, his tone growing harsh as though I've angered him.

"Yeah, after we lost three lives, Marc. Stop talking to me for a while, okay? You pushed me off when you were determined I was a traitor. Now I'm pushing you away because I know you are one."

There's a shuffling before his heavy boots plod across the glass to my side. In a hushed voice he says, "I pushed you away because I had chosen you over my brother and knew I'd do it again. I blamed it on you being a traitor. But as it's been revealed to you, I didn't care about any of that. I don't care about what's on your inside, what your genetic makeup is or whose side you're on because I'm on your side, Kylie."

I crane my neck to look up at him. His stoic expression brings me a comfort I reject. When our eyes meet, his shoulders slacken, and he exhales as he rolls his eyes to look away from me. "When you were ordered to execute Luke and I, had that Vojin not interrupted, you would've done it. No?"

He shakes his head. "Never." His answer comes out as a whisper. "I knew he was going to be interrupted. Only recent events had not gone as planned. Everything else was as we expected."

I wave my hand dismissively.

"Tonight, Sean and I will help you, Jord, and Seits escape. As soon as the lights dim. The night guards will have other arrangements this evening." He flicks his gaze to Noranti, and she nods, agreeing. "With our alliance, they'll free all of us and lead us through the halls to our exit. The room we'll have to pass through will unfortunately alert those gray Vojin, so one of the blue ones has agreed to sacrifice itself for our freedom. We'll shoot him, and he'll explode to kill the others, even the one responsible for killing Luke. I'll get your mask for you and make sure you have your weapons before you leave your cell. Once the gray Vojin are out, we're home free. We'll get back, save our country," he scoffs, correcting, "our *world*, and be done with the whole thing." He goes silent, and then asks, "You in?"

"Duh, Marc. I wouldn't choose to sit here."

He sits beside me and grabs my hand. "When we get home—"

"When I get home, just stay away from me. I know my mission. I don't need help from you to accomplish it."

Fool me twice, shame on me...

Grumbling, he stands. "I'll be back in a few hours."

"That's right," I call behind him as the bars rise. "You go keep up appearances."

He halts, back to me. His head bows forward as he groans, and then he continues onward, and the bars close behind him.

That's the end of this sneak peek of CULMINATED... Finish the series today.

Thanks for reading

Felisha Antonette

FELISHA ANTONETTE

SALIENT
INVADERS

THE SEPARATION TRILOGY
— BOOK TWO —

BETRAYAL NEVER COMES FROM THE ENEMY